I0593817

THE

NEW

NORMAL

a novel

K.N. CRIGHTON

THE

NEW

NORMAL

a novel

K.N. CRIGHTON

Bordeaux
Street
Books

The New Normal
Copyright © 2019 by K.N. Crighton

All rights reserved. No part of this work may be reproduced or
transmitted in any form or by any means without permission in
writing from the author.

This novel is a work of fiction. Names, characters, businesses,
organizations, incidents, and dialog, except for specific depictions
of historical public figures as characterized in this book's
acknowledgments, are the product of the author's imagination or
are used fictitiously.

ISBN: 978-0-9980343-1-7

Published by Bordeaux Street Books, New Orleans

Cover design by Melissa Williams Design

Formatting by Melissa Williams Design

How lonely sits the city
that once was full of people!
How like a widow she has become,
she that was great among the nations!
She that was a princess among the provinces
has become a vassal.

—Lamentations 1:1

for Ethel

JULY 29–AUGUST 30

FRIDAY, JULY 29

"What the hell, Howard?"

Four o'clock on a Friday afternoon. That's when Howard always fired people. In twenty-seven years with Parker Publishing, I'd seen him do it any number of times. And now he was doing it to me.

When Howard calls you into his office late on a Friday, it's never good news, but I'd thought this summons was most likely about some great idea he'd suddenly had over lunch that involved my working all weekend while he was out playing golf. In fact, he was still wearing his lunch on his tie. Red sauce today, on a pink tie his wife Ruth must have picked out for him. Creole? Italian? Howard likes his lunches with Important People, often at famous old restaurants in the French Quarter: a corporate executive, a state senator, someone from the mayor's office. He's still hoping to have lunch with the mayor himself one day.

"Now, Maggie, let's not get all upset about this. You knew this was coming."

"No, I didn't. What's going on?"

"Things just haven't been going well lately. Advertisers are telling us the magazine is getting stale. Same old same old. It needs a fresh approach."

"I'm open to making changes. We've made them before. There's certainly no need for this drastic move. Especially since this is the first I've heard of it."

"Now, you know that's not true. We've talked about this." He shook his head. "Frankly, you've gotten into a rut, doing the same pieces over and over. *New Orleans Now!* isn't Now. It's Yesterday. The magazine needs new blood."

"Code word for somebody younger?"

"Don't try to put words in my mouth. It's time for us to part ways. We both need to seek new horizons."

"Is that what you call firing your hardest-working employee after twenty-seven years?"

He smiled a fake smile, one I'd seen before when he was delivering bad news. He opened a file folder on his desk, removed a sheet of paper filled with legal-looking text in small type, and slid it across the desk toward me. "We need your signature on this. It's a very fair offer."

I skimmed it quickly. It was an offer of severance. Not a lot of money considering my years of service, but Howard always was a cheap son of a bitch. The offer was contingent upon my stating that I was resigning of my own will and that I wouldn't seek unemployment compensation or take legal action against the company. Or work for a competitor for the next two years, the term "competitor" not being defined.

"I'll have to have my lawyer take a look at this." He knew damn good and well I meant George. There have been many times over the years when it's served me well to be married to a lawyer. And I knew the last thing Howard wanted was for me to show this paper to him.

"Now, Maggie, we don't have to get contentious about this. We've been friends for a long time. Let's be civil and not get into any adversarial positions."

"Adversarial positions? Howard, you're firing me out of the blue after I've worked here for nearly thirty years. I'd say that's pretty adversarial."

"This is a very generous offer. We need your answer now."

I slipped my cell phone out of my pocket. "Okay, I'll call George right now and read it to him."

"Maggie, let's keep the lawyers out of this, shall we?"

"Hell, Howard, your lawyers drew this damn thing up, so don't give me that crap."

"I'm sorry you're reacting this way. I had hoped we could end on a better note." He took the paper back and tucked it into a file. For a moment I wondered if he would forge my signature on the document. I wouldn't put it past him.

He stood up and gestured toward the door. "Kevin will help you clear out your desk. Goodbye, Maggie." He didn't offer to shake my hand. I wouldn't have, anyway. His was probably still sticky with red sauce.

I had the humiliation of having the mail clerk stand over me while I frantically collected my personal belongings in a couple of empty copier paper boxes. For the record, Kevin looked pretty humiliated himself. The whole office was watching. Finally Amy, my assistant editor, came over, not looking me in the eye, and carried one of the boxes out to my car for me.

And that was it: out the front door of the converted shotgun double house that served as the office of Parker Publishing Company, into the blast furnace of a midsummer Friday afternoon in New Orleans. I screeched my red Mustang out of the unpaved parking lot, spraying gravel like buckshot against the side of Howard's black Mercedes, and slammed into a gap between two cars in rush hour traffic on South Carrollton Avenue. My dramatic exit slowed immediately to a bumper-to-bumper crawl, and my last Friday afternoon drive home from work turned out to be pretty much like any other.

It was a bad dream come to life. From the time I started working there, I was always afraid of being fired. The publishing industry in New Orleans is tiny. I'd given up a career in the magazine business in New York City to come home and get married. I didn't regret the choice, but it meant I had few options to do the kind of work I loved.

Howard and Ruth own Parker Publishing, and they pretty much do as they please as far as their employees are concerned. Louisiana is a right-to-work state, and you really don't have a lot of recourse if your boss just decides one day that he wants you gone. Federal employment laws against discrimination for being married or having a baby? There are ways around them. I've seen it.

There's always a lot of screaming coming from his office at the back of the building, the sound of a fist slammed on a desk. Howard's favorite line is "Goddammit, because I said so, that's why!" There is no negotiation. There is no listening on his part, only on yours.

I've seen some people fight back. I've seen some storm out the door. I've seen some beg for their jobs. Howard never takes anyone back.

I got home before George did. My usual Friday evening beverage is a glass of Chardonnay, but this wasn't a Chardonnay evening. I dropped two ice cubes in a glass and poured a generous amount of bourbon over them. Tucking the bottle under my arm, I carried my drink and an ice bucket out to the glassed-in sun porch at the back of the house. Setting the bottle and the ice bucket down on the drink cart, I dropped onto the flowered cushion of the chaise with a small grunt.

"I'm not suicidal," I muttered. "I'm homicidal."

I was well into my second drink when George got home. He'd already ditched his jacket and tie and unbuttoned his collar. "Hot as hell out there. Almost makes you wish for a hurricane to come along and cool things off." He took one look at my glass and the bottle on the cart and said, "Rough day?"

"They fired me. Kicked me out the door like a dead cockroach."

"What?"

"Yup. They need fresh blood. Sounds like they want someone younger."

"Oh, Maggie, I'm so sorry."

I burst into tears. "You're a lawyer," I said. "Sue the bastards. Age discrimination. Put the fear of God into them."

"You know I'm not a labor lawyer." George is a founding partner in a firm that practices maritime law. In a port city the size of New Orleans, there's never a shortage of work.

"No, but you must know somebody."

"I'll look into it. But you know that taking legal action is a big step. Word gets around, and maybe nobody else will hire you for fear you'll sue them too. Meanwhile, your case could drag on for years in the courts. You might never see a dime."

George was always being pragmatic, something I both hated and loved about him. I didn't need pragmatic right now. I needed support. "I'm three years from getting my full pension. They've screwed me."

He sighed. "All these years you've complained to me about how badly they treated you. I'm really sorry this has happened, but I can't say I'm surprised." He went over to the drink cart and picked up the bottle of twelve-year-old single malt Scotch from the lower shelf. It was George's private splurge. He fixed his drink and sat down beside me as I continued to rant.

"How am I going to tell Caroline? I was working there before she was born. She's going to Syracuse because I did. She wants to be a journalist too."

He took a sip of his drink. "She's twenty-one. Full of her own life. This probably won't mean much to her."

"Thanks a lot," I hissed. My career is in shreds. Doesn't anybody care?

TUESDAY, AUGUST 2
At City Coffee Shop

It's Eloise's day to clean the house. I left before she arrived because I didn't want to explain to her why I wasn't at work. I feel like I've let her down.

Other people might think that's crazy. You don't want to tell your cleaning lady you lost your job? But Eloise is far more than my cleaning lady. She's also my friend. We've known each other for twenty-one years.

We first met when I hired her to take care of Caroline right after she was born. Eloise had a child of her own, a boy named Isaiah. Eloise's mother stayed with Isaiah while Eloise was at work. Eloise sacrificed time with her own child to take care of mine. I know she had to work to support her family, because her husband's salary wasn't enough to cover all their expenses. My husband made good money, enough that I could have stayed home to raise my child, but I wanted the career I'd worked hard to have. Eloise was a nurturing caregiver to my daughter, just as I'm sure her mother was to Isaiah. But still, our reasons for not being home with our own children were different.

Isaiah grew up, and right after 9/11 he joined the Louisiana National Guard. He was part of a construction brigade that was sent to Afghanistan to build permanent buildings for the military. Last year he was killed after stepping on a mine. He lost a leg and bled out before he could get medical treatment. Eloise and her husband Robert were devastated. Still are.

Eloise gave up those years with Isaiah so I could have the career I wanted so much, and now I've lost my job. I can't bear to face her.

I got to the coffee shop around nine, thinking it would be nearly deserted after everyone had picked up coffee on their way to work—as I used to do. Instead, the place was jammed: mothers with babies in strollers, college students hunched over books or laptops, people meeting clients and doing business at the tiny jammed-together tables. Outside on the patio, a couple of dogs tied to wrought-iron tables waited while their owners were inside getting coffee.

This is a whole daytime world I didn't know existed. People who spend their days surrounded by the panels of an office cubicle have no idea what people in the outside world are doing. Not that I spent all my time in the office. *New Orleans Now!* is a magazine about dining and entertainment in New Orleans. I was often out of the office during the morning, talking to owners of restaurants and nightclubs at a time when they weren't busy with customers. I'd tour the kitchens, meet the chefs, get a feel for the place.

I did write about a few new coffee shops. But I didn't hang out in them as a matter of course. Now here I was, avoiding Eloise and going back for another vanilla latte.

I finally called Caroline last night and told her I'd lost my job. I was so worried she'd be upset. But George was right. She's wrapped up in her summer internship at a talent agency in Los Angeles, and my grief over the loss of my job hardly registered with her.

"What a bummer, Mom. I'm sorry." Then she told me with great excitement how she'd met some rock star who came into the agency on Friday, somebody I've never heard of but who apparently is known to everyone her age.

What could I say? "That's great, honey." Well, when I was twenty-one, I guess my parents' problems didn't register with me, either.

She and her boyfriend Jason drove out to L.A. after he graduated from Syracuse in May. He's got an entry-level job on a new television series. She still has a year to go before she graduates, but she got the summer internship at the talent agency. It was quite a coup. They rented an apartment. I'm okay with them living together, even if George isn't as sanguine as I am.

She's ambitious and driven, even more than I was at her age. She's going to stay in Los Angeles for the fall semester as part of a special program Syracuse offers students in her television-radio-film major. In the winter she'll go back to campus for her last semester and, God willing, graduate next May.

I'm a little worried that she might decide to stay out there with Jason and not go back to finish school. Let's face it, Los Angeles in January is a whole lot more appealing than upstate New York. And leaving behind a serious boyfriend just makes it worse. I hope she goes back and graduates.

There are people standing around me, coffee in hand. Now I have something else to feel guilty about: hogging this table. Hell with it. I'm going home. If Eloise is there, I'll just tell her what happened.

3:30 p.m.

She was mopping the floor of the sun porch. I asked her to come sit with me at the kitchen table. Without a word, she set the mop aside and followed me.

"They let me go, Eloise." My eyes got hot and I fought the tears.

Her expression hardened. "That is just so wrong." She shook her head. "It's gonna be all right, baby. Don't you worry. God's gonna take care of you."

She leaned toward me across the table. "You listen to me now, you hear? Those people never treated you right. When Caroline was just a little bitty thing, I remember how scared you were that they were going to fire you. For what? For having a beautiful little baby? What kind of people act like that? I remember you used to call here from a pay phone at lunchtime to see how she was doing. I could hear people talking in the background and dishes rattling, so I knew you weren't at work. At first I thought you were in a bar somewhere. But then I figured out you were on your lunch break. You told me not to call you at work unless something bad happened, like she needed to go to the hospital. I didn't know you then like I do now, and at first I thought you just didn't care about your baby. But when you explained to me about those people you worked for, I understood. I've seen people like that. They've got rocks where their hearts ought to be."

I remembered those calls from the sandwich shop as clearly as yesterday, although that was back in the days before I had a cell phone. There was no phone booth in the place, just a small wooden frame on the wall that did little to give the user privacy. I'd press one ear against the nasty-smelling receiver, crusted with other people's body oils, and hold a finger to the other ear to try to hear Eloise over the yelling of orders from the counter to the kitchen, the background chatter of customers, the clatter of dishes and silverware. Every word she said was precious to me: Caroline took her bottle; she was sleeping; she was fussy today. I suspect Eloise was the one who heard her first words, but she was careful never to tell me. The tears overpowered my efforts to stop them, and I dug into my pants pocket for a tissue.

"I don't mean to be speaking out of turn," Eloise continued, "but why didn't you get yourself another job somewhere else? You're a smart lady."

I wiped my eyes. "There's just not a lot out there in my field. I was afraid that if they found out I was looking, they'd get rid of me, and then I wouldn't have anything." There were people standing in line to have the job I had. I saw the résumés come into the office. I took some of the phone calls from people looking for work. The Parkers could have replaced me in a heartbeat.

"Now they have, and you didn't even do anything to make that happen. I'm so sorry, honey. But look. I'm here for you. Always. You know that. You were there for me when Isaiah got killed last year. You came to the house and sat with me and Robert all that night. You came to the funeral. I'll never forget that. And I'm gonna be here for you now. But I'm telling you, those Parkers just aren't worth fussing over. You're gonna be all right. You know a lot of people. You'll get another job. Don't you worry."

God bless Eloise. Not even George has been so supportive. She's right, I should have gotten away from that dysfunctional situation years ago. But it was more than fear that kept me where I was. My job was my identity: Maggie McBride, editor of *New Orleans Now!* I was a media personality. Not as famous as the ones you saw on television, but people knew me for what I did. And I loved that.

I'm still Maggie McBride, even if I'm no longer editor of *New Orleans Now!* It's time to see just how much that name still means in this town.

Wednesday, August 3

I can't think of anything more humbling than asking someone who started her career as your assistant if she will hire you. At least Penny took my call. She was a bright young thing just out of LSU when I hired her, maybe ten years ago. She was smart enough to realize quickly that she wouldn't move up fast or make a lot of money working for Howard, so after she got the minimum necessary experience, she left for more money elsewhere. As I should have done when I was her age. Now she's the editor of a new local business weekly that's getting a lot of buzz. Sure, my expertise is writing about restaurants and bars, but they're a big part of the New Orleans economy. Penny was friendly but noncommittal, told me to send her a résumé and keep in touch. Pretty much what I would have said in her position.

I used to get calls from people I knew who were down on their luck and needed a job. But most of them Had Problems, and everybody in the business knew it. Alcohol, cocaine, just plain flaky. I don't Have Problems. Except I'm fifty-one years old in a world where people over forty are considered too old, too slow, too expensive.

Right after I got off the land line with Penny, my cell phone rang. "Hey, Mags, when the hell are you going to run my article?"

I laughed. "Hey, Mickey. How'd you get this number?"

Mickey Donnelly was a freelancer who used to write for me regularly. His Irish charm had saved his bacon with me any number of times when he was late with an assignment.

"I told Amy you'd loaned me a laptop and I needed to give it back. What's the deal? She said you no longer work there."

I sighed. "They let me go on Friday."

"What the hell? What did you do to piss off Howard this time?"

"This time?"

"You know what I mean. It's always something with him."

"He said they were taking the magazine in a new direction. So I have no idea what they're going to do with your article."

"If they don't run it, I want a kill fee. I worked hard on that piece."

"If they don't use it, maybe you can sell it somewhere else."

"It's a work for hire. Says so in those damn contracts you always made me sign when you gave me an assignment. The rights to the piece don't belong to me."

"See what you can do with the new editor, whoever that is."

"Right. So, Mags, what are you going to do now?"

"I've got some feelers out."

"What are you looking for? I write for a lot of people. I may hear of something. You never know. Tell me what kind of job you're looking for, and I'll keep my eyes and ears open."

I'd always thought of freelancers as powerless, untethered creatures, not connected to any employer, leading a fragile existence dependent on the whims of editors for that next assignment and quirky accounts payable departments when it came to putting checks in the mail. But Mickey, with his stable of regular clients, probably knew things I didn't about what was going on in the local publishing market.

"Thanks, Mickey." Another humbling experience.

Thursday, August 4

I looked at myself in the bathroom mirror this morning as the early light came through the window. When I was a teenager, I had wild curly red hair framing my face, in a day when other girls had long straight hair, preferably blonde, down to their breasts. And freckles, lots of them. For a long time I wished desperately to look like everybody else, until it finally occurred to me that standing out from the crowd could be a good thing. I learned that laughing was attractive. So was tossing those red curls. I was quite the flirt. Maggie Callahan, Irish to the core, had a lot of boys pursuing her back then.

Now the flaming red hair of my teenage years has faded and the curls have softened. I keep my hair much shorter than I did back then. The gray is creeping in around my temples. My freckles have faded, too. I use a lot of sunscreen these days because I keep hearing I'm at high risk for skin cancer with my fair coloring. I've got lines on my forehead and around the corners of my eyes. My mouth seems drawn down in a perpetual frown. What happened to laughing Maggie?

It's been two months since I've had a period. I'm having hot flashes. I keep telling myself it's summer in New Orleans and of course I feel hot. But this is different. It starts in my chest and builds and spreads out to my arms and hands until I'm dripping. It lasts about five minutes, then it fades. My clothes are soaked with sweat and I'm freezing. Thirty minutes later it happens again. It's got to be menopause. I'm the right age for it. I guess I should go to the doctor to make sure. I wonder how long these hot flashes will go on.

I'm getting old. Still, I'm not ready to stop working. But who's going to hire me when there are so many young things running around, eager and hungry and willing to work for practically nothing?

FRIDAY, AUGUST 5

George and I are going to White Linen Night in the Warehouse Arts District tomorrow with Seth and Noreen Dupree, our friends from down the street. It's always hot as hell the first Saturday evening in August, but White Linen Night is fun. Maybe this will help me feel better.

The Warehouse Arts District is a transformation of a grimy industrial neighborhood to a thriving downtown residential and retail district. It's all happened in the last twenty years. When I was growing up, my Uncle Frank owned a three-story warehouse on Julia Street in the heart of the district. It was a dirty, scary part of town where homeless people wandered in search of enough spare change to buy a bottle of Thunderbird wine and slept in open boxcars alongside the warehouses. The windows of the old brick buildings were opaque with years of dust—the ones that didn't have their panes broken out. The streets smelled like rotten produce and urine.

By the 1980s, though, the warehouses were closing or moving to the suburbs. The old brick and cypress buildings were converted into upscale apartments, condos, art galleries, restaurants, and trendy shops. The Julia Street

Wharf became a port of embarkation for cruise ships. A mall of high-end stores, The Riverwalk, opened beside the wharf to cater to cruise passengers.

Uncle Frank died years ago. Today his warehouse is home to a children's museum. The arched windows on the top floor, no longer grimy, are like half-shuttered eyes lazily watching the ships pass on the river.

Now, every year on the first Saturday of August, the arts crowd celebrates the renaissance of the Warehouse District on White Linen Night, an evening street festival. You're supposed to wear white, of course, because it's classy and gives the illusion of coolness. But it's still New Orleans in August, and even after dark, the streets are as hot as the inside of a boxcar. Still, it's fun to drift from one gallery to another, sipping white wine, nibbling hors d'oeuvres, and running into friends.

The only downside this year is that I'm no longer the editor of *New Orleans Now!*, the authority on nightlife in the city. Well, legal nightlife, anyway. In years past, I'd be covering the event with a photographer. This year, I'm just going for the fun of it. At least I hope it'll be fun.

Saturday, August 6

Seth and Noreen came over around five for drinks. They bought a house down the block a couple of years ago. He's a cardiologist; she owns a high-end consignment shop on Magazine Street. They're younger than we are, late thirties, maybe. No kids. They seem to dote on their dogs, a couple of golden retrievers who sit sentinel on their front porch much of the time.

We walked two blocks to St. Charles Avenue, caught the streetcar down to Carondelet and Julia, and walked past the barricades that blocked cars so pedestrians could roam the streets. The late afternoon sun was descending behind the buildings, and it wasn't quite as hot as it had been earlier.

The local public radio station had a tent. We met the new general manager, who's just come here from Georgia. I gave him my card. Who knows? Maybe I can pick up some freelance assignments.

We visited a few galleries, had a couple of plastic cups of wine, saw a demonstration of glass blowing, and watched a pastry chef create amazing designs with molten sugar. The faint scent of cotton, lumber and rice once stored in the warehouses still lingers. Built in the nineteenth and early twentieth centuries, the warehouse walls are thick, made of cypress timbers and brick.

I imagined selling our house Uptown and moving into a new condo down here, carved out of an old warehouse. Now that we're empty nesters, it might make sense to move to a smaller place with no yard to worry about. I said, "If The Big One ever comes, this is where I want to be. These walls will stand up to anything."

The Big One is never far from anyone's mind, especially this time of year. August and September are peak hurricane months in the Gulf of Mexico, and we've already had a couple of close calls this year. Pensacola is still devastated from a major hurricane that hit there last year. It was headed straight for New Orleans and shifted east at the last minute.

We were standing just outside Uncle Frank's old warehouse when we ran into them.

Howard and Ruth Parker were talking with a real estate developer who advertises in several of their magazines, but not as often as they'd like him to. Jack Wright, the advertising director who was my friend up until last Friday, was with them. When Jack saw me, he looked like he'd just swallowed a bad oyster.

There was a young man with them. Early twenties. He wore a sleeveless black t-shirt, black jeans and running shoes. Did anyone explain to him why they call this White Linen Night? His arms were covered with tattoos. He had olive skin, thick black glasses, and a mass of curly black hair. Sweat was running down the sides of his face and neck.

Howard's eyes shifted from the advertiser to me, and I heard his sharp intake of breath. "Maggie, good to see you," he said, although his expression suggested he didn't think it was good.

"Howard." I stared at him, not moving.

Ruth, tall, heavyset, and imposing as always, stepped between us. "Maggie, this is my nephew, Zach Meyer. He's just moved here from New York."

I extended my hand to the young man. "Maggie McBride."

His eyes widened. Clearly he'd heard my name before. And probably not in a good way.

Jack just said, "Hey, Maggie."

"Hey, yourself." It's how we used to greet each other every morning at the office.

Howard turned back to his conversation with the advertiser. Ruth said to me, "Have a good evening," effectively terminating our conversation, and turned to speak to someone who had just come up. The young man nodded at me, shrugged, and turned in the direction of his aunt and uncle. Jack leaned toward me and whispered, "I'll call you."

I heard Howard tell the advertiser, "Zach's just joined us as editor of *New Orleans Now*! He's got some great ideas for the magazine."

The hot flash came on me without warning. They usually start as a warm feeling, then slowly build up to a heat beyond bearing. Not this time. It was instant blast furnace. I could feel my face redden and the sweat break out on my head, face, arms, and torso.

I must have blanked out for a minute. All I remember is George's hand, tight as a blood pressure cuff around my upper arm, dragging me down the street.

Noreen asked, "Are you all right?" and Seth, the cardiologist, looked concerned.

"I'm going to kill them," I said between clenched teeth. "I'm going to sue the shit out of them."

Noreen's eyebrows shot up. Seth assumed his best noncommittal clinical expression and stared, not saying anything.

George said, "It's okay. Little too much wine on an empty stomach. She just needs to get a cup of water, something to eat. Maybe we'll catch up with you later." Still gripping my arm, he pulled me away from them, out of the crowd, and headed toward the river.

After about half a block, the hot flash dissipated, leaving me bathed in a cold sweat. I was shivering in my sleeveless sheath. I stopped at a corner and leaned against a telephone pole.

"You can let go of my arm now."

"Maggie. No death threats in public places." He spoke to me the way he did to Caroline when she was little and threw a temper tantrum in the grocery store.

"They fired me and gave my job to Ruth's *nephew*? He's Caroline's age! I'm going to kill them!"

"Maggie!"

"Yes, Counselor. No death threats. Don't want it used against me later in court."

"I mean it. You're better than they are. Act that way."

And that was all he said. And all I said. But I was trembling with rage.

We ended up at the food court in the Riverwalk shopping mall. I got a scooped-out loaf of bread filled with redfish courtbouillon, which is a spicy fish stew poured over rice, and George had broiled catfish with crabmeat dressing. We took our plates outside to a table on the deck overlooking the river.

The wind was blowing, scattering napkins and plastic tableware. The sun was setting and a thunderstorm was drifting up from the Gulf of Mexico. Dark clouds gathered over the West Bank, contrasting with the lights on the twin Crescent City Connection bridges just upriver from where we were.

As it heads toward the Gulf, the Mississippi River turns east and makes a crescent loop around the city of New Orleans. From our vantage point on the Riverwalk deck, the west bank of the river was actually to the east. It's one of those crazy things you get used to when you live here. Nothing is as you think it ought to be.

"Maybe we should get out of town for awhile," George said. "It's August. I haven't got a lot going on at the office. And you need to get away from all this crap. It's driving you crazy."

"Leave town? Why? Here we are in the most romantic city on earth. I'm eating redfish courtbouillon and looking out over the river. The wind is blowing and a thunderstorm's coming in. I can't imagine any other place on earth I'd rather be."

The wind blew over my plastic cup of Chardonnay. George tried to catch it, but it splashed onto my white linen sheath. I blotted it with a paper napkin. "At least it's not merlot," I said. I counted silently the glasses I'd had this evening, including the wine we shared with the Duprees at home before we left. Four. Well, those two at the galleries were in kiddie-size plastic cups legal for carrying on the street in New Orleans. And the one that just spilled on me was not much bigger. So, I told myself, maybe two and a half real glasses, tops. I wasn't drunk. But I could feel myself melting like a wax crayon into my chair. Just mellow, relaxed. Good dinner, good wine. I even smelled like wine now.

Practical George nodded toward the darkening sky. "We're about to get soaked, and we didn't bring an umbrella. Let's head home."

We caught the St. Charles streetcar at St. Joseph Street, across from the Sewerage and Water Board offices. There were a lot of people getting on, but it wasn't yet as crowded as it would be later. We were standing at the back, next to the open windows, when it started to rain. A gentle shower quickly intensified into a downpour, punctuated with thunderclaps. The rain felt good on my face. I started to cool off, emotionally as well as physically.

I leaned against George, relaxing into his warmth and familiar scent of sandalwood aftershave. He rested his chin on the top of my head and put one arm around me, while with the other he held on to the window frame of the rocking streetcar. After twenty-seven years of marriage, he feels comfortable to me, like a favorite shirt. I let out a deep breath I hadn't realized I'd been holding.

By the time we got to our stop, the rain had slacked, but you could still smell the earthy scent of it. Steam rose from the pavement like fog. It was everything the old-time movies about New Orleans would have you believe this city is all about. Maybe those old movies got it right sometimes.

We made love that night for the first time in a long time. It was slow, sensual, awesome. I hadn't realized how much I really needed it. The menopause thing that started this summer has taken a lot of desire away from me. Sometimes I forget how wonderful sex can be. And last night, well, it was like old times again. After all that's gone on this past week, and the tension it created between George and me, I think we both needed this.

Sunday, August 7

Late this afternoon Jack called as he'd promised. He started at the company as an ad salesman on straight commission about the same time I was hired as a lowly editorial assistant. Now Jack is ad director over all the company's magazines.

He said, "The kid is Ruth's sister's son from Long Island."

"How did he end up here?"

"He went to Tulane. Majored in economics, can you believe that? He wanted to live here and write."

"So Howard and Ruth gave him my job, just like that?"

"There are a lot of rumors floating around, and I advise you to take them all with a grain of salt. No telling what the real story is. But the one I think makes the most sense is that Howard and Ruth borrowed a lot of money from Ruth's sister's husband to keep the company afloat. The brother-in-law is a big-time investment manager. You know advertising revenue at the company has been down for quite awhile. I see the spreadsheets they won't show you, and frankly, we've been losing money hand over fist for years. I can't tell you how many times we've been on the brink of shutting down. So, anyway, the story goes that Zach's dad loaned them a lot of money. And as part of the deal, he wanted them to give the kid a job."

"Hell, if he's an investment manager, why couldn't he give his own son a job? You said Zach had a degree in economics. I'd think his dad would want to help him get into the business."

"Well, his older brother is already working for his father. But I don't think Zach wanted to do that. He wants to write. He's been out of Tulane more than a year, didn't have a job yet, and he wanted to live in New Orleans."

"Shit," I said. "I came into the company with a magazine degree and three years' experience in publishing in New York. I wanted to write, but they had me making coffee and running the copy machine. He comes in, he gets the whole enchilada. What does he know about New Orleans nightlife besides the college bar scene?"

"I've talked to him. I think he really likes the city and wants to live here. Howard says he's got some good ideas, wants to do cutting-edge stuff with the magazine and cater to a younger audience—"

"Watch it, Jack. You're on dangerous ground."

"Hell, I'm sorry, Mags. You know I don't mean to tromp on your feelings. I'm not happy about what they did to you. How am I supposed to sell advertising for a magazine that caters to kids who run around to the clubs every night? You know who our bread-and-butter ad clients are: luxury real estate properties, medical advertisers, high-end retailers. Our readers have high incomes and can afford an upscale lifestyle. And now I'm supposed to do what? Sell ad space to beer companies? Shoot, I don't think kids today even read magazines. This could be a disaster."

His voice was starting to get a little shaky. "Tell you the truth, I'm not sure I'll have a job much longer, either. Howard has been on my case for years, telling me I'm not doing enough. Who knows, he may decide to hire some kid to replace me, too. Maybe even on straight commission. Save them a lot of money."

Suddenly I felt very old. Maybe I *am* old.

"Maggie? Are you still there?"

"Yeah. Just feeling a little obsolete."

"Me too. We think we're on top of the world, that we've finally made it to the big time, and then some kid comes along and pushes us over a cliff."

"Jack, you're not making me feel good here."

"Sorry. Didn't mean to be so negative. Hey, would you like to get together for a drink sometime? You know, for old times' sake? Just you and me? Do you think your husband would mind?"

I thought of all the times Jack and I had gone out for drinks when we worked together. He's been divorced a long time and has had girlfriends over the years. But there was never anything romantic between us. Sometimes he went with me at night when I was doing a story on a club somewhere, especially if the place was in a dangerous neighborhood—and many of them were. Officially he was accompanying me to develop relationships with the owners and managers of these establishments that might lead to an advertising contract, but I knew he was also looking out for my safety. George knew about the arrangement, and after a few conversations with Jack, he was okay with my going with him. Hanging out in clubs during the week wasn't George's speed, anyway.

None of this answered Jack's question. But I knew it was highly unlikely we'd ever get together for that drink. It was just something to say before we ended the conversation, to pretend this wasn't the end of our long working relationship.

"Sure, let's do that. Like old times."

FRIDAY, AUGUST 26

It's been four weeks, and I don't have another job, not even any good prospects. George and I decided to go to New York for Labor Day weekend to catch a Broadway show and do some sightseeing. It's giving me something fun to look forward to.

On another note, there's a category 1 hurricane named Katrina moving west across Florida this morning after causing some damage in Miami. It's supposed to go into the Gulf of Mexico, make a right turn and head north, and then make another landfall on the Florida coast.

Here in New Orleans, though, it's a sunny, hot morning. I had to water the plants in containers on the front porch. They dry up so fast in this heat.

SATURDAY, AUGUST 27

Eloise called a little after eight this morning, not customary for her. She said, "What are you going to do about this hurricane?"

"*What* hurricane?"

We didn't watch TV last night. Seems Katrina didn't turn north after all. It kept heading west into the Gulf, where the water temperatures are around 90 degrees. Now it's blown up into a major hurricane. And it's headed right for us.

"Robert and I aren't going anywhere. People are saying we ought to leave, but we're gonna stay in our house and be safe. I'm not getting stuck in traffic on some interstate when I don't know where I'm going. What would I do if we ran out of gas?"

Eloise was the one who would have to drive in an evacuation. When Robert was growing up on a farm in St. Francisville, a town outside Baton Rouge, he was injured badly in an accident when his right leg got caught in some farm equipment. It had to be amputated above the knee. He has a prosthetic leg and manages pretty well, but he doesn't drive.

"I don't know what George and I are doing," I said. "This is the first I've heard of Katrina coming this way. We'll have to talk about it. I'll let you know."

Even before I hung up, George had the television on. As soon as he heard the basics, he said, "We're leaving."

"Are you crazy? We're native New Orleanians. We've never evacuated for a hurricane. I'm with Eloise on this one. I'm not getting stuck in all that traffic. Let's stay where we're safe."

He gave me that look that said this one wasn't subject to negotiation. And I gave him my look right back, the one that said, "You're damn right, I'm not negotiating."

"How much gas do you have in your car?" he asked.

"I don't know, maybe half a tank."

"Go fill up. The city's going to run out of gas. Stay or go, you'll need it. I filled up on the way home last night."

Okay, we *were* negotiating after all. I've learned enough from George to know that you start the process with points all sides can agree on. He'd just opened with one. There was going to be a run on gas, and a lot of places would sell out. If the power failed—and it probably would—nobody would be pumping gas.

So I climbed into the Mustang and headed out. On my way down our street, I spotted Seth and Noreen. We hadn't had a conversation since White Linen Night, just waved at each other when we drove down the street. They were in their driveway, loading the dogs into their Mercedes SUV. A container was lashed to the roof with bungee cords.

"You're leaving?" I asked. Well, obviously they were.

"We're going to Houston to stay with my parents," said Noreen. "How about you?"

"Don't know yet. I'm going to get gas."

"Better make up your mind soon," said Seth. "The roads are going to be jammed."

We exchanged cell numbers. As I drove away, they followed me down the street. I turned left at the corner, and they continued straight ahead. I had a sinking feeling that George was going to prevail on this one. His law firm has an office in Houston. That's probably where he'd want to go. Ugh. I hated Houston. Freeways and traffic.

The line of cars at my regular gas station blocked the right lane of the street for the length of a football field. I shook my head and pulled in behind the last one.

As I waited, I called Caroline on my cell phone. It wasn't quite seven in Los Angeles, and I'm sure I woke her and Jason up.

"We're fine," I assured her. "Don't worry. You know we've been through this before. It will probably turn at the last minute and go somewhere else."

"Okay, Mom," she said. She sounded sleepy and not particularly concerned. "Just let me know what you and Dad decide to do."

"I love you, honey."

"Love you too."

I finally got the tank filled. Now what? I'd been to the grocery yesterday, thank God, so I didn't need to get into the bread-and-milk-and-beer craziness. I had a stash of canned goods in the closet in the guest room upstairs. I stock up every June at the start of hurricane season and donate most of it to a food pantry in November.

Cash. I went to the bank and hit the ATM.

I came home to find George struggling with the sheets of plywood we keep stored in the garage to board up the windows that don't have shutters. We spent most of the rest of the day covering the French doors with plywood and closing the old wooden shutters. I love having real shutters with slats that actually open and close, but these have been painted so many times that the edges no longer come together properly so you can latch them. They have to be tied shut with rope. Several had wasps' nests behind them that had to be sprayed with a fast-kill insecticide. There were still a few angry wasps flying around as we tied the shutters closed.

We brought in all the porch furniture, flowerpots, and containers so they wouldn't become flying objects. By afternoon the wind was picking up, but it was still hot outside. George's face was red. We were both soaked with sweat and dirt from struggling with plywood sheets, dusty shutters, porch chairs, and flowerpots.

In all that time, we hadn't said anything more about whether to leave or not. Again, we were doing something we both could agree on. Securing everything in preparation for a hurricane is just a normal household task in New Orleans. Some years we're lucky and don't have to do this. Some years we do it more than once. In the past few years we've had a lot of near misses from hurricanes, but this time the weather reports we were getting throughout the day didn't sound good. Still, I've never run from a hurricane, and I was shocked that George would even consider it.

Around five o'clock we finally collapsed on the sofa with sweating glasses of iced tea. That's when he told me that while I was out getting gas, he'd called his old fraternity buddy from Tulane days, Jeff Winters, who was his best man at our wedding and is now an architect in Atlanta.

"I know how much you dislike Houston. So how about Atlanta? Jeff and Maribeth said we could stay with them. Just think of it as going to visit friends for a few days. We'll be back soon."

"One word," I said. "Contraflow." I'd seen the crazy maps of spaghetti-like red, blue, and green lines that attempted to explain how traffic would be rerouted on major roads to force everyone to travel in the same direction, even on both sides of an interstate. This was supposed to make the traffic flow better, but all I could think was what a confused mess it would be.

"Another word," I added. "No."

George shook his head. "We've stayed for a lot of them, Maggie. Not this time. This one is different. We have to leave."

I stood up, picked up my glass and his. "Want more?"

"Yes, please." I went to the kitchen and refilled our glasses. I handed George's to him and sat beside him.

"What about Mister Whiskers? Will the Winters let us bring him?"

Mister Whiskers is Caroline's cat. He was a stray kitten, black with white whiskers and white paws, who showed up in the back yard when she was ten. Someone had shot him in the leg with a pellet gun and he was limping. The vet said it would be too risky to remove the pellet. But he's managed to live a normal life anyway. Since Caroline has been away at college, he's graciously accepted our attention as a substitute for hers, but when she comes home on holidays, he's definitely her cat.

I could see from George's expression that he hadn't thought to ask. "I'm sure it'll be all right," he said. "If not, there must be a vet around there where we could board him."

He took a long swig of his iced tea. "Look," he said. "Just pack a bag, all right? In the morning we'll see where the storm is going, and we'll decide."

Pack a bag? I don't even know what to take. It's not like going on a vacation to visit friends, no matter what he says.

SUNDAY, AUGUST 28

George won the negotiation. The infrared image of Katrina on television this morning showed an angry red blob of a monster swallowing the entire Gulf of Mexico. I was convinced. It didn't matter if this thing turned at the last minute. We were all going to get clobbered: New Orleans, South Louisiana, the Mississippi Gulf Coast. Okay, I got it.

George packed the SUV, telling me to throw away all the perishables in the refrigerator and freezer. It killed me to toss out all the meat and milk I'd just bought on Friday. But the power almost certainly will go out, and it'll all go bad anyway. I packed a cooler of drinks, sandwiches and snacks to take in the car, but there just wasn't room for everything I wanted to save. When I was done, he put the garbage can in the garage where the wind wouldn't blow it away.

I watched George carry a crate of file folders downstairs. "Insurance policies," he said. "Checkbooks and credit cards. Investment statements. Tax returns. You never know." I rolled my eyes, but I knew better than to argue. My lawyer husband was planning for every contingency.

"Should we pack your mother's silver, too?" I asked.

"No, it'll take up too much room. Besides, if anything happens to it, it's insured. But if you have some favorite pieces of jewelry, you might want to pack those in your suitcase."

"Jeez, I was making a joke about the silver."

"It's not a joke. The house could get looted while we're away."

"Now you're *really* scaring me."

I wanted to take my Mustang too, but he vetoed it. "Gas is going to be hard to find along the way, and trying to fill up both tanks in long gas lines is going to take too much time. And with all this traffic, we might get separated."

"Then why did you send me out for gas?"

"Might need it when we get back. Chances are the power will be out, so the pumps won't work."

I parked my beloved Mustang in the garage with the garbage can that's going to stink to high heaven by the time we get back. I put the keys in my purse. If a looter wants a red Mustang, at least he won't find the keys in the house.

The wind was starting to blow really hard. The old cypress shutters rattled like skeleton bones in a scary movie, but they were holding. The wind forced itself through the tiny spaces between the front door and the door frame, creating a shriek like a high note on a harmonica. My God, what's it going to be like tomorrow, when this thing makes landfall?

Just before we left, we saw the mayor on television calling for a mandatory evacuation of the city. "Okay, I got it," I muttered. "I give up. I'll go."

I made the mistake of getting out the cat carrier before I had Mister Whiskers in a place where he couldn't run away. George was headed out the back door with our weekend bags in both hands, and Mister Whiskers shot out the door. I saw a streak of black go through the iron bars of the fence, and he disappeared under the house next door.

I called him, shook a bag of cat food, tried all the usual tricks, but he wasn't going to be fooled. George was yelling, "Come on, Maggie! We've got to go!" I put a couple of big bowls of dry food and water under our house, out of the wind. I hope he'll be all right. I'll ask Eloise to come over after the storm passes and check on him. Dear God, how am I going to tell Caroline that we left her cat behind? By now she must have seen the live broadcasts on CNN and The Weather Channel. She knows how bad it is.

SUNDAY AND MONDAY, AUGUST 28-29

It was ten-thirty Sunday morning when we pulled out of our driveway. I looked back at the house one last time. The French doors upstairs were boarded up, the shutters were tied closed, and there was nothing outside—no porch furniture or container plants or even a garbage can. The house looked abandoned, and we hadn't even pulled away from the curb yet. The mimosa tree in the side yard was almost bent double from the wind.

Sneaky tears caught me by surprise. I am not one of those women who gets weepy over sentimental cards or cries at sad movies. I. Don't. Cry. But I did as we drove away.

I thought we'd never get out of New Orleans. Despite all those contraflow maps that the television stations were distributing earlier in the summer, nobody knew which road to take. If you wanted to go east toward Atlanta on a road that was designated westbound only, you were out of luck. The state police wouldn't even let you get off at an exit so you could find a different route. Traffic was stopped everywhere we went.

There are only so many ways out of town. You have to cross a body of water whichever way you go: north on the 24-mile Lake Pontchartrain Causeway, west on I-10 across the Bonnet Carré Spillway, east on I-10 over the narrow eastern neck of the lake, or south across one of the Mississippi River bridges.

We ended up going north across the Lake Pontchartrain Causeway. Once we were across, George drove through residential neighborhoods in the Northshore towns to avoid the roadblocks. We took back roads until we were well into Mississippi, past the parts of I-59 designated for contraflow. But when we got onto the interstate, surprise! The traffic was even worse there than it was in the contraflow.

So many people had clearly never been on an interstate before and didn't know how to drive on one. And it seemed like many of them had no idea where they were going. They only knew they had to get out of town. We saw caravans of cars—families, church groups, ten cars or more—pulled over onto the shoulder. Maybe someone in their group got lost and they were waiting for them to catch up. Maybe someone ran out of gas. Maybe they needed to confer about where they thought they were headed. Who knows? All the traffic would slow down as the cars pulled over one by one, and then everyone driving by would slow down to gape at the line of cars on the side of the road. I could see George's face getting red as he muttered under his breath.

For several hours we listened to WWL-AM radio, which has a powerful signal, getting updates on the progress of the storm. People were calling in to talk about where they were, what they were doing, and what the weather was like where they were. Some of them were scared. Some of them were trying to convince you that they weren't. Some were really confused. After awhile I couldn't stand to listen anymore and shut it off.

As the hours passed, I began to feel like I was having one of those dreams where I'm trying to run away from something and my legs won't move and I end up crawling, pulling myself along with my hands, just trying to get away. Holy cow, are we only as far as Poplarville, Mississippi? Is this just Meridian? Surely we ought to be in Atlanta by now. By the time we got to the Alabama Welcome Center, I thought we were almost there. No, George said, we're only about half way. Dear God.

I was ready to give it up by the time we got to Birmingham. We had driven three hundred and fifty miles in twelve hours, about twice as long as the drive usually took. It was well past dark as we stopped at a fast food restaurant for supper.

"Come on," I said as we finished eating. "It's after ten o'clock. We're both exhausted. Let's find a hotel room somewhere."

George's expression was grim. I could see the exhaustion around his eyes. "There are no hotel rooms left in Birmingham. There are no hotel rooms anywhere. We have to keep going."

I knew he was right. I crawled into the car, wincing as I settled my butt into the passenger seat. After twelve hours on the road, it hurt to sit.

We saw huge RVs, many towing cars, and I decided I would never again make jokes about what gas guzzlers they were. At least those folks had a place to spend the night.

By the time we got to Atlanta, in the Eastern time zone, it was three in the morning. I-285, the beltway around the city that is usually like the parking lot of traffic we'd been driving on since morning, was deserted. George had insisted on driving the whole way, and when he hit open road at last, he stomped on the gas. He must have been doing ninety miles an hour. I knew how tired he was, but I knew better than to say anything.

The Winters live off a major road called Georgia 400, north of Atlanta in a town called Alpharetta. George had been calling Jeff and Maribeth on his cell phone to apprise them of our progress—when the phone worked, that is, because just about everyone in area code 504 was on their cell phone, and the circuits were often tied up. They directed him when he got off the main road and started down winding streets toward their subdivision.

We finally pulled into the driveway of a brick two-story colonial that to me looked like every other house on the street except for the number on the mailbox. When I got out of the car and tried to stand, my legs gave way and I had to grab the door handle to keep from falling.

Jeff and Maribeth had been up most of the night waiting for us, so they were exhausted too. They helped us unload the essentials—George's crate of file folders can stay in the car for the duration—and showed us upstairs to the guest room and bath. At that point, anything better than sleeping in the car would have looked like a five-star hotel to me.

We fell into the double bed as it was starting to get light. I thought I would fall asleep in minutes, but I was so strung out by everything—the hurricane, the trip, the unfamiliarity of this place—that my thoughts were a staccato clatter, back and forth, back and forth, like when I was a child banging away at my father's old manual typewriter on the desk in his study. The last time I looked at the alarm clock on the bedside table, it was quarter to seven.

George was very still, lying back to back against me in a bed much smaller than our king-sized one at home. I guess he'd fallen asleep immediately.

I slept, but not for long. I awoke when I heard a car start up in the driveway. That must be Jeff leaving for work. It was 7:45 on a Monday morning, a normal workday in Atlanta. I sat up on the side of the bed and found my slippers and robe in my open suitcase on the floor.

George stirred next to me. "Go back to sleep," I said. "No need for you to get up." I grabbed some clean clothes and staggered off to the guest bath for a shower.

As I came downstairs, I saw from the window a second car going down the driveway. That must be Maribeth. George had told me she was a professor at Emory University. I had a vague idea where Emory was—nowhere close to Alpharetta—and knew she must have a hellacious commute. In the kitchen, she'd left us a note to help ourselves to coffee and whatever we wanted for breakfast.

The house was quiet and dark. Outside, it was overcast but not raining. I found the light switches in the unfamiliar kitchen and flipped them on. Recessed lights in the ceiling revealed a large room, longer than it was wide, with dark cabinets, black granite countertops, and dark gray stone flooring. An island with a gas cooktop, an extra sink, and a food preparation area divided the kitchen. There was a walk-in pantry and a well-stocked wine cooler. At the far end of the room sat a large wooden table and six chairs. It was very different from the small kitchen of our hundred-year-old Uptown house.

The countertops were bare, no appliances anywhere. I fumbled through the cabinets, looking for the coffeemaker, coffee, and filters. Eventually I found them all—just not all in the same place. I'd never seen a coffeemaker like this one before—I favor the basic kind you buy at a discount store, not this gourmet brand—but eventually I figured out how to use it.

The coffee was stronger than I'd intended. I'm so accustomed to our strong New Orleans coffee that when I have to use a different brand, I assume it's not as strong and add a lot more to the basket than I normally would. I found milk in the refrigerator and heated it in the microwave to make some serious café au lait—half milk and half coffee.

What to fix for breakfast? The very thought of an egg right now made me nauseous, and I was hesitant to use

Maribeth's immaculate gas cooktop on the granite island. As someone who spent nearly thirty years racing to get out of the house in the mornings, I don't often fix a traditional eggs-and-bacon breakfast. In the walk-in pantry I found five different kinds of cereal. I opted for raisin bran and a banana I found in a bowl on the table.

Halfway through my breakfast, I heard footfalls on the stairs. George, in his rumpled terrycloth bathrobe and pajamas, hair sticking up and eyes bloodshot, looked like he'd been out drinking all night. It wasn't his normal morning appearance.

I pointed to the coffeepot across the room. "Strong."

"Can't be strong enough." George poured a cup and took the chair next to me. "What's going on?"

"Well, they both left for work, and it looks like we have the house to ourselves till Maribeth gets home. She left a note on the counter. Said she'd be back around four o'clock."

"That's not what I meant. What's going on with the storm?"

"Oh. Right." I looked around the room but didn't see a television. "They've got every convenience in the world in this kitchen. You'd think they'd have a TV."

George got up and began opening cabinets. "Here it is."

"God forbid they'd have a TV out in the open where anyone could see it and discover how bourgeois they are."

"Maggie, stop it. I know you don't want to be here, but Jeff and Maribeth have been really gracious to invite us. Don't criticize the way they live."

I sighed. It was more than that. They lived in suburban Atlanta. Neither of them had any idea what it was like to live from June to November with your upstairs closet full of canned goods and gallon jugs of water and a list of what to take with you if you only had hours to get out. But now was not the time to get into it with George.

He found the remote and turned on the television. On a cable news channel, there was a live shot of a reporter standing just outside the glass front doors of a hotel on Canal Street, under a canopy and out of the wind. The camera panned out to Canal Street. Gusts were whipping the rain down the street in sheets. Flat signs and other objects I couldn't identify flashed past.

For some reason the reporter decided to venture out to the sidewalk. We watched as he cautiously stepped out from the shelter of the canopy. A gust of wind caught him and sent him sailing sideways. He grabbed the handle of the pull-down lid of a mailbox at the curb. The lid tore off and sailed down the street, the reporter still clinging to it.

I spit my cereal and milk across the table. We were both laughing so hard we were gasping for breath. It was the first time we'd laughed since I got the phone call from Eloise Saturday morning.

"What an idiot!" I was trying not to choke on what was left of my mouthful of cereal. "Doesn't he know any better than to go out in the middle of a hurricane?"

George shook his head. "Wonder where he's from."

"Someplace far, far inland. Stupid!"

We sat there all morning, switching from news to weather reports. The national news coverage was all about Katrina. It was bizarre to watch scenes from streets we traveled almost every day, live on national television.

There were no more funny moments. All of it was terrifying. We saw sections of the domed roof of the Superdome in tatters, whipping in the wind like desperate flags calling for emergency help. There were people in that stadium. The city had designated it a shelter of last resort, and not even this great football stadium could hold up to the winds. My God, what must it be like in there?

And if the Superdome was coming apart, what was going on at our house? If the roof of the Superdome was peeling off, what was happening to our roof? Or windows? Or walls? Was it flooding? Nobody was sending a news crew Uptown to see what was going on. Certainly trees were coming down. Even in a windy summer thunderstorm, a live oak or two would occasionally topple over, its roots giving way in the waterlogged soil. I had a fairly good idea what St. Charles Avenue must look like right now, with trees and branches down everywhere. Probably some of the catenaries—the supports for the electric lines that powered the streetcars—were getting hit by downed trees. What a mess.

And what about Eloise? The last time we spoke was when I managed to get through on my cell phone from somewhere in Alabama early Sunday evening. She said they was fine. But that was yesterday. I picked up my cell phone from the table, but I couldn't even get a dial tone. I tried to call Eloise's home phone from the Winters' land line and got an annoying wheedle. A mechanical female voice said, "Your call cannot be completed at this time. Please try again later." I sneered at the phone and hung up.

"Not only are the land lines out, the cell phone towers must have come down," said George. "All our calls on 504 cell phones have to be routed through New Orleans. Our phones are probably going to be useless until the phone company can reroute the calls."

We sat at the kitchen table all morning, drinking too-strong coffee, glued to this real-life disaster movie set in our hometown as it unfolded on national television.

The shots from the Mississippi Gulf Coast were even worse than the ones from New Orleans. The storm surge had gone inland for miles, even crossing I-10, which had been built several miles away from the coast for the very purpose of keeping it out of the range of storm surges. The town of Waveland, where we used to vacation in the summers when I was a child, was completely under water. Gone.

Every now and then I'd feel my eyes grow hot, and the tears would slide down my cheeks. I dabbed at them with a napkin. Sometimes I'd sneak a look at George. His face was impassive, betraying no emotion. George was always the rational, analytical one, basing his decisions on logic and reason. He could get angry, but he never let his temper make decisions for him. Sometimes I wished I were like him, and this was one of those times. I didn't like to cry and certainly didn't like anyone to see me cry, not even this man I'd been married to for twenty-seven years.

"What do you think's going on at our house?" I asked.

"Roof's probably coming off. And I'm sure some of the trees in the yard have taken a hit. If the pecan tree's fallen, it might have taken out the glass wall in the sunroom."

"Oh, God." I hadn't thought of that.

"There really wasn't a good way to board up the windows in that room. With all that glass, there wasn't anything to nail the plywood to, and I didn't have enough sheets of it to cover them all anyway. But the floor is tile. It should be okay if it gets wet."

I thought of my beloved sunroom, where I'd pictured myself setting up shop with my computer and writing articles, maybe even a book. All those plans seemed lost forever now.

"Do you think the house will come down?"

"Don't know. We'll find out when we get back."

"But what will we do if it does come down? Where will we live? What will we do?"

"Maggie!" His voice was sharp, like when he would yell at Mister Whiskers to get off the kitchen table. "Stop catastrophizing! We won't know what's happened until we get home, so stop worrying about what might be. We'll deal with it when we know what we're dealing with." It was a favorite line of his, and it always made me angry, because I like to think about how I'd handle different outcomes. But more often than not, things play out in a way I'd never anticipated.

"In case you hadn't noticed," I said icily, "this is a catastrophe." The remaining cereal from my breakfast was hardening on the side of the bowl. I picked up the bowl and my coffee mug and took them to the sink.

"It's a catastrophe we can't do anything about. Don't invent the next one. Let it go." He got up from the table. "I can't watch this anymore. I'm going upstairs to lie down awhile."

George and I were most likely to get into A Really Big Fight when we both were exhausted. And we were on the edge of a big one. Crazy as it seemed, I was still upset about not riding out the storm in our own house. If I were there, at least I'd know what was going on.

He gave me a quick kiss and headed upstairs. It was his way of saying, "I'm not happy right now, but I love you anyway. Now I'm going to give us both some space." He often did this when I was in a mood to argue. It used to annoy me, but over time I've noticed that it works. My mood will pass and I'll let go of whatever was annoying me, and things will be okay between us again.

I watched him go up the stairs, then retrieved my mug from the sink and poured myself another cup of coffee. The coffeemaker had shut off long ago, so I heated it in the microwave and sat down again to watch the news coverage.

MONDAY, AUGUST 29
The end of a day I'll never forget

It was nearly two o'clock in the afternoon and I was satiated with the news coverage. There was very little information that I hadn't already seen several times in the last hour. The taste of coffee in my mouth was sour.

Watching all this reminded me of the day the Twin Towers came down. I'd been out well past midnight the night before, working on an article, so I'd planned to go in to the office a little later than usual. Instead, I never left the house all day. I sat at the kitchen table watching television, just as I'd been doing today all through the morning and into the afternoon. The television networks replayed the scenes of the towers going down again and again. I finally had to shut it off. Still, the images of clouds of smoke and debris flashed like a slideshow in my brain, and my body wouldn't stop trembling.

Watching this hurricane slash parts of downtown New Orleans where I'd walked so many times was like watching the horror of 9/11 four years ago. Only this time it was my own city that was under attack. Not by terrorists, but by a force of nature beyond anyone's control. I was watching history unfold, and not knowing how the story would turn out was agonizing.

The news channel was still replaying footage of the Superdome roof in shreds. I shut the television off. French doors at the far end of the kitchen opened onto a screened porch overlooking the back yard. I slipped outside and sank into a chaise. The air was warm and humid, the sky still overcast, but the wind was picking up. How much of Katrina would make it all the way to north Georgia?

I must have fallen asleep out there, because the next thing I heard was a car pulling into the driveway. Maribeth? I got up and went inside.

I didn't know her as well as I knew Jeff. They hadn't begun dating when Jeff was in our wedding. We'd had dinner with them once or twice over the years when I accompanied George to meetings in Atlanta, but that was about it. I knew she was from Birmingham, and from the no-nonsense, uncluttered look of her kitchen, I guessed she was big on keeping things orderly—much more orderly than I kept my own home, even with Eloise helping to keep things tidy. She and Jeff had never had children. In my opinion, after you have kids, you learn to tolerate a little messiness. At least that was what I told people to justify my less than perfect housekeeping.

She marched into the kitchen, a bundle of unleashed energy after being confined in the car in traffic for more than an hour. "Well, Maggie, what do you hear from home? I've been listening to NPR off and on during the day and it—it sounds like things are pretty bad down there."

"I don't hear anything from home. The phones are out."

"Have you been watching the news?"

"We did for a while, but it was too intense. I had to turn it off."

She nodded, tried to smile, then perhaps thought that was a bad idea. "Of course." She looked around. "Where's George?"

"He's upstairs taking a nap. He drove the whole way yesterday, and he spent the day before we left boarding up the house. He's worn out."

"Poor man."

"In fact, I think I'll go check on him," I said. "Excuse me."

The door to the guest room was closed. When I opened it, the room was in semidarkness. The window shades were drawn. He still lay on his side, turned away from the door. How long had he been there—four hours? George was not one for long naps.

"Are you awake?"

No response. Normally I would have let him go on sleeping. But something about him just wasn't right. He was too still. The bedspread wasn't moving up and down with his breathing. I touched his shoulder and shook him gently. He didn't move.

"George? Honey, wake up." I sat beside him on the bed, rolled him over on his back and turned on the bedside lamp.

His eyes were closed, but his mouth was open. I touched his face. It was warm. I put my hand on his chest.

It wasn't moving. I felt for a heartbeat but I couldn't find one.

"George, you're scaring me. Wake up!"

What did they do in the movies to check for a pulse? Carotid artery. I ran my fingers along his neck, but my hand was shaking so badly I couldn't tell if he had a pulse or not.

I shook his shoulder, yelling, "George! George! Please wake up!"

I heard Maribeth's footfalls on the stairs. "Maggie, is everything all right?"

"I—I don't know."

"What's wrong?"

"I can't wake him up."

"Is he breathing?"

"I don't think so."

"I'll call 911. Do you know how to do CPR?"

I had a fleeting memory of a class I'd taken years ago at the country club. "Um, maybe."

"Well, do what you can." She picked up the phone on the bedside table and dialed. After a moment I heard her say, "Dammit."

"What?"

"If it's an emergency number, why do they put you on hold?"

I was trying to remember what I'd learned in CPR. One hand on top of the other. Push hard on the middle of the chest. Three compressions and a breath? Turn his head to the side in case he throws up? But George hadn't drowned.

All he'd had was black coffee. I started pumping his chest as hard as I could.

The clock beside the bed indicated it was 5:15. Rush hour in Atlanta. How long would it take an ambulance to get here? I stopped the chest compressions and stroked George's hair. I wanted to memorize every detail of him, right now, because this was my last chance before they took him away. Twenty-seven years of marriage, and you'd think I knew every freckle, the curve of his cheek, the shape of his nose, the dark brown hair now graying at the temples. We were the same age, fifty-one. We'd graduated in the same high school class. I had known him since ninth grade. And in that moment, it seemed as if I hardly knew him at all.

"Maggie, are you tired? Do you want me to take over?"

"No," I said, and went back to the chest compressions.

Sirens screamed in the distance. They grew louder, and I heard the ambulance pull into the driveway.

And then they were trotting up the stairs, two very efficient young people, a man and a woman in white uniforms, toting bags of gear. They nodded to me and went straight to George. I stepped back and stood by the door.

Maribeth and I watched silently as they worked. It was hard to see what was going on. The EMTs were bent over George, speaking in low tones, hooking up various devices, but their backs were blocking my view and I couldn't see much. Eventually I figured out they were trying to get his heart started with a defibrillator. The female EMT said, "Clear," and I heard the snap of the paddles and saw a flash of movement. And then she said, "Again."

"Keep trying," I said.

"We're doing the best we can, ma'am."

After an eternity, I heard the woman say, "Got a heartbeat."

He was alive.

They slid George onto a stretcher, secured his body with straps, and carried him down the curved staircase. I remember the ambulance door slamming shut. It seemed to take way too long before they pulled out of the driveway. Maribeth asked them which hospital they were going to and told me to get my purse. When I went back upstairs, I saw George's worn brown wallet on the bedside table. Insurance cards. Oh, right. George would always think of things like that. I could feel him standing next to me now, telling me to put his wallet in my purse because I was going to need it at the hospital.

And that's when I started to cry.

Maribeth came in, put her hand on my shoulder, and guided me downstairs and out to her car. She told me to put on my seat belt, as if I were a child. Maybe at that moment I was. She backed skillfully out of the driveway, maneuvering around George's SUV, and took off. She called Jeff on her cell phone and told him to meet us at the hospital.

Steel magnolia from Birmingham, I thought. Maybe she's got more going for her than I thought she did. Or maybe there's something to be said for not being emotionally involved in a terrible event. She dropped me off at the emergency room entrance and went to park the car.

The hospital was a confusion of corridors and official people at desks telling me to go here and wait there. I did need George's wallet and insurance cards. Stupid, stupid, stupid. My husband is in some curtained-off space somewhere and I don't know where he is or what's going on, and all these people care about is filling out paperwork. But they won't let me see him until I play their silly games and sign these forms that say God knows what. As if I'm going to sit there and read all that fine print at a time like this. Not that it matters. If I objected to anything in that fine print, too bad. Hospitals don't negotiate contracts with patients' family members in the emergency room. I sighed and signed.

Eventually I ended up in a chair in a waiting room. Maribeth and Jeff showed up a few minutes later and came to sit with me. Jeff wanted to know what happened. I started telling him about what we had been watching on TV all day. He said, "No, no, I mean what happened to George?"

"I'm trying to tell you. This is our home town being destroyed. Have you any idea what it's like to watch that? And he hadn't had much sleep, and he went upstairs, and when I went to check on him, he wasn't breathing and I couldn't feel a heartbeat."

"You're upset, Maggie. Understandably. Maybe it's not as bad as you think. Maribeth said they got his heart going again. Maybe they can bring him around."

At that point someone at the desk called my name. She directed me to an olive-skinned young woman with long dark hair wearing green scrubs. I followed her down a corridor to a tiny room with a sofa and chairs. I knew if she wasn't taking me to George, it wasn't good.

"Your husband had a massive heart attack, Mrs. McBride. When the emergency personnel treated him at your house, they were able to get his heart started. But he went into cardiac arrest again as he was arriving at the hospital. We did everything we could. I'm sorry."

This time I was the steel magnolia, holding on to whatever inner strength I had for as long as I could. "I want to see him."

She nodded. "Come with me."

More corridors. A small private room with walls, not flimsy curtains, thank God. George was on his back. His eyes were closed but his mouth was sagging open, struggling for one last breath. Just like my father looked after he died.

This isn't real, I thought. I'm asleep, I'm stressed out from everything that's happened, and I'm having a nightmare. I want to wake up now. I bit my lip, hard. It hurt. But I didn't wake up to a different scene.

"I'd like a few minutes alone with him," I told the doctor.

"Of course," she said. "Take as long as you like." She left the room.

I touched his face, smoothed his hair back from his forehead and stroked it. This couldn't be the end, not like this. We had so many things yet to do together. Caroline's wedding. Grandchildren. Retirement. Travel. Wake up, George. I don't want you to miss all this.

How do you touch someone after they die? The way you do when they're alive? I held his hand in both of mine and kissed the tips of his fingers. I didn't know what to do. He could have been asleep, but he wasn't. His body was growing cold. Part of me wanted to sit there with him and keep him company, while another part just wanted to run out of the room, out of this hospital, get as far away from this dead body as possible. But this wasn't a body out of some horror movie. This was George. It was all so confusing.

Oh, God. Caroline. I needed to call Caroline. I looked at my watch. We were in the Eastern time zone now. Three hours earlier in California, still the middle of the afternoon. Where would she be right now? At school? Her internship was over and classes had started. Maybe I should wait a couple of hours to call her. My area code 504 cell phone was quite dead, and hers must be also. I'd have to call Jason's cell. Every now and then my phone would give a sad bleat, advising me I had a voice mail that I couldn't retrieve.

Call her tonight, I thought, when she and Jason are both at home. Call her when the two of them are together. She's going to need him.

I eased myself onto the side of the narrow hospital bed and lay on my side next to George, my arm across his chest. How many times had we lain like this? How could this be the last time? Tears slid from the corner of my eye onto the pillow. I lay there until I had to sit up on the side of the bed to blow my nose.

I don't know how much time passed. I heard the click of the door and someone I hadn't seen before, a nurse, perhaps, asked, "Do you need anything?"

What did she mean by that? Did she really want to help, or was this a code for "Okay, time's up, we need the room, please get on with it."

"I need a lot of things," I said. "But I don't think you can provide them."

"Of course," she said.

As long as I could stay there with him, time would not pass. Outside that room, the future waited like a train that would carry me away from George, hurtling down the tracks into an unknown night. I didn't want to get on that train. But I had no choice.

I bent over and kissed his open mouth. Only it didn't feel like his mouth. It was rigid and didn't respond. I touched his face. "Goodnight, honey." I couldn't say goodbye.

Out in the corridor, the train was already at full throttle. The nurse said there would be an autopsy, but where would I want them to send the body afterward? I had no idea. I'd have to find a funeral home in Atlanta, I supposed. And then what? Have his body shipped back to New Orleans? I told her I'd have to talk to someone and let her know.

Jeff and Maribeth cried when I told them George was dead. We stood together in that waiting room with our arms around one another, sobbing.

As we left the hospital, it was getting dark. The wind was blowing hard now. What was left of Katrina was headed inland. We'd get some of the storm here after all.

Maribeth mentioned the name of a local funeral home. She said she'd call her church tomorrow and arrange for a minister to meet with me.

After that, we drove back to the house in silence. Maribeth pulled bowls of food out of the refrigerator, a meal she'd made yesterday when she expected us to arrive by suppertime. I shook my head and went into the darkened living room to sit while she and Jeff ate in the kitchen.

The phone call to Caroline was the hardest thing I'd ever done in my life, even harder than giving birth to her. Just a month ago I was agonizing over how to tell her I'd lost my job. What a joke.

"Caroline, honey, we've had a bad day."

"I know, Mom. I've been watching on television every chance I could."

"No, honey, it's worse than that. Daddy—" My voice broke. "Daddy died of a heart attack this afternoon."

She screamed. She screamed like I screamed when I was in labor with her, before they gave me the epidural. If only an epidural would help the pain now.

"But Daddy was in such good shape. He worked out every morning. He played golf."

"I know. But it was so hard on him, all the physical work of boarding up the house. He insisted on driving the whole way to Atlanta, and it took forever. And the stress of watching the storm—" My voice broke. "The doctor said all the hospitals around here are seeing a lot of patients from New Orleans coming into the emergency room."

At that moment it occurred to me that I might not be the only New Orleans wife evacuated to Atlanta who lost her husband today. And we all thought we'd be safe if only we could get away from the hurricane.

"What are you going to do about a funeral, Mom? You're going to bring him back home, right? The storm has passed. It should be okay to go home in a day or two."

"I don't know yet. I'll have to let you know."

I could hear Jason's voice in the background. "What is he saying?"

"He says to wait until the weekend to have the funeral, so we both can come. It'll be Labor Day weekend, and Jason will be able to get off from work."

I'm still getting used to the idea that my daughter is now part of a couple. Like her father and me.

"I'll see what I can do, honey."

We talked for a few more minutes, but there was little more to say. I was exhausted. I'd been running on adrenalin for much too long, and it had finally played itself out. My words weren't making sense. I felt as if I were drunk, but I hadn't had anything to drink.

Maribeth fretted about where I should sleep. She didn't think I should sleep in the room where my husband just died. There was a third bedroom, but Jeff used it as an office and it didn't have a bed. It had a small sofa. She asked if I wanted to sleep there. I told her I'd be fine in the guest room. I wanted to lie in the little double bed where George and I had slept fitfully for a few brief hours early this morning. It helped me feel close to him.

But I didn't sleep. That train kept rushing away, each minute another mile away from him, and there was no going back.

TUESDAY, AUGUST 30

I lay awake most of the night. I last looked at the clock around five, and when I opened my eyes again, it was after eight. I could hear someone moving around downstairs. Maribeth didn't have to go in to teach a class until afternoon, so she said she'd help me make arrangements. Arrangements: what a word. Nice, tidy, vague. And polite.

I got up and went into the bathroom, showered, dressed, and came downstairs to the kitchen. Maribeth waved a coffee pot at me. "Bet you'd like some of this."

"Yes," I said. I sat down at the table and let her pour me a cup.

"Now," she said in that no-nonsense, steel magnolia tone I was both coming to appreciate and grow weary of hearing, "I've got some time to help you this morning, but unfortunately not a lot. I can call a funeral home for you and set up an appointment. I can call my church and get a pastor to meet with you, if you'd like. I remember George was Presbyterian. We're Methodist. Do you mind if I call a Methodist pastor?"

"Um. I was raised Catholic. I'm afraid I don't know a lot about Methodists."

"All churches are the same, really. Don't worry about it."

I haven't set foot in a Catholic church since George and I got married, but I do know they're not the same as Methodists. I was in no mood to argue the point. But I knew if I didn't set some boundaries with Maribeth, she'd be running my life for me.

"What I really need to do this morning, Maribeth, is contact some people we know to tell them about George— his law partner, Tony Richards, for instance. My cell phone isn't working, and I'm not sure if Tony's is, either. Would it be all right if I made some long distance calls on your land line? I'd pay you for them, of course."

"Not a problem. Make all the calls you need."

"And I need to get into George's computer and check his emails, but I don't know his passwords. I hope I can figure that out. Oh."

"What?"

"I just remembered. George insisted on bringing a crate of file folders with us. They're still in the car. Maybe he had a list of his passwords."

And, as it turned out, he did. In a short time, while Maribeth was calling her church and the funeral home, I was on his laptop. When I opened his email program, the list of new emails ran on for pages. Most of them had headings reading "Where are you?" and "Are you okay?"

Oh my God. How am I going to tell all these people that George is dead?

One thing at a time. I emailed Tony and asked him to call me on the land line where we were staying. I added, "It's urgent." Didn't want to give him this news in an email.

In a matter of minutes, the phone rang. The caller ID had a 713 area code. Houston.

"Maggie? Are you in Atlanta?"

"Alpharetta, Georgia, Tony. You're in Houston?"

"Yes. You know the firm has an office over here. That's where I am. Sleeping in the office, actually. George said you hate Houston and he was having enough trouble trying to get you to leave without suggesting you come here, but he figured he could get you to agree to go to Atlanta."

I winced. George hadn't told me that.

Tony chuckled. "Just as well you went over there. You wouldn't believe how long it took to get to Houston. Seems like whoever didn't evacuate to Baton Rouge is here, and it's a mess. Are you guys okay? Where's George?"

Deep breath. I was going to be saying this many times over the next few days. "Tony, I have bad news. George died of a heart attack last night."

"Oh, Maggie. Oh my God."

I could hear him on the other end of the phone. It sounded like he was gasping for air. Or maybe he was crying. Tony probably spent more time with George than I had all these years. Waking hours, anyway.

"He's still at the hospital—" I realized it sounded as if George was still alive, just a patient waiting to be released and sent home. If only. "They're going to do an autopsy, then release the body. I thought I would make arrangements with a funeral home here to send him back to New Orleans, now that the storm has passed, and we could have a funeral there, maybe on Saturday. I know it's Labor Day weekend but—"

"Send him back to New Orleans? Maggie, have you seen the news this morning?"

"No, what?"

"The levees have breached all over the city. The worst one is at the 17th Street Canal in Lakeview, not far from our house. It breached yesterday morning, but with communications down, we didn't know how bad it was until today. The whole city is flooding. The Ninth Ward and New Orleans East, not surprising, because they've flooded before, years ago. But this time, with the 17th Street Canal levee breach, the flooding is just about everywhere. There's even water around the Superdome where all those people are stranded."

"How could water from Lakeview get down there? It's miles away."

"It's a hell of a breach. Maybe the size of two football fields. The storm surge in Lake Pontchartrain is pushing up into the canals and through the breaches. The Lower Ninth Ward is flooding from a breach on the Industrial Canal. The London Avenue Canal in Gentilly breached too. And water is coming up the Mississippi River Gulf Outlet and flooding St. Bernard Parish, downriver from the city. It's all under water, Maggie. We can't go home."

I slumped in the kitchen chair. It couldn't be. Was our house flooded? It had never flooded in our neighborhood. Was everything really gone?

"Maggie, are you still there?"

"Yes. I just can't take all this in at once."

"I know. Me either. But look. Let me give you a word of comfort about your situation, at least. George had life insurance, a lot of it. He wanted to take care of you and Caroline. He told me he wanted to be sure, if anything happened to him, that Caroline would have enough money to graduate from college. Even go to grad school. And you wouldn't have to worry about losing the house or being able to pay the bills. You two are going to be all right from a financial standpoint. Don't worry about that."

"He brought all these papers with us when we evacuated. Insurance policies, bank statements, stuff like that."

"Sounds like George."

"I need to get hold of our financial advisor."

"Jerry. He's our advisor, too. He went to Baton Rouge. I'll give you his number."

"I guess I should plan to have a service here in Atlanta, then. I'm not sure who will come. Maybe some of our friends evacuated here, too."

"Let me know what the plans are, and I'll catch a flight up. I'll certainly be there for you."

"Thanks, Tony."

After I hung up the phone, I turned on the television. The news channel was showing pictures of neighborhoods flooded to the rooftops, of people standing on their roofs waving white rags, of other people pulling them from those roofs into boats. I couldn't figure out what part of the city they were in. All the landmarks I might have spotted were under water. After a few minutes I had to shut it off. It was like watching a disaster movie filmed in my own city, only it was real.

Maribeth came in from the living room, her cell phone in her hand. "I've set up an appointment at the funeral home at eleven. And I've talked to someone at my church. One of the associate pastors is going to meet us there. Oh, Maggie, you don't look so good. You're white as a sheet."

"New Orleans is gone," I said.

SEPTEMBER

Thursday, September 1

On Tuesday morning we met with the funeral director and the associate pastor of Maribeth's church, an attractive young woman with short blonde hair, not my idea of a minister, but she seemed kind and supportive. So was the funeral director, a courtly Southern gentleman from Georgia who spoke in a soft accent that sounded like he didn't want to bruise his words—not at all like the melting pot of German-Irish-Italian-immigrant English that one still heard in parts of New Orleans. The two of them are probably used to dealing with people stunned by grief, but all of this is new to me.

We planned a service on Saturday morning. I decided to have George's remains cremated so I can have his ashes with me and bury them when I can. We'd never talked about what we wanted, but I always figured we'd be buried together in New Orleans. Right now, that's just not going to happen.

The news reports say eighty percent of the city is under water. Actually, that number gives me hope. Our house is on high ground near the river, in the older part of the city. We just might be in the twenty percent that didn't flood.

When I sat down at my own laptop on Tuesday afternoon, I had hundreds of emails, just like George did. Everyone I ever knew has been trying to find me. Our friends are scattered all over the country, but most of them are within driving distance of New Orleans. Some are even in Atlanta. I finally composed a single letter about what happened to George and copied and pasted it to each one.

Everyone expressed shock and offered condolences. Some said they would try to get to Atlanta by for the service.

One of the emails cluttering my inbox was from the airline, advising us that there was a problem with our flight from New Orleans to LaGuardia on Friday. Oh, God, I'd totally forgotten that we were supposed to go to New York for Labor Day weekend. A problem with our flight? Oh, yeah. The whole airport is shut down with no power or air conditioning, and there are sick people in the main area of the terminal lying wall-to-wall on blankets on the floors, waiting to be transported to hospitals elsewhere.

We'd made hotel reservations and bought Broadway tickets. More stuff to deal with. I wonder if I can get any of that money back.

My phone was finally starting to return to life. They must have rerouted the cellular service to other towers. I could get a few calls in and out this morning. Even after talking to our financial advisor, I was worrying about money. The funeral home wanted to be paid, and I didn't know if I'd even be able to use my bank account because of the storm.

No problem, I found out. The bank was far better prepared for a disaster than the City of New Orleans. They moved all their operations to Baton Rouge and were doing business as usual.

Just before we left for the funeral home, Seth Dupree called. He wanted to know how we were doing and if I had any news of what's happened on our street. He and Noreen and the dogs were at her parents' house in Houston. I didn't have his email address, so I hadn't written to him about George.

When I told him, he said, "George was a good man. I really liked him. He was honest, a man of his word. If he said he'd do something for you, he would. I'm so sorry, Maggie."

"Seth, I—I have to ask. You're a cardiologist. I mean, I know you weren't his doctor, but you knew him as a friend. He was in good physical shape. How could this have happened? Why? I'm sorry, I know I shouldn't be asking you, but I've had to deal with doctors I don't know, a hospital I don't know . . ." My voice trailed off as the tears spilled down my cheeks. "Oh, God."

There was a long silence on the other end of the line, and for a moment I thought the connection had been lost. Finally he said, "I'm so sorry this happened, Maggie. You're right, I wasn't his doctor. All I can say is that sometimes the first symptom of a heart attack is sudden death. I know that sounds harsh, and you probably don't want to hear that right now. But the hard truth is, a lot of people who evacuated for Katrina are dying right now. Some were already very sick, and the stress of getting out may have hastened their deaths. But there were others, like George, who seemed healthy enough and then just died without warning. He may have had some underlying medical issues that you weren't aware of. He may have had chest pain and decided it was indigestion and ignored it. Or maybe he didn't have any symptoms. It's hard to say. I wish I had answers that could give you comfort. I get asked questions like yours a lot. It's the hardest part of my work."

My nose was starting to run, and I couldn't find a box of tissues. "I didn't mean to put you on the spot. I just—I just had to ask."

"Of course."

"The service is Saturday. In Atlanta."

"I don't think we'll be able to come. Our situation is kind of in flux right now. It looks like my practice is going to relocate to Baton Rouge, and we need to find a place to stay. But we want to send flowers. Just tell me where."

I gave him the information. "Thank you, Seth. Give my best to Noreen."

FRIDAY, SEPTEMBER 2

I haven't been able to get hold of Eloise. Her home phone
and cell don't answer. All I get is an electronic voice that
tells me her voice mailbox is unavailable. Where is she? Her
home is in Hollygrove, in the Carrollton neighborhood, and
that part of town did flood. I saw horrifying pictures on the
news of a block of houses on South Carrollton Avenue
across from the Catholic seminary that caught fire, possibly
due to a gas leak. They burned all the way down to the water
line, the flames reflected in the murky floodwaters. There
was no way for a fire truck to get to them. I hope that didn't
happen to Eloise's house. I hope she and Robert got out. I
know she'll call me when she can. Oh, dear God, I can't take
any more losses right now.

Caroline and Jason are flying in from Los Angeles
tonight and should arrive around midnight. Monday is
Labor Day, and Jason has to get back to work on Tuesday.
He'll fly back around noon on Monday. Caroline is going
to stay with me for a few days. The school has given her time
off for bereavement purposes.

I had to buy a dress and heels and panty hose to wear
to the funeral. I'd only packed some slacks and shorts and

t-shirts for the trip—after all, we figured we'd be gone just a couple of days. It was strange to be in a shopping mall in Atlanta, seeing people wearing black and gold New Orleans Saints t-shirts and knowing they were evacuated too.

I'm not sure what we're going to do after the weekend. Maribeth acts very kindly toward me, but I can see the wheels turning in her head. If New Orleans is shut down, where am I going to go? Does she think I plan to stay in her guest room forever? None of us thought George and I would be here more than a couple of days. We'd go home after the storm passed. But now the city is shut down and the National Guard won't let anybody in. Where am I going to go, indeed?

SATURDAY, SEPTEMBER 3

Jeff drove me to the airport last night to pick up Caroline and Jason. I was grateful because I don't know my way around, and the Atlanta airport is a long way from Alpharetta. They were tired and rumpled, not having slept much on the plane. They'd talked about staying at a hotel, but even here in suburban Atlanta the hotels are full of evacuees.

Maribeth said, "Of course they can stay here. We'll just have a big old house party."

I figured they could have the guest room and I'd sleep on the sofa in Jeff's office. But when we got back to the house, Maribeth had already planned the sleeping arrangements. "Now Caroline, you and your mother have a lot to talk about. You two can stay in the guest room. Jason, you can sleep on the sofa in Jeff's office, or on the living room sofa if you prefer—it's longer."

I saw the flash of anger on Jason's face. I opened my mouth, then closed it. As clearly as if he were standing next to me, I heard George say, "Maggie! Her house, her rules!"

Jason and Caroline exchanged a look. She was clearly embarrassed. Jason said evenly, "I'm sure the office will be fine."

Maribeth beamed. "Great. Just follow me." She headed up the stairs.

I mouthed "I'm sorry" to Caroline, but she just shook her head.

It was around three in the morning before we finally went to bed, and we were up at seven. Some day I'll catch up on my sleep, but I'm not sure when. We had to be at the church by nine-thirty, and people started arriving at ten for the visitation before the service at noon.

Maribeth and her woman associate pastor did well. They even arranged a punch-and-cookies reception after the service in the fellowship hall, put together by some church ladies who'd heard we were evacuees from New Orleans. Complete strangers went out of their way to be kind when they learned what had happened to George.

I was surprised by the number of people who came. Some were friends who had evacuated to Atlanta. Some, like Tony, came from as far away as Houston. Sophie Abrams, my roommate from Syracuse days, sent flowers. Jeff and Tony gave eulogies. Jeff told some funny stories from our wedding, stuff I hadn't thought about in years. To my surprise, I laughed. I didn't think I could laugh at my husband's funeral.

At the reception afterward, people stood around for hours talking. Not so much about George, but about what had happened to them in the last week. Each one had a story to tell about how they got out and where they ended up. Talking to them helped to take my mind off my own pain.

Some people had evacuated to one place and now had moved to another when things didn't work out where they were. People who evacuated to their weekend homes within a relatively short driving distance from New Orleans got caught in the path of the storm as it moved inland. Trees down, no power, no water if they were on a well with an electric pump. They had to cut their way out with chainsaws and go to a place that had power. Some people found motel rooms but had to leave them. Some slept in their cars.

Some were talking about buying houses in the places where they'd landed. Many were staying with friends or relatives and, like me, knew they were wearing out their welcome and couldn't stay much longer. And also like me, they were wondering where to go next. Some people knew that their homes had flooded and they couldn't go back. Some weren't sure what had happened. It was all so strange, but it was our new reality, and it was good to be with people who shared my bewilderment.

A few people had stayed for the storm and by the grace of God didn't end up on their rooftops. The ones whose homes hadn't flooded had to deal with gaping holes in roofs and rain pouring in. With no electricity, no television, no phones, and unreliable news reports on the radio, they really didn't know what was going on. But on Thursday, water started bubbling up from manhole covers in the street. That's when they realized how bad the flooding was, and they had to get out. The city shut off the water and natural gas—something that had never happened before in my memory. The big fears were that the water supply had been contaminated by leaking pipes and that ancient underground gas lines might have broken from the weight of flood water and would cause explosions and fires.

Getting out of town four days after the storm wasn't easy, not even with a full tank of gas. Rumors were being reported as facts: armed gangs roaming the streets, drug addicts who'd run out of drugs, a city where the police and firefighters weren't going to come because they were too busy trying to rescue people. Nobody knew what to believe, but everyone was terrified of looters and shooters. You couldn't cross the Mississippi River Bridge because law enforcement on the West Bank had set up a blockade. A shopping mall across the river had been torched. No one trusted anyone.

The stories were crazy and scary. It just didn't seem real—that ordinary folks I'd known for years had gone through the things they were telling me.

And I had wanted to stay, just like they did. What if George had had the heart attack while we were at home during the hurricane? With the phones out, there would have been no way to call for help, and nobody would have come anyway. He would have died there in the house, in the heat and the darkness at night. What would I have done, alone, watching my husband die? And then sitting with his body for days in the heat?

It was late afternoon before we got back to Jeff and Maribeth's house. I was exhausted, the voices of all the people I'd talked to still bouncing around in my head:

Flooded cars everywhere. Oil, gasoline, brake fluid, everything washing into that flood water. Raw sewage backed up. Dead animals floating in it. Dead people. It's a toxic soup.

It's going to take ten, twenty years for the city to recover. Maybe never.

We're leaving. We never want to evacuate again.

We're buying a house in Baton Rouge.

My job is gone. I haven't gotten my paycheck for August. I don't know how I'm going to pay my bills.

Maggie, you can make a fresh start. Stay in Atlanta.

I sank into Maribeth's gold living room sofa, looking around the room. White walls. Wood-burning fireplace with a gilt-edged mirror above it. Floor-to-ceiling windows covered in pale green silk drapes that spilled onto the floor. Off-white carpet with a deep pile. French doors leading out onto a covered porch. It was a lovely room. But it wasn't my living room. And I wanted to be in my living room so badly right now. From the conversations I'd heard today, I was pretty sure my neighborhood hadn't flooded. But how much damage had the house sustained?

Caroline came in, Jason beside her. She cradled the bronze urn containing George's ashes like a beloved child. Carefully she set it on the coffee table, then she and Jason sat down beside me.

"I can't quite get my head around it, that this is Daddy," she said. "Maybe it would be real to me if I'd just seen him one last time."

I put my arm around her, resting my head against hers. "Neither one of us got to tell him goodbye. It's so hard."

Jason cleared his throat. "I wish I'd gotten to know him better. We only met that one time, when you came to Syracuse to visit last spring. I think we would have gotten along well."

"I'm sure you would," I said. "He had a great deal of respect for you." Not entirely true. George had been decidedly unhappy when the two of them moved in together, but he was wise enough not to say anything to them. But at a time like this, it was best to let that go.

I couldn't decide how I felt about Jason. He was quiet and reserved, hard to get a bearing on. I thought I was picking up a tension between him and Caroline, but I wasn't sure what it was about. Nerves? Here they were, relatively new as a couple and so young, dealing with their first big personal crisis—the death of Caroline's father. Jason was among strangers here. Except for me, he was meeting everyone for the first time. Maribeth's insistence on separating the two of them in the sleeping arrangements probably didn't help matters any.

All I could do was hope he'd be good to my daughter. How they weathered this crisis together would set a precedent for the future of their relationship.

That evening, we got on Jeff's computer and did a search of satellite images of the city in the wake of the storm.

Jeff's pretty good at this, and so is Jason. They managed to find a grid of our neighborhood and zoomed in as high as the resolution would go. Houses, streets, trees appeared. We could see shadows, suggesting the sun was out when the images were taken, so this had to be a few days after the storm passed.

We saw flooded streets, but it was hard to tell how deep the water was. We recognized a hospital about a mile from the house by the circular down ramp at one side of the parking garage. It was surrounded by water. The streets were straight rivers with trees on either side.

We scanned slowly through the satellite image until we could see pavement, indicating an area was dry. Here was St. Charles Avenue. No flooding. We could see the massive oak trees the street was famous for, but they appeared to be blocking the roadway. Of course. Limbs or entire trees would have fallen in the storm. But the landmark buildings were recognizable: schools, a library, a drugstore. A cluster of dots at one unflooded intersection, we realized, were people. It was a staging area where rescuers had brought them by boat or helicopter to wait for buses to take them out of the area.

Where was our street? Our house? I held my breath. One block, another, another.

"There it is!" Caroline pointed a finger at the screen. I saw the roof, the brick-lined garden beds, the front sidewalk. No water. I exhaled.

Jeff said, "The resolution's not good enough to tell if you have damage to your roof. But it does look like there's a tree pretty close to it."

"Pecan tree in the back yard," I said, remembering that George had warned me it might fall on the house.

"It didn't flood," said Caroline. "Oh, Mom, the house is all right."

"Maybe not all right," I said. "If the roof was damaged, water probably got inside. But you're right, that's not as bad as if it had flooded."

Later that night, as Caroline and I were getting ready for bed in the guest room, she said, "Have you been able to get hold of Eloise?"

I shook my head. "When I call her cell, I just keep getting a recording. Of course, the phones are so messed up right now, that doesn't necessarily mean anything. If they evacuated somewhere out of state, with the 504 phones not working, they may have gotten a new phone with a different area code, like some of the people who came to the funeral."

"Surely she'd call to let us know where she was, wouldn't she?"

"My phone's only working now and then. Hers too, probably, if she's still got it. I don't know if she memorized my cell number. If she had to get a new phone, my number wouldn't be stored in it."

"We need to find out what's happened to her."

I sighed. I'd seen the photos of flooding in Carrollton. I hoped Eloise and Robert managed to get out of their house before the water got too high. But if their car flooded, then what? Would they have been among those tiny dots we saw on the satellite image, people rescued from their flooded neighborhoods who were waiting for buses to take them to Baton Rouge and Houston?

Or did they drown in their house? I couldn't bear to think of the horror of Eloise and Robert standing on a sofa or table in their own home, trying to keep their heads above the flood water, but it kept rising, and then . . .

No. I wasn't going there.

"I hope she and Robert are all right. But I have no idea how to find them, except to keep trying the number and hoping that eventually the call goes through."

"We have to find her. And I have to know what happened to Mister Whiskers, too."

"Honey, I'm so sorry he got away. I did leave him food and water under the house. I'm guessing he rode out the storm there. He'll be okay."

"The food and water have probably run out by now." She jutted out her chin, like she did when she was little and demanding her way. "I want to go home. I want to find Eloise. And Mister Whiskers."

"We can't go back. The city is shut down. Nobody can get in."

"There's got to be a way. You and I both know a lot of back roads. The National Guard can't possibly have blockades on all of them."

I hesitated. Caroline had just given voice to my own deepest longing. I wanted to go home, too. I wanted to make coffee in my own kitchen and drink it at my own table again. And I wanted to find Eloise, but if she was in her house, she was probably dead. And if she wasn't in her house, she probably wasn't in New Orleans at all.

To go back to the city right now felt like walking into a pitch-dark room where we didn't know where the furniture was. There were so many unknowns. What if we got back to our house and found it unlivable? Where would we go? "I don't know, honey."

"Mister Whiskers has been my cat since I was ten. I have to find him."

I sighed. Caroline lost her father without seeing him one last time, and now she wanted to find her cat, who disappeared before she could see him one last time. Got it. As for Eloise, well, I doubted we'd find her alive in the city, but maybe we could learn what had happened to her.

"I can think of a dozen reasons not to do this. You know there aren't any utilities working or gas stations or grocery stores open."

"It'll be an adventure, Mom. The two of us."

I shook my head. "I can only think of one reason to do this, baby. I want to go home just as much as you do."

"I'm not a baby. Don't call me that."

"You've been away from New Orleans too long. Even the checkout ladies in the grocery store call you 'baby.'"

She laughed. "You're right. I'd forgotten."

I hugged her. "Okay, baby. Let's go home."

SUNDAY, SEPTEMBER 4

Jeff and Maribeth went to church this morning. They invited me to join them, but I declined. I'm not sure how I feel about God right now. A few idiot TV preachers are saying Katrina is God's judgment on New Orleans for hosting the Southern Decadence festival over Labor Day weekend. Jeff assures me that their church doesn't believe in that hogwash, but I'm still not in a mood to hear any more about God than I heard yesterday at the memorial service. It was a nice service, and I thanked the minister for it, but I'm not sure I want to believe in a God who let Katrina happen and let my husband die too soon.

Caroline and Jason bowed out of church too. They took the SUV and went out for brunch and did some shopping. I think they needed some time together to do normal things, to talk without having all these other people around eavesdropping.

I was looking forward to having some time alone to regroup and process the last few days, but Tony called and wanted to drop by before he headed back to Houston. As it turned out, his timing was good. We needed to talk privately about George's financial affairs.

We sat down at the kitchen table with coffee. Tony said, "I want to lay out some things you need to know to start the process of settling George's affairs. Louisiana law is different from other states. It follows the old French Napoleonic Code. What we have to do is called opening a succession in Louisiana."

"I know. I had to deal with my father's succession."

"Good. You know some of the basics. What makes this one a little tricky is Katrina. In a way, you're lucky George died here. You won't have any trouble getting death certificates to file for his life insurance. In New Orleans right now—" He sighed. "It's absolute chaos. City Hall was flooded. The courts were flooded. God knows how long it will be before any of that is up and running again."

The anger hit me unexpectedly, like a bullet to the chest. "Excuse me," I said. "Did you just say I was lucky? My husband dropped dead on Monday in the middle of the worst disaster ever to hit New Orleans, I don't know what's happened to my home, the National Guard won't let me back into the city, and you're telling me I'm lucky?"

Tony ducked his head. "I'm sorry, Maggie. Poor choice of words. No offense intended." He ran a finger around the rim of his coffee cup. "This has been a nightmare for everyone. We're all feeling a little raw. None of us had any previous experience to prepare us for a disaster like this. Right now I'm trying to find a little bit of hope wherever I can. When you told me on Tuesday about George—well, it was the last thing I expected. We'd known each other for so long."

He picked up his cup, then set it down untouched. "George named me his executor in his will. The original is in the files at the office downtown. We're on a high floor, so I know the office didn't flood, and with the power out, I doubt that any looters would climb that many flights of stairs to steal paperwork out of a law office. I'm guessing there's a copy in those files you brought with you."

"I found it. I'll go get it."

I went upstairs and retrieved the box of papers and brought them down to the kitchen and set the box on the table. Tony went over the will with me, paragraph by paragraph. I pulled out my reporter's notebook from my purse—I still carry one, a journalist's habit—and began making notes.

After Tony left, I suddenly remembered I'd gotten a notice for jury duty in Orleans Parish some time later this month. I laughed to myself. "Don't think I'll be going."

Caroline and Jason returned around mid-afternoon, toting shopping bags from an electronics store. Not the shopping I'd thought they were doing. I'd envisioned clothes, not gadgets. "What did you get?" I asked.

Caroline waved a hand dismissively. "Just some stuff I need for school. Video equipment."

I smiled. "You picked the right major. Even when I was in college, the broadcast majors told the newspaper and magazine majors that print was dead."

"Print *is* dead, Mom. Think about it. Where are you getting your information about Katrina? Not from printed newspapers. From television news networks and the

Internet. From emails and chat groups online. And videos people are posting."

"You're right. Everyone from New Orleans and the Gulf Coast is scattered all over the country and desperate for news of home. We couldn't read a local print newspaper right now if we wanted to. The papers are publishing online. Even the local television stations are finding ways to broadcast to other cities where a lot of people have evacuated, like Houston. I don't understand the technology, but I'm glad it's there."

The five of us—Jeff, Maribeth, Caroline, Jason, and I— had dinner together in Maribeth's stately dining room: crystal chandelier, Oriental rug, polished mahogany table, chairs upholstered in ivory silk. Jeff sat at one end of the table, Maribeth at the other. Caroline and Jason sat together, and I sat across from them. It felt so strange not to have George beside me. Maribeth had quietly removed the sixth chair from the table so I didn't have that reminder next to me, but the empty space was still there.

Jeff asked Jason about his work on the television show. Quiet Jason finally opened up, talking at length about work he clearly enjoyed, even though it was an entry-level position. I watched him, animated at last, sitting directly across the table from me. He had tousled black hair, a round face that still hadn't lost its child's softness, and black-framed, squared-off glasses. Kids probably thought he was a nerd when he was growing up. But I saw his black eyes flash with delight when he laughed, and I saw the way my daughter turned to him and laughed with him, not a forced laugh but an easy one that comes from being comfortable with the person beside you.

Please don't break her heart.

Over dessert and coffee, Maribeth turned to me. "Maggie, this has been such a difficult time for you and your family. We never dreamed all this would happen, and we—Jeff and I—are glad that we were able to be here for you."

"I'm so grateful for your hospitality and all your help with the funeral, Maribeth. I'm a stranger here, and I wouldn't have known which way to turn. Thank you."

"We are blessed, Maggie. But—"

I knew there was a *but* coming. I waited.

"—we were wondering what your plans are. I mean, what you're going to do. I know Jason is leaving tomorrow and Caroline is staying on for a few days, and . . ." She waved her hand.

What you want to say, I thought, is *when are you going to leave?*

"Caroline and I are going home," I said.

Jeff's spoon clattered in his coffee cup. "What? You can't go back. The city is shut down."

"We have to find our friend Eloise," said Caroline. "We haven't heard from her."

"Do you think she's still in the city?" asked Jeff. "I heard everyone had to leave."

"It's a place to start," she said. "And I want to look for Mister Whiskers, my cat. He ran away when Mom and Daddy were evacuating."

I saw Jason shoot her a look, and I saw her deliberately ignore him.

"And I need to see firsthand what's happened to the house," I said. "Nobody from the news channels has gone into the areas that didn't flood and sent back a report, 'Hey, looks pretty good here, Joe.' I know the house didn't flood, but I don't know what damage has been done."

Jeff nodded. "I understand. But what will you do after you get there? You can't stay. What have they been saying on the news about going into the city? 'Look and leave'? There's no power, no water. It's dangerous for the two of you to be alone there right now. No telling what's going on. You'll have to find someplace out of the city to stay. Do you know where you'll go after you've seen the house?"

"We'll just have to figure that out when we get there, I guess."

"I don't know, Maggie. I think you need to have a plan."

Jeff was right. I didn't have a plan. I just wanted to go home.

I saw Jason give Caroline another look. *He doesn't like this idea either,* I thought.

"Caroline and I are working on a plan," I said. "We'll let you know."

After Jeff and Maribeth had gone upstairs to bed, Caroline and Jason and I stayed in the living room and watched a DVD of a movie we found in the media cabinet. For two hours, we had an escape from the reality of the past week.

After an hour and a half, Caroline fell asleep leaning against Jason. He was having trouble keeping his eyes open, too. When the movie ended, I hit the button to slide the DVD out of the player. The sound of it woke Caroline. She looked up, startled.

I crossed the room to the sofa where they were, leaned over and whispered, "It's Jason's last night here. The two of you take the guest room. I'll sleep on the sofa here."

Caroline said, "No, Mom, it's all right."

I grinned. "Go ahead. What Maribeth doesn't know won't hurt her."

"Thanks, Mrs. McBride," said Jason.

I watched the two of them tiptoe up the stairs so as not to disturb Maribeth, who I hoped was sleeping peacefully by then. If she got up early and found me on the sofa, I could make something up about falling asleep after the movie. Or not. What could she do, anyway?

My cell phone rang in my pocket. It was one o'clock in the morning. The number was from the 504 area code. I answered it quickly, hoping it hadn't wakened Maribeth.

"Mags, where the hell are you?"

"Mickey? Where are you?"

"In New Orleans, darlin'. Again I ask, where the hell are you?"

"Outside of Atlanta. What are you doing in New Orleans? I thought everybody had to leave."

"The media lie. You ought to know that by now, being part of it yourself. Hell, I'm working. Biggest news story of my career. I've got freelance assignments out the wazoo.

Every big media outlet wants a reporter on the ground, who knows his way around the city, covering Katrina. I'm their man. What are you doing in Atlanta? You ought to be here, picking up some awesome freelance work. They're paying big bucks."

"Mickey, are you drunk?'

"It's midnight in New Orleans. Of course I'm drunk. Everybody else is."

"Why are you calling me?"

"Because I was thinking about you and wondering where you were. But don't get your head all swelled. I've been calling a lot of people, just trying to track them down."

"Where are you staying? What's it like in the city?"

"I'm at my house on Tchoupitoulas Street. Sliver on the river. You know, high ground in the older part of town. No flooding. Got a couple of guys staying with me. Fellow journalists. No power, no water, no baths, no shaving. We all stink."

"Where are your wife and children?"

"In Charlotte, at her parents' house. The kids are already enrolled in school. They're going to stay up there at least through the semester. No schools open here."

"Mickey, can you do me a favor?"

"Let me guess. You want me to check on your house."

"Yes."

"You and everyone else I've called. Sure. Give me the address."

I gave it to him, wondering if he was writing it down, and if not, if he'd even remember in the morning that he'd talked to me. "My daughter and I want to drive back in the next few days. We want to check on the house, but after that I'm not sure where we'll go."

"You and your daughter? What about your husband? Is he going to stay in Atlanta?"

Deep breath. "He died of a heart attack the day of the storm."

"Aw, jeez, Maggie, I'm sorry. That's awful. A lot of people have lost family members in this thing. I'm hearing stories every day."

"Thanks, Mickey. This is so hard."

"Well, I'll check on your house for you. And come on back. Things are not great here, but they're not as bad as people are telling you. There really are people staying in the city, not just emergency workers and journalists. Some never left, especially Uptown where it didn't flood. I live across the street from the riverfront wharves, and the Port of New Orleans is open for business. It reopened as soon as ships could navigate the Gulf of Mexico after the storm passed. People are working on the docks. Entergy and crews from all over the country are fixing the power lines. People who own businesses are trying to put things back together. Not a lot of folks around, but we're here. Come on home. I can put you in touch with some national editors who are looking for writers. We can get you up and running again."

"Mickey? One other favor?"

"Sure. What?"

"I'm trying to find someone. Eloise Jackson. And her husband Robert. She works for me. I haven't been able to reach her on the phone. They live in Hollygrove." I gave him the address.

"Mmmmm. I hate to tell you, but that whole area flooded badly. Water up to the rooftops in some places. Nobody's living back there. Only way in right now is by boat."

"Still?"

"Still. The water's starting to go down, but all those streets are still flooded. The National Guard has the area blocked off. I'll see what I can do, but I can tell you, she's probably not there."

I closed my eyes. Either Eloise and Robert had evacuated, or they were dead. "Thanks, Mickey."

WEDNESDAY, SEPTEMBER 7

Caroline and I left Alpharetta before dawn this morning. On Monday, Labor Day, she and Jeff and I took Jason to the airport, then came back and had a cookout in the Winters' back yard. On Tuesday, we bought stuff to take back with us: coolers to fill with ice, drinks, canned food, four battery-operated lanterns and lots of extra batteries, Mister Whiskers' favorite cat food, a dozen gallons of bottled water. I know I've got canned food and bottled water in the upstairs closet—my "hurricane stash"—but I'm not sure how many days it will be before we can buy supplies again. Better to have more than we need than to run out.

Our new purchases, Caroline's luggage and electronics-store bags, and everything George and I had brought with us filled the entire back seat and storage area of the SUV. I wrapped the urn containing George's ashes in one of his polo shirts and tucked it gently inside his weekend bag with the clothing and toiletries he'd brought with him. The bag smelled like him, a mix of aftershave and toothpaste and a hint of sweat. There was something comforting in the thought that he was coming home with us. Looking out for us on the journey.

The early morning North Georgia air was cool on my face and arms as I shut the back of the SUV and climbed into the driver's seat. It wouldn't be this cool in New Orleans for another six weeks. It hadn't rained in the city since the storm passed, and there wasn't any in the forecast for the immediate future. The temperatures were running in the high 90s in the afternoons.

I love air conditioning. I'm not going to be happy living without it.

Mickey called late Monday night. "I went by your house. Walked up the driveway and looked around. It doesn't look like anyone's broken in. You've got a tree down that's leaning against the house. It looks like it took out a section of your roof. Not sure how much damage there is. Oh, and your famous red Mustang is all right. I looked through the garage window and saw it. Can't believe you left it, Maggie. I know how nuts you are about that car."

"Who knew it was going to be this bad?"

"Yeah, you're right. As for your friend's house in Hollygrove, I got somebody to take me into her neighborhood in a boat. The flood water is coming down, but you can see the water line's up to the roof. There's a dormer window that's been smashed. Could have been from flying debris, or maybe somebody broke it to get out of the attic."

"You think they had to go up to the attic?" I'd seen the news footage of people on their roofs, waving bed sheets and holding signs begging rescuers to save them. I closed my eyes. Dear God, not Eloise.

"If they didn't get out before the water came up, the attic was the only place they could go. I saw a car in the driveway, still partly submerged. Did they have two cars? Maybe they took the other one."

"No, just one. Tan. Toyota, I think."

"That was it. No one's going to be driving that car again. If they got out, it was either by boat or helicopter."

Or they drowned inside, I thought, but quickly forced myself not to think about it.

I told him of our plans to leave on Wednesday, and he told me which roads were open.

"The roads along the Mississippi Gulf Coast are all flooded, so you can't come in that way. The storm surge took out the twin bridges over the east end of Lake Pontchartrain. You can't come that way, either. Take I-20 from Atlanta through Birmingham and go on to Jackson, then head south on I-55 into Louisiana. The National Guard has the interstate shut down just south of Ponchatoula, but you can get off and take U.S. 51, the old two-lane, to LaPlace."

He gave me directions to get to the high ground along the Mississippi River levee, and I wrote them down in my reporter's notebook. "I think I can find it," I said. "How do you know all this?"

"Got people coming into the city, bringing me supplies," he said. "They tell me which roads are open. It's crazy here, Maggie, like living in a war zone. Roadblocks everywhere. Soldiers with guns. And some of the troops that are here, well, they've actually been in a war zone. Iraq. Afghanistan. Stuff like that. I've talked to some of them."

"I thought you told me things weren't so bad."

"Not as bad as you may have heard. Hell, I haven't eaten anyone's pet dog. At least not yet."

"Oh, that's comforting."

"You know what I mean. Some of this stuff you're seeing on the news is just crazy. You'd think there are looters everywhere, running around the streets with automatic weapons, shooting at people. I've been to a lot of neighborhoods in the last week, and I've talked to a lot of scared and angry and hurting people. But a lot of these stories you're hearing are just rumors and can't be substantiated. Come on home and see for yourself."

So in the darkness Wednesday morning, Caroline and I pulled out of the Winters' driveway. Jeff and Maribeth stood together by the garage door, his arm around her in the pre-dawn cool, and waved goodbye. I promised to call and let them know how we were doing. But as I turned into the street and drove away, I felt an enormous sense of relief to see their house in the rear-view mirror. They had been kind. It wasn't that. Everything terrible that had happened to my family in the last ten days had taken place or had been witnessed on television in that house. I let out a long sigh.

"Glad to go home, huh, Mom?"

I smiled. "Oh, yes. You too?"

"Pedal to the metal. Let's go."

From Alpharetta we drove south on Georgia 400, headed west on I-285 and west again on I-20 toward

Birmingham, retracing the route George and I had taken ten days earlier. I'd made sure to leave before the infamous Atlanta morning rush started. We saw some cars on the roads as the sky began to lighten, but we didn't see real traffic until we got to I-20. Fortunately, it was headed in the other direction, toward the city we were leaving.

I still had flashes of anger that all these people were carrying on with their normal lives, going to work or school or whatever they did, while for all of us from New Orleans and the Mississippi Gulf Coast, well over a million people, life was no longer normal and might never be normal again.

But I was still alive, and I had my daughter with me, and my house was still standing and hadn't flooded. These were things to be thankful for.

We crossed into Central Daylight Time at the Alabama state line and hit Birmingham just in time for that city's rush hour. We got off the interstate and found a Waffle House. The pre-dawn coffee we'd drunk in the car was long gone, and we were both ready for breakfast.

A waitress took our order and brought us fresh coffee. As we waited for our food, Caroline said, "Mom, do you think Eloise is dead?"

I shook my head. "Eloise is tough. She's a survivor. She found a way to get out of her house. I'm sure of it."

"In my reporting class, they talked about how to track down people you want to interview. I know you've probably done that lots of times. How would you find Eloise?"

It hadn't occurred to me to look at this from the standpoint of a reporter, but Caroline was right. "I can't reach her on her phone. It could be she lost it in the evacuation. It could have fallen in the water, I don't know. Maybe wherever she ended up, she got another phone. Or borrowed someone else's. I don't know if she's got my cell number memorized, but I'm sure she knows the land line by heart after all these years. One way or the other, we'll hear from her eventually. It might take some time, though."

"You're depending on her to call you. What can you do to track her down? Would you contact the Red Cross? The police?"

"I could try. But they probably have requests to find thousands of people right now. I did get my friend Mickey to go over to her house. He says it's still flooded over there. I guess I'd go back again after the water goes down."

"You're saying all we can do is wait?"

"Maybe Mickey will have some ideas. He seems to know people. I don't think she's at her house, but maybe we can find a clue there as to where she might have gone."

But I was worried. When Mickey told me he'd found her car in the driveway, I knew she hadn't left before the water came up. She and Robert could well be still in the house. Dead.

When we left the restaurant, Caroline offered to drive, and I was more than happy to hand over the keys to her. I was tired, and it was still morning. It was a hot, sunny September day with a promise of even hotter temperatures to come as we drove south. Sitting on the passenger side, I pushed my seat back and closed my eyes. I must have dozed, because when I looked up we were crossing from Alabama into Mississippi. I saw a flattened road sign, then the jagged trunks of pine trees snapped off along the side of the road.

Caroline shook her head. "This much damage, this far from the coast. How many miles inland are we, do you think?"

"A hundred and fifty, at least. Can you believe this?"

We made a stop for gas. The tank was still half full, but I was worried about gas shortages. The station was accepting cash only, no credit cards, with a twenty-dollar limit on purchases. Gas prices had shot up dramatically all over the country on the fear that oil platforms in the Gulf or refineries in Louisiana and Texas might be damaged by the storm and shut down. Some of that panic had eased, but gas was still far more expensive than it had been just two weeks ago.

I had George's wallet in my purse. Fortunately, he'd brought a lot of cash when we evacuated. I knew there was more hidden in the house for emergencies. I had a hunch we might be living in a cash-only economy for a while. I bought twenty dollars' worth of gas and told myself to be glad I could get it.

At Jackson, Mississippi, we picked up hamburgers from the drive-through of a fast-food restaurant. We weren't really hungry, but as with the gasoline, I wasn't sure what would be open as we traveled further south. There was relatively little traffic on the road, and we were making good time. Not at all like the trip north when we evacuated.

It was around noon, and the temperature was well into the nineties. As we drove south on I-55, we saw more and more damage from the storm: billboards with sections missing, metal supports for road signs bent over, stands of trees flattened, metal barn roofs tossed casually into overgrown pastures. Two hours after leaving Jackson, we pulled into a gas station and convenience store in Hammond, Louisiana, about sixty miles from New Orleans.

"You have got to be kidding me," said Caroline. A beer truck making a delivery was blocking our way to the gas pumps. She managed to maneuver around it and pulled up to a pump, shaking her head. "People don't have food and water, but the convenience store is getting a delivery of beer?"

I laughed. "For some folks around here, that's a priority."

She gave a derogatory grunt as she shut off the engine.

This time I was able to fill the tank and pay for the gas with a credit card. We loaded up on packaged snack cakes from the convenience store—no beer—and dumped fresh bags of ice into the ice chests. I seldom eat snack cakes, but right now they looked like a luxurious dessert. No telling when we'd have a chance to buy them again.

I drove the last stretch of highway into New Orleans. As Mickey had warned me, the elevated interstate was closed just south of Ponchatoula, reserved for emergency vehicles only. I exited onto the old narrow two-lane highway and took it south to Laplace. Caroline read me the directions I'd written down, and we worked our way to the road that runs along the Mississippi River levee—the highest ground in the area—where we were fairly sure it hadn't flooded. There were no other cars around. I drove faster than I'd ever driven down that stretch, past houses with roofs gone, some with blue tarps already covering the damage. The levee side of the road had no trees, just grass, so we didn't have to drive around fallen limbs.

We bounced across railroad tracks into Uptown New Orleans. So strange to have no traffic. In a few minutes we were on Magazine Street, which divides Audubon Park in two. Caroline gasped when she saw the military tents pitched under the ancient live oaks.

"Soldiers," she said. "Bivouacked in Audubon Park. Right in front of the stables where I took riding lessons when I was little."

"It's like living in Iraq," I muttered. "Dammit, this is my home."

"I know they have to be here, but—"

"They'd better not try to stop me from going to my own house. That's all I have to say."

But we encountered no military roadblocks on our way. We had to detour a couple of times to avoid fallen trees blocking the streets, but in a few minutes we were in front of the house.

When I saw it, I started to cry. It looked just like it did when George and I left eleven days ago, except the grass in the front yard was now at least five inches high. The windows were still boarded up—the work that I suspected had contributed to George's heart attack—and the roof, at least in the front of the house, was intact. Caroline jumped out of the car and opened the black iron driveway gate.

I drove all the way to the back of the house and stopped in front of the garage. When Caroline and I turned to look toward the house, we both said, "Oh." The pecan tree had snapped in two and fallen on the roof, as Mickey had said. It was blocking the back door. One large branch had smashed the glass of my beloved sunroom.

"How are we going to get into the house?" I asked. "We locked the front screened door when we left and went out through the kitchen." The entire front porch was screened, and I hated to rip the screen to get inside. "Do you think we can get past the broken glass and into the house through the sunroom?"

Before Caroline could answer, I saw a flash of movement in the rear-view mirror. Someone was walking up the driveway toward us. Someone black. Someone wearing a lime green t-shirt I'd gotten from a charity walk five years ago.

"Eloise!" I yelled and jumped out of the car.

"I thought you'd never get here!" she cried and hugged me. Then Caroline ran around behind her and hugged her from the back. The three of us were in a group hug like children, laughing and crying at the same time.

As we broke apart, Eloise turned to Caroline. "Baby girl, what are you doing here? They let you out of school?"

"Yes. Oh, we were so worried about you. We've been calling and calling—"

"Cell phone's dead. No way to charge it."

"We knew your house had flooded. But you got out."

"Yeah," she said, a slow, drawn-out word. She looked toward the car. "Where's George? Didn't he come with you?"

I looked at Caroline, then back at Eloise.

"What? What happened?"

"George passed away the day of the storm, Eloise. He had a massive heart attack."

"Oh, Lord. Oh, Lord, no."

"And Robert? He's with you? Is he inside?"

She shook her head. "He's dead, too."

"What? Oh, no, Eloise, no. What happened?"

She began wavering from side to side, her eyes not focusing. Her knees buckled. I grabbed her under the arms and pulled her toward the car. Caroline opened the passenger door. "Turn on the air conditioning," I said.

Eloise leaned back limply into the front seat as I directed the air conditioning vents toward her face. "Oh, Lord, that feels good," she said. I got a bottle of water out of the ice chest in the back seat and opened it for her. She downed half of it before putting it down.

Caroline was in the driver's seat. I wriggled into the back seat behind her where I could see Eloise. "What happened to Robert?" I asked softly.

She wiped her brow with one hand. "We made it through the storm. It was bad, real bad. The power went out before daylight, and we were in the dark with all that wind and rain. But then it passed, and we thought we were going to be all right. But the next day the water started coming up, real fast. It got into the house. Pretty soon we realized we were going to have to go up into the attic. There aren't any stairs. There's just a wooden square cut into the ceiling in the hallway. So I moved the kitchen table into the hall and we climbed on it and pushed open the cover in the ceiling. I pulled myself up into the attic and then helped Robert get up. It was hard for him. You know he's got that artificial leg. And the attic doesn't have a floor. You have to walk on the rafters. There's insulation, too, those big pink batts, so you have to feel your way around to find the rafters. And I could hear the rats running around in the walls, trying to get up out of the water, just like us.

"And oh, God, it was stifling hot. We could hear the water lapping under us in the house. There was a dormer window in the front of the attic. When I looked out I could see water rushing like a river down the street. I never saw anything like that in my life."

"It got so hot up there I thought I would pass out. Robert went to kick out the glass in the dormer window to get some fresh air coming in. That's when he slipped and lost his balance. You know he's got that artificial leg. He fell through the rafters and broke through the ceiling. I tried to catch him, but I was too far away. I could hear him down there, thrashing around in the water and screaming for me to help him. He can't swim. But I couldn't reach him. I—I kept calling him to come over to where I was, but he never did. Maybe he got caught under a table floating in the water. I don't know. After a while he stopped screaming, and I couldn't hear him anymore." She was crying now.

"Oh, Eloise," said Caroline, reaching over and taking her hand.

"I climbed through that busted window onto the roof and just waited for someone to come help me. The storm was over and the sun was out. It was like sitting on a hot stove up on that roof. But it was worse in the attic. I probably would have died if I'd stayed in there. I just kind of braced myself in the corner where the dormer meets the roof. I was up there a day and a night. No food, no water. Then one morning, I think it was Thursday, a white man came along in a boat, looking for people. He got me down off the roof. He gave me a bottle of water and a candy bar. He took me to a drop-off place at Carrollton and Claiborne and told me to wait for a bus. A bus! I said, where's that bus going to take me? He said he didn't know. But I thanked him for getting me out of there. And I don't even know his name.

"I bet there were a hundred people or more at that drop-off place. Nobody could tell me where this bus we were waiting for was going to take us. I thought about it. I had my cell phone and my wallet and my keys in my pants pockets. I had the keys to your house on my key ring. And I knew it never floods up here. So I just took off on foot on Carrollton Avenue, heading toward the river. There was some water in the street, but it wasn't deep. And the farther I went, the less there was of it, until finally the street was dry. I went around the bend where the streetcar turns onto St. Charles Avenue. There were so many trees down on St. Charles that I had to go over to the side streets and work my way over here. A lot of power lines were down, but I figured they were dead. Still, I didn't touch any of them." She finished the bottle of water.

"When I got here, I tried to get in the front door, but you had the screen latched. So I went around the back, and I found all this—" she waved in the direction of the tree limbs. "I climbed into the sunroom through the broken windows. There's some damage upstairs where the rain got in through the hole in the roof, but otherwise the house is all right." She turned around to face me. "Maggie, I'm so sorry, I borrowed some of your clothes. I didn't have anything to wear but what I had on my back." She laughed. "And I wore some of your underwear. I'll pay you for them."

I smiled. "Don't worry about it."

"I knew you kept that hurricane stash up in your closet. I've been eating your food and drinking your water. I was so hungry and thirsty. Oh, those Vienna sausages were so good."

"We brought more," said Caroline.

Her eyes widened. "You mean you're planning to stay here? There's no power. The water is back on, but the gas isn't. Can't cook. No hot water. I been listening to your radio with the batteries you got in your stash. They say not to use the water for anything but flushing the toilets." She shook her head. "But I've been sweating so much in this heat, I've been taking baths in it anyway. Not dead yet."

"I see that," I said. "Actually, we haven't decided what to do. We don't really know of any other place to go right now. We thought we'd stay here a couple of days and figure out our next move."

She shook her head. "You have no idea what it's been like here for the last week. You don't know what you're getting yourselves into."

"No," I said. "I guess we don't. But you have no idea how glad I am to see you. I didn't know what had happened—" My voice broke. "I was afraid you had died."

"Almost did," she said. "These last few days, I've had nothing to do but think and pray. I just don't know why I survived and Robert didn't. Sometimes I wish I had died up in that attic. But God must want me to live. I don't know why. Lost my boy last year. Now I've lost my husband. I'm hurting so bad inside. What's left for me?"

"You're alive, Eloise. That's what counts. The rest will take care of itself."

She shook her head. "I've been asking God to give me strength. I'm not feeling very strong right now, I tell you. But God sent the two of you to me, and that's something."

Caroline asked, "Do you need another bottle of water?"

"Not right now, thanks." She pointed toward the garage. "I hate to tell you, Maggie, but if I could have found where you put the keys to that Mustang, I would have been out of here in no time."

"They're in my purse. I didn't want anyone breaking into the house and finding the keys and stealing it."

"Like me."

"No, of course not. It never crossed my mind that you— that this would happen."

We sat quietly in that blissful cool of the air conditioning for several minutes. Then I remembered.

"Eloise, did someone come by here a couple of days ago, checking on the house?"

"Maybe. A couple of times people came up the driveway. Can't remember exactly when. And the neighborhood patrol has come by, too."

"The patrol? Really? They're back?"

"Yeah, I've seen their truck go by. No police, though."

"I asked a friend of mine to come check on the house. He never mentioned seeing you. But you were here, weren't you?"

"Well." She looked a little bit embarrassed. "Whenever anybody came around, I went and hid in the powder room under the stairs. I didn't want them arresting me or hauling me out of here and putting me on a bus to who knows where."

I blinked. "What?"

"I'm a black woman staying in a white family's house when everybody's gone. Why wouldn't they think I was a burglar or something? You know, your neighbors in the back never left, the ones with the grocery store. That lady, Mrs. Giannini, she knows I'm here. She knows who I am, that I work here. But she's been looking at me like she thinks I'm going to take all your stuff and maybe hers too."

I groaned. "Oh, Eloise, really?"

"Yeah, really. Don't you believe me?" There was an edge of anger in her voice.

I nodded. No point in arguing. "I'm so sorry. I'll speak to Mrs. Giannini."

Sitting in the car, we were facing the chain link fence that divided our back yard from the Gianninis'. Under their back stairs, I could see a generator with an orange electrical cord connecting it to the breaker box for the house, but it wasn't running.

Eloise said, "They go over to the store during the day, trying to clean things up so they can open again. They're home at night. You can hear that generator running. Sounds like a lawnmower."

"And I bet nobody tells them they have to get out and go on a bus to Houston," said Caroline.

"And nobody's going to tell us to go, either," I said. "Come on. I want to see the inside of the house."

Reluctantly, Caroline shut down the engine and the wonderful air conditioning. We climbed out of the SUV, and each of us took a weekend bag. I carried George's, the one that contained the urn with his ashes. We walked up the driveway toward the front door, which Eloise had unlocked.

"Eloise," asked Caroline, "have you seen Mister Whiskers?"

She laughed. "That cat! Your mama called me from the road on her way to Georgia and told me he ran away when they were leaving. She wanted me to come over here after the storm to look for him. When I got here, who do you think comes sauntering around the corner of the house, looking for me to feed him?"

"You found Mister Whiskers?"

"More like he found me. That cat never liked me until now. He knows to be nice to me because I've got his food. Did you bring more? His stash is just about out."

"Oh yes," Caroline said. "His favorite kind."

When we entered the house, it was dark. The shutters were closed and the French doors boarded up with plywood. It wasn't as hot as I'd expected. But even in the shadowy darkness I did see something black, about the size of a soccer ball, behind the white railings at the top of the stairs.

Caroline squealed. "Mister Whiskers!"

He came trotting down and headed directly for Caroline as if she'd left just yesterday, rather than months ago on her last visit before going out to Los Angeles. She scooped him up in her arms and he wrapped his big paws around her neck. Even from a distance, I could hear his deep purr.

"He's your cat, all right," I said. "We were an adequate substitute, but he knows who he likes best."

While Caroline and Mister Whiskers were reuniting, I walked from the front hall into the living room. The catalogs and magazines that had arrived on the Saturday before we left were still on the coffee table. George's reading glasses were on the mantel where he always left them. I choked a little when I saw them.

"Like nothing happened," I whispered.

I passed through the dining room and into the sunroom. A large branch of the pecan tree had smashed through the glass wall. Leaves and green pecan husks hung limply on the dying branch. They were like unexpected intruders in the house, unable to find their way back out to the place where they rightly belonged. But something wasn't quite right.

"There's no glass on the floor," I said.

"I swept all that up," said Eloise, standing behind me. "Didn't have nothing else to do in this house all day long. Can't stand a mess. Getting that tree out of here, though, now that was more than I could handle by myself."

"I'll pay you, of course—"

"I ought to pay you for room and board. Been eating your food, sleeping in your guest room, borrowing your clothes."

I laughed. "I think we can work something out."

In the kitchen, the remaining canned goods and bottled water from my hurricane stash were lined up on the counter. The room was surprisingly silent without the familiar hum of the refrigerator.

Eyeing the dwindling stash on the counter, Caroline said, "I hear Jefferson Parish is open. It's just across the 17th Street Canal. We can buy gas and food there. Long lines, of course, but we can do it. We've got this car and Mom's car. Maybe the power will come back on soon, and then we'll be fine."

I climbed the stairs, feeling the temperature rise with each step. The house has four bedrooms, two facing the street and two facing the back yard. Our bedroom and the room that George used as a home office are in the back; Caroline's room and the guest room are in the front.

When I reached the top of the stairs, I could smell the mold. In our bedroom there was a hole in the ceiling where the tree had fallen on the roof. When I looked up, I could see blue sky. The shutters up here were closed also, and the light coming through the roof provided the most illumination to the room.

During the storm, rain had come through the hole in the roof. Like Eloise's attic, ours didn't have a floor, either. The moisture had soaked through the thick pink batts of insulation between the joists into the plaster ceiling, and the batts and plaster had fallen into our bedroom. Chunks of plaster had landed on the bed. Their inch-thick edges had a sandy texture like pieces of cement. The white bedspread had a dark wet stain across the middle. No doubt the mattress was ruined. Our marriage bed.

"I'm sorry I didn't clean this up, Maggie. I started to, and then I thought maybe the insurance people would need to see it."

"Don't worry about it. Probably not safe to be in here anyway. More plaster could fall. If it hit you in the head, it might kill you."

I peeked in the closet. It was empty, but there was mold starting to grow down the walls. I frowned. "Where are all the clothes?"

"I took them all out of there," said Eloise. "Some were wet. I spread everything out in the front bedrooms."

George's office hadn't fared well, either. Some of the roof shingles had peeled away in the wind, and water had soaked through the ceiling here too. A chunk of plaster lay in the middle of his desk. Streaks of grayish-blue mold ran down the outside wall nearest the opening in the ceiling. I eased my way carefully over to the desk and picked up a small framed photo of me holding Caroline when she was two years old. George took that picture one spring day under the live oaks near the sea lion pool at the Audubon Zoo. Caroline was laughing and squirming, wanting to get down and run off, and I was trying not to drop her.

I turned, and she was right behind me. A grown woman now, but always my little girl. She held out her hand and I gave her the photo. She smiled. "I always liked this picture."

"Keep it," I said. "Your daddy would want you to have it." Her eyes filled with tears.

We moved to the front bedrooms—Caroline's and the guest room. Miraculously, they were unscathed.

"Do you think you'll be able to sleep up here?" I asked. "It's going to be awfully hot, even at night."

"I'll be okay," said Caroline. "Eloise, what's it been like?"

"Hot," she said. "I've been sleeping in the guest room. But you can have it now, Maggie. It's your house. You ought to have a bed to sleep in."

"I can sleep on the sofa in the living room," I said. "I've had my share of naps on it."

We went back outside to finish unloading the car, carrying food, bottled water, and other supplies into the house. It should have felt like coming home from a normal trip to the grocery store. But it didn't.

"It's so quiet," I said. "Too quiet. No cars, no people."

"No birds," said Caroline. "Do you think they were killed by the wind?"

"Huh," said Eloise. "I don't see any dead birds around, do you? They all evacuated. They're smarter than humans. They knew to get out of here. Wish I'd been as smart as those birds." She started to cry. "We could have gone home to St. Francisville. Robert's people would have taken us in. But I was afraid to go on the interstate. Afraid of that contraflow. I should have gone anyway. Robert would still be alive."

"Don't second guess yourself, Eloise," I said. "I didn't want to leave, either. George made me go. And he died from the stress of leaving."

I went outside and walked around to the back of the house, skirting the pecan tree. I got down on my knees and crawled underneath the house to retrieve Mister Whiskers' food and water dishes that I'd left for him after he ran away. They were empty. The sandy soil under the house, that had not known rain since the house was built a hundred years ago, was as dry as old ashes.

"It didn't flood," I breathed. "It really didn't flood here."

THURSDAY, SEPTEMBER 8

I haven't slept much since the Saturday night before we evacuated. But I thought that once I got home again and knew that my house was still standing and hadn't flooded, I would sleep soundly. It didn't happen.

After a dinner of canned spaghetti and meatballs heated over a propane camp stove—another item from the hurricane closet—we all decided to turn in early. Caroline and I were exhausted from the long trip home, and Eloise just seemed worn out. We could hear the Gianninis' generator roaring like an oversized lawnmower on the other side of the chain-link fence. I wondered if they would run it all night, perhaps to keep a window unit air conditioner running, but Eloise said no, they didn't do that. They couldn't sleep with all that racket any more than we could.

Sometime around nine o'clock, the roaring lawnmower stopped. The silence was both surprising and unnerving— at least to me. It was as if our neighbors had suddenly disappeared, perhaps beamed up into a passing flying saucer, and we were the only ones left on earth. I scolded myself for my overactive imagination and tried to embrace the quiet. But the quiet left too much space in my head to think about things I didn't want to think about. Like how much I wanted George back with me and Caroline tonight, keeping us safe.

I stretched out on the brown leather sofa in the living room, where I've enjoyed many a pleasant afternoon nap over the years. In air conditioning. In daylight. I'd never slept here in complete darkness and utter silence and hot, still air. There were no streetlights to cast shafts of light through the louvered shutters. There were no voices or music in the street, no car doors slamming and engines starting as guests departed at a late hour or residents left early for work or to catch a six a.m. flight. There were no wailing babies in nearby houses, no clatter of distant streetcars—all the things I was accustomed to hearing in my neighborhood at night. If I opened my eyes, I couldn't see anything. I felt like I was sealed in a coffin, buried alive. I had a moment of panic, when I fought to breathe and struggled to see.

The sofa was unyielding beneath me, the leather squeaking against my sweaty body like chalk on a blackboard. I wriggled myself upright to a sitting position and took deep breaths, telling myself, "You're not in a coffin. You're in your own living room. There's plenty of air." I groped around the coffee table until I found the battery-operated lantern, fumbled with it, and finally managed to turn it on. I blinked in the bright blue-white light. It hurt my eyes.

A trail of sweat slid from my armpit to my waist. Or was it an insect crawling down my torso? A spider, perhaps? Another moment of panic. I was wearing nothing but an oversized t-shirt. I patted the cotton knit fabric against my body, soaking up the sweat. The possible insect stopped crawling.

Caroline and Eloise were sleeping upstairs, where it was much hotter than in the living room. Before it got dark, the three of us struggled to open bedroom windows that had been painted shut years ago. We forced screwdrivers between the windows and their hundred-year-old cypress frames, deeply gouging the beautiful wood, but we finally forced the windows up. The ancient green shutters were still tied closed, but the evening air came through the louvers. That was the way they had been designed to work when the house was built, long before anyone had air conditioning. So at least Caroline and Eloise had some air moving over them as they slept in their beds.

But downstairs, we'd decided not to try to open the windows for safety reasons. We locked the door to the sunroom, lest anyone think the broken glass was an open invitation to come in and loot the house. There was no air movement downstairs. We might have to rethink this. There were shutters on the downstairs windows, too. Maybe we should open the windows as we'd done upstairs. It was probably going to take someone with more carpentry skills than the three of us to remove the plywood George had nailed over the windows and French doors that didn't have shutters.

The battery-operated lantern was just too bright to function as a nightlight, but I wanted some light in the room to keep my claustrophobia at bay. On the mantel was an oil-burning lamp that had been in George's family for God knows how long. It had come from their old summer home on the Mississippi Gulf Coast. For years now it had been sitting on the mantel, just a decorative piece. It appeared to have oil in the base.

I went into the kitchen and got a box of long matches—a household staple for lighting the gas burners on the stovetop when power outages make the electric pilots unusable. Removing the glass chimney on the oil lamp, I lit the wick. It had dried out from years of disuse and quickly burned down into the base. I picked up the lamp and carefully sloshed the oil until it soaked the entire wick, then used the little wheel on the side of the lamp to raise the wick above the base and tried again. This time the match caught the oil in the wick, and it began to burn with a steady flame. The odor of kerosene spread across the room. I replaced the glass chimney and put the lamp back on the mantel.

I'd heard on the car radio as we drove down that all the experts were saying not to use oil lamps or candles because of the danger of fire. Yet our parents and grandparents had used them routinely. As long as the lamp didn't fall over, it wasn't going to catch fire. When the wick ran out, it would simply burn out.

The biggest danger was that Mister Whiskers might knock it over. But he was probably sleeping upstairs on Caroline's head—his favorite place—and I was pretty confident that at his advanced age, his days of jumping on the mantel were over. I left it there.

With the soft light of the oil lamp outlining the furniture and walls, I could breathe again. I knew that I wasn't buried alive in a coffin. I lay back down on the sofa and tried once again to sleep. It took a long time, but eventually I drifted off.

Even so, I awakened before dawn. Where just a few short weeks ago, unable to sleep as I fretted about losing my job, I listened to the birds call the sun into rising, now there was only silence. I wondered if the birds would come back. Silly, of course they would. But what about the humans who had lived in the city before Katrina?

A sudden roar from beyond the back fence sent me leaping off the sofa. Jesus, what time was it? I pushed a button on my watch to make the face light up. Four-thirty. The Gianninis were awake early, cranking their generator. I walked to the sunroom and looked out through the wilted leaves of the pecan tree and saw lights in the house beyond the fence.

I heard a toilet flush upstairs. A few minutes later Caroline came down, carrying one of the battery-operated lanterns and looking much perkier than I felt. "Don't forget to use the bottled water to brush your teeth, Mom. I think we can get away with bathing in the tap water so long as we don't swallow it or get it in our eyes."

"Um," I said. My daughter was now giving me advice. One day I'll be in a nursing home and Caroline will be talking to me the way I talked to her when she was four.

"The generator woke you up too, huh?"

"I was already awake. Think Eloise is too. It's really hot up there. Hard to sleep."

"It could be awhile before we get the power back. Do you want to stay here, now that you've found Mister Whiskers? Or would you rather leave? I don't know where we'd go, but eventually we'd find someplace to stay."

"No." She lifted the lantern and pointed toward the sofa. "We need to talk."

We need to talk? I made my way back to the sofa and perched on the edge of the cushions, suddenly feeling as if the roles between mother and daughter really had reversed, and now I was the child. I didn't like it.

Caroline set her lantern down on the coffee table, next to the one I hadn't turned back on. The oil lamp still glowed on the mantel. In the light from those two, her expression was hard and unyielding, as serious as I'd ever seen her.

She took a deep breath. "There's something I didn't tell you before we came back here. It's about school."

Oh, God. "Caroline, you're not dropping out because of all this, are you? You're so close to graduating."

"No, of course not. But before I left Los Angeles, I spoke to one of my professors about doing a special project. I'm going to make a documentary about survivors of Katrina living in the city. That's why I bought the video equipment in Atlanta. I'm going to spend three weeks here shooting it, then go back to Los Angeles to edit it and put it together."

"A documentary? You mean go out into the streets and interview people who got flooded out? Like in the Lower Ninth Ward? Is that what you're talking about?"

"Yes." Now her face was animated with excitement. "It's a terrific opportunity. If I make a really good film, I can use it to help me get a job after graduation. It might even be nominated for an award or something."

"The Lower Ninth Ward? By yourself? Do you have any idea how dangerous that is? No way, young lady. I forbid it."

She sat ramrod straight next to me, and her expression hardened again. "I was afraid you might react this way. With all due respect, Mom, I'm an adult now, and you can't tell me what to do. I am a journalist, and I'm here on an assignment."

Oh my God. I felt a vibration, a buzzing in my head, as if I were going to faint. The heat must be getting to me. Or maybe it was the Gianninis' generator.

"You have no idea what you're going to find, Caroline. You could get mugged or raped or even killed."

"I'm a journalist now. Just like you. Katrina is the news story of a lifetime, and it's still happening, right here in my hometown. This documentary has the potential to kickstart my career."

I fell back against the sofa cushions, covering my face with my hands. Was I really hearing this? From my baby girl?

"I'm not ready for this, honey. You're so young. I really can't let you do this." I wish George were here. He'd back me on this. And he'd find the right words to say to turn things around.

"I'm going to do this. I wish I had your blessing, Mom, but if I don't, well, that's just how it will have to be."

I had a sudden flash of her and Jason at Maribeth's dinner table the night before Jason went back to Los Angeles, Jason had shot her a look I'd interpreted as annoyance when she said she wanted to go home to look for Eloise and Mister Whiskers. "Caroline, does Jason know about your plans?"

"Yes."

"And he's not happy with this either, is he?"

She stiffened. "We talked it out."

I bet you did, I thought, remembering some of the "talkings-out" I'd had with George about my work, particularly when it involved going to clubs in dangerous neighborhoods at night. "And Jason is okay with this?"

"Do I need Jason's permission, too?"

"Not permission. The point of talking about things like this, with people you care about, is to get feedback from them. And the feedback you got from him, and that you're getting from me, is that this is not a good idea." Thank you, George. I know you just put those words in my mouth.

"My professor thinks it's a terrific idea."

"Your professor doesn't have the emotional investment in you that Jason and I do."

She shook her head. "My mind is made up. I'm going to do this. Now that I'm actually here, I want to do some looking around. Get some ideas of how to do this thing. Get a vision."

I sighed. "Just think about what I've said, okay?"

You're still my baby, I thought. *You always will be. And when you have babies of your own, you'll understand.*

At that point, Eloise came downstairs with another lantern. I wondered how much of our conversation she'd heard. Over the last twenty-one years, she's probably heard a lot of private conversations in this household, so this was just one more.

"That generator," she said. "Like an alarm clock. They're up at four-thirty every morning. They must go in to their store early."

"I wish we had a generator," I said. "Not that I'd know how to use it. But it would really be nice to have lights. And a working refrigerator. And maybe one window unit air conditioner."

"I bet we'd learn how to use one," said Caroline. "Can't be all that hard."

"I doubt you can find one anywhere right now. At any price."

"Put it on the list for next time."

"I don't want to hear a word about next time. This can never happen again."

"Except it can, you know. The climate is changing. It could happen again this very hurricane season."

"Caroline, I don't want to hear it, all right?" I heard the edge in my voice. I was still angry about—what? That she was going to do something dangerous, or that she hadn't

told me about it until now? But what would I have done if
she had? Dropped her off at the Atlanta airport on my way
out of town?

"I'm sorry," I said. "It's just all been too much."

"You got that right," said Eloise. "But a pot of hot coffee
will help. Show me how to turn on that propane stove you
fired up last night to heat supper. I'm going to boil some
water and make coffee in the old drip pot."

My mother's white enamel drip coffee pot, a staple
kitchen item in New Orleans households when I was a
child, had become as much of a decorative piece on a
kitchen shelf as George's parents' oil lamp had been on the
mantel. Until now.

"Coffee. That sounds good," I said.

"I'll help you with the stove, Eloise," said Caroline.
They headed outside, and I went into the downstairs
powder room where I had put my toiletries.

When I came out, I got dressed and went out the front
door and around to the back yard. The sky was lightening.
The thermometer by the back door read eighty degrees, the
coolest it would be all day. Maybe in another two or three
weeks the temperature would start to drop, but it was
definitely still summer.

Eloise had a pan of water simmering on the camp stove.
The old coffee pot sat on a nearby metal table, a bag of New
Orleans-style coffee and chicory beside it. The pot didn't
hold a lot of liquid—back in the day, a cup of coffee was
only about four ounces—but we could always make another

pot. I figured we could all get a small cup out of the first batch.

When the water had come to a full boil, Eloise slowly poured a small amount into the top of the coffeepot. The water passed through the grounds, swelling them. She put the pan back on the stove and waited.

"You remember how to do this," I said.

"Of course. This is how we did it before we had those fancy electric coffeemakers. And the coffee was a lot better back then, too."

"Stronger," I said.

"The slower you pour the water through, the stronger the coffee."

Eloise poured a little more water into the top of the coffeepot. I tried to listen for the tiny metallic sound of the coffee dripping through, but the Gianninis' generator drowned it out.

"How will you know when the pot is full?" asked Caroline.

Eloise grinned. "You pick up the top and look inside. Carefully, because it's hot."

"I don't think I've ever seen anyone make drip coffee before. I mean, I've seen the pot on the shelf, but I don't think we've ever used it."

"Welcome to the past," I said.

The coffee was, indeed, strong. I took mine black, the way George used to, because we didn't have any milk. Caroline made a face when she tried to drink hers and went inside to get some sugar. Eloise drank hers black also.

"Thank you for making the coffee," I said. "I needed this."

"Haven't made drip coffee in years. I'm surprised it turned out like it was supposed to."

"We brought more coffee with us. We actually found some New Orleans coffee in the grocery store in Atlanta."

"That's good," Eloise said.

We stood together in silence a few moments. Then Eloise said, "She's right, you know."

"Who?"

"Caroline. She *is* a grown woman now. You can't tell her what to do anymore. She wants to go out there, make her mark on the world. You can't stop her."

"But it's dangerous out there. You know that better than I do. You've been out in these streets."

"I know. But she's got to find that out for herself. You've got to let go, Maggie."

At that point Caroline appeared around the corner of the house with a spoon and a bag of sugar. "I think I'm going to put the whole bag in this coffee. How can you two drink this stuff?"

"You get used to it," I said. I set down my cup. I wasn't ready to have Eloise taking Caroline's side. "I'm going around the corner to let the Gianninis know we're back."

What was normally a simple trip around the block had turned into an obstacle course. When I walked around the corner to the street connecting ours to the Gianninis', I found that a camphor tree growing in the grassy area between the sidewalk and the street had been uprooted in the storm. The tree had fallen in the street, and its roots had buckled the sidewalk when they came up. I picked my way over a small hill of broken pieces of concrete and tree roots. The air had the sharp medicinal smell of camphor, a welcome relief from the odor of rotting meat coming from the garbage can in our garage, the contents of refrigerators hauled out to the curb, and who knows what dead animals that had washed down the sewer drains. Good for George to insist I throw out everything in the refrigerator, or the three of us would be struggling to haul our refrigerator out to the curb, too.

I went up the front steps of the Gianninis' house and knocked, wondering if they'd hear me over the racket of the generator. But Mrs. Giannini must have seen me coming, because she quickly opened the door. She wore an old-fashioned flowered housedress and a white apron. Her steel-gray hair was pulled back in a messy bun, and beads of sweat dotted her forehead.

"Maggie! Welcome back!"

"Stella, I'm so glad to be back. How are you?"

"As well as can be expected. Come on in." I followed her through the living room, down a hallway past the stairs, and into a small kitchen. A standing fan oscillated blessedly cool air in my direction. Lights were on and the refrigerator was running. A coffeemaker was gurgling on the counter.

"I saw your car in the driveway last night, so I figured you were back. You don't have power, do you?"

"No. It was pretty hot last night."

"For us, too. We only run the generator a few hours a day when we're here. It's too noisy for us to sleep, so most of the time we do without at night. You get used to it. Want some coffee? There's milk."

"Yes, thanks. How do you keep your refrigerator cool if you don't have the generator running all the time?"

"We keep it packed with ice from the store. We're getting supplies in."

"Are you open yet?"

"No, we don't have power over there, but they're telling us it won't be long. We're going to open as soon as we can. The neighborhood needs us. I hear the big supermarkets won't be open again for months. We can't wait that long. This is our livelihood. When we're not open, we don't make any money." She got milk—blessed milk!—out of the refrigerator and handed me a mug of steaming coffee.

"You were here for the storm?"

"Yeah. It was really bad. The power went out about four-thirty on Monday morning. We sat on the floor in the hallway, as far from the windows as we could get. A couple of them broke. But we'd put a new roof on the house last year, so it stayed on. But oh, God, the wind and the rain! I never want to go through that again." She shook her head. "I heard the crash when your tree came down on your roof. I know it's bad, but your insurance company is going to pay for your new roof. We paid for ours by ourselves."

"I've got damage inside my house from the rain coming in. My bedroom is ruined. I think I'd rather have paid for the new roof."

"Well, yeah, I can see that. Anyway, my husband and son went over to the store as soon as the storm passed. Ever since, one or the other of them has been sitting out front 24/7 with a shotgun to keep the looters away. My daughter and I have been working inside the store, cleaning out the coolers, disinfecting everything with bleach, getting rid of stuff that's gone bad or that we're not allowed to sell because the power was out. My husband stayed there last night. I'm headed over in a few minutes to bring him some breakfast."

"The store didn't flood?"

"No. Some blocks around us had water in the street from the rain, but the deep water from the levee breaches, no, we didn't get that. I don't know what those poor people are going to do. You still can't get into a lot of neighborhoods for the water in the streets. There's a rowboat parked on the sidewalk just a few blocks away from here. That's how close the water came."

"I saw the satellite images when we were in Georgia. It's awful."

"Anything I can do for you, just let me know. You need to charge your cell phone or something, come on over. You'll know we're home when you hear the generator running." She grinned.

"Thank you."

"Do you have a grill? I might be able to give you some meat we can't sell. It's not spoiled. It was frozen."

"That would be lovely. We're eating canned goods."

"Let me see what I can do." She paused. "You know, that colored woman you've got working for you, she was over at your house."

I stiffened. "You mean Eloise."

"Yeah. I'd forgotten her name. I saw her over there. Didn't know what she was doing there, with you being evacuated. Didn't know if you knew she was there. Lot of stuff going on right now, you know what I mean?"

"Eloise has keys to the house. She can come over whenever she wants to."

"No offense meant. I'm just telling you, I've been in business for years, and I've had people working for me I thought I could trust, and then they'd do stuff you couldn't imagine. You never know what someone is going to do when your back is turned."

"Eloise is living with us now. Her house flooded and her husband drowned."

Stella wiped her hands on her apron. "I'm sorry to hear that. Give her my condolences."

"I will. I just wanted to come by and let you know we were back. Thanks for the coffee." I turned and left the cup on the counter. I'd only taken a couple of sips. The oscillating fan whirred at my back, stirring my sweat-damp hair. I was going to miss that fan. But not her attitude.

When I got back to the house, Eloise and Caroline were still out in the back yard. Eloise had made another pot of coffee. Caroline asked, "So what's going on with them?"

"Stella offered to let us charge our cell phones. And maybe she can give us some frozen meat for the grill."

"Huh," said Eloise. "She didn't offer me anything."

"Yeah," I said, and let it go at that.

Caroline held up a box of granola bars. "Breakfast," she said brightly. "Think of it as camping on the trail."

"Mmm, yummy," I said.

At that moment a car horn blew at the end of the driveway. A white Honda sedan was parked in front of the gate. As I started toward it, the driver got out. He was wearing jeans and a dark green t-shirt that looked like it hadn't been washed in a while.

"Mickey!"

"Hey, Mags! Welcome back!"

I opened the gate and hugged him. "It's so good to see you! My God, you're growing a beard!"

"Yeah," he grinned. "Been looking for an excuse."

"Come on back! We've got coffee."

He pulled a white paper bag out of the car and held it up. "Brought you a little something." He opened the bag to let me see and smell.

"Doughnuts! Where did you get them?"

He grinned. "Fresh from Baton Rouge. I've got sources." He followed me up the driveway.

"This is my daughter Caroline, and this is Eloise Jackson. Caroline, Eloise, this is Mickey Donnelly. He's a writer friend of mine."

"Hi, Caroline. Your mother brags about you all the time. And Eloise, you must be the friend Maggie's been trying to find. You live in Hollygrove?"

"Yes."

"I went to your house the other day in a boat to look for you. Your dormer window was broken. Did you get out through the attic?"

"Yes. Did you go inside my house?"

"No, the water was still too high."

"My husband—he's in the house. We were in the attic, and he fell through the ceiling. I think he drowned. I need to get him out of there."

Mickey sighed and looked down. Then he looked up at Eloise again. "I'm so sorry for your loss, Mrs. Jackson."

I realized it was probably not the first time he'd said that. And I was touched that he'd called her Mrs. Jackson out of respect.

"Thank you," said Eloise. "But you don't have to call me Mrs. Jackson. Eloise is fine."

"Eloise it is, then."

"Would you like some coffee?" I asked. "Sorry, but you'll have to take it black."

"No, I won't. Got another present for you in the car. Milk. Eggs. Bread. Cold cuts for sandwiches. And a cooler of fresh ice."

Caroline said, "Don't get me wrong, Mickey. I have a boyfriend. But I love you right now."

"Don't get me wrong, either, but I'm married, and anyway, your mother would kill me."

"Where did you get all this stuff?" I asked as we helped him unload the car.

"Some big-time media people in New York hired me to cover the storm. They've been taking good care of me. They send me stuff every day. Got more supplies than I know what to do with."

"Mickey, this is awesome!"

Eloise cooked scrambled eggs on the camp stove, and we ate them with jelly doughnuts and café au lait, sitting in chairs in the back yard. For someone who lost her husband eleven days earlier and had come home to a damaged house and a city in ruins, I was deliriously happy.

Caroline was telling Mickey about her proposal for a documentary, and he was listening intently. As I watched her, I saw the excitement on her face and her determination to show him, a professional journalist with New York connections, that she was capable of doing this project. For the first time I began to see my daughter as a colleague, a fellow journalist, just like Mickey and me. Maybe even a better journalist than I was at her age.

Caroline was brainstorming ideas with him, and he was playing devil's advocate: What about this? Have you thought about that? No, that won't work. Maybe . . .

Finally he said, "This isn't going to be a long documentary, is it? Not an hour or more."

"No, maybe fifteen, twenty minutes, tops. I mean, it's a class project, and it's just me working on it."

"Well, then, this isn't something you want to take a macro view on. You won't have the luxury of time to explore everything. You want to focus on a small area that represents the bigger picture. Tell the human side of this story. Maybe find one person or one family and show what they've gone through, what they're doing now, what challenges lie ahead for them. Make your audience care about them."

Caroline was silent a moment. "That's a great idea. I think I can do that. But I wonder where I'd find someone to be my subject—someone I could persuade to trust me with their story. Do you have any ideas?"

Mickey sat back, looking around the yard. "Your subject might be closer than you think."

"Who? Us?"

He motioned toward Eloise, who was shutting down the propane stove. "Your friend here has been through quite a lot. And now she's trying to get back into her house to find her husband."

"You mean film a documentary about Eloise?"

"No," I said. "Absolutely not. You will not exploit Eloise in her grief."

Eloise raised her head from the stove and pointed a fork in my direction. "I can speak for myself, thank you. Don't you patronize me."

I felt the heat rise from my neck to my face. Maggie McBride, control freak, caught in the act. Again. "I'm sorry."

"Caroline, you want to make a movie about me?" Eloise asked.

"Well, how would you feel about that?"

"I never thought I'd be a movie star. What would I have to do?"

"Just be yourself. Let me follow you around with a camera. Talk to you, just like we normally would talk."

"Maybe your mother could help you," said Mickey. "You're going to have your hands full trying to video this and conduct interviews at the same time."

I stared at him. *Mickey, I'm going to get you for this.*

He was grinning at me. "Of course, it means Caroline is in charge, and you'll be taking orders from her."

"I like the sound of that," said Caroline.

"I gotta see this," said Eloise.

I smiled, but I wasn't happy like I had been just a few minutes ago. I was outnumbered. Now I was just trying to be a good sport.

Eloise turned to Mickey. "You said you went to my house in a boat."

"That's right. A guy I know took me back there the other day."

"You think he could take me? I got to see my house."

Mickey scratched his beard. "Maybe." He took out his cell phone and dialed a number.

"Billy? This is Mickey. Remember you took me over to that house in Hollygrove on Monday, the one with the dormer window smashed out? I'm with the owner of the house now. Her name is Eloise Jackson. You got a minute to talk to her?" He handed Eloise the phone.

Caroline waved a hand in Eloise's face. "Ask him if I can come too."

When she got off the phone, she said, "He can take us back there. He said to meet him about ten o'clock."

"I can drive you," said Mickey. "Offer him some money for gas. He probably won't take it, but do it anyway."

"I'll get my equipment," said Caroline. "I charged the camera before we left, and I've got backup batteries."

"What about me?" I asked. "Am I invited on this trip too?"

"He doesn't have a lot of room in his boat," said Mickey. "I'm not going. I'll drop them off, then I've got to meet someone for an interview."

I followed them in the SUV to the place where they were to meet Billy. He was black, fiftyish, with a graying beard. He wore overalls, a dirty short-sleeved shirt that had once been white, and a Saints cap. Mickey had vouched for him. I decided to trust him with my daughter and my best friend—not that they'd given me a choice in the matter.

"Call me when you're back, and I'll pick you up," I said. Then I drove up River Road into Jefferson Parish.

Life on the other side of the levee breach was a different world. Yes, there had been flooding where water from the breach doubled back into some exclusive neighborhoods in Old Metairie. Workers who staffed the pumping stations had been evacuated early to safer locations across the lake, and the drainage pumps had been turned off. As a result, rainwater had overflowed the banks of some of the open canals and flooded nearby homes. As I drove around, I saw piles of ruined carpet at curbsides and people cleaning up fallen limbs in their yards.

But some areas had power, and I found a few stores open. People were lined up outside some of the big-box stores—there were so many customers that security guards were only letting a few in at a time. I had Eloise's cell phone with me, and I managed to find a new charger for it. I decided to take Mrs. Giannini up on her offer to let us charge our phones. And Caroline's video camera. And my laptop.

A lot of everyday things were sold out: batteries, flashlights and lanterns, bottled water. I was glad we had stocked up before we left Atlanta. As I looked around for things we might possibly need, my thoughts were far from this store and the meager inventory on the shelves. I was thinking of Caroline and Eloise in a boat with a stranger, navigating their way around God knows what submerged in the street: fire hydrants, stop signs, trash cans. And what about people? Dead people floating in the water. People who might try to hijack the boat or pull a gun on them for whatever they might be carrying with them.

I couldn't take it anymore. I stood in line for thirty minutes waiting to pay for the charger for Eloise's cell phone. After I finally got to the cashier and paid for my purchase, I practically ran to the parking lot. I got in my car and drove back to the spot where I'd left Caroline and Eloise near the Jefferson Parish line, where they walked through the nasty water until it was deep enough for the boat to float, where they'd climbed in and Billy had started the engine and they'd headed down the flooded street toward Hollygrove.

It wasn't long before I saw the boat in the distance. My cell phone rang. "Is that you down there, Mom?"

"Yes. Are you all right?"

"Sure. Be there in a minute."

When they got out of the boat, they were wet and dirty. Caroline had a muddy smear across one arm. Eloise's face was grim.

"The water's lower now than it was when that man got me off the roof, but we still can't get into the house. We managed to wade out of the boat and get up on the porch, but we couldn't get the front door open. The key wouldn't even turn in the lock."

"I tried," said Billy. "But that wood is swollen up from all the water. It won't budge. I asked her if she wanted me to break it down, but she said no."

"The windows are boarded up," said Caroline. "There was no way to get in there, either."

"Even if we had, I've got burglar bars on those windows," said Eloise.

"We'll go back later," said Caroline. "After the water goes down. It shouldn't be more than a few days. We'll find a way to get inside."

Caroline had been filming as the boat made its way down Eloise's street, and she got the scene of Eloise and Billy trying to get the door open. Eloise had burst into tears when they had to give up. I winced when Caroline told me later, privately, of the emotional drama. As a journalist, I could appreciate how powerful this documentary was going to be. But the person at the heart of it was not a stranger. It was Eloise, someone Caroline and I had known for twenty years. It just didn't seem right to me.

After we got back, I mixed a few drops of bleach in buckets of water. Caroline and Eloise washed off their arms and legs and feet where they had been exposed to the flood water. It wasn't the greatest disinfectant, but under the circumstances it was the best we could do. The tap water wasn't certified safe to use, either, but it had to be cleaner than what they'd waded into.

Later, Caroline and Eloise sat down in camp chairs in the back yard to film another scene for the documentary. I operated the camera as Caroline interviewed Eloise about what had happened to her and Robert during the storm and how she had escaped her flooded home. Eloise broke down and wept when she came to the part about Robert falling through the ceiling. Tears ran down my own cheeks as she spoke.

Nothing in my own career has prepared me to cover a story like this. I've been writing about restaurants and nightclubs for the last fifteen years. I've never covered murders and car wrecks and all the other tragedies a newspaper or television reporter would consider part of a day's work. But this is personal.

When we were in Atlanta, watching television news at Jeff and Maribeth's house, I saw reporters break down on camera as they tried to tell the story of their own home towns being devastated by the storm—not only in New Orleans but on the Mississippi Gulf Coast. Telling the story of a close friend's loss is like that. If Caroline can survive the emotional toll of putting together this documentary, she is going to be one hell of a journalist.

Friday, September 9

Mrs. Giannini, true to her word, came by this afternoon with a cooler of ribeye steaks from the freezer at her grocery. I called Mickey and invited him to dinner. He arrived with a six-pack of beer just as Caroline was putting the meat on the grill. Caroline and Eloise declined a beer, but I joined Mickey in a cold one as the steaks cooked.

"Amazing," I mumbled through a full mouth of meat. "Best meal I've ever had."

"I'll drink to that," said Mickey.

I remembered that I'd intended to be judgmental of Mrs. Giannini for her attitude toward Eloise, and now I was greedily eating her steak. Oh well, call it a peace offering and let it go. We had all been through a lot.

As we were polishing off the last of our meal, Mickey asked, "Is your land line working?"

"I don't think so," I said. "The phone hasn't rung since we've been back."

"Do all your phones need electricity?"

I thought a moment. "Yes. They're all cordless now. "They won't work until the power is back on."

"But you might have phone service anyway. If you had an old corded phone, it might work if you disconnected all the other phones."

"There might be an old phone in a closet somewhere. If it works, it could be handy to have a land line."

"What I'm thinking is that if your land line works, maybe you can get dial-up Internet service. It would be slow, but at least you'd have access to email."

As it turned out, the land line did, indeed, work. It was like being in the twentieth century again after living in the nineteenth. The twenty-first century would have to wait for the electricity to come back on.

After Mickey left, Caroline and I took turns with our respective laptops to check our email. It was the first time either of us had been online since we left Atlanta, and we both had fifty or more emails. I sped through mine as quickly as possible, mindful of the limited battery time on my laptop. But one email stopped me in my tracks.

Dear Maggie,

I don't know where you are or how to contact you except through this email address. I apologize for not writing you a real letter, but this will have to do. We are in Houston. We ran into Tony Richards today and he told us about George. We were shocked to hear the news.

George was a wonderful man. He did so many kind and generous things for the community and rarely took credit for them. I suspect not even you know about all of them. He will be dearly missed.

Our house in Lakeview sustained major damage, so we will have to remain in Houston for quite some time. But if there are things we can do for you, we will be glad to be of assistance.

Our deepest condolences to you and Caroline.

Sincerely,
Bitsy and Mark LeBlanc

"I'll be damned," I said.

Caroline looked up from her laptop, where she was loading a file from the camera. "What?"

"Tell you in a minute." I quickly dashed off a reply.

Dear Bitsy,

Thank you for your kind note. Caroline and I are back home—she is taking a short break from her studies to be with me. Our house is damaged, but we are living like pioneers in it.

Losing George so suddenly has been a great shock, but we are comforted by the kindness of friends.

I hope you and Mark will be able to get your house repaired quickly so you can come back to the city. These are extraordinary times, and New Orleans needs its people to come home.

Sincerely,
Maggie and Caroline McBride

I shut down the laptop and closed the lid. "I got a condolence email from possibly the last person I ever expected to hear from—Bitsy LeBlanc."

Caroline shook her head. "That name doesn't ring a bell."

"No reason why it should. She's someone your father and I used to know socially. But we parted ways more than ten years ago over the Dorothy Mae Taylor business."

Eloise turned sharply in my direction.

Caroline said, "I remember the name, but not the connection."

"You were little when it all happened. Not surprising you wouldn't remember."

"What was it all about?"

I sighed. "It's a long story."

"Huh," said Eloise. "You got that right."

Caroline looked from me to Eloise and back. "Now I really do want to hear."

"Dorothy Mae Taylor was a black New Orleans city councilwoman who had been in the forefront of the civil rights movement here. In the early 1990s, she proposed an ordinance to force the gentlemen's luncheon clubs that put on some of the old-line Carnival parades to stop discriminating in their membership. These groups were male-only and Gentile whites-only—no blacks, no Jews, no Italians, and frankly, no Yankees either. My father was a well-to-do publishing executive, but he was never asked to join because he was from New York State."

"Are you kidding me? No Yankees allowed?"

"That's right. Anyway, Mrs. Taylor's ordinance was struck down in the courts, but she proposed another one banning discrimination in membership by groups that sought parade permits in the city. It was a way to keep hate groups like the Ku Klux Klan from staging marches, but it also kept the Carnival organizations that discriminated in their membership policies from parading—especially the ones that kept their members' names a secret. The ordinance stood up in court because it involved providing city services like police protection and sanitation, and the city could refuse to use tax dollars to provide services to groups that discriminated. The Taylor ordinance set off a firestorm in the high-society, white Uptown community. People hated her and mocked her. Whites called her the Grinch that Stole Mardi Gras. She didn't steal it. She dragged the good old white boys kicking and screaming into a majority-black city whose existence they'd been denying for years."

"You got that right," said Eloise again.

"Some of the newer Carnival organizations—the krewes—were much more inclusive, much more representative of the population of the city. Organizations like Endymion and Bacchus, the superkrewes with the huge parades on Saturday and Sunday nights before Mardi Gras and the huge balls open to just about anybody who could afford it, were wildly popular. They were growing, but the old-line organizations were not. The children and grandchildren of the old-liners were moving to other cities where the professional jobs were more plentiful than in New Orleans. In the end, just a couple of those groups refused to comply with the ordinance and stopped parading."

"Okay, but I still don't get it. What does all that have to do with this woman who sent you the email?"

"I supported the ordinance in a very public way, and she took offense."

Eloise snorted. "Your mama finally stood up for something important."

"What did you do, Mom?"

"I wrote an editorial in the magazine supporting Dorothy Mae Taylor's position. I said it was almost thirty years since the Civil Rights Acts of 1965, and it was high time for white New Orleans society people to quit pretending it never happened."

"Mom! Howard let you publish that?"

I groaned. "Not exactly. Let's just say I dropped it into the magazine at the final proofing stage, and he didn't see it until it was printed."

"That's the first time she ever stood up to that man," said Eloise. "She should have done it a lot sooner."

I grimaced. "As things turned out, yeah, you're right."

"Darn straight," said Eloise.

"I was taking a calculated risk. I knew he agreed with me. We'd talked about it many times. His mother was Jewish. That was enough to keep him from being invited to join any of those clubs, either, and he was mad as hell about it. The biggest business deals in the city were made over lunch in those very private clubrooms. Howard hated those guys for excluding him. He could have fired me for that editorial, but I suspected he wouldn't. He yelled at me, but that was about it."

"What effect did your editorial have on the magazine?"

"Oh, a couple of advertisers pulled out. We got some rather colorful hate letters, a death threat or two. We were just about the only white-owned publication in town that supported Dorothy Mae Taylor."

"I'm surprised you didn't get your butt kicked out of there over the lost advertisers. From everything you've told me about Howard, it's all about money with him, not principle."

"I'm sure he thought about it. But one day a group of black business owners came to the office and met with him. They thanked him for supporting the ordinance and pledged to buy advertising. The look on Howard's face when they left was priceless. They kept their word. They bought long-term advertising contracts in the magazine. It all worked out."

"Good for you, Mom. But I still don't see where this Bitsy woman comes in."

"It never occurred to me that my editorial would affect us as a family, professionally and socially, but it did. Some of your father's colleagues and clients were not happy. Some of them were members of these clubs. They pretty much told George to make his Yankee wife shut up. And he pretty much told them to go to hell."

"Good for Dad! But you're not a Yankee. You were born here."

"My father was from upstate New York, and I went to college in Syracuse. That makes me a Yankee, as far as some of those folks are concerned. Anyway, the law firm lost a couple of clients over my editorial. As for Bitsy, she was queen in her debutante year of one of the Carnival organizations that stopped parading, and her husband was a member—I know the membership is supposed to be secret, but we knew who was who. Anyway, one night your father and I were having dinner at the country club, and Bitsy and Mark LeBlanc walked in. They saw us, turned around, and walked out. They were really obvious about it, too. I haven't heard a word from them since that night, more than ten years ago, until I got this email."

"Wow," said Caroline. "Why do you think she contacted you now?"

"Because she and her husband remained friends with your dad. He and Mark used to play golf together. I was the problem, not your father. Bitsy wrote the condolence note because that's what wives in that social circle do. When someone dies, they pretend the conflict never happened. If Tony Richards gave her my contact information, you can be sure he gave her my cell number as well as my email address. She could have called. But an email gave her more distance. She didn't have to talk to me directly."

"Oh."

I shook my head. "When I took a stand on the ordinance, I didn't think about the difficulty it would cause your dad in certain social circles. He actually resigned his membership in one of those segregated gentlemen's clubs. But one thing that worried him was that alienating these society people might prevent you from making your debut when you were old enough."

Caroline laughed. "My debut? Are you kidding me?"

"Your father grew up in that society, where such things are important. His mother had been a debutante and a maid in the courts of some Carnival balls. When you were born, he imagined escorting you on his arm at a debutante ball, in your long white dress. But as you grew up, it was quite clear that you weren't interested in such things."

"I never knew any of this."

"If you had said something about wanting to be presented to society, I'm sure your dad would have found a way to make it happen. But we let you be your own person and chart your own course. We both could see that from an early age, your interests lay elsewhere."

"Wow," said Caroline. "White gowns and Carnival balls. Never in a million years."

"I'm quite happy that we spent the money to send you to Syracuse instead of paying for your debut. Your college education is a much better investment in your future, as far as I'm concerned."

"All that fuss," said Eloise, "and after all these years, those clubs are still around, and the only black people welcome there are the waiters."

"Yes," I agreed, "but the old white boys live in a dream world. They think they still control what goes on in this city. They don't. And they haven't for a very long time."

Caroline shook her head. "I can't believe we're having this discussion. We're sitting here in the middle of a devastated city that's still under water. We've got no electricity, no grocery stores, no mail, no garbage pickup, and we're talking about Mardi Gras and Carnival organizations and debutantes. Seriously, who cares about all that right now?"

"Believe it or not, there are people who do. And most of them are in Houston and Baton Rouge right now, trying to figure out if there will be a Carnival season next year."

"Well, I think it's crazy. After what I saw, riding in that boat down Eloise's street, Mardi Gras is the last thing on my mind."

"I agree with you. This is the biggest crisis the city has ever known. Maybe one of the biggest crises the whole country has ever had to deal with. We need help right now, all the help we can get."

Monday, September 12

Eloise said, "I need to go back to work."

Before the storm, Eloise cleaned offices at night in Metairie, the suburb on the other side of the 17th Street Canal in Jefferson Parish. With her cell phone working again, she was able to contact some of her employers. Parts of Metairie had flooded, but some were unscathed. A couple of the offices where she worked were open, albeit with only some of their staff, but when she called them, they were glad to hear she was alive and well and wanting to come back to work.

I gave her the keys to the SUV, and she headed off to Metairie in the late afternoon. There's a curfew at six o'clock in New Orleans, and she'd be coming back later than that. But she hoped that if she explained she was coming home from work, the National Guard would let her pass any checkpoint she encountered.

She usually wore a uniform and a badge on a lanyard, but her clothes and her badge were still in her house and undoubtedly ruined. Fortunately, she'd put her key ring with all her work keys on it in her pocket when she and Robert had gone up to the attic.

I was concerned that the National Guard might not believe that she was coming home from work if she was dressed in slacks and a t-shirt. I offered to write a note for her to carry if she was stopped, indicating that she worked for me and asking that she be allowed to come to my house, but she waved me away.

"Don't need you to be giving me a note, Maggie. You make me feel like a slave, needing a pass from the white lady to get past the patrols."

Her words hit me like a slap. "Eloise—I never intended—I want to help—"

"You think you mean well, but you don't understand. I thank you for letting me use your car so I can get to work. Now let me go about my business, please."

I could feel my face redden. Eloise had never spoken so harshly to me. There was a gap between us that I hadn't been aware of until now. Or maybe I had been aware of it at some level but hadn't wanted to acknowledge its existence. I was white and she was black. There were things Eloise had to deal with on a regular basis that I never had, and never would.

All I could say to her was, "Be careful out there."

It was after ten o'clock when she returned. Caroline had gone upstairs to bed, but I stayed up to wait for her, struggling to read by the light of a lantern on the coffee table.

Apparently she had found a spare uniform at work, because she was wearing a black apron over her clothes with her name embroidered on one side. She grunted in response to my "I'm glad you made it back safely" and went into the kitchen, tossing the car keys down on the table. Carrying the lantern, I followed her as she pulled a can of soda out of the ice chest that functioned as a refrigerator, opened it, and drank half of it while standing beside the table.

I couldn't make out her expression by the light of the lantern. "Eloise, are you all right?"

"I got stopped on my way back, over on Saint Charles Avenue."

"A checkpoint?"

"Hell, no. They pulled me over."

Hell, no? I'd never heard Eloise use the word before. "Why?"

"Because a black cleaning woman isn't supposed to be driving a Lexus SUV, that's why. They thought I stole it. And having George's name on the registration and insurance card didn't help matters any."

I covered my face with my hands. "Oh no."

"I told them I worked for him and was out running errands for him. I said I was using his car because mine got flooded. I told them I'd give them the cell phone number if they wanted to check it out. I was going to give them your number and hope when they asked for him, you wouldn't say right off the bat that he was dead. If they knew that, they'd think for sure I stole the car. I was hoping you'd figure it out and cover for me."

"They didn't call."

"Yeah. They must have bought my story. They let me go."

"Eloise, I am so sorry."

"Yeah, well, sorry isn't going to do it. I can't drive that car. I'm just going to get stopped again."

I picked up my purse, dug out the keys to my car, and tossed them across the table. "Maybe they won't stop you for driving a six-year-old Mustang."

"You won't let Caroline drive that car."

"Yeah, well, Caroline is twenty-one. You're not. Take it. I'll drive the Lexus."

"I can't drive your car."

"You don't know how, or you don't want to?" She just shook her head. "It's an automatic. You can drive it."

She blew a breath through pursed lips. "No."

"What are you going to do? You can't walk to work. There is no bus. And I'm not going to drive you around when there are two cars in the driveway and you've got a valid driver's license. Take the Mustang, Eloise."

"Shit," she said—another word I'd never heard her use before. She dropped the keys into the pocket of her apron.

Tuesday, September 13

Eloise took the Mustang to work this afternoon. Caroline and I heated canned beef stew and green peas on the camp stove and ate in the kitchen.

"I heard you and Eloise talking when she came in last night," she said. "I've never heard her so angry."

"Me either."

"Do you think she's so upset because of what happened to Robert?"

"I'm sure it hasn't helped matters any. Everyone's nerves are frayed by now. But no, I think there's more to it. Eloise has a legitimate point. She was stopped and questioned at length last night. You and I might have been stopped under the same circumstances, but I think after a routine check, they would have waved us on. It never occurred to me Eloise would have a problem because of the car. And," I added, "because of the color of her skin."

"Really? In this day and age?"

"Really. You've heard the stories about looting and shooting in the city, supposedly by black people. So much of it is unfounded rumors and never should be reported on the air without verification. But right now it's hard to confirm what you've been told. You don't know if it's true or not. It sounds like the patrol saw a black woman driving an expensive car and thought she might have stolen it. I don't blame her for being angry. I bet it's not the first time something like this has happened to her. She's just never vented that anger in front of me before."

Caroline paused, her fork in midair. "So, after all the controversy about Dorothy Mae Taylor, did that whole business do anything to change attitudes about race in the city? Or are we still back where we were in the civil rights era?"

I sighed. "For the whites who were willing to listen to what the black community had to say, it got them to re-think some things they'd always taken for granted about Mardi Gras. The way the membership policies of the all-white organizations resembled those of hate groups like the Klan—that was the big eye-opener. To borrow a phrase we used back when I was your age, Dorothy Mae Taylor did a lot for consciousness raising about race in this city.

"But we've still got a long way to go. In a crisis like this, people tend to go back to their old prejudices and knee-jerk reactions and not think things through. They see a black person and they assume the worst."

I thought briefly of my conversation with Mrs. Giannini. I'd never told Caroline what she'd said about Eloise. I decided to let it go.

Caroline pushed her plate aside. "I wonder," she said.

"Wonder what?"

"I wonder if Eloise would let me ride with her to and from work. Would she think I was trying to protect her by having a white person in the car with her?"

"Is that what you're trying to do?"

"I don't know. Maybe."

"You could make it part of your documentary. Take your camera. Film her going to work. Talk to her about what that's like, trying to go back to her normal life when nothing is normal. Not just all this—" I waved my hand around the room to include the chaos all over the city "— but personally for her. She's just lost her husband and hasn't even been able to recover his body yet, much less have a funeral. And she's going back to work."

"I'll talk to her. It's such a sensitive thing. You're right, Mom, about how hard it is to do a story about someone close to you, that you care about, who's going through such a tragedy."

"In a way, I'm amazed that Eloise agreed to this at all. But you know how much she loves you. She trusts you. She thinks she's just helping you with a project you're doing for school. But if you do a really good job with this documentary, and I fully expect that you will, it may get a far wider audience than either you or she anticipate."

"I've thought about that. What's happening here is a story I want to tell the world."

"As well you should. But when you go out in the car with her at night, if you do get stopped, don't try to film the National Guardsmen. They might take the camera away from you and not give it back. That would be the end of your documentary right there. It's happened before."

"Might be hard to explain to my professor. Sort of like 'the dog ate my homework.' Maybe a little more believable, but still, I wouldn't have anything to turn in."

"Right now, anything goes out there. Your rights and the law don't mean a whole lot. It will all be sorted out later, but in the meantime, you've got to be very careful. If you get stopped, be polite but firm about where you're going and why. But just do what they tell you."

"Right." She paused. "How would you feel, though, about being alone in this house after dark while Eloise and I are out?"

I laughed. "Don't you think I can take care of myself? If some machete-wielding madman came in here to steal the canned goods, do you think we'd be any safer if all of us were here? If Eloise is willing to have you with her, then go."

We shared a can of peaches for dessert. Caroline said, "Work is what's going to keep us from going crazy right now. Eloise has her evening jobs, I've got my documentary. We need to get you back to work, too, Mom."

I looked up from my peaches, a slight smile on my face. "Have you heard of any leads?"

"I was thinking that maybe you ought to start writing a blog."

"A what?"

"A blog. It's like a column written on the Internet. You could talk about what's happening here in the city right now. You just said there's so much unverified information out there. You could write about what you've seen with your own eyes, what's really happening. There are people you know who are still evacuated, and they're hungry for news from their neighborhoods. They're not getting that from the television reports."

I finished my peaches and set the dish aside. "Any idea how I could get the word out about my blog, so people would read it?"

"You said you had a ton of emails from people you know who are living all over the country. Send them a group email and tell them what you're doing. They can sign up to get notifications every time you post something."

I thought for a moment. "If I could write one blog entry that everyone could read, it would save me a lot of time and computer battery sending out emails to everybody."

"And it will get you exposure. People who like what you're writing will tell other people to check out your blog, and then more people will read it. Who knows, it might get the attention of some editors out there. You might pick up some paying assignments."

I grinned. "Okay. Caroline, teach this old dog some new tricks. How do I set this thing up?"

By the time Eloise got home—this time after an uneventful trip, thank goodness—I had a web page set up for my blog. I wrote an introductory entry and posted it online. I titled the blog "I'm Still Here" and in the space for the tag line, I wrote, "My name is Maggie McBride, and I am a New Orleanian."

The first entry:

September 13.

If you watch the news, they will tell you that everyone has been evacuated from New Orleans by now—those who aren't dead. Imagine a city of hundreds of thousands of people, who were here living their everyday lives just three weeks ago, with no thought that anything would be different in a matter of days—all gone. Scattered to Baton Rouge and Houston and Atlanta and Memphis, places all over the South and all over the country. Now houses stand empty, streets are devoid of life, and there's not even the sound of birds anywhere.

What they don't tell you on the news is that some people are still here. Some never left. Some came back. Some have jobs that require them to be here: emergency workers, medical personnel, city officials, people who work at the Port of New Orleans—which is open, by the way. Some are business owners whose livelihoods depend on getting things up and running again: grocery stores, drug stores, restaurants. Building contractors are about to become the toast of the town.

Some people are here because they were just too stubborn to leave. Some came back because this is the only place they want to be. I'm one of them. I'm Maggie McBride, and I live here, dammit. This is my home.

I don't have electricity. I don't have gas. The water quality is questionable. It's hot as hell. But people lived like this in New Orleans a hundred years ago and survived. If they could do it, so can I.

I am writing this blog to tell you, wherever you are, about what I see going on around me in the city right now. I'm not going to write about what I've heard other people say. I'm only going to report what I've seen for myself. I've been a journalist in this town for nearly thirty years, and this is the biggest story this city has known in my lifetime. I'm going to cover it as honestly as I can. This blog is for you who are far away and want to know what's really happening here.

As I finished writing, I realized that if I was going to fulfill that promise to my as-yet unknown readers, I was going to have to get out of the house and do some reporting. This is going to be good for me. Career-wise, I've been adrift ever since that Friday afternoon in Howard's office. At last, I'm going back to doing what I know best: investigate and report.

I feel better already.

WEDNESDAY, SEPTEMBER 14

Caroline was sitting on the front porch this morning hunched over her cell phone. I happened to be in the doorway, about to join her with my coffee mug in my hand, when I realized she was trying to have a private conversation. I admit it, I eavesdropped. I didn't hear much, but I gathered she was on the phone with her professor about the documentary. From her end of the conversation, it sounded like her project hadn't been approved as she had breezily suggested it was.

I went back inside until she was done. When she came in, I asked her how things were going with the documentary.

"They're going okay."

"How does this work as far as school is concerned? Did they give you permission to take time off to be here?"

"Were you listening to my conversation?"

"Just a bit. Not a lot."

She sighed. "Normally, if a student wants to do a documentary as a project for credit, everything has to be approved in advance. Usually there are a lot of academic hoops to jump through. But for this project, the story is too immediate. Katrina is such an unprecedented event in the life of America. And with my losing Daddy on top of it . . . well, to make a long story short, they're going to let me cut through the red tape and film Eloise's story. I can do the paperwork later."

"Oh, Caroline. I know you'll do your best. If you need me to go to bat for you with any of your professors, I'll vouch for you."

"Mom, it's not like I'm in fourth grade again and I need you to talk to the principal for me. I'm a senior in college. I'd look like a spoiled kid if my mother started calling up faculty members. Have you heard the term helicopter parent?"

"I get it. 'Please don't, Mom, I'm a big girl now.' Right?"

"Right."

THURSDAY, SEPTEMBER 15

It wasn't a madman with a machete who came to the house while I was alone. It was four National Guardsmen in an armored vehicle.

It wasn't quite dark. Caroline had gone to work with Eloise to shoot film for the documentary—and to run interference if she got stopped again, although she didn't tell Eloise that. I'd had dinner and was on the sofa in the living room with my laptop, working on a blog entry. They must have seen the light from the lantern on the coffee table.

I heard the vehicle pull into the driveway and knew by the sound of it that it wasn't Caroline and Eloise in my Mustang. I looked out and saw the soldiers in tan and black camouflage uniforms getting out of a Jeep. They were carrying rifles.

I ran to the kitchen and grabbed a carving knife from the drawer. A little voice in my head—George?—was saying, "Maggie, this is stupid. You can't take on four armed soldiers with a knife." Another little voice—me?—said, "No, but if they try to force their way into my house, I'm going down fighting."

Someone knocked hard on the door. Holding the knife behind my back, I walked through the front hall and stood just behind it. Through the glass panels on either side of the door, I could see two men. I wasn't sure where the other two were. I figured they probably had seen me approaching—or at least had seen a shadow moving in the darkness inside.

"What do you want?" I yelled at them.

"National Guard, ma'am. Can we come in?"

"No," I said. "This is private property."

"Anyone else in the house with you?"

"This is private property," I repeated. "I am the owner. Leave. Now."

"Ma'am, the city is under mandatory evacuation. You need to leave."

"The hell I do. I'm a journalist. I'm working here, covering the storm."

"Who do you work for?"

I hesitated. "Parker Publishing. Our offices on Carrollton Avenue are flooded. I'm working out of my home." Partly true. Carrollton Avenue *was* flooded. I just didn't work for Parker anymore. But they had no way to check that.

"Can I see your credentials?"

"No. You are on private property. Leave."

"Would you open the door, please?"

"No."

"Can I have your name?"

"Maggie McBride. I've been a journalist in this city for twenty-seven years. How old are you, soldier?"

"Ma'am, there's no need to be patronizing. We're checking every house in the city. You know it's not safe here. The police and firefighters and EMTs aren't going to come if you have an emergency. We understand there are reporters here on assignment. But if you're by yourself in this house, I need to tell you that you're not safe. You really need to leave. Now."

"Thank you for your concern. I have neighbors who are still here. And our security patrol is on the streets."

The soldier said something to the man next to him. They conferred for a moment, then he turned back to me. "Do you understand we can't guarantee your safety?"

You can't do that under normal circumstances, I thought. "Yes, I understand."

"Be careful, ma'am."

"I will," I said. I watched them go down the front stairs and back to their Jeep. After they left, I opened the door and walked outside, still clutching the carving knife. One of the soldiers I hadn't been able to see had spray-painted a big orange X on the siding on the front of the house. In the quadrants formed by the X were letters or numbers. All I could identify was the date, 9-15, in the top quadrant.

"Goddammit," I said. "Goddammit."

When I came inside, I was shaking. Fear, rage, all of the above. I put the knife back in the drawer. I needed a drink. I found a bottle of bourbon in the cabinet in the dining room and poured two fingers in a glass. No, make it three. There was ice in the cooler, but it wasn't particularly clean. Hell with it. I'd drink the bourbon neat.

It burned. Wow. But it felt good. I made my way to the sofa, pulled my cell phone out of the pocket of my jeans, and called Mickey.

"The National Guard was here," I said.

"I'm surprised they didn't come sooner."

"They spray-painted an X on the house. Like a bunch of teenage vandals."

"They have to do that. They're working in teams, checking every house in the city for bodies. They need to mark them so other teams will know that a house has been checked."

"It's my house, goddammit. They have no right to deface it."

"If they don't put that X on your house, you're going to have team after team knocking on your door. Do you want that?"

"No. I want them to leave. New Orleans is still part of the United States of America, the last time I checked. These are American soldiers throwing Americans out of their own homes. Who gave them the right to do that? This isn't Iraq."

"We need them, Maggie. They're here to keep order. The police department is in chaos right now. Make peace with these folks. They're going to be here for quite a while."

"I want my city back."

"Don't we all. It's going to take time."

The tears were sliding down my cheeks again. I hate to cry, and I've been doing it too damn much these last three weeks.

"Maggie? You still there?"

"Yes."

"I've got some good news for Eloise. The water has gone down in her neighborhood, and her street is probably dry now. The National Guard still isn't letting people back there, but I might be able to talk them into letting us go in to look for her husband."

"I'll tell her. She and Caroline have gone to Jefferson Parish. She's working again, cleaning offices at night, and Caroline is filming her for her documentary."

"You were by yourself when the Guard showed up?"

"Yes. I had a carving knife behind my back."

He whistled. "Jesus, Maggie, I never want to get on your bad side."

I laughed. "It was a pretty stupid thing to do. They might have shot me if they'd seen it."

"You're right about that. Don't do that again."

"Okay, Mickey. Thanks for letting me rant."

After we ended our call, I noticed that my laptop had gone into sleep mode. Oh, right. I'd been working on a blog entry when the Guard arrived. I slid my thumb over the touchpad and woke up the laptop.

September 15.

Stella Giannini says the family's grocery store, Giannini's Fine Foods, will reopen as soon as the power comes back on and the store can be inspected by the health department. The family remained here during the storm and went to work removing spoiled foods and cleaning everything the very next

*day. They look forward to welcoming back
customers and serving the community.*

Did I really want to publish that in my blog? It sounded
so folksy, like something you'd read in a neighborhood
newspaper. I deleted it and started over.

*The National Guard came to my door tonight and
tried to make me leave my home. Yes, we're under
a mandatory evacuation order. No, I'm not
leaving. I managed to persuade them to let me stay,
but they spray-painted graffiti on the front of my
house before they left: a big orange X with some
obscure letters and numbers around it. I'm told
every house in the city will be sporting this tattoo
before they're done. Be prepared to do some
painting when you get back.*

Would publishing this on the Internet get me in trouble
if someone in authority happened to read it? Could they
force me to leave my own home? Deported from the city?
No, that was just too paranoid.

I clicked the "post" button.

Eloise and Caroline got back around ten o'clock. Eloise
was grumbling, but Caroline was excited.

"Mom, we got stopped by the National Guardsmen on
our way home, just a few blocks from here!"

"Yeah," said Eloise. "Again." She took a can of Vienna
sausages and some crackers from the pantry and fixed

herself a plate. Caroline snagged some of the crackers and nibbled them.

"What happened?" I asked.

Caroline said, "There were four of them. The one in the lead asked Eloise for her license and registration. They asked for my license too. When the soldier saw your name on the registration, he asked Eloise what her relationship was to you. She told him she worked for you. Then he looked at me and asked if I was your daughter, and I said yes. He said, 'You've got some mama there, miss.' I asked him how he knew that, and he said he'd met you."

Caroline has my curly red hair. At least, the curly red hair I once had, before I got to be fifty-one. Not surprising that the soldier had made the connection, once he saw my name and address on the car registration.

Caroline pointed to the glass in my hand. Either she'd just noticed it, or perhaps she'd caught a whiff of what was in it. "Rough night, Mom?" Just like her father used to say.

"Yes," I said. "They were here earlier."

"What did you do? You sure made an impression on him." I told her briefly, omitting the part about the knife.

"That explains a lot. He asked if the three of us were living together, and I said yes. He asked me what you did for a living, and I told him you were a journalist. An award-winning journalist."

"Thank you." Big sigh of relief.

"He asked us what we were doing out this late, and Eloise told him she worked out in Jefferson Parish, cleaning offices, and we were just coming home. I told him I was working with her. I didn't think it was a good idea to tell him I was a filmmaker. You're right, I don't want anyone taking my camera away from me."

"They let you go, obviously."

"Yes. They told us to be careful."

"The soldiers didn't spray-paint an X on the car, did they?"

"Huh?"

"Take a look at the front of the house tomorrow morning and you'll understand what I'm talking about. I'm just glad they let you come home."

In the excitement of hearing their story, I forgot to tell Eloise what Mickey had said about her street being dry. I needed another two fingers of bourbon before I could fall asleep.

FRIDAY, SEPTEMBER 16

In the morning I remembered to tell Eloise about the water going down in her neighborhood. She wanted to go over there immediately. I called Mickey to see if he could meet us, but he was working on a story and couldn't get away. The three of us piled into the SUV. Eloise drove, Caroline was in the passenger seat with her camera, and I sat in the back.

We passed through mostly deserted streets in Carrollton to Hollygrove. Along the way we saw evidence that others had come back, although they may not have stayed. Refrigerators stood like silent sentinels along the curbs, wrapped in duct tape. Even with the doors closed, the deathly stench of their rotting contents hung in the air. Some still had magnets on the sides. Some had humorous slogans scrawled in spray paint:

> *"For Sale, Cheap!*
> *"Free Gumbo Inside!"*
> *"Big Easy? Big Stinky!"*

I thought of our garbage can and the unbearable smell in the garage. Eloise and I had dragged the can down the driveway to the curb, gagging all the way. Not that anyone is going to be picking up the garbage any time soon, but I had to get that can out of the garage. I wanted to throw up every time I went in there. When the power comes back on, I hope our refrigerator will be salvageable.

I spotted the row of houses on Carrollton Avenue that had caught fire while surrounded by flood waters. The had burned all the way down to the water line. The wood framing that remained looked like black jagged teeth pointing up to the sky.

For twenty-seven years I drove this street to work every day. I'd passed these houses literally thousands of times. They can't be gone, I thought. These things happen in distant countries. Not here. Not in New Orleans.

Getting into Hollygrove wasn't easy. A lot of streets were still barricaded. And just as I expected, a National Guardsman stopped us at a checkpoint. Eloise rolled down her window.

"I'm trying to get to my house, sir." She gave him the address.

"I'm sorry, ma'am, but you can't go back there."

"I understand the street is clear of water now."

"You can't go back there, ma'am."

"Please, sir. My husband is disabled. He was in the house. I have to find out what happened to him."

"We're checking all the houses. If he's back there, we'll find him."

At that point, Eloise sat up very straight in the driver's seat. "Sir, I really appreciate all that you folks are doing to help us. I'm glad you're here, keeping us safe. My son, Isaiah Jackson, was in the National Guard. He was my only child. He was killed in Afghanistan last year. I know if he had lived, he'd be here with you folks today, doing his duty."

I could see the soldier's expression soften a bit. "I'm very sorry for your loss, ma'am. I served in Afghanistan too."

Eloise gave him the name of Isaiah's unit and the date and place of his death. He nodded. "I've heard of his unit. They took some losses." He told her the name of his unit and where he had served.

Eloise said, "I'm glad you got to come back from over there. God bless you and keep you safe."

He stepped back from the car and waved us through. "God bless you, ma'am. I hope your husband is okay."

As we drove away, Caroline turned around in her seat and hissed at me, "I never again want to hear you say this is like living in Iraq. Is that clear?"

"Yes," I said meekly, wondering when I had stopped being the mother here. My daughter was giving me orders. But I had to admit, grudgingly, that she was right.

I'd been to Eloise's house four or five times over the years. It wasn't in the best of neighborhoods, although I've been in worse. But I wasn't prepared for what I saw as we drove down her street. The lines of debris left behind by the flood waters were up to the roofs of the houses. At least half the houses had a section of roof open to the rafters. A couple of them had jagged holes in the shingles where the occupants had used an ax to cut their way out of the attic, not having a dormer window to kick out. One house had collapsed, falling over on its left side, leaning precariously against its next-door neighbor. I hoped no one had been in it when it fell. Every house on Eloise's street had that spray-painted X by the front door.

The road was dry, but some of the yards still had black water standing in them, covered with a multicolored sheen of oil. There were flooded cars on the street and in driveways. Grass and shrubbery were brown-dead as if from a long drought, instead of just the opposite. I saw the bloated remains of a dog in a front yard. The smell of death was everywhere. The neighborhood was deserted.

Eloise's house was built on brick piers about a foot off the ground. The house was one story, with white wood siding and a single dormer window in the attic. It was probably built in the 1940s, after the era of the shotgun house. It sat on the typical New Orleans thirty-foot-wide lot. The house was narrow enough that there was room on the side for a gravel driveway.

Eloise's Toyota was still there, not that anyone would have driven it anywhere. The windows were covered with silt from the flood water. I couldn't see a water mark, so I guessed the water had been over the car's roof.

She parked the SUV in front and we got out. Caroline was filming the scene. Eloise walked up to her car, wiped the silt off a small section of window, and tried to look inside. There was a thick layer of condensation on the inside of the glass.

"Can't see anything," she said. "I hope the insurance company gives me enough money to buy another car."

We climbed the steps to the front porch. The door had been kicked in.

"It wasn't like this the last time we were here," said Eloise.

I saw the big red X beside the door. The top quadrant read "9-14" and the bottom had a "1."

Eloise was shaking. I put an arm around her shoulder. "We don't have to go in if you don't want to."

"I've got to." She went inside, Caroline following her with the camera. I took a quick look around the neighborhood to see if anyone was watching us. The street was empty and hot and still. Shrubbery was brown below where the water line had been and green above it. Cars and houses were layered with silt. It was as if we had landed on an uninhabited planet.

When I followed Eloise and Caroline inside, the first thing that hit me was the smell. Mold. Death. My eyes immediately started to water.

The house was dark except for the light coming from the open door. Someone, a neighbor, perhaps, had nailed sheets of plywood over the windows, as Robert wouldn't have been able to do this. The large front room was a combination living and dining room. Even in the dimness, I could see that it looked like it had been ransacked, but it was the rising water that had moved everything. Tables and chairs had been tossed around. A lamp lay on its side on the floor. The only things that were still in place were the sofa, which was waterlogged, and the china cabinet, which had too many heavy dishes on the bottom to float. The refrigerator had fallen over on its side and was blocking the entrance to the kitchen. Slimy carpet squished under my feet.

We climbed over the refrigerator into the kitchen, moving chairs out of our path. A hallway led from the kitchen back to the bedrooms. By now, we were too far from the light coming through the front door to see anything. Caroline's camera wasn't going to get this scene.

"There's a flashlight in the car," I said. "I'll go back for it."

Eloise was sobbing. "I thought he'd be in the living room. That's where he fell through. But I don't see him. He must be around here someplace."

I put a hand on her shoulder. I was pretty sure what the "1" under the X meant. Someone had already found Robert's body and probably had removed it. But Eloise wasn't ready to hear that yet.

When I returned with the flashlight, I shined the light on the living room ceiling. Eloise had said he lost his balance trying to kick out the glass in the front dormer window, so he must have fallen through somewhere around here. I found the hole, just where she thought it would be. But Robert wasn't in the living room.

The dining table, which had been at the far end of the room, had floated into the living area. It was upside down on the floor. Perhaps Robert hit it when he fell and was injured. Maybe he'd overturned the table, or maybe he'd been pinned under it. If he'd hit his head, he might have been knocked unconscious. It was hard to figure out what had happened, especially since there was no body.

Eloise and Caroline had made their way down the hallway to the bedrooms. I followed them, pushing aside a table in the middle of the narrow hall. It must have been the one Eloise and Robert had stood on to climb into the attic. When I shined the flashlight upward, I could see the square opening to the attic that Eloise and Robert had climbed through.

Eloise was moving around in the near-darkness in her bedroom. I could make out her silhouette but couldn't see her face. Caroline was standing a little to one side, holding her camera at her side. It was too dark to film in here, and I was glad.

Eloise was frantic. "He's not here. He's not here. Where could he be?"

I shined the light around the room. "I'm not sure why he'd be in here. The hole in the ceiling is up front, in the living room."

"But he's not in there. Maybe he came back here."

The bed was waterlogged like the sofa. The chest of drawers hadn't moved, either, but the nightstand was on its side and the table lamp had fallen on the bed.

"Maybe he got out the back door," Eloise said. "Maybe he swam out and found a tree somewhere to hang on to. Maybe he got rescued."

We went out into the hallway. The back door at the end of the hall, leading to the yard, was bolted shut from the inside. "I don't think he got out this way," I said.

I knew she was desperate to believe he was still alive. I remembered how I'd tried to wake up George in Maribeth's guest room, three weeks and a lifetime ago.

"Eloise, honey." I had never called her "honey" before. "Let's take another look at the living room, okay? I'm pretty sure that's where he fell through. We might find something."

Because the front door was open, it was lighter in the living room than in the rest of the house. I watched Caroline turn on her camera and film the room, panning up to the hole in the ceiling.

I examined the overturned dining table more closely. It was covered in silt and mold. If Robert had hit it when he fell, would it have splintered? Could he have overturned it, then been pinned under it and drowned?

The smell of decaying flesh was strong in this room. I was fairly sure this was where he had died.

There were footprints in the wet carpet. Some were ours, some might have been those of whoever kicked in the front door. But there was no disturbance of the silt on the table to indicate that someone had picked it up or moved it.

"I think he was here, lying on the sofa," I said, although I had no way to know that. It just sounded more comforting. "I think this is where the searchers found him."

"But where did they take him? What if I never find him?"

"We'll find him, I promise you. I'm going to help you find him."

I half-carried her out of the house, down the front steps, and over to the car. My eyes were streaming from the mold inside, and I was coughing. I think Caroline filmed us, but I didn't turn around to look. I helped Eloise into the car and started it, turning on the air conditioning.

This time I drove, with Eloise in the passenger seat and Caroline in the back. Eloise had her hands over her face.

On the way out, we stopped at the National Guard checkpoint again. I spoke to the same soldier Eloise had talked to earlier.

"We didn't find my friend's husband in the house, but we think his body may have been removed. There's a date on the X, two days ago, and a one beneath it. Where do you think his body might have been taken?"

"There's a morgue being set up in St. Gabriel, a town on the way to Baton Rouge. Do you know where it is?"

"I can find it."

"If I were you, I'd wait a few days to go over there. His body may not have arrived yet. They're being transported in refrigerated trucks. You might go all the way there and not find out anything."

"Thank you," I said.

As we drove away, Eloise said, "I want to go there right now."

"But you heard what he said."

"I don't care. I've got to find Robert. You said you'd help me."

It wasn't easy to get to St. Gabriel. We negotiated checkpoints and roadblocks, took back roads, had to search for gas. But two hours later, we drove into the town. St. Gabriel, population about six thousand, is south of Baton Rouge near the Mississippi River, and all I knew about it prior to today was that it was the location of a women's prison.

The morgue is in a big warehouse behind the city hall. It's run by a federal agency called D-MORT, which stands for Disaster Mortuary Operational Response Team. I was apprehensive about what we'd find here. I've heard so much since the storm about bureaucratic bungling and government red tape that I feared we'd never find Robert. I wanted to shield Eloise from callous civil servants who might treat her with indifference at a time when she was devastated by grief.

But a very kind woman named Marie met with Eloise and listened to her story with compassion. Of course there was paperwork to fill out, but Marie was patient and caring. She told her, as gently as possible, that they were still getting things set up at the morgue and, as the soldier had told us, it was likely that Robert's body hadn't arrived yet. There were so many.

She told her that family members weren't being allowed to see the bodies. Many were decomposed past the point of recognition, and it really wasn't a sight family members would want to remember for the rest of their lives. Even if they saw the body, it was possible they'd identify the wrong person. Remains were being identified by things like dental records, DNA, and serial numbers of orthopedic devices, like Robert's prosthetic leg. Marie said Robert's leg might be the best shot they had at identifying him.

Eloise wrote down what she knew about his medical records and the name of his dentist. But where would she find DNA in a house that had flooded up to the ceiling?

When Marie told Eloise to check back in a week or so, I saw the anger in her face. "I'm gonna call you every day until you find him," she said.

Marie was gentle but firm. "I know you want answers now, Mrs. Jackson, and I wish I could give them to you. But please give us time. Calling us every day will only frustrate you. I promise we'll contact you when we have a positive identification."

"You find him," she said.

Caroline wasn't allowed to film the meeting between Marie and Eloise, but she interviewed Eloise outside the building afterward. Eloise was crying, but she answered Caroline's questions.

We drove back to New Orleans in silence, stopping only to get a late lunch at a fast food restaurant along the way. I never thought I'd consider a hamburger and fries a luxury, but it tasted like the finest meal I'd ever eaten.

I took a few back roads to get Uptown and managed to avoid the checkpoints. I was afraid if we got stopped this time, they might not let us back in. And that was something none of us needed, not today.

We got back late in the afternoon. Eloise took the Mustang and headed to work, this time without Caroline. She'd shown no emotion since we left St. Gabriel. I had no idea what she was thinking, but I wished I was half as brave as she was.

Saturday, September 17

We went back to Eloise's house this morning to help her begin the process of removing what could be salvaged. We took cleaning supplies and garbage bags and rubber gloves and bandanas to use as makeshift face masks—the mold and the smell in the house are overpowering. Figuring we'd be there all day, I packed sandwiches and snacks and bottles of water.

The same Guardsmen who'd been on duty yesterday were there again today. They recognized us and waved us on.

Eloise still wasn't saying much. Her mouth was set in a grim line and her jaw was clenched. She led the way, climbing the four steps to her front porch and pushing open the battered front door.

"Doesn't look like anybody's come in since we were here yesterday," she said.

"That's good," I said. "Where do you want to start?"

"That lady at St. Gabriel, Marie, said they could probably identify Robert from the serial number on his prosthesis. Trouble is, I don't know what happened to his medical records. They might have gotten flooded, too. And nobody is working in those doctors' offices right now anyway. So she said maybe they could identify him if they had a sample of his DNA. Now where am I going to find a sample of his DNA in this house?"

I looked around the living room. "Under normal circumstances, maybe some skin cells in the cushion of a chair he usually sat in. Or hairs or skin cells on a brush or comb he used. Or on some clothing he wore that hadn't been washed. But . . ."

"These aren't normal circumstances," said Caroline.

"You got that right," said Eloise.

"Maybe we can find something that didn't flood," I said.

Eloise shook her head.

Mold was climbing the walls in small round blotches of varying sizes and colors, like some bizarre Impressionist painting. I remembered the walls as white, but now they were a sepia tone beneath the mold. The sofa, which had been covered a floral pattern, was dark and slimy from dirty water and mold. It was still waterlogged. A bookcase on one wall had what looked like a set of encyclopedias on the bottom shelf that had kept it from floating around in the water. Cookbooks and paperbacks and knick-knacks were on the middle shelves, and several framed photos still sat on the top shelf, with a brown water line across the glass. There was a photo of Eloise and Robert, several small photos of Isaiah as a child, and one of him in his military uniform. All looked like they had mold on them under the glass.

Eloise picked up the photo of Isaiah in uniform. "I wonder if I can save these pictures."

"Sure going to try," I said. "Let's bring them back to the house, see if we can get them out of the frames without damaging them and dry them out."

She carried them out to the SUV and laid them in the back cargo area. When she returned to the house, I could see the glitter of tears in her eyes. But the expression on her face wasn't grief. It was anger.

"Help me move some of this furniture outside," was all she said.

We pulled on rubber gloves and set to work. I shook my head at the waterlogged sofa and the beds. They'd have to wait for a crew of strong men. But we moved chairs and tables and other lighter pieces out to the curb and started to pile them up.

"The refrigerator," said Caroline. "It's blocking the doorway to the kitchen. We really need to get it out of here."

It took all three of us to get it upright. "Should we empty it before we move it?" I asked.

Well, yes, that would make sense. It would lighten the load. But we all coughed at the smell when we opened it. I held a garbage bag as Eloise and Caroline tossed stuff into it: milk, butter, ketchup, mayonnaise, packages of lunch meat, brown shrunken fruit that might have been peaches, a bowl of unidentifiable something. Eloise tossed the whole bowl into the garbage bag. Next, cans of soft drinks and a plastic container that might have been iced tea. In the freezer were packages of meat and seafood that stank like death. For a moment I thought I'd throw up, but I didn't.

When the refrigerator was empty, the three of us pushed it across the sodden carpet to the front door. It was an effort to get it over the lip of the door and onto the porch.

I looked at the four steps down to the front sidewalk. "How are we going to get it down?"

"Push it," said Eloise.

We turned it so it would go down on its side, which was smooth, rather than get hung up on the coils in the back or the door handles in the front. It bounced on the steps, slid down, and landed on the front sidewalk with a crash that could be heard all over the neighborhood, although as far as I could tell, there was no one around to hear it. We picked it up again and pushed it out to the curb.

"We need to seal it," said Caroline.

"Yeah," I said. "Don't want any children playing in it. Like there are any children around here. Or any who would want to play in something that smells so bad."

"Still, we need to seal it. Eloise, do you have any duct tape?"

"I think I've got some in a kitchen drawer. If we can get it open."

The wooden drawers were swollen shut. We pulled on the handles until the fronts came off.

"That didn't go well," I said.

Caroline was able to snake her slender arm inside the drawers and pull things out: twist ties, rubber bands, pencils, sodden grocery receipts, plastic bags, all the things one stuffs in a kitchen drawer without thinking about it. She finally came up with a wet roll of gray duct tape and a pair of scissors.

"Think it's still sticky enough to work?" I asked.

It was. We wrapped the refrigerator in several layers of duct tape.

"Wish we had some spray paint," said Caroline.

"What would you write on it?"

"I don't know. Eloise, it's your refrigerator. What would you want to say to the world?"

"Never again," she said.

"You got that right," I said.

It was hard, dirty, nasty work, but after a couple of hours, we could see progress. The pile out by the street was growing. We took a break for lunch, cleaning up with a bottle of hand sanitizer. We sat on the porch floor—the two metal chairs that had been on the porch had either floated away or been taken—and ate our sandwiches.

Caroline asked, "How are you doing, Eloise?"

"Not so good, child."

"I wish I could do something to help."

"You are. You and your mama are helping me clean this stuff out."

"That's not what I meant."

"I know. But it's all you can do. Can't bring them back."

By "them," I knew she was talking about Isaiah as well as Robert. Caroline took her hand. Eloise squeezed it. "Just pray, honey. Just pray."

"I'm not very big on prayer. But for your sake, I'll try."

"Thank you, baby."

Caroline had bristled when I'd called her "baby." But she just nodded when Eloise did. Different situation, I reminded myself. But it stung anyway.

"Tell me about Robert," she said. "When did you meet?"

Eloise sat back, leaning against the wall of the house. "We both lived in the country outside of St. Francisville. We went to the same high school. This was back when the schools were segregated, and we went to the black school, Dawson High, by the bridge. It wasn't that big a school, but it was big enough that he and I didn't really know each other. I was fifteen and he was sixteen and we were in different classes.

"But everybody in the school was talking about him when he had the accident. He and his cousin were out on a farm and they were fooling around, like boys do. His cousin was pulling a combine behind a tractor. I don't know exactly how it happened, but his cousin ran over him with the combine. They had to amputate his leg above the knee.

"He was out of school for quite a while, and when he came back, he was in a wheelchair. Everybody was talking *about* him, but hardly anybody was talking *to* him. We were all just kids. I guess most of us didn't know what to say to somebody in that situation, so people just kind of avoided him.

"I would see him in the lunchroom sitting by himself in that wheelchair, and it just didn't seem right to me. So one day I went up to him and asked if I could sit with him. He said yes, and we started talking. It was a little awkward at first, but he was glad to have someone to talk to, and I was pleased that a boy would talk with me. I was never very pretty or popular, so I liked the attention." She wiped her face with her t-shirt. Sweat, tears, both?

"Do you remember what you talked about?"

"Oh, girl, silly stuff, like boys and girls do. I guess we talked about our teachers and complained about the homework. We both wanted to get out of St. Francisville and go to New Orleans. This was the big city, where everything was going to be better. Robert laughed and joked with me a lot, but he was really having a tough time with the leg. Not only did he have a lot of pain with it, but he thought it was the end of all his plans for his life. He didn't think he'd ever be able to get a job. Most jobs for black people back then—and a lot of them still—are manual labor. You need two good legs to do that." She sighed, rubbing her own legs.

"In the end, he decided to get a college education so he could get a job working in an office. He went to Southern University in Baton Rouge and got his degree in accounting. It wasn't easy for him. By then he had a prosthetic leg, which made it a little easier to get around than being in a wheelchair. He got student aid, worked in the library, had a part-time job as a file clerk in an accounting office.

"After I graduated from high school, I took care of my grandmother till she died. In St. Francisville back then, black girls just didn't go to college. And nobody in my family had every gone, anyway. I'd see Robert when he came home from Southern. He didn't drive, so he could only come when he could get a ride with someone. But we were in love, and after he graduated, we got married." She smiled.

"My father didn't like the idea of my marrying a crippled boy, but my mother was pleased that I had a husband with a college degree. She told my father Robert would be able to support me. We moved to New Orleans after we got married, just like we'd said we would. He got a job as an accountant with an insurance company. It was a black-owned firm, of course. That's just how it was in those days—if you were black, the white firms wouldn't hire you."

"Some of them still don't," I said.

Caroline shot me a look. "Not now, Mom. Go on, Eloise."

"We couldn't make it on Robert's salary alone, so I got a job taking care of an old lady who couldn't get out of bed. But then Isaiah came along, and I had to quit.

"My father died of a heart attack not long after that, and my mama came down here to live with us. She started taking care of Isaiah so I could go back to work. The family of the lady I'd worked for had hired someone else, but they recommended me to your mama. You had just been born, and she needed someone to take care of you so she could go back to work. And I've been working for your mama ever since."

Caroline waved a hand at the house. "You and Robert and Isaiah and your mother were all living together? Here?"

"That's right. We were renting the house at first, but then the owner died and his children sold it to us. We've been here, let's see, thirty-three years."

"Wow, that's a long time."

"Yes, indeed." Eloise took a swig of her water. "Child, you've known me all your life, and you didn't know all this about me?"

Caroline looked embarrassed. "I was a little kid. I guess I never asked."

"Maggie, what about you?"

I coughed, partly from the moldy air I'd been inhaling all morning, partly from embarrassment. "You've told me some of this over the years. I didn't know the story about how you and Robert met, though."

"Huh," said Eloise.

"I remember when your mother died," I said. "It was what, maybe five years ago? It was before Isaiah was killed."

"Thank God she didn't live to see that. She loved that boy so." Eloise's eyes filled with tears again.

"What family members do you have left?"

"My sister. My aun-tie. Robert's parents and his brother. Some cousins. They're all up in St. Francisville."

"Have you talked to them?"

"I managed to get hold of my sister, and she called Robert's brother. When those people in St. Gabriel identify Robert, I'm going to have a funeral in St. Francisville. Can't have one in New Orleans, not after all this. We'll bury him up there with the rest of his family."

"That's where you buried Isaiah. I remember going there."

"Yeah. His family told me there was a place for me too."

"But not yet, Eloise. Not yet."

She looked up and down the street at the devastation around us. "Sometimes I wish I hadn't lived through this. Maybe it would have been better to die with Robert."

"You don't mean that."

"Yes, I do. That's my whole life in there. It's all gone."

I shook my head. "You made it through, Eloise. You survived. That means there's more."

Eloise grabbed the porch railing and hauled herself to her feet. "More of what?" She turned and went back into the house.

Caroline stared after her but didn't get up. "Did you hear her, Mom? Eloise has been taking care of other people her whole life. Her grandmother, the old woman, me, even Robert."

"You're right. I hadn't thought about it, but Eloise is one of those people who spend their lives taking care of others."

"And now she's got no one to take care of."

"It's time someone took care of her." I smiled. "If she'll let them."

"Well, that's what we're doing now. Come on, let's go back inside."

TUESDAY, SEPTEMBER 20

There is Another One out there, heading into the Gulf of Mexico.

This one is Rita, now passing over the Florida Keys, following much the same path as Katrina did. Early predictions are that Rita will pass us by and make landfall to the west, somewhere in south Texas. The projected track will take it due south of New Orleans as it crosses the Gulf of Mexico, but we're going to get rain and wind. Right now the levees have temporary repairs. They can't take the pressure of another storm surge.

George's law partner Tony called from Houston this evening. He and his wife have rented a house there, as their home in Lakeview was just blocks from the levee breach on the 17th Street Canal. He said people in Houston, Galveston, Corpus Christi, and Beaumont are terrified of this coming storm after what happened in New Orleans, and everybody's evacuating. Tony and his wife are going to Dallas.

It was the first time we'd talked since he came to Atlanta for George's memorial service. He'd read my blog and was shocked to learn that we'd come home.

"You and Caroline? And Eloise? But the city's still shut down."

"Yeah, we know. Don't get me started about the National Guard checkpoints."

"Was your house damaged? Do you have electricity?"

"Yes to your first question, no to your second."

"You mean you're living in a damaged house without power?"

"Why yes, Tony, it *is* hot as hell. I confess I've gotten used to the cold showers, but I haven't gotten used to the heat."

"Are you crazy? Do you know how dangerous New Orleans is right now?"

"Probably less dangerous than Houston, from what I hear. Everyone is saying the drug dealers all evacuated there."

He grunted. "There's been some trouble, yes."

"Please don't get too comfortable over there. New Orleans needs you back."

"I wish you and Caroline and Eloise would come over here. Houston isn't a bad place to be."

"You've got a hurricane coming, and you're evacuating for the second time in a month. I don't think so."

"Point taken. But I worry about you."

"Thanks, Tony. Be careful going to Dallas."

WEDNESDAY, SEPTEMBER 21

The National Guard came to the house again and urged me to leave. They were pretty insistent. I thanked them as politely as I could and said I would consider it. Both cars have nearly full tanks of gas. We could leave if we wanted to. I knew I didn't want to go, but I wasn't going to speak for Caroline or Eloise.

"What do you think?" I asked them after the Guardsmen had left.

Eloise shook her head. "It's not coming here."

"I'm in if you're in," said Caroline.

"Have you talked to Jason lately?" I asked.

"Yeah."

"What does he say?"

"What he always says. 'Get the hell out of there.' And I say, 'Not till I'm done filming this documentary.' He doesn't get it."

"Are you sure you want to stay?"

"Absolutely. We're living in the middle of history here. Rita is going to be a part of that history. I can't run away from it."

"Eloise, you're sure too?"

"I'm not going anywhere. Not till they find Robert."

Every morning, Eloise goes out to the front porch, sits in the rocking chair, and pulls her cell phone out of her pocket. The reception is better outside. She calls Marie at St. Gabriel to find out if they've identified Robert's body. So far, nothing.

Then she and Caroline go to her house to continue cleaning it out. I went with them the first few days, but breathing the mold gave me a terrible sinus infection and a violent cough so powerful I nearly threw up a couple of times. Caroline told me to stay home, because none of our doctors are here and no hospitals in the city are open.

They've been bringing things back that they've managed to salvage from the house—utensils and dishes and glassware, mostly. We're storing them in the garage. When the power is back on and the water is considered safe, we can sanitize them in the dishwasher. Her cast iron frying pans were rusted and covered in mold. They went to the trash pile.

Just about everything in her house is ruined: furniture, clothing, bedding, linens, curtains, carpet, televisions, phones, kitchen appliances, cabinets, the stove, the window unit air conditioners, the floor furnaces. She and Caroline have been hauling everything they can carry out to the curb. Caroline says the pile is now about six feet high and as wide as the lot. She's showed me some of the film she's shot. A lifetime's worth of possessions in a mountain of trash, waiting to be hauled away—who knows when?

Eloise came back one day carrying a still-sodden Bible. The pebbled leather cover was gray with mold and the pages bulged unevenly. "It was on the nightstand in our bedroom," she said. "I would read it every morning and every night. I want to keep it, but I know it's ruined. Maggie, do you have a Bible I could read?"

I coughed. I'd been raised Catholic but walked away from church as soon as I was old enough to make my own decisions. George had been Presbyterian. He didn't go to church either, but his mother had attended regularly.

"Um, there may be a Bible in George's upstairs office. I think it was his mother's. You're welcome to read it."

"Thank you." She went upstairs and came back a minute later with a worn leather Bible not much different from hers, except it wasn't wet and covered in mold. "It was on the shelf." She set it down on the kitchen table. "I've missed reading my Bible. I need it right now."

I nodded. I still don't want to think about God, especially not a God behind storms like Katrina and now Rita. It makes me angry to hear these preachers say God is punishing us for our sins. Babies have died in this flooding. Is God punishing them? Or their parents? If so, then I don't want anything to do with their God.

Time to change the subject. I asked Eloise if she had flood insurance. She looked a little embarrassed.

"We had to carry it when we had a mortgage on the house, but we paid that off a few years ago. We'd never had to use it, and because the house was raised on piers, we didn't think we needed it. We let it go. It was expensive."

"I'm hearing that FEMA may be able to help. You're not alone here. A lot of people are in the same situation. We never thought the levees would fail so catastrophically and cause this kind of flooding."

"FEMA?" She snorted. "The government's gonna help me? Like they helped all those people in the Superdome and the Convention Center? When?"

"I don't know, Eloise. But it seems to me they've got to do something. Too many people are living in shelters all over the region. They can't come home because they no longer have a place to live."

"When that man dropped me off from his boat and I saw all those people waiting for buses, I said to myself, 'Unh-unh.' Who knew when these buses were coming? Or if they were coming at all? And where were they going to take us? I don't know where all those people ended up. I'm so glad to be here in this house, Maggie, even if we don't have any lights or air conditioning. It beats being in some shelter, sleeping on the floor with all those other people."

"I'm glad you found your way over here. You're welcome to stay here as long as you want."

She nodded. "Those people in shelters are sitting around all day doing nothing. Not because they want to, but because they don't have any choice. Their jobs were here, and now they've got no jobs to go back to, with the city shut down. I'm glad I've still got my jobs to go to at night and can make some money. It won't be enough to rebuild my house, but at least I can pay my expenses. Pay you for the food I'm eating, and for living here in your house."

I raised my hand in protest, but she cut me off. "No, Maggie! I'm paying my way, you understand? I'm not a charity case."

"No, you're not a charity case. But sometimes people need help, Eloise. You've been helping other people all your life. Let us help you now, when you need it."

"I can pay for myself."

"Okay. I got that. But if the government offers you money to help fix your house, take it."

"I'll take it if I ever see it."

FRIDAY, SEPTEMBER 23

We got a lashing of wind and rain from Rita as it moved south of us in the Gulf. We stayed in the house all day, listening to news broadcasts on the battery-operated radio as the rain pounded against the sides of the house. The windows are still boarded up and the shutters closed, so very little natural light gets inside. But today it was even darker than usual.

At one point I heard a crash upstairs and took a flashlight with me to investigate. In my bedroom I found huge chunks of sodden plaster on the bed and the floor. The rain was causing even more damage where the roof is open to the sky. Nothing I can do about it until I can get a contractor in here. And as long as the city remains officially closed, that's not going to happen. I shook my head and went back downstairs.

Caroline and Eloise were listening to a report that the Industrial Canal levee had breached again and water was pouring into the Lower Ninth Ward. The canal connects the Mississippi River to Lake Pontchartrain. The storm surge in the lake backed up into the canal and overtopped the temporary repairs to the levee. Then the levee started to leak and a number of breaches appeared. Now water was roaring into neighborhoods that had flooded just three weeks ago in Katrina. This time, at least, nobody was living there.

My bedroom was rapidly filling with chunks of wet plaster, and stalactites of mold were tracing a path down the walls. But compared to what we were hearing on the radio, it was like a mosquito buzzing around your face while enemy aircraft are flying overhead.

"Some people are saying the Industrial Canal levees were deliberately breached to save the 17th Street Canal levee from breaching again," said Eloise. "Let the Lower Nine take the pressure off the 17th Street Canal levee and save the houses of those rich white people in Lakeview. Who cares about those poor black folks?"

I opened my mouth to protest, then closed it. History records that in the great Mississippi River flood of 1927, levees south of the city were dynamited to carry off some of the flood water and relieve pressure on the levees surrounding the city. And it was poor people who were flooded out and lost their homes and farms. Some drowned. There was definitely a precedent for thinking this could happen again.

I looked at Eloise. "Your neighborhood floods in a heavy rain, even when the pumps are working."

She closed her eyes. "House is already flooded. Car too. Doesn't really matter now, does it?"

Caroline said, "All that stuff we piled out at the curb is either going to blow around in the wind or float away in the water. I never thought of that when we were cleaning out the house."

"Can't do anything about it now," I said. "Besides, there's already debris everywhere."

From time to time we peeked outside to see if water was rising in the neighborhood. Pools of water in the street spilled over the curb out front onto the grass between the sidewalk and the street and eventually covered the sidewalk. The water hovered at the edge of the front walk to the house but didn't come any closer.

After dark, the rain finally stopped. The wind rose as it shifted to the south with the passing of the storm. The air was warm and smelled like a sea breeze coming off the Gulf of Mexico. It brought back memories of summer trips George and I had made to the Mississippi, Alabama, and Florida coasts. I had so many pleasant associations with that warm scent of sand and salt. Not this time. Now Rita was moving westward to wreak devastation on the Louisiana-Texas border. I hope Tony and his wife will be okay.

I want my life back. I want to go back to those days of sea breezes off the Gulf and walks on the beach with George. Would someone please let me out of this disaster movie and open the doors to the world I used to know?

Sunday, September 25

I think I'm getting used to taking cold showers. Actually, they're closer to lukewarm. By late afternoon, the water is warm just from the heat of the day. What I can't get used to is the towels. We wash them in the bathtub and hang them outside to dry. They come off the line stiff and scratchy. It feels like drying off with sandpaper. I never thought I'd miss my clothes dryer so much.

Today, before I got in the shower, I stepped on the bathroom scale. I hadn't weighed myself recently, and I was shocked to discover I'd lost ten pounds. I thought my pants had gotten looser, but I hadn't really paid a lot of attention.

Later, while we were eating, I mentioned it to Eloise and Caroline. "Have you weighed yourselves lately?"

Eloise said, "I've lost twelve pounds in the past month."

Caroline said, "Maybe a couple of pounds."

I narrowed my eyes. Caroline looked tired, and she wasn't eating much. Working around all that mold in Eloise's house couldn't possibly be good for her. Or for Eloise either. But there was no stopping either of them.

"We're not eating as much in this heat," said Eloise. "And we're sweating it off."

"It's not like we're eating diet food here," I pointed out. "All this canned food is full of carbohydrates, fats, and preservatives."

Caroline sighed. "I am so tired of eating Vienna sausages. I'm starting to get nauseous just smelling them."

"You used to love them when you were little," said Eloise.

"Yeah, but I didn't have to eat them every day."

"Those steaks Mrs. Giannini sent over were wonderful," I said. "But that little windfall came to an end quickly." I sighed. "What I would love right now is a big, juicy hamburger. Rare. Dripping. With lots of ketchup and mayonnaise."

Caroline said, "I miss salads. And fresh vegetables."

"Living in California is changing you," I said. "You've gone healthy on us."

Eloise said, "I would love to make a big pot of seafood gumbo."

"With a side of hot French bread, just out of the oven," I added.

"And ice cream for dessert," said Caroline. "Oh, do I miss ice cream."

We all moaned.

"Maybe California hasn't turned you into a complete health nut yet," I said.

Eloise said, "We're gonna gain that weight back, soon as we get power for the refrigerator and gas for the stove. Maybe gain ten pounds more than we lost."

"I don't care," I said. "It'll be worth it."

MONDAY, SEPTEMBER 26

Caroline is leaving on Sunday. She has to be back in Los Angeles for school next week. I'm going to miss her so much. It's been a godsend to have her with me these last four weeks since George's death. I've never leaned on my daughter for support before. I hope I've supported her, too. She's so young to have lost her father.

She's been fretting about the video. So many loose ends to the story she's trying to tell. Eloise still hasn't heard anything from the morgue at St. Gabriel. Caroline hoped Eloise would find Robert's body before she left, so she could include it in the video. But there's no telling when that will happen. It could be weeks, or it could be much longer. I hope not.

We were sitting out in the back yard in late afternoon shade, drinking bottles of water. Eloise had left for work. It wasn't exactly cool, but a light breeze made it cooler outside than in the house.

"I don't know how to end it," she said. "I want to tell Eloise's story, but it feels like I'm cutting it off in the middle."

"Real life doesn't always comply with our journalistic deadlines. Sometimes you have to go with what you've got, without any kind of resolution to the story. If you have to finish the video without knowing what happened to Robert's body, well, that could be a story in itself. You could frame it in the context of the ongoing story of Katrina, that it will take years to work through what happened here."

"I just wish Eloise could get some closure on this. And I wish I could show it."

"It will happen. And I'll be here for her when it does."

"I hate to leave the two of you. I feel guilty about going back to L.A., where they have electricity and grocery stores and hot showers."

"We'll be okay. The mayor has given permission to reopen the city on Friday. You'll be here to see it and put it in your video. I think things are going to improve quickly after that."

"What about you, Mom? What are you going to do?"

"Keep writing my blog. When the city reopens, I should be able to travel around more freely, without all the roadblocks and checkpoints and restricted access. I don't have a legitimate press pass, like Mickey does—that's how he's been able to go into areas that I can't. When they loosen the restrictions, I'll have more to write about."

"Will you be able to find someone to repair this house?"

"I've been in touch with Steven, the contractor who built the sunroom for us. He's over in Florida right now with his family, where they evacuated. He said he'd get a crew over here to start the repairs as soon as the city reopens. I'll be busy with him and his workers, too."

"I worry about how you're going to manage. I mean, with Daddy gone . . ." Her voice trailed off.

"I know, honey. This is something I'm just going to have to face, that's all. Eloise, too, dealing with all of this without Robert. We'll be here for each other, her and me. We'll get through this."

"I miss Daddy so much."

"I do too. But if he were still alive, you know he'd never have agreed to stay here under these conditions. He and I would be in Houston with Tony and his wife, and you'd be at school in Los Angeles. We wouldn't have come back and found Eloise here, and you wouldn't be making a documentary."

"Daddy always did like things neat and orderly."

"Caroline." I was struggling for words. Finally I said, "I am sorry."

It was quiet in the yard. Caroline looked at me, looked away, looked back again. "Sorry for what?"

"For the things I've done when I didn't think about how they would affect you. I could have waited until after you got to Atlanta to have your father's remains cremated. I just wasn't thinking very clearly."

"No, you weren't." Her face turned red and I saw her brush a tear from her cheek.

"I know you're upset that you didn't get to see him again. I've been to funerals, Caroline. A body that's been made up by embalmers isn't the person you knew. It's like a wax figure. Cold. Maybe you think it was important to see your father in a casket, but what's really important is the father you see up here—" I tapped my head "—and the memories you have of him. Remember his voice. Remember the things he said to you. That's what's important. Never forget."

In the high voice of a small child, she cried, "I want my daddy back."

I wanted to hold her the way I had when she was small, to let her cry against me, but her ramrod-straight back told me this wasn't the time. "I know."

TUESDAY, SEPTEMBER 27

Tony called last night to let me know he and his wife were back in Houston after evacuating to Dallas for Hurricane Rita. Everything seems to be okay at the house they were renting.

"When they reopen the city, we're going to drive in to check on our house in Lakeview to see if anything can be salvaged. And I'm going to the office. I'm hoping the power will be on and the elevators working. We're on the twenty-fifth floor. If there isn't any power, that means I'll have to climb the stairs."

"Jesus, Tony, are you up for that? And in this heat, too."

He laughed. "I guess I can just take my time. I heard there was some flooding on the ground floor, so the elevator machinery might be damaged. I'm thinking that even if they get the power back, it may be awhile before the elevators are in service again. Twenty-five floors. I'd better put in some serious time on the elliptical at the gym."

"Let me know when you're coming," I said. "I'd like to join you when you go to the office."

"Why?"

"I want to see George's office. When he left that Friday, he thought he was coming back on Monday. I'd just like to see it as he saw it that last day. I'd feel close to him there."

"Okay, Maggie. I'll let you know."

FRIDAY, SEPTEMBER 30

The mayor finally reopened the city today. We are now officially allowed to be living here—now that we've been here more than three weeks and fighting the National Guard just to stay in a house that I own.

We had finished breakfast and were sitting at the kitchen table when it happened. The clock on the stove suddenly began to blink 12:00 in blue-green numbers, and the room was filled with the humming of the refrigerator starting up. An impatient beep behind me announced that the microwave had returned from the dead.

"Oh my God!" cried Caroline. "The power is back!"

Eloise and I jumped from our chairs. She opened the refrigerator door, and the light came on. We all cheered, despite the musty smell inside.

"I can get this clean," Eloise said. "Bleach and water. I'll take all the shelves outside and clean them."

I had turned off the central air conditioning units—one each for upstairs and downstairs—to protect them from being damaged by a power surge when the electricity returned. "Do you think I ought to wait to turn them back on, in case the power goes out again?"

"No," said Caroline and Eloise in unison.

I went to the downstairs thermostat and flipped the switch. A few seconds passed that felt like hours. Then the compressor outside roared to life. We all cheered again.

George and I had turned off all the lights before we evacuated, a lifetime ago. I started to walk through rooms, flipping light switches, marveling as the lights came back on.

Eloise tried the electric pilot on the gas stove. It clicked like a cricket, just as it was supposed to. But the blue flame didn't leap up on the burner. "No gas yet."

"I guess they have to check every house before they can turn the gas back on," I said. "At least we have the microwave and the refrigerator now."

"Not until I clean the refrigerator," said Eloise.

At that point, her cell phone rang and she answered it. "Hey! Where are you?" She listened for a moment. "I'll meet you over there. Give me twenty minutes." She hung up.

"What's up?" asked Caroline.

"People from St. Francisville. They're coming over to my house to help. I got to go over there."

"We'll go with you," I said.

We cleared the table and were out the door in five minutes. I would have loved to sit in my house all day, reveling in the return of air conditioning, but I wanted even more to be with Eloise when her friends arrived.

By the time we got to her house, they were already there. A black Ford pickup truck was parked just down the street from the pile of household goods at the curb. As we pulled up, two men got out, one about Eloise's age and one about Caroline's.

Eloise jumped out of the car and ran to them. Caroline followed with her video camera. I watched as the older man hugged Eloise.

"Thank the Lord, Birdy!" the older man said. "I'm just so glad you're alive!"

"Birdy?" I asked.

"That's what everybody in St. Francisville been calling her ever since she was a little bit of a thing," the man said. "She used to run around like a little bird."

Eloise smiled shyly. "Maggie, Caroline, this is Robert's cousin Lamar. And this is his son Bobby."

I shook their hands. "Bobby. Named for Robert?"

"Yes ma'am," he said.

Caroline and I shared a look but said nothing.

"We're so glad you're here," I said.

"Been waiting and waiting for them to give us permission to come into New Orleans," Lamar said. "When we found out about Robert—and that Birdy had gotten out alive—we wanted to come down and get her. But she said no, it was too dangerous. She was afraid the soldiers might think we were looters. She thought we might get arrested. Or shot."

Of course. They were from out of town, so their vehicle wouldn't have an Orleans Parish inspection sticker on the windshield. That would be a red flag to law enforcement that they weren't locals coming to check on their homes. And they were black. Unfortunately, since the storm, many white people in the city were automatically assuming the worst about people of color. Hell, that had been going on long before the storm. But I understood. Eloise had good reason to be afraid for them.

"We've been taking good care of her," I said. "And she's been taking care of us."

"She said you all didn't have any electricity or gas. And the water might not be safe."

"The power came back on just before you called," I said. "And the water hasn't killed us yet."

"Well, Birdy, we can still take you back to St. Francisville with us. If you want to go."

She looked first at me, then at Caroline. "I appreciate that. But I've got my jobs at night. I need to make a living, now that Robert's gone."

Lamar nodded. "I understand. But if you change your mind, we've got room for you at our house."

"Thank you. But my place is here, for now."

"What can we do to help you out here? Looks like you've gotten a lot of stuff out of your house already."

"Yes, but there's a lot more. Heavy things. The sofa. The beds. And then the cabinets in the kitchen and bathroom need to come out. And the walls need to be gutted."

"We brought tools. Let's get started."

The two men got a lot done. They removed the plywood boards from the windows to let more light into the house so they could see what they were doing. Now Caroline could film inside. They took out the heavy furniture and ripped out the cabinets. They'd brought a wheelbarrow in the back of the pickup truck, and we filled it with debris. Bobby helped us get it down the front steps, bump, bump, bump, and out to the curb.

By late afternoon, we were all worn out. I invited them to come to my house for dinner.

"There's a six o'clock curfew," said Lamar. "We're going to have to head back to St. Francisville."

The curfew hadn't stopped Eloise from going to work, but I knew well how many times she'd been stopped on her way back at night. Two black men in a pickup truck that didn't have an Orleans Parish inspection sticker on the windshield, yeah, they could run into trouble after dark.

"And I have to go to work," said Eloise. "Got to get cleaned up first."

"We'll be back," said Lamar. "We'll gut your house for you. We're going to do everything we can for you, Birdy."

Her eyes filled with tears. "God is so good," she said.

Later that night, after she returned from Jefferson Parish, I asked her the question that had been on my mind ever since that morning. "Was Lamar the cousin who ran over Robert's leg with the combine?"

"How did you guess?"

"He named his son for Robert."

"He did. He's never forgiven himself. He was crying when he first talked to me on the phone after the storm. He said if Robert still had his leg, he never would have fallen through that ceiling. He would have gotten out alive."

"There's no way to know that."

Caroline said, "But if he hadn't lost his leg, the two of you wouldn't have started talking in the lunchroom. Maybe you never would have started dating."

"He would have been better off with two legs than having me." Eloise was starting to cry.

"I don't agree," said Caroline. "I don't think he would have, either."

"I'm with Caroline on this one," I said. "Robert loved you more than the whole world. And he died trying to save your life by kicking out that window."

"I don't want to talk about this," said Eloise. She turned and went upstairs.

OCTOBER

SATURDAY, OCTOBER 1

This morning Caroline rummaged around in a closet and found an indoor television antenna—what we used to call "rabbit ears." She brought an old portable set downstairs from her bedroom and set it on a card table in the living room in front of the set we normally watched.

"Your new high definition set doesn't even have the connections to hook up an indoor antenna," she said. "I'm going to have to go old-tech here." She connected the antenna to the television, plugged everything in, and turned the set on. It blinked into life, giving us a fuzzy picture of a couple of local anchors reading the news while a banner of headlines streamed across the bottom of the screen: where to get emergency food stamps, apply for help from FEMA, or pick up donated bottles of water.

"Your father insisted on keeping those old rabbit ears just in case the cable went out. I thought it was silly, but now I'm glad we have them." I laughed. "This is what television was like when I was growing up. See what you missed, Caroline?"

"In a way we're lucky that Congress has delayed the change to a digital signal," she said. "Otherwise, we wouldn't be able to see anything without a converter box. All the televisions in the house are analog."

"I knew there was a reason to send you to Newhouse. I'm sure you learned all that in your broadcasting classes. None of what you just said even existed when I was there. Thank you for setting up a TV that actually works."

"Consider it my going-away present to you and Eloise," she said. Her eyes clouded and I could see she was about to cry.

"Now, none of that," I said. "You're going back to the future tomorrow. You'll have cable TV and restaurants and everything. We'll be right back here in the past, fiddling with those rabbit ears and cooking frozen dinners in the microwave." I managed to get a smile out of her.

"At least the power's back on. I don't feel quite so guilty about leaving you guys here in the twentieth century."

"We'll be fine. Mrs. Giannini says they're opening next week. We'll be able to get groceries right here in the neighborhood. And hey, we've got a refrigerator again."

Earlier that morning, Eloise and I had removed the shelves and storage compartments from the refrigerator and carried them outside, where we dunked them in a big plastic tub of bleach and water. I oversaw the dunking, rinsing everything with a strong blast from the hose and wiping the shelves and compartments dry with paper towels. Eloise wiped down the interior of the refrigerator and the freezer section with cloths soaked in disinfectant.

Once more I silently gave thanks to George for his insistence on removing the entire contents before we evacuated. I was hearing stories that you couldn't find a new refrigerator in a store anywhere in the Southeast because the demand was so great. At least that was one headache we didn't have to deal with.

But even as I worked, I nursed the heartache of knowing that my beloved daughter was leaving in the morning. I've grown accustomed to having her back home with me again, and I'm proud of the adult woman she's become in the years she's been away at college. If I let her see my grief, she'll never go back. But she has to. She really is going back to the future—her own. Her education, her budding career as a filmmaker, and her relationship with Jason are waiting for her in Los Angeles. Her future isn't here. But mine is. And so is Eloise's.

Sunday, October 2

We took Caroline to the airport in Baton Rouge this morning to catch her flight to Dallas, where she would change planes for a nonstop to Los Angeles. She started crying before we left the house, when she said goodbye to Mister Whiskers. I had intended to be brave and put up a good front, but if she was going to cry, so was I.

"You take good care of him, you hear, Mom? No letting him get out of the house again. He's not a young cat anymore."

My eyes filled with tears, but it wasn't about the cat. "I'll be careful with him, honey. Don't you worry."

Mister Whiskers, purring in Caroline's arms, gave me a look of smug disdain.

Baton Rouge was a traffic nightmare. So many people from New Orleans have evacuated there. The population may have doubled or even tripled since the storm. The main roads were jammed, and cars moved at a crawl or not at all. Fortunately, we'd left early.

It took nearly four hours to make what was normally an hour and a half drive. Even so, we got to the airport two hours before Caroline's flight time. I hadn't been so glad to get out of the car since the seventeen-hour drive when we evacuated to Alpharetta.

The airport was as crowded as the roads leading to it. Very few flights were going in or out of New Orleans, so Baton Rouge had become the alternate airport for the region. It wasn't designed to handle this many passengers and their entourages.

We both hugged and kissed her before she went through security, and she started to cry again. She shook her head and turned away. "Sorry. I didn't mean to make this worse. I'd better go."

I watched her walk through the scanning equipment and caught a glimpse of her picking up her things from the belt on the other side. She walked toward the concourse without looking back at us.

I don't know how long I stood there, staring at the spot where she'd been. Finally Eloise touched my arm. "Come on, Maggie. Let's get out of here. I don't like this place."

Probably the last time she saw Isaiah was in a situation just like this, as he boarded a plane to go back to his military duties. Merely being here was probably bringing up a lot of memories she didn't want to revisit.

My daughter wasn't going off to fight a war, I reminded myself. She was only going back to college. I could be fairly sure I'd see her again. Although anything could happen— to her or to me. *Don't go there*, I told myself.

I nodded. "Let's go back to New Orleans."

We were both silent on the ride home. I was thinking about how different things were between Eloise and me now, compared to the way we were before the storm. Back then I thought of us as longtime friends, but I was still her employer and she was my employee. We joked around and talked about things that touched us deeply. I thought we had a cordial relationship. But Eloise never spoke to me harshly, never criticized me, never defied me. I was her boss.

Now I was seeing a side of her I'd never seen before. It may have always been there, but she'd been careful not to let it show when she was around me. She was openly angry about being stopped by the authorities, angry at her helplessness to do anything to locate Robert's body, angry at me for not understanding the differences between us, and not hesitant to speak her mind. It's been an eye-opener for me to realize, all these years after the civil rights legislation of the 1960s, how differently a black woman is still treated versus a white woman. Or a black man, for that matter, as I thought of Lamar and his son having to leave the city before nightfall.

I've been angry too, but the things that set me off are petty compared to what Eloise is dealing with. I could stand up to four National Guardsmen at my front door and send them away by the force of my authority as an Uptown white woman living in a big house. But Mrs. Giannini had suspected Eloise of being a thief for staying here, even though she knew Eloise had worked for me for years. And Eloise knew Mrs. Giannini didn't trust her. Because she was black.

I'd never thought about Eloise and me seeing the world through very different perspectives based on race, but now I realize that's a barrier between us. And I feel foolish for not recognizing that barrier or how high it is until now.

Is it insurmountable? We've known each other for twenty years. Maybe not as well as I thought we did, but we've still got a history together.

Is this something we can have a conversation about? I don't even know where to begin. Or how. Or when to have it. I don't think now is the right time—I sense that she's got a lot of anger built up. A conversation might turn heated quickly.

Or maybe I'm just scared to have the conversation at all.

Monday, October 3

Steven the contractor arrived promptly at seven this morning with a crew of three men. I actually hugged him, even though I hadn't seen him in a couple of years.

"I get that a lot these days," he laughed, hugging me back.

"You have no idea how glad I am to see you," I said.

"So you've been living here since the storm, huh? When did you get your power back?"

"Friday morning."

He whistled. "And you came back when?"

I told him. He shook his head. "You're tougher than I am. We've been living over on the Florida Panhandle. Got the kids in school over there. But now the guys and I are staying in an apartment in Gonzales, south of Baton Rouge, so we can drive in every morning to work on houses here in the city."

"And your house?"

"It's a couple of miles toward the lake from here. Broadmoor. Got about five feet of water."

"Oh, Steven, I'm so sorry."

"It's like the shoemaker's kids who are barefoot. It'll be the last thing I get to. I've got too much other work right now. My wife and kids are okay over in Florida. They can stay there through the rest of the school year, and I can go back on the weekends. It's not too far."

"You seem so upbeat."

"Hey, I've got enough work to keep me busy as far out into the future as I can see. What's not to like?"

"I like that you're getting lots of work, but I don't like the reason why."

"Gotcha. Okay, show me what happened."

I led Steven and his men upstairs to the bedroom, where we all looked at blue sky through the jagged hole in the ceiling. If it hadn't been my bedroom, I might have found something beautiful in the stalactites of yellow mold and the Impressionist paintings of spotted blue-gray mold on the ceiling and walls. But it was my bedroom, and there were chunks of gray plaster scattered across the bed and on the Oriental rug.

Steven looked around, making notes on a pad. "You're not the only one with a room like this. Don't worry, we can take care of it. We'll get a blue tarp over the roof first. Your insurance adjuster been here yet?"

"He's supposed to come this morning."

"Good for you. Those guys are hard to get hold of. They're stretched to the max with claims."

We went downstairs and I showed him the fallen tree, its withered leaves and green pecan husks still poking through the shattered glass wall of the sunroom. "This is my favorite room in the house. I have loved being in it every day since you put it in. I've really missed being able to use it."

He glanced around the room, making more notes. "I can get someone to take the tree down. What else have you got?"

"Do you think your crew can take the wood panels off the windows? It's been so dark in this house. I'd love to see the sun again."

They set to work taking down the plywood sheets and opening the shutters. It was a shock to see the morning sun pouring in the windows. Now the living room walls that for weeks had seemed a dull, faded white in the dim light suddenly turned the color of butter. The room was beautiful, serene, and cool. The way it used to be.

"Thank you so much," I said. "You have no idea what a difference this makes."

"Glad to do it. Now we'll get up on that roof and secure it. I'll work you up a price on all of this. Don't worry, Maggie. This isn't as bad as you think it is."

I thought of Eloise's house, flooded almost to the ceiling. No, compared to hers—or Steven's, for that matter—this wasn't bad at all. Unlike Eloise, I had insurance that would pay for most of this. And money in the bank to cover what the insurance wouldn't pay. Without flood insurance, what was she going to do?

What she was doing right now. She was at her house, gutting the Sheetrock with a crowbar Lamar had left her. He and Bobby both had jobs in St. Francisville and could only get down here on the weekends. They could do the heaviest work, like removing furniture, appliances, and cabinets. Much of the rest was up to her.

And I had a contractor to do all of it.

The insurance adjuster, a sandy-haired man with a frown on his face and a clipboard in his hand, arrived while Steven's workers were scuttling around the roof with the tarp. Steven had left to see another client, so he and the adjuster didn't meet, which was probably just as well.

He moved around the house silently, making notes, measuring with a tape, shaking his head now and then. I followed him around, thinking George would probably tell me not to volunteer any information lest it be used to lower the amount they would pay. I was quite sure my gender was enough of a factor against me when it came to negotiating money. I had relished using that "My husband is an attorney" card when dealing with people who were trying to overcharge or low-ball me in some financial transaction—most recently Howard in his severance offer. Now I was on my own. I adopted a stern look, folded my arms across my chest, and tried to look as powerful as I could while saying as little as possible.

He finished touring the damage, said he'd be in touch, and got into his truck with the magnetic sign on the door with the name of the insurance company. I sighed, wondering how little the insurance would pay with respect to Steven's bid, which I was quite sure would be high. At least I was dealing with a licensed, insured contractor whose work I knew, not someone who had stuck a bunch of hastily-made signs on the medians of the streets. I'd seen quite a few of those. I went into the kitchen and poured myself another cup of coffee, thankful once again for a working coffeemaker.

Steven's crew worked for several hours. After they put a blue tarp on the roof, they hauled the ruined furniture out of the bedroom, down the stairs, and out to the curb. I watched my marriage bed march out of the house to be tossed in a pile of trash at the street. The dresser that had belonged to George's parents followed. Eloise had removed everything from it even before Caroline and I returned. They rolled up the Oriental rug and stacked it on top of the pile.

There goes the private life that George and I shared. Now I will have to create a new room. And a new life.

When the crew started up the stairs with crowbars, I knew what came next. They were going to knock the plaster out of the walls, and I wasn't up for that. I checked my watch. It was about nine.

I'd heard the neighborhood post office was open. It was one of the few that hadn't flooded. We couldn't get our mail delivered yet, but we could go to the post office to pick it up. I gave the workers a spare key so they could come and go as needed, got into the SUV, and left the crew to their work.

I found a parking place in front of the post office. There were only a few people ahead of me in line. I had two pieces of mail, both bills a month old that I'd already paid online.

On the way home, I drove past City Coffee, where a lifetime ago I'd hung out one morning because I didn't want Eloise to know I was out of work. The building was dark. I was fairly sure it hadn't flooded, but like Giannini's Food Store, it would have to pass an inspection by the health department before it could reopen. And the employees would have to come back from wherever they'd fled to.

The neighborhood drugstore was open. I stopped to pick up a few things. Unlike the post office, this place was packed. I stood in line at least half an hour to pay for my purchases. Afterward, I went to the bank. Same thing. I was in line at the drive-up for half an hour. The waiting is frustrating, but it's also a sign that people are coming back to the city. And that's good.

When I got home, I found a small hill of gray plaster at the curb. Steven's workers had left. Eloise had left early to work on her house in the cooler morning temperatures. The house was quiet.

I missed Caroline's voice, her laughter, her energy. She'd called last night to let me know she made it back to Los Angeles safely. Now she was plunging back into her busy life as a college student. And back to her relationship with Jason. For her sake, I hope it all works out. Meanwhile, I really am an empty nester. And newly widowed. I'm glad to have Eloise living with me. For now. We both need each other.

I fixed myself a ham sandwich—on toast made in the electric toaster oven, what a treat!—and carried it into the living room. I ate in the warm sunshine pouring in through the windows and splashing off the butter-colored walls, sitting on the sofa I'd been using as a bed for weeks. Now that the air conditioning makes it bearable upstairs, I'm sleeping in Caroline's room. What a luxury to sleep in a bed again!

Another luxury: listening to the radio for pleasure instead of emergency information. I tuned it to the public radio station, my preference back when life was normal. They were broadcasting from the studios of a sister station in Atlanta. I remembered meeting the new general manager at White Linen Night, when he'd told me he'd just come to New Orleans from Atlanta. I guess his connections from his old job helped the station get back on the air, although the technicalities elude me. I do know that their studios near Lake Pontchartrain flooded in the storm surge.

The lush strains of Tchaikovsky's "Romeo and Juliet Overture" washed over the living room. It was as if none of this had ever happened. But it had.

It's funny how you never appreciate how interconnected our world is until everything goes away at once. People evacuate and there's no one to work at the bank, the drug store, the grocery store, the restaurant, the post office. Businesses and city government can't operate. People can't go to work and aren't getting the regular paychecks they've come to expect without question, and they're panicking. Even parts of the city that didn't flood can't get services like electricity, gas, water, phone, and cable.

I see cars traveling the wrong way up one-way streets. At first it made sense because so many streets were blocked by fallen trees. But even after they were cleared away, people were still ignoring one-way signs. Stop signs are being ignored, too. I have to be very careful. There are very few traffic signals working, and sometimes a signal that works one day doesn't work the next. You have to treat every intersection with a traffic light as a four-way stop and hope everyone else does, too.

Street signs are missing, and it's not just because they blew away in the storm. People are stealing them. Not just stop signs and one-way signs, but signs with the names of streets on them. People come back to clean out their houses and take the street signs as souvenirs of New Orleans as they leave, figuring they'll never be back. Meanwhile, only the people who know their way around can make sense of where they're going. I find myself giving directions like "turn right at the yellow house," because the street sign is gone.

It's like all the rules have been tossed out the window. With everything up for grabs, it seems like anything goes in this New Normal. I don't like it a bit.

But for a few minutes, I can listen to the "Romeo and Juliet Overture" and pretend everything is the way it used to be.

Tuesday, October 4

Tony arrived this morning. He and his wife are staying with friends in Baton Rouge. They'd both come in yesterday to see their house in Lakeview. It flooded so badly he thinks it will probably have to be demolished. His wife is devastated.

But today he came in without her to check on the office. He stopped by my house first, knowing I wanted to go with him. We sat in the living room and drank coffee as if it were a normal social call on a normal day in a normal house in a normal city. But Tony had to burst my bubble of illusion.

"Maggie, I don't mean to insult you, but you look like hell. Your clothes are hanging off you, your face is pale, and your hair—I don't know. You just don't look the way you did when I saw you in Georgia a month ago. You and Caroline and Eloise should never have stayed here without any electricity. And the mold in this house—I can smell it. It's not healthy for you to be here. Pack a bag and come back to Baton Rouge and stay with us."

"Tony, I'm fine. I've lost a little weight in the heat, I'm not wearing any makeup, and I need a haircut. So what? The power is back on and we have lights and air conditioning. We should have gas for hot water and cooking in a few days. Caroline hooked up the television with rabbit ears before she left, and we can get some local stations. That's all we need until the cable service is restored. My contractor and his crew put a blue tarp on the roof yesterday. We're going to be up and running again in no time."

He ran a hand through his hair. "After all these years, I ought to know better than to argue with you. But why do you want to go down to the office? It's going to be a nightmare, climbing those stairs, and I don't think you're in the physical shape to handle it. What do you want so badly in George's office that you'd do that?"

I sighed. How to put it into words? "It's the last place George was before the world changed. That Friday in the office was his last normal, ordinary day. When he left that afternoon, he thought he'd be back on Monday. I just want to see his office, sit in his chair, look at the things he looked at, maybe read an unfinished memo on his desk. If I do that, I can be with him again for a little while."

Tony shook his head. "My reaction is the opposite of yours. You want to go there to get a glimpse of his last day at work and feel like he's with you. But it's going to be hard for me just to go into the office and not see him. I mean, we worked together for so many years. It's like I've lost my right arm."

"Yeah. I've been living with that part for the last month, being in this house without him. Having Caroline here was a big help. Eloise too. But now with Caroline back in California, reality is starting to settle in. And it's hard."

"Well," he said, setting down his coffee mug, "we'd better get going. It's a little cooler than it was a couple of weeks ago, but it's still going to be a warm day. And we've got twenty-five flights of stairs to climb."

It only took about ten minutes to drive downtown. There were very few other cars on St. Charles Avenue. The traffic lights were blind sentinels without power. Crews were clearing limbs and other debris off the streetcar tracks. Some of the T-shaped supports for the streetcars' electrical wires were bent or snapped by fallen trees, and the wires waved aimlessly in the light breeze.

I miss the sound of the old streetcars on St. Charles Avenue late at night. There was always something comforting in knowing they were there, running on their appointed rounds, and that people were traveling on them all night long. The old olive green ones on the St. Charles line, which dated from the 1920s, had survived in a car barn on high ground, but the new red-and-yellow ones on the Canal Street line had all been destroyed in the flood.

I thought of the night George and I came home on the St. Charles streetcar in the rain after White Linen Night. I think that was the last time I rode one. Certainly it was the last time I rode one with him.

We parked on the street in front of the high-rise that housed the law office George and Tony had founded more than twenty years ago. How strange to actually have parking places on the street downtown on a Tuesday morning. A security guard at the entrance to the building scrutinized

Tony's ID badge, then looked at me. I handed him George's ID.

"I'm Mrs. McBride," I said. "Mr. McBride died in the evacuation."

"Sorry for your loss, ma'am." He waved us through.

A raucous generator rattled on the marble floors, powering large fans in the lobby. The elevator doors were open, but the entry was blocked with sawhorses. The fans were there to dry things out, I figured. I knew there had been water in the building, but I wasn't sure how much.

The door to the emergency stairwell was propped open. Obviously we weren't the only ones trying to get up to an office. "Last chance," said Tony. "Sure you want to do this?"

"Do you want to go first, or shall I?"

"I've been working out at the gym. I'm in better shape than you are," he said.

"Yeah, but I've been living in the heat for the last month, and you've been in cushy air conditioning in Houston."

"Touché," he grinned, and we set off.

The stairwell was lit, if you could call it that, by emergency lighting. It was dim, but we could see where we were going. The first three flights weren't too bad, but after the fourth, I had to stop and sit on the stairs. Tony joined me. We sat for a few minutes, then tackled the next flight.

Being from the flat country of south Louisiana, mountain climbing was never my sport. After a while, I was stopping after every flight, and sometimes on the landing halfway between one flight and the next. If Tony was faring better than I was, he was hiding it well. At least he had the foresight to bring a backpack with bottles of water for us.

It took us more than an hour to get to the office. I was overjoyed when I finally saw the number 25 painted on the concrete block wall beside the exit door. We stumbled through the doorway into the carpeted hallway that ran alongside the elevators and made our way down to Suite 2500.

"McBride and Richards, Attorneys at Law," read the dignified raised gold letters on the mahogany door. Tony unlocked it and we entered the reception area.

The office was hot, and a musty odor emanated from the carpet. But I could feel a breeze moving through the room, and it was a welcome relief after the stifling stairwell.

"Oh my God," said Tony.

I followed his gaze. Beyond the reception area was a glassed-in conference room with floor-to-ceiling windows offering a panoramic view of the Mississippi River. The windows had shattered, and the drapes were billowing out into the open air.

"I was afraid this had happened," he said. "The force of the winds and the difference in pressure between the inside and outside caused the windows to implode. My guess is they're all like this." He started down a hallway, trying doors. Most were unlocked. And yes, most of the windows had shattered.

He and George, as founding partners, had corner offices at opposite ends of the building. I walked down to George's office and unlocked the door with his key.

There was glass all over the carpet, the sofa, the top of his desk. Papers were scattered everywhere. The drapes were dry but badly stained from the rain. So much for my quaint idea of seeing George's office just as he left it that Friday.

I brushed glass shards off the seat of George's desk chair, my feet crunching on bits of it on the hard plastic static guard over the carpet as I sat down. A small battery-operated clock on the desk told me it was 11:47 a.m. Here was one thing he would have seen before he left for the day that Friday. I picked it up and put it in my purse.

When I looked up, Tony was in the doorway. "Not what you expected, huh?"

"No," I said. "What does your office look like?"

"Pretty much the same. Ironically, the junior members of the firm and the support staff all had offices on the inside, without windows. Those are fine. Looks like the files are okay, too. So much for the status of a window office."

"Yes," I said. "And now you have open windows."

"I need to go check on some things. Take as much time as you need, Maggie."

A sudden memory: that's what the doctor had said to me when I was in the hospital room with George after he died. *Take as much time as you need.*

Aside from the broken windows with the drapes flapping through them, here was the scene George would have seen each day: a view of the Mississippi River and the two Crescent City Connection bridges, side by side, crossing it. The view wasn't so different from where we'd seen it on White Linen Night when we had dinner at the Riverwalk, except I was much higher up. And yes, there were ships moving on the river. Just as Mickey had told me, the Port of New Orleans was back in action.

George would sit at this desk and write out his notes in longhand. He had a computer, but he preferred to take notes on a yellow legal pad and have his secretary type them up. I knew he liked to use an antique fountain pen that had belonged to his grandfather and father. I hadn't found it when I'd cleaned out his desk at home. Maybe it was here.

The long narrow drawer across the width of the desk was locked. I fiddled with his key ring until I found the key that opened the desk.

Yes, there it was, in a wooden tray at the front of the drawer. I took it out, admiring the patina of age on its surface, the gold cap. I should save this for Caroline, I thought. It might make a lovely graduation gift—if she cared about such old technology as a fountain pen. But because it had been her father's, I knew she would treasure it.

I spotted something else in the drawer. Not a pen. A square piece of plastic. I reached in and picked it up. It was a green American Express credit card.

I thought I had found all of George's credit cards and canceled them, but this one was new to me. I looked at the front. Yes, it was in his name, not the firm's. But perhaps he used it for business purchases or taking people to lunch.

I tapped the edge of the card on the desktop, frowning. Something didn't make sense. If it was a card for business use, why wasn't it in the name of the firm?

I opened the two drawers on the right side of the desk. It didn't take me long to find the credit card statements. There were a couple of years' worth, held together with a paper clip. George did like to keep statements. "Just in case," he'd say. His name and business address were at the top of each one. I flipped through them.

All the charges were for hotel bills, roughly one a week, each for one night's stay. All of them were in the downtown area.

Suddenly the air went out of my lungs, as if someone had punched me in the stomach. I was gasping, trying to breathe. The room around me was growing dark. For a moment I thought I'd faint. I gripped the sides of the desk with all my strength.

It took a few moments, but slowly my lungs refilled and the light came back. I reached for the water bottle I'd set on the edge of the desk. Instead of drinking it, I splashed it on my face.

When my breathing returned to normal, I looked at the credit card statements again, page after page. The charges were for different hotels, all very upscale, and the pattern of stays was regular. I'd have to check a calendar to be sure, but it appeared the stays were on the same day every week. The most recent statement had a closing date in early August.

George had been having an affair. But with whom?

Of course, he could have been seeing call girls. But he just didn't seem the type. And I didn't think he'd be using hotels this expensive to sleep with prostitutes. And on the same day every week? He was methodical, but not that methodical. He was meeting someone who could get away on a certain day without arousing suspicion.

He was the founding partner of a law firm. If he left the office one afternoon a week, who would say anything? He could be meeting clients outside the office. I thought of Howard's lunches downtown with Important People. But those were real lunches, as far as I could tell. He always brought back souvenirs of them on his ties.

But George? Careful, precise, methodical George? Having wild whoopie with some woman in a downtown hotel room in the middle of the afternoon?

I didn't see any restaurant charges, but no two hotel bills were for the same amount. Of course. They'd order from room service. He wouldn't take the chance of being seen by someone who knew him. Or who knew her, whoever she was.

What would they order? Champagne and strawberries?

"Stop it, Maggie," I said aloud.

I looked at the American Express card again. "Member since 1993," it said. Had he gotten the card just for the hotel bills? Had he been having an affair for twelve years? And I had never even suspected. I felt myself growing woozy again.

Did Tony know? They were partners and close friends since law school. Would he have destroyed the card and the statements if I hadn't come with him?

He must have heard me, because he was back in the doorway. "I heard you say something. Everything okay?"

I could have just said yes. I could have pretended everything was, indeed, okay. Instead, I held up the sheaf of papers. "I found the credit card statements."

He sounded genuinely puzzled. "What credit card statements?"

"George's secret American Express account. The one he used to pay for the hotel rooms."

I heard the air wheeze out of Tony's lungs.

"Did you know?" I asked.

"Don't ask me that, Maggie."

"I just did. Who was she?"

"Maggie, George was my best friend. But he didn't confide his personal business to me."

"But you suspected. He was spending one afternoon a week out of the office."

"Is this the real reason you climbed twenty-five flights of stairs? To find out if George had been hiding things from you?"

Had I? So I could search his office before Tony had a chance to destroy any evidence? I'd put Tony in a terrible spot, caught between loyalty to his dead friend and truthfulness to his friend's widow. But the journalist in me recognized that he'd just tried to shift the subject to put me on the defensive.

"No," I said. "I was not expecting to find this. But did you know he was having an affair?"

He didn't answer.

"Okay, I get it. You're caught between a rock and a hard place. But I didn't come here to snoop. And now I know, but I don't know much. Do you know who she is?"

"You may think you didn't come here to snoop, but you did. And you found something. We all have secrets, Maggie. If you died tonight, what secrets would you leave for Caroline to find? George left some credit card statements. I don't know what's in them or why you think he was having an affair. If you tear his desk apart, you might find something else. I don't know. Would it make you feel better if you did? I doubt it."

"Who is she, Tony?"

"George named me as executor of his succession. That means we're going to have a lot of conversations over the next several months. But we're not having this one. Is that clear?"

I drew back, startled. In one brief moment, the relationship between Tony and me had jumped from what I had considered a friendship to strictly business. I stared at him, the sheaf of statements still in my hand. Finally, I tossed them across the desk with the credit card.

"Fine," I said. "You're the executor. You figure out if there were any outstanding charges on this card, and you pay them. I'm done." I leaned back in the chair and crossed my arms, just as I'd done with the insurance adjuster.

He picked up the card and the statements and walked out of the office.

WEDNESDAY, OCTOBER 5

Tony drove me back to the house yesterday afternoon in silence. I sat in the living room, this time with the radio off, until Eloise came home that night.

Who was George having an affair with?

Certainly not his secretary. Mrs. Dubois had been his father's secretary. She was well into her seventies, maybe even eighty. I'd heard she had evacuated to her daughter's home in Lafayette and wasn't planning to return. I bet she knew something was going on, but even if I tracked her down, she would be too loyal to George to tell me anything.

The Other Woman probably wasn't someone from the office. She'd have to disappear for those long lunches at the same time as George, and that would have caused a lot of gossip.

Who, then?

Had he ever brought her to the house? Had he slept with her in our bed?

And if he had, did Eloise know?

I wasn't going to ask her. I wasn't going to tell anybody what I'd found. But I really wanted to know who George's mistress was.

Did she know he was dead? If not, would she try to contact him? I still have his cell phone. Would she call? A number of his friends and business associates have called that number. But no one who called has raised any suspicions with me.

I didn't sleep much last night. By morning, I realized I was going to have to turn my mind to something else, because this was driving me crazy.

I started thinking about my old office at Parker Publishing. I hadn't driven past the place since my last day as an employee. I doubted anyone was there now. If I went over there, I probably wouldn't be spotted. After breakfast, I got in the SUV—not the red Mustang everybody knew—and headed to Parker's offices.

Carrollton Avenue is a long, straight street—most unusual in a city where everything bends with the river—running south to north, away from the river and out to City Park. Since we'd been back, I'd only taken it as far as the turnoff for Eloise's neighborhood in Hollygrove. Close to the river, the land is higher and didn't flood. But the farther north you drive, the lower it gets and the deeper it floods. About halfway between the river and City Park is a fairly deep underpass where a railroad track and Interstate 10 pass overhead. The underpass had been barricaded since the storm because the water was deep enough to drown anyone foolish enough to try to drive through it. But today the barricades were gone and the street was dry. I continued northbound, headed for my old office.

I began to see abandoned cars parked on the median, which sits several inches higher than the curb. It's customary for people to park there if the street is expected to flood. I could see the silt marks on the sides and windows of the cars where the water had risen. The farther I drove, the higher the marks were on the cars, until finally they were at the roof lines or not visible at all.

Finally I spotted the office. The red-and-white Parker Publishing sign was still nailed to the side of the building by the parking lot. The silt line was about two-thirds of the way up the sign, maybe six or seven feet. The waves created by passing vehicles had washed clamshells and gravel from the parking lot into the street and grassy areas. I pulled in, dodging piles of carpet, Sheetrock and roofing shingles, and parked. A cloud of dust hung in the air around my car, and I sat with the windows closed for a few moments waiting for it to subside.

Howard had bought this shotgun double house, five rooms back-to-back on each side, in the 1960s when he first started the business. In the early days he and Ruth lived on one side and operated the business on the other. As the company grew and the Parkers could afford to live elsewhere, they bought a house in Lakeview and converted the entire double into one big office, rearranging rooms on each side into offices and creating a hallway down the middle to connect them.

I was working there during the conversion and remember the mess. Fortunately, those were the days when we still used typewriters. There was so much Sheetrock dust everywhere that if we'd had computers, they would have been ruined. But when all was done, we had an office that managed to look like an office on the inside and a house on the outside.

Eventually Howard was able to buy the house next door on the corner and tore it down to create a parking lot. We thought that was heaven. Off-street parking is still a luxury in the older neighborhoods in New Orleans.

As I sat in the car watching the dust settle on the hood of the SUV, I wondered what I thought I was doing. I had no business being here. Still, I didn't expect to find anybody. The lot was deserted, and the only cars parked on the street clearly would never move again under their own power.

I was no longer an employee, and if I went inside, I'd be trespassing. But in this crazy world where people were stealing street signs for souvenirs, what the hell difference did it make? There was no one around to stop me. I got out of the car and walked around to the front of the building and up the steps to the front porch.

My God, it felt so familiar. Twenty-seven years of going up those steps. I almost dug into my purse for my office keys.

But I didn't have to. The door had been kicked in, probably because it had warped so badly from sitting for weeks in the flood water that it wouldn't open any other way. I saw the red X beside the door. Where Eloise's X had a 1, here was an 0. No bodies found.

I stepped inside. Someone had been here, probably several someones, cleaning the place out. The carpet had been ripped out and heavy things had been dragged across the floor. Some of the walls had been gutted, but not all. Black mold tracked down from the ceiling and up from the floor. The building smelled like, well, mold. Duh. My eyes started to water.

I picked my way through the mess to my office. It was always going to be my office, dammit. My red swivel chair sat in the middle of the room, no longer red, covered in mud or mold or both. My desk had a woodgrain laminate top and metal legs. The laminate was buckled. A metal filing cabinet was literally bulging where the paper files had swelled with water and pushed out the sides. Probably would never be able to get it open. And my computer—see, I still thought of it as mine—was gone. I wondered if someone had the foresight to get it out of there before the storm. It would be pretty stupid to steal it after it had been submerged.

"Hello?" A male voice was behind me. "Can I help you?"

I whirled around.

I'd seen those tattoos and the curly hair before. A lifetime ago. "Zach, right?"

"Yup. You're Maggie."

"Yes. We only met that once. I—I came by to see what happened."

"A lot of people have. Well, here it is."

"I'm so sorry, Zach."

"Yeah. Thanks. Shortest tenure of any editor of *New Orleans Now!*, huh? Four weeks."

"It'll come back," I said. I wasn't sure I believed that, but I needed to say something positive.

"No. My uncle says he's going to file for bankruptcy. He and my aunt are living in their condo in Naples. They're not coming back."

I wasn't surprised.

"I wouldn't work for them any more even if they did come back. They left me here. They were supposed to take me with them when they evacuated to Florida, and they just split. They knew I didn't have a car. I don't even have a driver's license. I get around on a bike." So that was why I hadn't heard him arrive.

"My father's mad enough to kill my aunt and uncle for leaving me here. He was frantic, trying to find me. They told him they thought I'd gotten a ride with some friends. It was a complete lie."

"So what did you do during the storm?"

"I live in an upstairs apartment a few blocks from here. I rode out the storm there."

"What was it like?"

"The roof came off, piece by piece. I got under the kitchen table and stayed there. I never want to go through anything like that again. And afterward—well, I couldn't get out. The water was about six feet deep. I had a little food in the house, but not much."

"So how did you get out?"

He grinned. "I wish I could say by grabbing a rope let down by a helicopter, but it was a guy in a boat. It was way cool anyway. I was out on the upstairs porch, waving and yelling, when he found me. The porch was about four feet higher than the boat, so he didn't want me to jump in and maybe capsize it. I had to jump into the water and swim to the boat. I literally got out with just the clothes on my back. I came back later, though, after the water went down, to get the rest of my stuff out of my apartment. My landlady, she's great. She's got a tarp on the roof and she's getting the place fixed. She may have me back in there by Christmas. Or January at the latest. Meanwhile, I've got friends I'm staying with whose place didn't flood, farther toward the river on Carrollton."

"So you're going to stay in New Orleans? What will you do if the magazine doesn't come back?"

"When I was in college I painted houses in the summer. I think I can find work around here fixing things up. Probably make some good money at it. Maybe even more than my cheap uncle was paying me."

I grinned. "I hear ya." I gestured around the office. "What happened to the computer equipment?"

"Some of us had the good sense to get the office equipment out of here before the storm. Loaded it on a truck and sent it to Baton Rouge. We were thinking looters, not flooding. The copy machine was too big to move, unfortunately, so it's gone. But all the computers are at somebody's house in Baton Rouge. I guess if we wanted to, we could get the publishing company running again from there. If we bought out my uncle. My father made a big investment in the company a few months ago. He may decide to seize the assets to recoup the money he put into the company. I don't know a lot about it. I only know he's really pissed off at Uncle Howard."

"What about the other employees? Do you know anything about them?"

He reeled off a list of names and where he'd last heard they were. I was listening for one in particular but didn't hear it.

"You know anything about Jack Wright? The ad director?"

He nodded. "You don't know?'

Something in my stomach clenched.

"They found him in his house in Lakeview. Not sure if he had a heart attack or drowned."

I grabbed the mud-caked swivel chair, not the sturdiest thing to hold me up, but it was all that was close. "Oh my God."

"I'm sorry. I guess you knew each other a long time, huh?"

"A very long time." I almost said *Since before you were born*, but I didn't.

"I thought you knew. Didn't mean to break it to you like that."

"No." The mold was getting to me. I was having trouble breathing. "Look, Zach, I've got to go. Do you need a ride somewhere?"

"I've got my bike. Thanks."

"Look." I pulled out a card. "Here's my number. Call me if you need anything. If you need a ride someplace too far to go on your bike. Or anything. I'm glad you're safe. I'm glad you decided to stay. I'm—I'm sorry about what happened, about your getting left behind. Howard is a shit. He's always been a shit. I was working for him before you were born—" oops, that one slipped out "—and he's never done anything that wasn't for his own benefit. Sorry I said all that, I know he's family—"

"Only by marriage."

"But he's a shit and he never should have left you here. So if I can do anything for you, I'll be glad to. I want you to know there were good people working here and we cared about one another and we looked out for each other. That's what this business is like. That's what people in New Orleans are like."

"I know. That's why I want to stay here."

"Take care, Zach." I half staggered out the door, down the stairs, and out into the parking lot to my car. I started the engine and turned on the air conditioning.

Jack and I would never get together for that drink. I sat in the car and cried.

I drove to the end of Carrollton Avenue at City Park and circled back by way of a winding road that runs along Bayou St. John. The water had been very deep here. On a higher grassy area beside the bayou, helicopters had landed to rescue people.

A few blocks later, the road became Jefferson Davis Parkway, a four-lane road divided by a median wide enough to be a park. The live oaks on each side had a much thinner canopy than the last time I'd driven this street. Some of the ancient trees had been yanked up by the roots by the wind and water.

Houses I used to pass regularly sat empty, striped with water marks and tattooed with red spray-painted X's. Driving this once-beautiful street was like walking across a battlefield the morning after the battle has ended and seeing the bodies of the soldiers, their lifeless faces turned up to the sky. And they were faces I had known all my life.

I haven't seen the Lower Ninth Ward yet, where some of the worst damage happened. I knew I needed to go down there, to see it for myself. Mickey told me it was horrific.

I was almost home when the front end of the car went down on the passenger side and started making thumping noises. I had a flat tire. No surprise. There are roofing nails everywhere. I remembered seeing a hand-lettered sign on a piece of old plywood propped against the pole of a non-working traffic light that read, "Flats fixed," with the name of the shop beneath it and an arrow pointing toward it. I limped over there. They were doing a brisk business, but they repaired the tire for me. I won't be surprised if I end up with more than one flat before all this is over.

If it ever is over.

THURSDAY, OCTOBER 6

This morning I went to the grand reopening of Giannini's Fine Foods. Some twenty people gathered around the front door as Mr. Giannini made a brief speech, thanking all for their faith in the future of the city by coming back and their loyalty to the store by being there. There was actually a red ribbon across the double doors, fastened to the burglar bars on each side of the glass. Mrs. Giannini cut the ribbon, their son opened the doors from the inside, and we all cheered and marched in.

There was free coffee back by the deli. We crowded around, pouring cups for each other, laughing and talking. Several people said they'd stayed in the city all along. Clearly Eloise, Caroline and I weren't the only ones who had defied the mandatory evacuation.

Someone touched my elbow. "Hey, Mags! How ya doing?"

"Hey, Mickey! Haven't seen you in awhile."

"Been busy. Got more work than I can handle. People are calling me all the time asking me to write stuff. You interested doing in a freelance piece?"

My former freelancer was offering me a chance to freelance. "Yeah, absolutely," I said. "What is it?"

"A guy called me the other day. He's the editor of one of the national trade mags for owners and managers in the restaurant business. He's looking for someone to do a piece on restaurants in New Orleans after the storm. What happened to their businesses, what they're doing to reopen, how they're finding staff, things like that. I told him I was up to my eyeballs in work, but I knew someone who knows the New Orleans restaurant scene like the back of her hand. You want it?"

"Oh, yeah. I can do this. Just tell me who to contact at the magazine."

"Attagirl. I've got the info in my notebook out in the car. When you're done in here, come on out and I'll get it for you."

Out in the parking lot, Mickey gave me the contact information for the editor. "Remember, it's a trade magazine," he said. "Don't expect them to pay you big bucks."

"You mean like the magazine I worked for? Which wasn't a trade magazine?"

He laughed. "Okay, you're right. It's just that I'm getting assignments now that pay serious money. I can afford to turn down work. No offense, Maggie. I don't mean to suggest I'm throwing you the dregs."

"But you are," I teased.

"More like offering you a piece that's right up your alley. Who knows? It could lead to other things."

"You're right. Thanks, Mickey. I'll call this guy as soon as I get home."

He leaned against his car. "I heard you ran into Zach the other day."

"You talked to him?"

"Yeah. Nice kid. He said he ran into you at the Parker office."

"I stopped by. Curiosity. Wanted to see how it looked."

"Pretty bad, huh?"

"I suppose it could be salvaged. But Zach said Howard was planning to declare bankruptcy."

"It's a shame his aunt and uncle treated him like crap. But that's Howard, huh?"

"Yep. Only thinks of himself."

Mickey looked at his watch. "Look, I've gotta run. Late for an appointment. Hey, Mags, let's do lunch soon, huh?"

"Lunch? Mickey, nothing's open."

"You don't get out much, do you? I know some places. You can call it research for your article. I'll check my schedule and call you."

"Sounds great."

He got in his car and took off across the parking lot, leaving me squinting at the phone number I'd scrawled on the back of one of my business cards.

When I got home, I called the editor. We discussed the article, my credentials, Mickey, and others in the business we knew in common. While we were still talking, I emailed him my résumé and a sample article I'd written. We talked about the length of the piece, deadline, and payment. He said he'd email a contract. Sounds like I got the assignment. And I didn't even have to use snail mail. Thank goodness for the Internet. And electricity and a phone line.

I've got paying work! Now I've got to track down some people I know in the restaurant business.

Friday, October 7

Mickey called this morning. "I'm free for lunch. How about you?"

"Absolutely."

"Did you got the assignment from the restaurant magazine?"

"I certainly did. Thank you for the reference."

"So you're buying, then? Expense account lunch?"

"Don't hold your breath on that. Where is this place?"

He gave me the address in an area of Carrollton near the river that didn't flood, and I drove over to meet him.

I'd spent hours on the phone yesterday tracking down some of my old contacts in the restaurant business. Some were open, some were struggling to get their employees back so they could open, but some were badly flooded and had no idea what they were going to do. I heard horror stories that made tears run down my cheeks. I heard stories of brave people who rescued others, and they made me cry too. The difference between the neighborhoods that flooded and those that didn't was stark.

This was my first visit to a restaurant in New Orleans since before the storm. A pink sheet of paper taped to the glass door said it had been inspected by the city health department and was permitted to reopen after Katrina. When we entered, there were only a handful of customers inside.

"Don't expect much," Mickey said. "They can't wash the lettuce and tomatoes because the water hasn't been deemed safe yet, so don't ask for them on your hamburger."

"Got it," I said, and ordered accordingly.

But hey, you could get a beer. In a bottle, no less. It felt wonderfully decadent, having a beer at lunch with an old buddy.

Mickey introduced me to the owner, and I told him about my assignment. He knew the magazine and nodded when I asked if I could talk to him about his experience. So as Mickey and I waited for our food, I scribbled in my reporter's notebook as the owner told me his story.

"Thank you," I said as our food arrived. "May I call you to continue this interview?"

"Sure," he said, and gave me his phone number. I thanked him and tucked it into my notebook.

As hamburgers go, I'd had better, but I'd had worse. It was the experience of eating out in a restaurant again that made it wonderful just to be there.

It was the first chance I'd had to talk to Mickey face to face without Caroline or Eloise around. As I looked at him across the table, I saw the folds of flesh beneath his eyes, the droop of his shoulders, the way his hand shook ever so slightly when he picked up his beer. He was trying his best to be the swaggering, laughing Mickey I used to know, but underneath he was struggling to process everything he'd been through since August 29. As we all were.

I remembered Tony telling me I looked like hell. So did Mickey. As far as I was concerned, looking like hell right now was a badge of honor. It meant we were survivors.

"Mickey, just between us, how are you doing?"

"My wife and kids are still in Charlotte. The kids' school here isn't open and I don't know when it will be. We had to pay the semester's tuition in advance before the storm, and now even though the school is closed, they won't give us the money back. There are lawyers who send their kids to that school. If they don't refund the tuition, there are going to be lawsuits—when the courts are open again. So we enrolled the kids in public school in Charlotte. It's all we can afford."

"Must be hard on your marriage, to be separated like that."

He shrugged. "I don't want them here right now. I see too much bad stuff out on the streets every day. I come home and I want to put my fist through a wall. They don't need to see the things I see, and they don't need to see me like this right now." He signaled the waiter for another beer.

"What about your house? I know it didn't flood, but did you have damage?"

"Last year we replaced the roof. It cost a fortune, but it was leaking so badly, we had to do something. Turned out to be the best money we ever spent. The roof stayed on in the storm. Had a couple of broken windows, but so what?"

"You said you had some other reporters staying with you. How did that work out?"

"I had three guys from the wire services for roommates. They turned up like drowned rats a couple of days after the storm. Their fancy downtown hotel had all its windows blown out and they needed a place to stay. The cell phone service was pretty spotty, but they texted me and I told them to come on over. I'll send their bosses a bill for rent later."

"Are they still living with you?"

"One of them is. One went to Biloxi to cover the Gulf Coast. The third, well, I had to throw him out. He kind of went nuts. There's a lot of that going on right now. A journalist can cover all sorts of wars, disasters, whatever, but when it happens in your own city, to people and places you know, it's different. Maggie, the stuff I've seen—bodies floating in the water in neighborhoods I've known for years, people on rooftops screaming for help that isn't coming, all those people waiting for buses outside the Superdome in the heat, the flooded hospitals and the nurses trying to get preemie babies out safely in helicopters—you cover these stories day after day, and it just gets to you."

"So how do you cope?"

He laughed. "Vast quantities of alcohol. I confess to looting the liquor section of one of the supermarkets a couple days after the storm. I'll pay them back when things are up and running again."

I leaned across the table and hissed, "Mickey! You *stole* stuff from the grocery store?"

He grinned. "It's not like they had any cashiers on duty to take my money. Come on, Mags. You got back ten days after the storm. Things were practically swell by then. You may be mad as hell about the National Guard trying to run you out, but let me tell you, be glad they're here."

"My daughter has already given me that lecture."

"In those first few days after the storm, it was everyone for himself. Nobody was coming to help, nobody. If you were going to survive, you had to look out for your own interests. I sleep with a shotgun next to me every night, in my house where I lived very peacefully with my wife and kids up until six weeks ago. I've fired it a couple of times when I heard suspicious noises. Don't know for sure if anyone was out there or not, but it got very quiet after I did."

I nodded. I'd heard a few noises I couldn't identify in the middle of the night. The utter quiet and darkness was eerie, but nowhere near as eerie as strange noises.

He took a long swig of his beer. "That's enough about me. How about that blog of yours, huh? How's it going?"

"I'm learning as I go along. I'm writing it for the people who evacuated and want to know what's going on at home. Some of them write me notes in the comments section. They seem to like hearing from someone they know who's living through it."

"I've been reading it."

"What do you think?"

"Honestly? It's good, Mags. But it could be better."

I made a face. "Thanks a lot."

"Well, you asked. It's just that I know you, know your writing, know what you sound like when you're really into it. And it seems to me like you're pulling your punches. It's clear that you want your readers to come back to the city. Maybe you don't want them to know just how bad things are."

I hadn't thought of that, but he was probably right. In the blog, I was trying to make jokes about not having electricity or hot water and eating canned Vienna sausages, but living like that was a struggle every day. "You may have a point," I agreed.

"Maggie, this stuff we're going through is raw. Our nerves are all shot. You're trying to write that blog with the old objective journalism stuff they taught you in college. They told you to keep yourself out of the story. But a blog is personal. You need to put all the raw stuff in there. Write it as if you're talking to a friend in a restaurant. Like me. Take your clothes off. Don't hold back."

I laughed. "Take my clothes off?"

"Hey, a guy can have fantasies, can't he?"

"Well, when you put it that way, I guess I can be flattered." Mickey is 36, fifteen years younger than me. He always used to flirt with me when he came into the office, but I wrote it off as an attempt to ingratiate himself to get more assignments. Of course, for the pittance Howard insisted we pay the freelancers, I probably should have been flirting with Mickey to keep him writing for me.

When the bill came, he paid. "I'm headed down to the Lower Ninth Ward to do an interview. Have you been down there yet?"

"No," I said. "I hear it's pretty bad."

"It is. Worse than pretty bad. Want to come along and see for yourself?"

I hesitated. "I don't like to play looky-loo at somebody else's tragedy."

"Maggie, you're not playing looky-loo. You're a journalist. You're covering a story."

"No, you are. You're the one with the interview."

"It's your story too. You're writing a blog about life here right now. Write about this. And write it raw. First person. Your readers deserve to know."

I nodded. "You're right. Let's go."

We left my SUV at the restaurant and got into his beat-up old Honda. The floor was littered with fast-food wrappers. But there aren't any fast food places open around here. Obviously Mickey didn't clean out the car very often. I crawled into the passenger seat, trying to ignore the smell of rancid french fry grease.

It was a long drive from Carrollton to the Lower Ninth Ward. From the refrigerator-lined streets of Uptown to the Central Business District, we bounced over potholes made by heavy equipment and Dumpsters. Downtown was still nearly deserted, an empty city in a post-apocalyptic world.

Crossing Canal Street into the French Quarter, we finally saw signs of life—on Bourbon Street. Of course. Not the crowds one would see on a normal Friday afternoon, but there were still people on the sidewalks and music coming through the open doors of bars. The Quarter, the original part of the city, was built on high ground and didn't flood.

"I heard that one of the Bourbon Street bars never shut down during the storm. Can't keep this place down, can they?" I asked.

"Nope. And the beer trucks were some of the first to make deliveries after the storm."

"When we drove back here from Atlanta, one of the first things we saw was a beer truck making a delivery at a convenience store." I laughed, remembering Caroline's outrage at the priorities of emergency supplies. At that point Mickey hit a pothole, and I tasted my own beer as I burped.

We crossed into the Ninth Ward, an old section of the city downriver from the French Quarter. Long, narrow mid-nineteenth century shotgun houses crowded the edges of thirty-foot-wide lots. The Ninth Ward is divided into two sections, upper and lower, by the Industrial Canal. The levees on both sides of the canal breached in Katrina's storm surge, then again in Rita. The Lower Ninth Ward caught the worst of the flooding.

The Lower Nine has always been poor. Most of the white population of blue-collar residents, known for their distinctive accent similar to that of Brooklyn, left the area years ago, and now the Lower Nine is almost entirely black. Or at least it was before the flooding wiped out everything.

I didn't come down here very often to write articles about the nightlife. Most of the nightlife in the Lower Nine involved drugs and gangs. Murders were commonplace, even just a few days before the storm. Not even the police wanted to come down here.

As we headed toward the canal, we bumped over what was left of the streets, which in some places were nothing but dirt. Houses built a hundred and fifty years ago had been knocked off the piers they were built on. The remains of houses, lathe and plaster and roofing materials, were stacked on vacant lots. Those that were still standing looked like skeletons, their roofs and walls gone, only the framing left.

I saw dead animals in the weeds on the side of the road, dark lumps so badly decomposed I couldn't tell if they were cats, dogs, or something else. The ubiquitous red X's spray painted on the old shotgun houses had numbers in the lower quadrant, indicating bodies had been found inside. It was six weeks since Katrina and two weeks since Rita, and the area still showed no signs of life.

When we crossed the canal into the Lower Nine, we could see from the top of the bridge the levee breach off to the left. A barge had gone through it and was aground in the middle of what had once been a neighborhood. Mickey turned the car in that direction.

We got as far as a National Guard blockade. Mickey spoke to the Guardsman on duty and showed him his press pass. The soldier squinted at it and shook his head. "Okay," said Mickey. "Maybe another day." He pointed in the direction beyond the blockade. "Look," he said to me. "It's all gone. Houses, businesses, everything."

The neighborhood could have been a Monopoly board, and a giant hand had come down and swept all the game pieces off the table. Where there should have been entire city blocks of houses built close together with only narrow alleys separating them, there was nothing.

Mickey said, "The levees breached in Katrina on Monday morning, after the eye of the storm passed. The east wind pushed the storm surge into Lake Pontchartrain, and it backed up into the canals. The force of the water pushed the levees aside like a layer on a cake sliding over the frosting. That's a concrete wall over there that gave way. When Rita passed, it happened again. And then there's the barge."

I felt sick. "The houses are all gone. Were there people in them?"

"Probably. They would have had no time to get out, the water came up so fast." He slammed his left fist into his open right palm to demonstrate. "How's that objective journalism coming, Mags?"

"My God," I said. "This is my home town. It looks like some city in Iraq you'd see on the news." I was fighting tears and my lunch wasn't sitting so well. Between the lurching car and the stench of death everywhere, I was swimming in nausea.

"But this is the Lower Ninth Ward. Your home town, Uptown girl? You come here all the time?"

"Yes, it is my home town. Shut up, Mickey." I wiped tears from my cheeks.

He turned the car around and drove for several blocks, then stopped in front of a shotgun house with a water line near the roof, its front door gaping open to darkness within. "This is the place," he said. A black man in a dirty white T-shirt and jeans came out to meet us. I couldn't guess his age. Twenty? Forty? The storm had aged all of us.

We got out of the car. My legs were wobbly, but I felt better outside the car than in it. Mickey made brief introductions, then he and the man, whose name was Deshon, went into the house.

I leaned against the car, taking deep breaths to fight the nausea. The death smell was everywhere, burning my eyes and nostrils. I decided to try walking. It was a warm day, not as hot as it had been just a couple of weeks ago, but warm enough. And it was quiet. No cars passing, no people talking, no birds singing.

Eloise's neighborhood had been devastated, but this was worse. In Hollygrove, the floodwaters had risen rapidly, but here they had come in a sudden surge that knocked over buildings. Here, no one who stayed for the storm had a chance to get out. The water had come through like a raging river.

I passed a vacant lot between two houses where the weeds were three feet high. A few feet from the crumbling sidewalk, a dark lump parted the weeds. It was too big to be a dog. Moving closer, I saw a tennis shoe in the grass. Wait. There was a bare leg on the other end of the shoe. A body.

Male, apparently, wearing shorts and nothing else, bloated and covered in dry gray mud. He lay face up. Between the mud and decomposition of the body in the heat, his features were barely recognizable as human. I couldn't even tell what race he was.

Something moved in the grass next to the bare leg. Funny how my brain was desperately denying what my eyes were seeing. A wharf rat, big as a small cat, was chewing on the leg. It noticed me and stopped, looking up with dark gleaming eyes as if to say, "You don't belong here." Then it slid quietly away into the tall grass, not running, just moving off.

I barely had time to lean over into the weeds before I threw up. Bitter, nasty bile. Beer, hamburger, everything. Tears sprang from my eyes and dripped on the ground. I wailed and threw up again. Don't faint, don't faint. I sank to my knees in the dirt and weeds, arms outstretched on the ground, waiting for the next wave to come up.

Mickey and Deshon came running. "Maggie, are you all right?" Mickey helped me to my feet.

"Body," I said, pointing. "Rat. Eating." I turned aside and started to throw up again, although not much came up this time.

Mickey took a step into the weeds and looked. Deshon nodded and pulled out a cell phone. Mickey went to his car and came back with a bottle of water. "Here," he said. "Wash your mouth out." I swigged some water and spat.

He helped me back to the car. I sat sideways in the passenger seat, facing the open door, my head down.

"You gonna write about this in your blog?"

"Stop it, Mickey."

"The world needs to know what it's like down here. Dead bodies and rats. This is still the United States of America, last time I checked. Stuff like this isn't supposed to happen here."

I shook my head. "I can't even tell Eloise. They haven't located her husband's body yet. I mean, I'm sure it was recovered, because he died in the house and he's not there now. But I can't tell her about this."

"Does she read your blog?"

"She doesn't have a computer."

"Well, then, blog about it. Too embarrassed to tell the world you threw up?"

"No. Yes."

"Everything they taught you about journalism, Mags— out the window."

We stayed until the D-MORT team and the ambulance arrived. With care and dignity they put up a curtain around the scene for privacy. I saw them load the black body bag into the ambulance. The sun was going down as they finished.

Mickey climbed into the driver's seat. "We don't want to be here after dark. Come on, I'll take you home. You can pick up your car at the restaurant tomorrow."

It was a long, jostling ride back Uptown, and it was well after dark before Mickey pulled into my driveway. In spite of throwing up just about everything in my stomach, my bladder was so full I could hardly walk when I got out of the car. All I could think about was getting to the bathroom.

Mickey followed me inside. "Got anything to drink?"

I waved toward the kitchen. "There's water and iced tea in the refrigerator." I made it to upstairs to the bathroom as fast as I could and shut the door. With a great sigh I sat down and emptied my bladder.

When I was done, I brushed my teeth for a long time and finished off with a big swig of mouthwash. I still had a burning sensation in the back of my throat, but my mouth finally felt clean. The rest of me wanted a long shower, even in cold water. In a little while, I told myself, after Mickey leaves.

I found him on the sofa in the living room with the bottle of George's twelve-year-old single-malt Scotch. He'd taken it from the drink cart in the dining room. The ice bucket and two highball glasses were beside the bottle on the coffee table, and one glass held a little more than two fingers of the golden liquid over ice.

"I see you found the iced tea," I said.

"Yeah. Can I fix you one?"

"No. I don't think my stomach's up to it right now."

He patted the sofa cushion next to him and I sat down, suddenly feeling like a guest in my own home. How had I let him take charge? Did I need someone else to take charge for awhile?

The ice clinked in his glass as he took a sip. "Good stuff," he said. "You know your Scotch. I would have taken you for a white wine person."

"I am. Most of the time."

"But that's changed, hasn't it? Since the storm?"

"Maybe. Or maybe since the day Howard Parker destroyed a career I'd spent nearly thirty years of my life building."

"So leaving wasn't your idea."

"Of course not. But I couldn't tell people that when I was looking for another job. I hate that man for what he did to me."

"Well, as it turned out, you would have been out of a job a month later. So what difference does it make that you got fired?"

"It makes a difference."

"Zach told me he first met you at White Linen Night. Said you threatened to kill him. Is that true?"

I could feel my face getting red. "Actually, it was Howard and Ruth I wanted to kill. I said it as we were walking away. I didn't realize Zach heard that."

"Well, when he ran into you at the office the other day, he thought he was toast. He said you were nice to him, though."

"Oh my God," I said. "I'm going to be explaining this the rest of my life."

"Get over it, Maggie. You think you're the only journalist in the world who ever got fired by a lousy boss for a stupid reason? And maybe said a few choice words? Hell, I've been fired too. More than once. Listen to me. You didn't get fired from your career. You got fired from a job. One job. You still have your career."

I leaned back into the sofa. "Yeah, I know. I just don't know what I'm going to do next. I mean, there's nothing out there right *now*. Literally. Nothing."

"Everything's crazy," he agreed. "The whole city is in flux. People are making all these predictions that New Orleans will never come back, or it will come back, only with a much smaller footprint. And of course there are a few idiots who say it should never come back. But nobody knows for sure what's going to happen."

He poured himself more Scotch, this time without additional ice. "Give it a few months. Things are going to be completely different a year from now. In the meantime, just keep writing. Document all this. Blog it and be honest about what you see and feel. We're living in the middle of a pivotal moment in American history. And America must never forget what happened here." He took a long swig. "But America has already forgotten Howard. You should too. What an asshole."

I laughed. And the next thing I knew, Mickey was kissing me, his tongue in my mouth, the flavor of twelve-year-old single-malt Scotch mingling with mouthwash. And then I was kissing him back with an intensity that surprised even me.

His hands were on me and mine were on him. It was sudden, passionate, surprising. He pulled off my t-shirt and I unbuttoned his shirt as fast as my trembling fingers could move. We were like a couple of frantic teenagers, only we were old enough to know exactly what we were doing. There we were, making love on my leather living room sofa—the sofa that had been my bed for three weeks. The surge of hormones pulsing through my limbs was like a drug, and I craved it.

I know what I'm doing, I thought. *I want this. No excuses.*

I reached a climax before he did, my body lifting and spasming as I gasped at how fast it came upon me. I heard him grunt in surprise, then laugh, and a few moments later he came too. We collapsed together, panting. He rolled over into the narrow space between me and the back of the sofa, his face inches from mine.

"You are one hot mama, Mags. I had no idea."

"You're not so bad yourself."

"I've wanted you for a long time. If I had known it would be like this, I'd have done it a lot sooner."

"I'm better after I've had a shower, actually."

"Okay, next time we'll do it in the shower."

"Next time? You think there's going to be a next time?"

"I'm counting on it. Remember," he said, pointing to the bottle of Scotch, "you can't say you were drunk. You didn't have any."

"Not drunk on Scotch. Drunk on lust."

He laughed. "I'm glad to be the object of your lust." He sat up and poured more Scotch into his glass. "Sure you don't want any?"

I hesitated. "Yeah. A little."

He dropped two ice cubes in my glass and began pouring the Scotch. "Say when."

"When," I said, but he still poured more than I wanted. I took a sip and began to choke.

"You really aren't used to drinking this, are you?"

"Actually," I said between coughs, "it was George who used to drink this."

He whistled. "So I just took George's Scotch and George's wife."

I shot him a look of annoyance. It was hard to act self-righteous when neither of us had any clothes on. "This," I waved my glass over the sofa, "was not about George."

But it was, wasn't it? Four days ago I found out that George had been unfaithful to me for years. Was this my way of casting him off? If it was, oh my God, it felt good.

"And it wasn't about Cassie," Mickey said.

Oh, yeah. Mickey had a wife. And two daughters. In Charlotte. But Charlotte might as well be in another dimension right now.

"So what was it about?" I asked.

He kissed me again. "Don't overanalyze, Mags. Just enjoy." He drained his glass. "I better get going. Need to get a story written tonight." He reached for his clothes.

"Are you okay to drive?"

He stopped in the middle of pulling on his pants, grinning at me. "Are you inviting me to spend the night?"

"No. Eloise will be home after awhile."

"Do you care what she thinks?"

"Let's just keep what we do between the two of us."

He zipped his pants. "O-kay, boss. Whatever you say."

I got dressed also, running a hand through my hair to try to straighten it out. I must have looked a mess.

He kissed me at the door. "I'll come by tomorrow and take you back to the restaurant to get your car. Say hello to Eloise for me. And I do want to do it in the shower." He grinned again and left.

Eloise got home a few minutes after Mickey left. She spotted the two glasses and the bottle and the bucket of melting ice on the coffee table but said nothing. She must have noticed the Lexus wasn't in the driveway, but she said nothing about that, either.

I got some leftover chicken out of the refrigerator and heated it in the microwave for the two of us. Eloise had hardly said a word since she'd walked in the door. "How'd it go today?" I asked.

She was standing in the kitchen behind a chair, her hands wrapped tightly around the chair back. "The lady in St. Gabriel called me late this afternoon. They've identified Robert's body."

SATURDAY, OCTOBER 8

Mickey came by this afternoon to take me to pick up my car at the restaurant. As we were on our way, he said, "That was some awesome Scotch last night. I woke up this morning with a hangover like to have killed me."

"That's it? That's all you have to say about last night? That you helped yourself to the Scotch and it gave you a hangover?"

He grinned. "That, and you, hot mama."

"That's better."

"When are we going to do that again?"

"The Scotch, or the other?"

"I can do both."

"Mickey, we've known each other a long time. This is something new. It changes everything between us. Maybe we should talk about it."

"I told you, don't overanalyze, Mags. Just enjoy. You did enjoy it, didn't you? Don't lie to me, girl."

"Girl? Did you just call me girl?"

"Yeah, I did. You're trying to change the subject. You enjoyed every bit of it. You know you did. You've been wanting this a long time."

Had I? Or was it a reaction to learning of George's affair? "May ... be," I said, drawing out the word in a manner I hoped was seductive. "How about you?"

"Hell, yeah. I've wanted to get in your pants since I first saw you."

"And all this time I thought our relationship was strictly professional."

"I think you were pretending it was. Don't look at me like that. You know you've wanted me too. What happened last night was no moment of weakness. You just don't want to admit it."

I leaned back in the passenger seat and exhaled. There he was again, forcing me to be honest. "I might have had a private fantasy or two."

"Well, the secret's out. You officially have the hots for me. Last night I saw the Maggie I always knew was there. And I want more of you."

What had happened to the woman I always thought I was, the faithful wife and mother, the woman who played by the rules? The woman who would never let her fantasies take her to places that she'd never acknowledge? She was sliding away from me. And I didn't care.

Mickey said, "Come home with me. I've got hot water. Let's do it in the shower."

And we did.

Afterward, we dried each other off and wrapped ourselves in towels.

"Oh, my God, that was awesome," I said.

"The hot water, or the sex?"

"Both."

"I think you liked the hot water better."

"Only because it came first. I haven't had a hot shower in a month. I'd forgotten what that feels like."

"Want to try the bed next?" he grinned. "You said you'd been sleeping on the sofa."

"Um," I said. "Where's your roommate?"

"Haven't seen him in a few days. I have no idea where he is or if he's coming back. And I don't care. Do you?"

I'd never been in Mickey's house before. It was a shotgun single, with the doorways lined up from front to back. You could stand at the front door, fire a shotgun, and it would go out the back door without hitting anything—hence the name. There was no real privacy. It had a living room, dining room, two bedrooms, a kitchen, and a bathroom, stacked one behind the other. I had glimpsed furniture, clothing strewn about, empty plates and glasses on the coffee table, and stuffed animals and dolls in the living room and front bedroom. I smelled smoke—cigarettes, maybe cigars, maybe both—and rancid food and garbage that hadn't been taken out, not that there were any garbage pickups. Men who weren't accustomed to picking up after themselves were living here. But before them, there had been a family with young children. I tried not to think about that.

"Let me take a rain check on the bed," I said. "I'm quite happy after our time in the shower."

"I'm happy too. I just want some more time with you. Don't go yet, Mags."

We curled up on the sofa, still wrapped in towels, my head on his chest. *This is crazy*, I thought. *How can this be happening? I'm fifty-one years old, and I feel like I'm Caroline's age. What am I doing?*

This is what I'm doing. I'm laughing in the shower and doing things I never did with George. I'm having fun and being silly and feeling wild and sexy and beautiful. To hell with what I look like in the mirror. The world outside has turned upside down. Upright citizens are looting liquor stores and stealing street signs. And I'm having an affair with a man fifteen years younger than me who's got a wife and two kids somewhere far away. And I don't care.

Maybe I do care, or I wouldn't be thinking about it. Mickey says don't overanalyze. Just let it go.

We've all been through hell. Time for some fun. No matter what happens today, tomorrow's going to bring more hell, so we might as well enjoy the moment while we have it.

When I got home, just before dark, Eloise was heating a frozen dinner in the microwave. We still don't have gas for the stove, but frozen dinners are a step up from canned spaghetti on the grill.

"You want one?" she asked.

"Yes, please. The chicken dinner."

She pulled it out of the freezer and prepared it for me. We sat together at the kitchen table and ate.

"You got your car back," she said.

"Yes. I left it at the restaurant yesterday when I went along with Mickey on one of his assignments. He brought me home afterward."

"Didn't that man tell us he was married?"

I put down my fork, suddenly aware that my hair was still wet. "His house has hot water. He let me wash my hair." Why did I say that? I didn't owe Eloise an explanation. Yet here I was, stuttering like a teenager confronted by her mother for doing something she shouldn't have.

"You just be careful, Maggie."

I could feel my face flush. I stared at her for a moment, then went back to my dinner.

SUNDAY, OCTOBER 9

I got an email from my college roommate, Sophie Abrams. She's a full professor now, head of her department in media studies—I think that's what they call it—at a university on the East Coast.

Maggie,

I just read your latest blog post. Oh my God, girl! Are you all right?

I'm on sabbatical this semester, finishing a book I'm writing on the future of journalism. I've sequestered myself at my husband's family's beach house in North Carolina. It's quiet and peaceful and I'm getting a lot of work done. But I could always use some company. Why don't you come stay with me for a few days? It sounds like you could really use some R&R. I'm worried about you, old friend. You need a break. You've been through way too much in the last few weeks. My door is open. Please come for a visit. I'd love to see you. It's been ages.

Sophie

I smiled and wrote her back.

Sophie,

You worry too much. You always did. I'm fine. Thanks so much for your kind offer. I've got some commitments here right now. The authorities have identified the body of my friend Eloise's husband, and I'm going with her tomorrow to make arrangements. I suspect Caroline will want to come back for the funeral—she's doing a documentary on the aftermath of the storm, focusing on Eloise's struggle to find Robert's body and to rebuild her home. And I'm working on a freelance assignment. Getting away isn't an option right now. Maybe later. I'll let you know, if that's all right.

Maggie

Monday, October 10

Eloise called her pastor Saturday morning and he agreed to meet her at the morgue today. He's been staying in Baton Rouge, holding services on Sunday afternoons in a church there. His congregation is scattered all over the country, but a handful of members evacuated to Baton Rouge and the surrounding area. He said he could do the funeral service next Saturday morning.

"He's talked to the pastor of Robert's home church in St. Francisville about letting us hold the service there," she told me. "That's where we're going to bury Robert, with his people."

I called Caroline with the news. Her reaction was immediate: "I'm coming, Mom. I'll book a flight right now."

I handed over the phone to Eloise and heard her say, "I'm all right, baby girl." I left the room to give her some privacy to talk.

A few minutes later she found me and handed back the phone. Caroline had booked her flights on her computer while she was talking to Eloise. She gave me the information and I wrote it down. She'd flown back to Los Angeles only a week ago out of Baton Rouge, but now she could get a flight into New Orleans by way of Houston. It was a good sign.

Eloise and I drove to St. Gabriel this morning to sign the paperwork to release Robert's body. Since the last time we drove there, much had changed. There's a lot more traffic on the roads. Just getting to the interstate took a long time. Streets were blocked off for construction equipment and bucket trucks. Workers were picking up the mountains of Sheetrock, plaster, lathe, carpet, refrigerators, and children's toys piled on the neutral grounds. It's a mess, but it means progress is happening. I'm willing to be patient.

There's more traffic on I-10, too, headed to and from Baton Rouge. Lots of trucks, but also more passenger cars. Many people who lost their homes in New Orleans are living in Baton Rouge and commuting back and forth, either to work or to clear out their houses or businesses.When we got to the old brick warehouse with the metal roof, it looked almost familiar, although I'd only been there once before. A tall black man in a suit stepped out of a white sedan a few cars away in the parking lot, and I realized it was Eloise's pastor. He'd been waiting for us. I'd met him last year at Isaiah's funeral, but I'd forgotten how young he was: in his thirties, maybe? No more than forty. He walked up to Eloise and wrapped her in a bear hug. I saw the tears come to her eyes.

"Sister Jackson," he said. "You don't know how glad I am to see you again. But I am so sorry that we are meeting here."

"Thank you, Pastor."

"I told the congregation on Sunday that Robert had been found. We are all praying for you."

"I appreciate that so much. Pastor Moses Anderson, this is my friend Maggie McBride."

"Mrs. McBride. Eloise speaks so highly of you. She has told me of your loss, also. I am so sorry to hear about your husband."

"Thank you, Pastor. We've met before. At Isaiah's funeral."

He cocked his head to one side, and I could almost hear him thinking, *Oh, yes, the white woman who sat in the back.* "I do remember now. You have been a wonderful friend to this family."

"Eloise has been good to me. We've known each other for more than twenty years."

We went inside the warehouse, and Eloise asked for Marie, the woman she'd been working with throughout this process. After a time, she was ushered back. Pastor Anderson went with her. I sat in a waiting area and tried to read.

I heard voices raised and recognized Eloise's, although I couldn't make out the words. Then murmurings. Someone was trying to calm her down. She raised her voice once more, and then it was quiet again.

It seemed a long time before they emerged. Eloise's face was like a stone, her jaw clenched. She wouldn't look at me.

"I wanted to be sure it was him. I wanted to see him. They wouldn't let me. But they said they'd matched the serial number on his prosthesis. I checked the numbers to be sure. It's the right one."

Pastor Anderson nodded. "It's all arranged. Brother Jackson's body will be transferred to a funeral home, and we'll have the service and burial in St. Francisville. It's only about a half-hour away. I've already talked to the church about having the service Saturday morning."

"My daughter is coming from Los Angeles. She's known Eloise her whole life. We'll both be there for her."

"God bless you, Mrs. McBride. I'm sure that will be a great comfort to the family."

"We love Eloise very much. We'll do everything we can to help her."

Pastor Anderson left, and Eloise and I drove to the funeral home. As I expected, it was one that provided services mostly to black families. Even in death, I thought, we're still segregated. I followed Eloise inside, acutely aware of my whiteness and feeling awkward. But the funeral director who met us was kind and welcoming. He went over the arrangements with Eloise. There was a long form. He pointed to a number at the bottom of a sheet, and she nodded.

"I don't have quite that much money in my account," she said, "but perhaps I could pay you so much a month?"

"I'll pay the difference," I said quickly. "There won't be a balance on the account."

"No, Maggie!"

"We're not arguing this one. Not here." I turned to the funeral director. "The bill will be paid in full," I said firmly. "Two checks. Hers and mine."

The funeral director looked at Eloise. Again I saw her jaw clench. "Yes," she muttered. "What she said. Paid in full."

"All right, then," he said.

In the car, Eloise exploded. "You had no business doing that, Maggie! You took away my dignity!"

"Maybe I did. But I also took away the opportunity for someone to charge you some outrageous interest rate on Robert's funeral expenses."

"You don't know that."

"You're right. I don't. I could be wrong. And if you want to pay me back, that's fine, but you know you don't have to. Consider it my gift out of respect for Robert and the fine man that he was." After a moment I added, "And the fine person that you are, too."

Eloise dropped her head and cried. I sat quietly beside her, remembering my own tears at George's death. No, don't think about George right now. Too complicated. Focus on Eloise.

"Why did all of this happen to us?" she cried. "What did we do, that God let this happen? First Isaiah, and then Robert."

I thought fleetingly of the pastor who made headlines by saying Katrina was God's judgment on New Orleans for its wicked ways. His church in the suburbs didn't flood. I am the wrong person to talk about God, that's for sure, but I didn't buy into what that pastor said.

"I don't know," I said. "I'm not really a believer, you know, but maybe God didn't do this. The levees failed. God didn't build the levees. The Army Corps of Engineers did."

Eloise eyed me sideways, still hunched over in the passenger seat, her head in her hands. "You always have to have an answer, don't you? Never mind, Maggie. Just take me home."

I started the car and headed out of the parking lot. We drove back to New Orleans in silence.

When we got home, there was a scrawled note from Steven the contractor on the kitchen table. "You have gas! I lit the pilot on the water heater. Happy showering!"

Well, at least we have one small victory to cheer about today.

WEDNESDAY, OCTOBER 12

Mickey came over in the late afternoon, after Eloise had left for work. With very little discussion, we ended up in the double bed upstairs in Caroline's room where I've been sleeping since she went back to Los Angeles. Being with Mickey is so different from being with George. He's bold, adventurous, exploring, eager to show me what he likes and demanding to know what I like. And we both laugh a lot.

My life in the last two and a half months has been hell. Mickey is fun and laughter and joy in a world that seems to have forgotten all these things. I still can't believe how much I want him—and how much he wants me. If George had lived, if Katrina hadn't happened, would I ever have fallen into this wild, incredibly erotic relationship with Mickey? Probably not. I need him right now for all sorts of reasons. Desire is the big one, of course. But it's much more than that. I need him because he reminds me that I'm still alive. That I didn't die with George, or the levee breaches, or this barren city devoid of people. Or with George's betrayal of me with some woman whose identity I may never know.

I don't know how long this relationship is going to last. I don't want to think about all the complications. I just want to drink in every moment as it happens and savor every bit of the pleasure I'm feeling right now.

After we made love, we ended up in the shower again—I've got hot water now, too! More giggles and slippery skin. We dried each other off, got dressed, and came downstairs. I fixed us supper: cheese omelets and bacon and toast.

"Breakfast for supper?" he asked.

"You have no idea how much I've missed cooking eggs and bacon on a proper gas stove," I said. "I can do this on a charcoal grill, but it's not the same. You can't regulate the heat the way you can with a burner on the stove."

"Whatever you say, Mags. As long as it tastes good."

"It will," I said. And it did.

Over supper, Mickey asked, "So I won't get to see you again until after Caroline leaves? I mean, first you didn't want Eloise to know. Now you don't want Caroline to know, either?"

"She's not going to be here very long. She comes in Friday. We're going to be in Baton Rouge and St. Francisville all day Saturday. And she leaves on Sunday. It's going to be a busy weekend."

"But that's not the reason you don't want me around, is it? You don't want her to see me with you. She'll figure it out, about you and me."

I sighed. "You're right. I just don't think she'd take it very well right now, that's all. I mean, I'm her mother, not one of her girlfriends."

"And what about Eloise?"

"Eloise knows. I didn't tell her. She figured it out."

"What did she say?"

"She doesn't approve."

"She said that?"

"Not exactly, but that's the gist of it."

"Eloise's approval is important to you."

I had a sudden memory of that morning when I hung out in the coffee shop, not wanting Eloise to know I had lost my job after she had worked for me for years, giving up her time with her own son, just so I could have my career. Yes, her approval was important to me.

"I didn't expect her to approve. She's, she's ..." I struggled for words. "She goes to church. She's got these high moral standards. She's the kind of person you'd be glad to have around your child when she's young, because she'll tell her about right and wrong."

He grinned. "And you're not a person of high moral standards? Because you're with me?"

I felt my face flush. "Hey, Mickey, what happened to your saying 'don't analyze'?"

"Just trying to figure out how I should act around people you care about."

A question grew in my chest like a balloon inflating. If I didn't ask it, something in me would explode. "What about Cassie, then? Would you want her to know about us?"

He shook his head. "That's a real can of worms, Mags."

"What happens to us when she comes back from Charlotte?" As soon as the words were out of my mouth, I wished I could snatch them out of the air and destroy them.

Had I really said "us"? As if we were a couple? As if I had any business thinking about some unknown tomorrow?

Mickey pushed his plate aside, staring down at it. He was silent for a long moment. I wanted to break the silence and apologize. But I waited. Always the journalist, waiting for an answer to my question.

Finally he looked up from the plate to me, and I was surprised to see tears brimming in his eyes. "I'm not sure she's going to come back."

"Oh," I said.

"It's complicated."

It always is, I thought.

"She and the kids are living with her parents. They're happy. She wants me to move to Charlotte to be with them. But I'm working here."

I nodded.

"Her father is an executive at one of the big banks in Charlotte. She says he can get me a job in the bank's PR department. A real job, as she puts it."

"As opposed to freelancing."

"Right. Regular hours, steady paycheck, health insurance, all that stuff."

"Wearing a white shirt and tie and jacket every day, dealing with the suits in the executive offices?"

"Yeah."

"I'm having a hard time picturing that, Mickey."

"So am I. Especially now, with all I've been through covering the storm. For the first time, I'm making a lot of money freelancing. And I'm getting my byline in some big-name publications. My career is taking off. I don't want to be some corporate PR hack, promoting the bank's new home equity loans."

"Even if the storm and all of the stuff afterward hadn't happened, I can't picture you doing that."

"Hell, no."

"And she doesn't want to come back to New Orleans?"

He sighed. "I told you it was complicated. Things haven't been good between us for a long time. She wanted to stay home and be a full-time mom, but we can't live on my income from writing alone. Her parents have been helping us financially. I mean helping us a lot. They gave us the down payment on the house. They paid for the new roof. They paid the kids' tuition for private school. They call it providing Cassie's salary for being a stay-at-home mom. And they never fail to let me know, in not-so-subtle ways, what a failure I am for not being able to support my family like that."

"I wondered how you could afford all that."

"Now you know. Her parents have had their claws in our marriage for a long time. Now they've got her and the kids right where they want them, and they're not letting go. Frankly, I can't stand them. They can't stand me. And I'm sure as hell not moving to Charlotte to live under their noses and let them run our lives."

"Oh, Mickey," I said. "I had no idea."

"I love my kids. I miss them so much. But they think Charlotte is great. They've already made new friends. Six weeks, and they're happy to stay right where they are." The tears overflowed and spilled down his cheeks.

"I'm so sorry."

He pushed back his chair from the table. "Maggie, maybe this isn't such a good idea, you and me. You shouldn't get mixed up in this. It's my problem, and you're just going to get hurt if you hang around me."

I got up and walked around the table to the back of his chair and wrapped my arms around him, my chin resting on the top of his head. "Too late. I'm already involved. I'm not backing away."

He began to sob like a small child. I felt the tears building in my own eyes. Since the storm, it's been so easy to cry. Six weeks after, here I was, in my kitchen, holding Mickey. At this moment, nothing else in the world mattered.

FRIDAY, OCTOBER 14

I picked up Caroline at the airport in the late afternoon. The parking deck was nearly empty, a sight I'd never seen before. Only a handful of flights were coming in and out of New Orleans, and the airport had the eerie feel of a ghost town. Not completely deserted, but not the bustling place I'd always known. Even at that hour, some of the newsstands and snack bars were shutting down for the day.

I waited outside security as passengers drifted down the concourse with their rolling luggage. They all looked a little uncertain, as if they weren't sure where they were. I wondered how many of them were visitors and how many were locals coming home, and how many—or perhaps how few—knew what to expect when they got here.

Caroline stood out from all of them. Well, she was my daughter, after all. But she moved with a confidence that the others seemed to lack. Her stride was long and purposeful. Her carry-on bag bounced behind her, struggling to keep up. She wore jeans, a denim jacket, and a black top. Very L.A., I thought. It was far too warm here right now for a denim jacket. But it had probably been much cooler there when she left for the airport early this morning, her time.

She'd had to change planes a couple of times to get here; her arriving flight was from Houston.

I felt a little shabby in my own jeans and short-sleeved white t-shirt and no makeup. I really need to find someone to cut my hair. God knows where my hairdresser ended up.

"Hey, girl," I said, hugging her.

But up close, that confidence I'd seen in her as she walked down the concourse faded. Her face was filled with weariness. It had only been two weeks since I'd last seen her, but she looked different. Something was sapping her strength. I'd thought that going back to the comforts of the twenty-first century in L.A. would make her life easier than it had been here, living without electricity in a sweltering late summer and helping Eloise clean out a moldy house. Apparently re-entry into her normal life was more difficult than I'd expected it to be.

"Hey, Mom, I finally got here." She looked around. "Is Eloise with you?"

"No, she went ahead to St. Francisville to be with family tonight before the funeral. I told her we'd drive up in the morning. They're having a repast at the church after the service."

"Repast? What's that?"

"A big meal after a funeral. Eloise has been on her cell phone with people all week, figuring out what everyone's going to bring. I think it's going to be quite a spread."

"Sounds very Southern to me."

"I'm sure it is. Did you check a bag?"

"Nope, this is it." We crossed the bridge to the parking garage, located the car, and headed home on Airline Highway.

"You look tired," I said.

"I just had to get a lot done before I left town. Didn't sleep much the last couple of nights, trying to get caught up. Schoolwork and stuff."

"Everything okay between you and Jason? He didn't seem happy about your being here for a month."

"Yeah, it's okay."

Probably it wasn't okay with Jason, but she'd tell me if she felt like it. Otherwise it was none of my business. Got it.

"What's been going on around here the last two weeks?"

I found out your father had an affair, and now I'm having one too.

"Well, you'll be amazed when you see how much Steven and his crew have gotten done on the house. They replaced the whole roof. They've gutted the bedroom and are working on the replacing the old plaster with Sheetrock. And they've just about finished replacing all the glass that was smashed in the sunroom."

"I'm still surprised how little damage to the house there was, compared to the neighborhoods that flooded. When I talk to people at school, they can't believe we were actually living in the city after the storm. The devastation that's been all over the news—they don't understand how anybody could live there."

"We're in the sliver on the river, the unflooded part. It's like night and day."

"I read what you wrote in your blog about going to the Lower Ninth Ward. I know we talked about it, too. I wish I had gone there with my camera. Do you think we could go while I'm here?"

"No." The word shot out of my mouth almost before she finished her sentence. Quickly I added, "You won't have time. We're going to be in St. Francisville all day tomorrow and you have to go back on Sunday."

"Maybe we could go Sunday morning. My flight isn't until afternoon. Maybe Mickey could take us."

"No!" This time I almost shouted the word.

"Mom? Are you okay?"

No, I'm not okay. I'm having an affair with Mickey, and I don't want you to see the two of us together, because you'll figure it out. And I sure as hell don't want to go back to the place where I saw a rat eating a human being for lunch.

"Caroline, it's just—It's not a tourist attraction. It's a death scene. Where the levee broke, the water came in like rapids on a river. It was a wall of water that swept everything away. Houses are just gone. People drowned. Children drowned. They're still finding bodies down there."

"All the more reason why I want to go, Mom. I'm a journalist and a filmmaker."

"Mickey's out of town right now," I lied. "After what I saw down there, I'm not going back, and it's too dangerous for you to go by yourself. Let's just have a Sunday morning together, just the two of us, okay? The power is back on, the gas is working, Giannini's is open again. We can have brunch at home. Just like at the downtown hotels before all this happened. Mimosas and eggs benedict. What do you say?"

She was silent a moment. I knew if she had the choice, she'd pick the Lower Ninth Ward over mimosas and eggs benedict. God bless her. My daughter, the journalist.

"Okay, Mom. Brunch it is."

SATURDAY, OCTOBER 15

We left early this morning for St. Francisville. It was about a two-hour drive. We took the interstate to Baton Rouge, then traveled north and east on U.S. 61 to St. Francisville. We were following the bends of the Mississippi River, although we never saw it. We passed some chemical plants that bordered the river. At one point we could smell the distinctive odor of a paper mill in the distance. What appeared to be peaceful countryside was actually fairly industrial.

I knew St. Francisville as the location of several plantations, some of which are open to the public. George and I had once visited Rosedown, now owned by the state and open for tours as an example of a working antebellum plantation. At the time of the Civil War, more than a hundred slaves lived there.

We passed two or three plantations along the highway on our way to the church. I said, "I wonder if Eloise might be a descendant of a slave who worked these plantations."

"She is," said Caroline.

I almost swerved off the road. "How do you know that?"

"She told me."

"When?"

"We talked about a lot of stuff while we were cleaning out her house. She was talking about growing up in St. Francisville, and I asked her if she had ancestors who worked the plantations. She said her grandmother told her stories of her own grandmother. I guess that would make her Eloise's great-great grandmother. She was born in 1832—at least that's what she told Eloise's grandmother— on Rosedown Plantation."

It had never occurred to me to ask Eloise a question like that. As a white woman, I would be embarrassed to ask. Furthermore, it would have to lead to another question: what if my own ancestors had been slave owners? Asking the question would mean opening a discussion about the history of race in the South—on a very personal level—that I didn't want to face.

Caroline's generation was different from mine. More forthright, less circumspect. She'd been born after the years of violence and anger of the civil rights movement, years that Eloise and I had lived through. There was still a gulf between white and black that I wasn't ready to cross. And, I grudgingly had to admit, her relationship with Eloise was more intimate than mine. After all, Eloise had changed her diapers and probably heard her first words.

The phrase "white woman of privilege" drifted through my head. In my last conversation with Mickey before Caroline arrived, he'd been skeptical about our going to the funeral.

"Don't be surprised if some of the black people there don't welcome you with open arms," he said. "There are some influential whites Uptown who think Katrina might just be their ticket to make New Orleans a majority white city again. Some powerful people are looking for ways to discourage African-Americans from coming back by dragging their feet on restoring power to majority black neighborhoods, or by declaring that certain flooded areas shouldn't be rebuilt but developed as green spaces."

"They can't do that!"

"I don't know, Mags. Everything's up for grabs right now. Most of the areas that didn't flood are majority white. A lot of the areas that did are majority black."

"Lakeview is majority white, and it was ground zero for the 17th Street Canal breach. A lot of national commentators are implying that the floods only hit black neighborhoods. You know that's not true."

"What I'm saying is that there are more white people living in the city now than there are black, and the city hasn't had a majority white population in nearly fifty years. The old guard white families are talking. There's probably going to be some action, or an attempt at action, to keep the city majority white. You told me you and Caroline may be the only white people at this funeral. I'm just saying, don't be surprised if you get some less than friendly looks."

We found the church without much difficulty. It was a small wooden building, painted white, set on red brick piers. An old cemetery flanked it on the left side and a gravel parking lot on the right. As we drove up, we could see a white tent almost as big as the church set up in the back—for the repast after the service, I guessed. We were early, and only a few cars were there.

We climbed the steps and entered the semi-dark entryway. I spotted the casket at the front of the church, covered in white flowers. It was closed. Of course.

An elderly black man in a suit greeted us. "Welcome," he said. "I'm Ronald Alexander. Mr. Jackson's family has been part of this church for years. We haven't seen much of him since he went to New Orleans, but a man's got to make his living."

"I'm Maggie McBride, and this is my daughter Caroline," I said. "We've known Mrs. Jackson for many years."

He nodded. "She told us to expect you. I understand she's been living with you since she lost her home in the flood."

"Yes," I said. "We are so sorry about Robert's passing. He was a good man and a good husband to Eloise."

Ronald handed us programs. A color photo of Robert as a young man was on the cover. Eloise had lost most of her photos in the flood, so I guessed this one came from a family member in St. Francisville. The dates of his birth and death were indicated as "Sunrise" and "Sunset." We made our way into the church and sat in a pew about halfway back. A few people were standing around in the aisles, talking.

I've never been much of a churchgoer, but this little country church was quite different from the soaring Gothic buildings I knew in New Orleans. The walls had dark wood paneling, and the ceiling, while slanting upward to a point, was not very high. There were small vertical windows on the side walls that looked like they had been covered with some sort of translucent red film—they weren't stained glass. The pews were the same dark wood as the walls. The floors, too, were wood, and worn with age. Ceiling fans turned slowly above us. There was no air conditioning, as far as I could tell.

An elderly woman in a dark print dress came up to us. "I'm Bessie Alexander. You must be Mrs. McBride."

"Yes," I said, "and this is my daughter, Caroline. We just met Ronald. Is he your husband?"

"Yes. I remember you. You came to Isaiah's funeral."

"I'd known him since he was a child. What a terrible loss."

"It was. Broke his mother's heart to lose him like that. But he wanted to serve his country."

"He wasn't much older than Caroline."

"And now Robert is gone, too. Eloise has had her burdens. But the Lord takes care of her. He always has. She told me she's been staying with you. God bless you for looking out for her."

Caroline said, "We were so glad to see her alive after the storm. We had no idea what had happened to her. She raised me, you know."

"She talks about you," said Bessie. "She is so proud of the fine young woman you've grown up to be."

"Thank you," said Caroline. "She's my second mother."

"Caroline is going to college in Los Angeles this semester," I said. "She came home to be here today for Eloise. She means a lot to both of us."

"Well, I know she appreciates it. So glad you're here." Bessie nodded and moved on.

A heavyset woman entered through a rear door and made her way to the electric organ at the side. She sat down, set up her music, and began to play.

The pews filled quickly. The seats next to us were the last to be occupied. Two older women hesitantly moved from the opposite end toward us. I smiled and nodded at them. *I get it*, I thought. *We're white. You don't know if you should sit next to us.* They nodded back and settled carefully a respectful distance away.

By the time the service started, people were standing along the walls. It was growing warm in the church with the press of bodies. Someone must have turned up a rheostat, because the speed of the fans increased, stirring the air around us.

The choir entered single file through a door at the front of the church and took their seats. Pastor Anderson and another minister, who I later learned was the pastor of that church, followed and sat down also.

Eloise and Robert's parents—I remembered them from Isaiah's funeral—led a group of family members down the aisle, settling into the front pews. I spotted Lamar and Bobby. The congregation rose as they entered, sending up a great creaking sound from the old wooden pews and a rumble of shuffling feet.

Eloise was wearing a white suit and a hat, and I realized she must have bought them yesterday in Baton Rouge. All the women around her were wearing white as well. I was wearing a black sheath dress and Caroline was wearing black slacks and a white top. Apparently it was the custom here for the family to wear white at a funeral.

Pastor Anderson rose and stepped to the lectern. He welcomed us all, noting how many had come from places where they had evacuated—Houston and Memphis and Shreveport and Jackson and Birmingham, among others. He said what a tribute it was to Brother Jackson that they had made the journey, and how grateful Sister Jackson was for their love and prayers and support. The choir rose and sang an old spiritual.

The service was similar in some ways to white funerals I'd attended, but it was very different in others. There was a lot of music and a lot of talk about homecoming and being welcomed by the Lord. Then Pastor Anderson got up to speak. I thought he'd talk about heaven and pearly gates and the wonderful place where Robert now was. He didn't.

"The prophet Jeremiah told us that the enemies of Jerusalem laid siege to the city until it surrendered. The people had no choice but to be marched off into exile in Babylon. They had to go where they were told or die. Jeremiah told them to settle in this new place and make homes and lives for themselves, until that day when they could go home again. Babylon was not home. It was a place to live until they *could* go home. Home is that place where they knew they belonged, among their own people, in their own city. Home for them was Jerusalem. Babylon was a place where they were strangers in a foreign land. When the day finally came when they were allowed to leave, they went back home to Jerusalem and rebuilt their city."

He continued, "The storm was our enemy. The levee breaches were our enemy. We all were told we had to get out of New Orleans or die. Some didn't want to leave or had no way to get out. Some thought they'd be safe if they stayed in their own homes. And some died in the storm and the floods, like our beloved Brother Jackson. And some who are here today have been scattered all over the country. You may have left on your own before the storm. Maybe you drove your own car, or maybe you rode with friends. Maybe you had no way out or you didn't want to go, and you ended up at the Superdome or the Convention Center or, like Sister Jackson, out on your roof. Maybe you ended up on some overpass in the hot sun, waiting for days for the buses they kept telling you were coming. When they finally came, you didn't have a choice where you were going. The soldiers told you to get on, and you went. Any place was better than the Superdome or the Convention Center or the overpass. Maybe you ended up in Houston, or Baton Rouge, or someplace else."

His voice rose to a thunderous pitch. "Those people from Jerusalem who ended up in Babylon had to stay where they were sent. But you don't! Look how many of you made the trip here to St. Francisville, to honor Brother Jackson and to be here for his wife and family. And another reason you're here is because you need to be back with your own people, the ones from your own church and your own neighborhood. Haven't you missed us? Don't you want to be back with us again? This thing that has happened, it's separated us, but it doesn't have to be forever. We *can* come home. We *need* to come home. We need to be a community again. We need to come back to New Orleans and rebuild our city, our neighborhoods, our churches. Nobody else is gonna do it for us. We have to show up and speak up."

He pulled out a handkerchief and wiped his brow. "The Babylonian army wouldn't let the people of Israel come home to Jerusalem. There's no army stopping us from going home. But there are people out there saying parts of New Orleans shouldn't be rebuilt. They mean *our* parts. If we're not there to stand up for our community, they're going to level everything we hold dear and make a park out of it. I am saying to you today, come on home. Yes, it's gonna be hard to get back. It was a free bus ride to Houston, but now we've got to find our own way home."

He shook his head vigorously. "Don't kid yourselves. Houston doesn't want us. Baton Rouge doesn't want us. But we want our homes back. And we have to stand together to make that happen."

I heard a few shouts of "Amen!" from the congregation.

"Now, Brother Jackson has come to his true home, that home that waits for us at the end of this earthly life. We rejoice that he is with Jesus at last. But we who are still on this earth need to come back to that place which is our home in this life, to be with our own people in our own city.

We need to come back together, to help one another grow strong again."

Mickey had been right. Pastor Anderson was well aware of the voices wanting to make New Orleans a majority white city again. And he was rallying his congregation, gathered from far and wide in this little country church in St. Francisville, to stand up to those voices and come home and make their own voices heard. It didn't seem quite the thing to say at a funeral, but perhaps this was the first chance he had had to address this many of them since the storm had scattered them all over the country.

I remembered the reception in Atlanta after George's service, less than a week after the storm. People had come from so many different places where they'd evacuated, and in that room they finally had the chance to talk to other New Orleanians who had been through what they'd been through. They drank punch and ate cookies like it was some wedding reception, but it wasn't.

None of them had stood out in the sun on an expressway overpass, then been loaded onto buses, destination unknown. When they left, they had a plan for where they were going, even if they ended up someplace else because there was no place to stay where they wanted to be. They talked about how they got out of the city and where they were staying now and what they knew about their homes. And what they were going to do next.

Today was exactly six weeks after George's service, and we knew a lot more now than we did then. But the people here today had had six weeks to begin to settle in other places. Some of them might like their new homes better than what they had in New Orleans. Would Pastor Anderson's impassioned sermon convince them to return?

After the service ended, pallbearers wheeled the casket down the aisle and out of the church. The pastors, Eloise, and the rest of the family filed out, with the congregation following. The procession made its way to a small tent in the old cemetery beside the church. I remembered this was where Isaiah had been buried, beside some of Robert's family members.

Eloise had held her head up throughout the service, and afterward she walked out with dignity. But when she got to the open grave, she broke down and began to wail.

Caroline hadn't filmed the service inside the church— whether out of respect for the family or because the lighting was poor, I wasn't sure. But when we got outside, she took her video camera out of her purse and turned it on. She filmed the procession making its way over to the graveside, then stood at a distance for a shot of the gathered mourners.

I looked over at her when Eloise broke down. Caroline's jaw was set and her hands were steady on the camera. She was in full journalist mode. I'm sure she was moved by the sight of Eloise's grief, but she didn't flinch.

Not me. I had tears streaming down my face. I wished I could go to Eloise, but there were several layers of people between me and her. I saw Lamar put an arm around her to keep her from falling. *Eloise has family,* I told myself. *You're not her family. Let them take care of her.*

When the graveside service ended, we made our way toward the big tent set up at the back of the church. There were plates and plates of food piled on tables: fried chicken, ham, gumbo, potato salad, baked macaroni, collard greens, cornbread, desserts, iced tea. The repast put the punch-and-cookies reception after George's service to shame. But we had been strangers in Atlanta. St. Francisville was the hometown of Eloise and Robert. People knew them and their family. Of course they would be there with food, lots of it.

Caroline made her way over to Eloise, who was still surrounded by a crowd of people. I trailed behind my daughter, feeling a little shy. I was such an outsider here. But Caroline didn't seem to care. She made her way through the crowd, and when Eloise saw her, she said, "Baby girl," and this time Caroline did cry. They wrapped their arms around each other.

I made my way through the crowd and stood next to them as they moved apart. "Eloise," I said. "It was a lovely service."

She nodded. "So many people. I had no idea they were all coming."

"What a tribute to Robert. And to you."

"There are people here I haven't seen in years. We left St. Francisville so long ago, and we didn't come back much, but they remember us."

Others were gathered around us, wanting to speak to Eloise, so we stepped back. Caroline and I got our food and found seats at a table. This time, unlike in the church, we were two white women asking to sit down at a table of three black women and one man.

I introduced us, and they did the same. "Where are you from?" I asked.

They were members of Eloise's church in Hollygrove and lived in her neighborhood. Right now they were staying in a motel in Baton Rouge. Pastor Anderson was holding services in a church that was letting them meet on Sunday afternoons. There were maybe fifteen or twenty people coming each week. He had told them about the funeral arrangements last Sunday.

"Have you been back to Hollygrove?" I asked. "Have you seen your houses?"

One woman nodded. "Flooded almost to the ceiling. Got no flood insurance. The house had never flooded, so why pay for it? When that levee broke, though, that was it. Those levees, they were supposed to protect us. They weren't supposed to break. Now what are we going to do? Got no money to rebuild without flood insurance. Homeowners insurance isn't going to pay for flood damage. Just the roof, and there's a big deductible for that. Hurricane deductible, they call it. They got you coming and going."

"I heard you could get a trailer," I said. "FEMA can put a trailer in your front yard."

"Got no money," she repeated.

"FEMA may be able to help you with that, too," I said. "There may be money."

Caroline said, "Do you want to go home?"

The woman snorted. "Want, sure. But I've got no money, I tell you. I've lost my job. I worked at one of the downtown hotels. They're closed. Flooded, windows blown out. They're telling us it could be years before they open again. Pastor says, come on home. But I got no home to come to and no job either. I'm trying to get me a job in Baton Rouge. But so is everybody else. It's hard out there."

I thought, *I've lost my job too. But I have money in the bank and my husband had a lot of life insurance. And my house didn't flood. White woman of privilege.*

Caroline said, "I'm making a film about what's happened to people after the storm. Would you be willing to talk with me on camera about that?"

The woman shrugged. "Sure. People need to know what's going on here. They think we're just lazy, don't want to work, get that government handout. Not so. We want to work. But with nobody living in the city, all the jobs have gone away. And our houses are flooded. We've got no place to live. It'd be nice to have a trailer in my front yard. But when is that going to happen?"

Caroline said, "Let me set up a place where we can talk." She left her food untouched and went to set up her interview.

I finished eating and got up. Pastor Anderson was talking to a group of people, and I went over to join the conversation. They looked at me—*who is this white woman?*—but Pastor Anderson introduced me and explained that I was a longtime friend of Eloise.

I said, "That was quite a sermon."

"Did something in particular stand out for you?"

"Yes. What you said about how important it was for people to come home and rebuild, and how there might be some . . . obstacles to that."

"Obstacles."

"Yes. Someone told me much the same thing you said, just the other day. That certain . . . individuals might not want some neighborhoods to come back."

"You heard that, did you?"

"Yes. And I was wondering . . . what can be done to see that every neighborhood has a fair chance at recovery?"

"You mean, what you can do?"

"Yes. Me."

"Sister Jackson has told me you are a writer. That you have something of a following."

"Well," I said. "I'm not sure how much of a following I have. I've been writing on the Internet since the storm. For people who haven't come back and want to know what's going on at home."

"But perhaps you know some people who know some people."

I used to, I thought. *Before I got fired.* "Maybe," I said.

"Talk to them, then. Tell them they don't own New Orleans. It belongs to all of us. And we all have a right to come back and rebuild. They don't know it, but they need us. We work in the hotels and restaurants and hospitals and schools. We work for the power company, the phone company, the cable company. We work for the city government. We work in construction. We're electricians and plumbers and carpenters and painters. We need to come back so everyone can rebuild. But to do that, we need places to live, just like everyone else. You tell them that."

"I will," I said.

He turned to speak to someone else, and I stepped back. It felt strange, having this black pastor tell me what to do, like an editor giving me an assignment. But it also felt right. We really did need one another to get the city up and running again.

I made my way over to Eloise, who was sitting at a table with a plate of food in front of her, largely untouched, as she continued to speak with people. I took a seat across from her, suddenly feeling at a loss for words.

She leaned toward me, and I realized she wanted to share something confidential. "I saw him," she said.

At first I didn't understand. Then, "You saw the body?"

"Yes. I looked inside the casket. I had to know it was him."

"And it was."

"Yes. I know they didn't want me to see him. It was awful. But I had to."

"I know." I reached across the table and took her hand.

"I have some peace now, Maggie. If I hadn't seen him, I always would have wondered. When he wasn't in the house, I just didn't know what had happened to him. But now I'm sure."

I nodded. "Can I do anything for you?"

"I'm all right. Everything is all right now." She waved a hand around the tent. "I've got my friends here. It feels like things are normal again."

"Normal," I said. "I miss normal."

"Tell me about it. Here in St. Francisville, they had a lot of trees come down in the storm. A lot of wind. The power was out for a while. But things are just about back to normal now. It's a relief. You know?"

"Yes," I said.

"I'm going to stay over here tonight. Tomorrow night too. I'll come in on Monday. Got to get back to work Monday evening."

"Caroline is going back to Los Angeles tomorrow."

"She told me. I'm sorry I didn't get to spend much time with her this trip. I do miss that child. But you two need to be together. She's grown up now and going out on her own. You aren't going to have much more time alone with her before she graduates from college, and then who knows how often you'll see her again."

"Yes," I said. "You're right."

Lamar came over to us then, standing beside the seated Eloise. "You need to eat something, Birdy. You haven't eaten all day."

"I'm not hungry," she said.

Something clicked in my head as I saw him standing next to her. Oh. Eloise and Lamar. I knew he'd made several trips down to help her clear out her house, but I hadn't picked up on this before. They had something going.

I thought of how I didn't want Caroline to see me with Mickey, because she would have figured it out immediately. I'd just figured this one out. And here I'd told Mickey that Eloise was too moral a person, a churchgoer, to approve of us being together.

Silly me.

SUNDAY, OCTOBER 16

I insisted that Caroline and I have that brunch, although it was clear that her heart wasn't in it. She declined the mimosa and only picked at her omelet. I had a sense she was disappointed about not going to the Lower Ninth Ward, maybe even a little bit angry at me for putting my foot down. Still, she'd gotten several good interviews at the funeral Saturday afternoon, including one with Eloise late in the day, after most of the mourners had left. She seemed pleased with the information she'd gathered about the difficulties facing people who really did want to come home. Her interviews were powerful, and I told her so.

Eloise repeated on camera what she'd said to me about needing to see Robert's body, even in the condition it was in, just to get some closure about his death. She had to be sure, she said, or she would always have wondered if he'd managed to get out of the house and survived.

"I know that's crazy talk," she said. "But you have to hope. You have to think maybe, maybe he's not dead. Maybe that's someone else they found. Maybe they made a mistake." She shook her head. "Now I know. It's so hard to face the truth. But I won't have to wonder any more. Facing it is better than always wondering."

Which, I thought, made a great ending to Caroline's documentary. I wouldn't be surprised if she wins an award for this piece. Maybe more than one. It's going to be much more than a semester's project for school. It's going to launch her career.

Still, I expected her to have a lot more energy and excitement than I was seeing this morning. Carefully I said, "You seem weary."

She sat back in her chair. "Just a little tired, Mom."

"How's it going with your professors and the documentary? Did you get it approved?"

"Still in process. I turned in a draft of my proposal. But as soon as I get back, I'm going to have to start the editing and production. It'll be hard to adjust it if they want big changes. I mght have to come back and do more filming, and I'm not sure when I could do that."

"Must be hard, living with all that uncertainty."

"It is. But everyone affected by Katrina is living with uncertainty right now. Just a different kind from mine. And theirs makes mine look petty by comparison."

"How are things going for you otherwise? I mean, now that you're back in L.A.?"

She looked down at her plate, then back at me. "It's just hard, this re-entry thing. I hadn't expected that. Being here for a month changed a lot of things for me."

"How so?"

She shook her head. "I'm just different now. When I'm with my classmates, all the stuff they worry about seems so . . . trivial to me, after what's happened here. I don't fit in with them."

"And what about Jason? Do you still fit in with him?"

She sighed. "It's hard. He has his new job and a whole different life from when we were in school. Meanwhile, I'm going through all the footage I shot, trying to put together a coherent story line. We're kind of moving in different directions right now."

I nodded. "The last time I saw Jason, when we were in Atlanta, the one thing that lit him up was talking about his work. And now you have this documentary that's consuming so much of your life. The two of you are going to have to figure out how to have a relationship in the middle of all these other priorities."

"Yeah," she said. "I know."

As we were leaving for the airport this afternoon, she pointed down the block. "Look, Mom. The Duprees' house is for sale." I spotted the pole in the front yard with the real estate agent's blue-and-white sign hanging from it on a chain.

We drove down to their house. Noreen's gray SUV was parked out front, and the two dogs were running around the yard. We got out and walked toward them. One of the retrievers bounded toward Caroline, and she hugged the dog in delight. "Look, she remembers me!"

Noreen came out the front door, and we greeted each other. "You're selling your house?" I asked, not that there seemed to be any doubt.

"Yes. Seth's practice is booming in Baton Rouge, and we're buying a house there."

"What about your consignment shop?"

She shrugged. "Not exactly a big market for consignments right now. Besides, there was just enough water in the building that the clothes got moldy. Can't sell them, can't find the people who brought them in to sell. It's all got to go, so I might as well shut down. I can find other things to do in Baton Rouge. Maybe even open a shop there."

"We're going to miss you."

She sighed. "I know. I'm going to miss everybody here. Except there aren't a lot of people here right now, are there?"

I nodded. A few neighbors had come back since the city reopened, but some just moved their refrigerators out to the curb, took a few things, and left. I suspected that this was only the first of many for-sale signs I'd see.

Noreen said, "The real estate market is crazy right now. People are paying unbelievable prices for houses that didn't flood. It won't be long before you have new neighbors."

"Hope they'll be as nice as you."

"Thanks, Maggie. And again, Seth and I were sorry to hear about George."

"Thank you."

Caroline and I got back in the Lexus and went on to the airport. To my surprise, there were long lines at the ticket counter. Very few flights, many people needing to get to their destinations. I heard a ticket agent say Caroline's flight was full. But she had a seat assignment, so I knew she'd get on the plane.

It was hard to leave her at the security checkpoint. I was surprised when those tears came again—for both of us.

"Call me when you get there," I said. What a way to say goodbye.

I was on my way to the parking deck when my phone rang. It was Mickey.

"Hey, is the coast clear yet?"

"Just leaving the airport now."

"Well, come on over to my place, hot mama. Spend the night with me."

For a moment I couldn't breathe. As casually as possible, I replied, "See you in a few."

When I got to his house, he was on the front step waving a bottle of wine. "Got your Chardonnay, just like you like it. It's even cold."

"What a treat."

"Plastic cup okay?"

"How very classy of you."

"Doing dishes is not my specialty." He poured two glasses and raised his in a toast. "To putting daughters on the plane. To spending the night together."

"Cheers," I said.

As we went inside, I could smell scents that made my mouth water. Tomatoes, garlic, oregano. "What's for dinner?"

"Spaghetti and meatballs."

It was wonderful, even if we did eat on paper plates at a tiny wooden table shoved against the back wall of the kitchen. I spilled pasta sauce on my t-shirt a couple of times. But hey, I have hot water again, and the washing machine works. I don't have to scrub my clothes in the bathtub anymore and hang them outside to dry. Amazing how the things I used to take for granted now give me such delight.

Through a mouthful of spaghetti, Mickey said, "I ran into the erstwhile editor of your erstwhile magazine yesterday."

"Zach? How's he doing?"

"He's gutting a double on North Carrollton. The owner is his landlady. I gather he lives upstairs, probably not legally considering the damage. But he seems happy enough."

"Yeah?"

"Uh-huh. He told me Parker Publishing has filed for bankruptcy."

"Guess you won't be getting paid for that story."

"No surprise there. But Zach said his father had made a big loan to the corporation a few months back. Howard hadn't made any payments, so he was going to call in the loan, and he thinks Howard filed bankruptcy to avoid paying him back."

I nodded. "With the company not operating right now, Howard could legitimately claim it has no income. Makes sense."

"Well, Zach's dad didn't get to be a big shot investment manager without having some high-powered legal advice. Howard may be collecting insurance money he can put a claim on. Should be interesting. Meanwhile, Howard and Ruth are living in their high-rise condo in Naples, happy as clams. It's the corporation that's in bankruptcy. Their personal assets aren't involved."

I shook my head and took a big gulp of wine. I'd thought I was over it, but even now, the very mention of Howard and Ruth still made me angry.

"I told you, Mags, the world has forgotten about them already. You've got a bigger career ahead of you than the one you left behind. Move on."

I sighed. "You're right. Everything is different now."

We finished the meal and tossed the paper plates in the trash. Hey, I kind of liked that easy cleanup. We quickly segued from the kitchen to the bedroom.

This time we took it slowly, savoring each kiss, each touch, each finger sliding down an arm, a breast, lower. He had my t-shirt and bra off and I was unzipping his jeans when I heard the front door open.

A woman's voice, somewhat slurred, called, "Mickey? Where are you?"

Jesus. I froze, but Mickey leaped off the bed and zipped his fly. "Coming, Cassie."

I grabbed for my bra on the side of the bed. Too late. She marched down the house, through the doorways, and lurched into the bedroom. "What the hell, Mickey?" Seeing me trying frantically to put on my bra, she screamed, "And who the hell are you?" Back to Mickey. "The kids are in the car! God, we drove all the way from Charlotte! I wanted to surprise you!" Back to me again. "Get the hell out of my house, bitch!" Back to him. "Jeez, Mickey, she's old enough to be your mother!" Back to me. "I said, GET OUT! NOW!"

She was so angry I wasn't sure if she was drunk or not. But I had the distinct sense she would do me physical harm if she had the chance.

The bra straps were twisted, but they were more or less in place. I pulled the t-shirt over my head and frantically tried to unroll it over my breasts. She was advancing on me.

Mickey grabbed her before she could grab me. "Surprise me, my ass. This is exactly what you hoped to do, find out if I was seeing someone. To hell with what the kids might see."

I shoved my feet into my tennis shoes, not bothering to tie the laces, and headed for the front door, grabbing my purse near the living room sofa. She was coming after me, screaming incoherently.

At the front door, I turned around. Her face was inches from mine. I could smell the alcohol on her breath. Scotch. Not that I was completely sober, either.

"If he means so much to you, why the hell are you living in Charlotte?"

Her mouth was open but no sound came out. I was shocked myself.

Mickey jumped between us. "Don't," he said to both of us.

"I'll kill you for that, bitch!" she screamed at me.

Mickey grabbed my arm and pulled me out of the house and down the steps.

"Get back in here, Mickey!"

I scrambled into the Lexus and shoved the key in the ignition. Mickey leaned over and whispered, "Sorry about this. I'll call you."

A blue SUV was parked behind me. I saw movement in the back seat. "Go see to your kids, Mickey." I put the car in gear and drove away.

Monday, October 17

I didn't sleep at all last night. My body was like a racing engine, throbbing, ready to take off at full throttle. All that energy and no way to get rid of it.

Mickey's wife. I'd known she was going to turn up sooner or later, but I'd tried not to think about it. Those few glorious days he and I had together were over. It was the end of pretending we lived in a magical world where she and those two children in the back of the blue SUV didn't really exist.

It was over, just like that. I was alone again. George's widow. George's betrayed widow. Maggie, old enough to be Mickey's mother. Well, not unless I'd given birth to him at fifteen. But it stung anyway.

When daylight came, I crawled out of bed and went to the bathroom. The face that stared back at me in the mirror looked every day as old as I felt. I brushed my teeth and washed my face, but I still didn't look any younger. I went downstairs, holding onto the banister as I put one foot in front of the other. Old enough to be—

"Stop it, Maggie," I told myself.

I went into the kitchen and made coffee. Too much coffee, actually. I'd forgotten that Eloise wasn't going to join me. Nor was Caroline. Oh well. I poured myself a steaming cup and went out to the front porch and sat down in a rocking chair.

The caffeine helped. The daylight helped. But there was a great hole inside me, a hole where my delight at being with Mickey had been. He made me feel alive in a way I hadn't felt in a long time. Even before the storm. Even before I lost my job. It had been fun just to be with him. The sex, yes. The sex was great. But it was more than that. It was having someone from my own professional world to talk to, someone who understood how crazy the business could be, who knew all the people and the personalities and could joke with me about it. Mickey could make me laugh again. Oh, I missed him so much.

I went back upstairs and took a shower. The hot water was energizing as it poured down over my body. But it also made me sad as I thought of Mickey's hands on me and the way we'd played in that shower. I turned my face to the showerhead and let the water wash off my tears. Damn, I've been crying too much lately.

I dressed, went back downstairs, fixed a couple of pieces of toast. I was halfway through the first one when I heard the knock on the front door. Mickey? I got up and ran to answer it.

Mark LeBlanc was the last person I expected to be standing there. I hadn't seen him or his wife Bitsy in more than ten years, not since that night at the country club when they'd turned their backs on George and me and walked out. His hair had gone gray and was much thinner, while he was a bit heavier.

"Maggie? How are you? I heard about George. I had to come to town on business, so I thought I'd drop by to see you."

"Mark, what a surprise. Yes, Bitsy sent me a note by email. Is she with you?"

"No. May I come in?"

"Oh, of course. Can I get you some coffee?"

"Yes, please. That would be good."

I ushered Mark into the living room, then went to the kitchen. I picked up the coffee pot and two cups, put them on a tray, and carried them into the living room.

"How do you take your coffee? I can get milk and sugar if you like."

"No, black is fine." He poured himself a cup.

What was Mark LeBlanc doing here? We hadn't spoken since I wrote that editorial supporting Dorothy Mae Taylor and condemning the racism of the old-line Carnival organizations. He and George had been in one of those organizations, and they used to play golf together at the club. After I took a stand on race and Carnival, George resigned from the organization. As far as I knew, they'd never played golf together again, although they may have had some business connections.

"What brings you here, Mark?"

He cleared his throat, putting down his cup. "Well, the business, you know. Bitsy and I are staying in Houston, but there are things to be taken care of in New Orleans."

Mark's family has owned a specialty spice business for generations in the Faubourg Marigny neighborhood downriver from the French Quarter. It's in the Upper Ninth Ward.

"Did your business flood?"

"Yes, it did. Not as badly as some places, but it only takes a few inches of water to shut you down when you're bottling spices for human consumption. I've been meeting with the insurance people, lawyers, all sorts of folks. We may have to sue to get the money we need to make repairs."

"But that's not why you're here," I said, waving my hand around the room.

"Er, no. I came to talk to you about . . . a delicate matter. Unpleasant, I'm sorry to say."

After all these years, what?

He took a deep breath. "Maggie, I'm sorry to tell you this, but after we learned of George's death, Bitsy broke down and confessed to me she'd been having an affair with him for the last twelve years."

I struck out with my hands, knocking over the coffee pot, but I managed to grab it before it hit the floor. "Bitsy? It was her?" Dammit, of course Tony must have known about the affair. That's why he told her and Mark about George's death when they were all in Houston.

"So you knew."

"I found out only a couple of weeks ago. I just didn't know who the woman was." I shook my head. Bitsy? It didn't make sense. The LeBlancs had shunned us ever since the Dorothy Mae Taylor episode. "Why would Bitsy and George have an affair?"

"She said she had loved George ever since they were in junior high. They went to all the same parties, did a lot of things together. She was devastated when he married you. She as much told me I was the consolation prize."

A consolation prize with a family fortune, I thought.

"Anyway, after that unpleasant business over the Carnival organizations, she contacted George at his office and met with him. She told him she knew he didn't go along with all the things you were saying, but he was obligated to support you because you were his wife. She said she was embarrassed for him and so on. And she told him she was in love with him. Apparently the feelings were mutual. They started to see each other once a week. She'd tell me she was having lunch in the Quarter with friends after her bridge group, but instead she was going downtown to meet George at some hotel."

The room was starting to swim around me. "Did you say twelve years?" I could hardly get the words out.

"That's what she told me. Now that I think back on it, that's about the time George rather abruptly told me he couldn't play golf with me anymore. Said he was too busy. Now I realize he couldn't face me."

Oh, God, all of this was beginning to make sense. "And I thought it was about, well, you know, my support of

Dorothy Mae Taylor. You and Bitsy walked out of the club one night at dinner when you saw us there."

"Actually, it was Bitsy who dragged me out of there. I realize now that it was about the affair. She was afraid I'd figure it out if I saw the two of them together." He finished his coffee. "I'm going to divorce her, of course. This is just too humiliating."

"George is dead, Mark. The affair is over."

"My marriage is dead too."

"I'm so sorry for you. All these years, and I had no idea. I feel betrayed too." Betrayed didn't begin to describe it. If Bitsy were here in this room, I'd rip her throat out. Tiny little bitch with platinum blonde hair plastered in place with hairspray. I pictured her in some hotel room with George, squealing like a pig when she reached orgasm. No, don't think about it. I picked up my coffee. My hand was shaking. I put down the cup.

Mark laid his hand over mine. "I know. I've always thought you were a beautiful woman, Maggie. So full of fire. Passionate. Much too good for George."

I looked at his hand on mine. What the hell?

"I've always been a secret admirer of yours. Always wondered what it would be like to be with you. And now you must be feeling ... very alone. Perhaps in need of companionship. Some comfort from a kindred spirit."

Oh. My. God. He was propositioning me. I drew my hand away.

"That's very flattering, Mark, but I'm afraid you're wrong about that. I'm doing quite well."

"Ah. Perhaps it's a bit soon. I apologize."

"Of course." I stood up. "I know you need to be getting on with your day."

He stood also. "Yes. Thanks for the coffee. Let's keep in touch, shall we?"

I smiled. *No, let's not.* "Take care, Mark."

After I shut the door behind him, I realized how badly I was shaking. It was only ten o'clock in the morning, but I really wanted a drink. I went back to the glassed-in porch—Steven's crew had done a great job repairing it—and took the bottle of bourbon from the drink cart. The hell with ice. I drank it neat, standing up, as I looked out over the ragged remains of the back yard. The pecan tree that had fallen on the house was gone, with only a fresh stump remaining. The grass hadn't been cut since before the storm and was six or more inches high, although it was flattened in places where the workmen had tramped around the yard replacing the roof.

The bourbon was like fire going down my throat. It was painful, but I craved the pain. It took my mind away from the emotional pain inside me. After a few minutes, though, I could feel myself starting to grow numb, starting with the inside of my mouth and spreading through my head, my hands, my whole body. I poured myself another drink. This time I sat down on the chaise.

I'd kill Bitsy if I had the chance. The woman had always been insufferable. Now I understood why she irked me so much. Of course. She'd been flirting with my husband all those years, long before the affair started. "If you value your life, you'd better stay in Houston, bitch," I said to the empty room.

Another Oh. My. God. I sounded just like Cassie. In fact, I *was* just like Cassie. A betrayed wife. The guilt hit me like a truck.

"Shit," I said, and took another gulp of my drink.

I must have fallen asleep on the chaise—I refuse to say I passed out—but the next thing I was aware of was the back door opening. "Maggie? You home?"

I looked at my watch. It was after one o'clock. "I'm out here, Eloise."

I heard something being set down, then a moment later she appeared in the doorway. "They sent me back with so much food, we won't have to buy anything for a week." She spotted the bottle and glass on the table beside me. "Oh."

I grunted.

"Something wrong, Maggie?"

"No," I said, sliding my legs over the side of the chaise and hauling myself into a sitting position. My head suddenly exploded in pain, and I winced.

"Can I get you something?"

"No. I'm all right."

She gave me a long look that let me know she wasn't buying it.

"I said I'm all right." Too sharp a tone.

"Oh-kay," she replied and walked back toward the kitchen.

I got up with a groan and followed her, in search of the bottle of aspirin on the kitchen table. I got some water and swallowed a couple.

Eloise said, "Saw a for-sale sign on the Duprees' house as I came in."

"Caroline and I talked to Noreen yesterday. They're moving to Baton Rouge."

"Lots of people leaving."

"Yes."

"Some folks in St. Francisville think I ought to move back there."

"But you won't," I said quickly.

"I don't know. I might."

"But what about everything Pastor Anderson said at the service on Saturday? About people needing to come home and rebuild their neighborhoods?"

She snorted. "Easy for him to say. Hard for people to do."

"Eloise, you wouldn't leave New Orleans, would you?" My head was really throbbing now.

"I don't know. What have I got here now, anyway? My husband's dead, my son's dead, my house is flooded, my whole neighborhood is empty. Might as well go back home. At least there I've got people who know me."

"Like Lamar?"

She stared at me. "Maybe."

"I'm sorry. I didn't mean to pry."

She began putting Styrofoam boxes of food into the refrigerator. "Can't say yet. He's kind of sweet on me. He's divorced, Maggie, and he's got a son. I don't know about that."

"But he wants you to move back."

"Well, maybe one or two others said something like that after the service. But he's the one who really wants me to, yes."

"Please don't go, Eloise." I blurted it out before I could stop myself.

She shut the refrigerator door and looked at me. "What?"

"I need you," I said.

"You don't need me, Maggie. With George gone and Caroline off on her own, you can take care of this house by yourself. Or you can move into someplace smaller."

"I'm not talking about you working for me. I need you, Eloise. You're my friend. You're all I've got right now."

She shook her head. "You've got more than you think you've got, Maggie. You've got this big house, almost all fixed up. George left you well off. You don't have to get another job."

I sighed. "You're right about all that. But everything is crazy right now. People are leaving. Some people I know have died. Nothing is the same. I need a friend, Eloise. And for twenty years, I've called you my friend. You know that, don't you?"

"You've been good to me, Maggie. You have, and I appreciate that. You were there when my boy died over in Afghanistan. You've been here for me while I was trying to find Robert. But Maggie, I work for you. Been working for you all these years. It's not like you and I have been going to lunch together and going out shopping or to a movie or something."

She was right. I was struggling, and the headache wasn't helping. "Is that what friendship is about? Going out shopping with someone?"

"You seem to do it with your other friends."

My white friends. Not that I had a lot of them. Mostly they were people I knew from work. I'd always been far too busy for relationships outside my own family.

"You had a life with your family. I had a life with mine, and with people I knew professionally. But now—things have changed for both of us. We're on our own. And I know I need you, Eloise, to help me get through this mess we're going through. This thing they're calling The New Normal. I'd like to be there for you, too."

"Well," she said. "Well. I'm going to have to think about that."

"Please," I said. I got some ice cubes from the refrigerator door and wrapped them in a dishtowel. "I'm going to go upstairs and lie down awhile. I'm glad you brought the food. Maybe I'll have some later."

Late in the afternoon, after Eloise had left for work, I awoke with the headache gone and the side of the bed wet from a dishtowel of melted ice cubes. I got up, went to my computer, and wrote an email to my college roommate Sophie Abrams in North Carolina.

Hey, Soph. You invited me to come for a little R&R with you at the beach. I could use a little time away from New Orleans right now. Can we talk?

TUESDAY, OCTOBER 18

There's another damned hurricane out in the Caribbean, this one named Wilma. We've had so many named storms this year that the names are up to W! It's headed for the Yucatan Peninsula and then into the Gulf of Mexico. The current projected path is the west Florida coastline. It's not coming toward us, not this time. They are saying this one is going to be one of the strongest storms ever in the Atlantic basin. What is it with this hurricane season? I've never known so many storms to form in one year.

We are all drawn down to the end of our reserves, exhausted from dealing with Katrina and Rita and running away and coming back and dealing with the devastation and worrying about what happened to people we care about. Enough is enough! But the storm clouds and the rain and the wind don't hear us and don't care.

I never heard back from Mickey, and I'm not about to call him. Maybe his wife came back to stay after all. She did have the kids with her. My head knows that what he and I had is over. But my heart misses him, and so does my body.

Sophie and I talked this morning. She's been staying at her husband's family's beach house for the past several weeks as she finishes the last chapters of a book she's writing on the future of journalism. She said she could use a break for a few days, and I'm welcome to come up and spend some time with her.

I managed to book a cheap ticket into Raleigh, leaving a week from now. Sophie will pick me up at the airport and we'll drive south to the beach house, about three hours away, on an island off the Atlantic coast near Wilmington. I've never been to that area. I could sure use a getaway right now.

I finished my article for the restaurant industry magazine and emailed it to the editor. He's asked for some more information, so I'll spend the next few days working on that. I should be able to wrap it up by the end of the week. It'll take my mind off Mickey, Cassie, George, and Bitsy.

And then there's Eloise. She left early this morning and didn't say where she was going. When she came in after work this evening, she took an envelope out of her purse and laid it on the kitchen table. "That's for you," she said. "Paying you back what I owe you."

I picked it up, puzzled. A glance inside showed me it was full of hundred-dollar bills. "Owe me for what?"

"The money you paid for Robert's funeral. Money for staying here with you. For groceries you bought. For letting me use your car."

"Eloise, you don't owe me anything."

"Yes I do. You said I was your friend. A friend doesn't take advantage of another friend. They don't take money and never pay it back. I'm paying you back."

My first impulse was to ask her where she got the money, but I stopped myself. A friend wouldn't ask. The question itself would suggest I didn't think she had this kind of money, and that was rude. And none of my business.

"Thank you," I said.

"I'm going to get myself another car. Mine is still sitting in my driveway after getting flooded. The insurance adjuster finally got over there this morning, and he said it's a total loss. They're going to tow it away and pay me for it. The money won't cover the whole cost of another car, but I can handle it. They said it wouldn't take too long. I'll be able to give you your Mustang back soon."

"No rush. I've got the Lexus."

"Yeah, but I know how you feel about that Mustang. I know you miss driving it."

Actually, with the condition of the streets right now, I don't. That car rides low to the ground, and the streets have sunk in some spots from the flooding and are gouged with potholes in others from Dumpsters being dragged around to collect debris.

"When you go car shopping, see if you can get a good deal on an SUV. They handle the bad roads better than something close to the ground. It's like driving off-road around here right now."

"You're not kidding. And I'm working on getting a place to live, too. I've been calling and calling about having a FEMA trailer placed in my front yard. They tell me it's going to happen soon."

I've seen her in the mornings, sitting in the rocking chair on the front porch, the cell phone to her ear. She's silent, and I know she's been placed on hold again. Rocking and rocking. First it was the phone calls to St. Gabriel, trying to get information about Robert. Then it was calls to the insurance company about her house and her car. Then FEMA.

"Have you thought any more about whether you'll move back to St. Francisville?"

She sighed. "I don't know what I'm going to do. I'm still clearing out my house. There are some church groups who want to come down here and work on houses for people who don't have flood insurance. One of those groups might be able to help me get it fixed. But it's not going to happen any time soon, because there's no place to put them up. We don't have room in this city right now for people who live here to come back to work, much less a bunch of volunteers from out of town."

"Sounds like you're still thinking about staying."

"I am." She shook her head. "St. Francisville, I don't know. I've got family there. But it's been a long time. I've been living in New Orleans close to thirty-five years. I've got a job here. Not much work up there. Small town."

I hesitated. "And what about Lamar?"

She nodded. "He's been good to me, it's true. But it's too soon for me to think about getting involved with another man. Besides, I think he still feels guilty about what happened to Robert when they were boys. He told me he thinks if Robert hadn't lost his leg, he might not have fallen in the attic. He feels responsible. He shouldn't think he needs to take care of me because of Robert. I don't want a man to be with me out of guilt."

"I can see that."

"It's good to have someone. It's good not to be alone. I just haven't made up my mind yet."

"You're taking your time."

"Yes. For now, I'm gonna work on getting my house fixed. Later, I don't know. I'm keeping my options open."

"Sounds like a plan."

She nodded. Took a deep breath. "What about you, Maggie?"

"Long term, I don't know either. I'm going to visit Sophie for a few days. See if I can clear my head."

"Things didn't work out with Mickey, did they?"

I stiffened sharply. Of course she knew. She'd seen me with the bottle of bourbon yesterday morning.

"No," I said quietly, "they didn't."

"I'm sorry. You were looking so happy there for a while."

"You were right. He's married. Not a good thing."

"Something's going to work out for you. You're still young. You can find somebody."

I smiled. "And so can you. Maybe Lamar. Maybe someone else. We've both got time."

"Yes we do. It's going to be all right."

I nodded. If only it were all right now. I miss things being all right.

Tuesday, October 25

I landed in Raleigh early this afternoon, flying from New Orleans to a connection in Atlanta. I grabbed lunch in Hartsfield-Jackson International Airport and had just enough time to make my connecting flight to Raleigh.

The plane out of New Orleans was completely full, and a lot of standby passengers didn't get on the flight. I hope the airlines realize we need more flights in and out of the city. We're up and running again—okay, stumbling a lot— and people are making regular trips between New Orleans and wherever their evacuation home is. Others are coming into town to evaluate the state of the city's recovery and learn what they can do to help. It's heartening to see that we're connecting with the outside world again.

I hadn't seen Sophie in twenty years. The last time we'd been together was when she'd come to New Orleans for an academic convention. She'd been six months pregnant with her second child. Caroline was an infant. We were young mothers, still amazed that we had brought these tiny lives into the world. And we both were struggling to figure out how to juggle these new family responsibilities with the demanding careers we were pursuing.

I spotted her outside security, waving her arm and grinning. She was a few pounds heavier than when we were in college but still fit and fashionably dressed in a flashy red, white and black top and designer jeans. The thick curly dark hair I remembered from college—almost an Afro—was tamed now and short enough to show off her gold hoop earrings.

"Scarlett! Girl, it's so good to see you!" She hugged me.

"No one's called me that since Syracuse. Wow, Sophie, it's good to see you too!"

Scarlett was the nickname she'd given me when we first met. I had flaming red hair, and I was from the South. She'd never met a Southerner before, so she figured I must be the embodiment of Scarlett O'Hara. At first I'd been angered by the stereotype—if I was Southern, I must be a Southern belle, straight off the plantation—but in time I learned to laugh it off and even make jokes about my Southern-ness myself.

Sophie held me at arm's length and looked me up and down. "It's been awhile, I know, but I have to ask, are you all right?"

"Do I look that bad?"

"No, not bad. Just a little rough around the edges. Like you've been through some serious shit."

"I have."

"I know. I've read your blog. We can talk about it. Did you check a bag? Let's get your stuff and hit the road. You look like you could use a sunset walk on the beach."

We talked nonstop on the drive from Raleigh to Wilmington. Sophie was racing to finish her book in the next few weeks. Her in-laws, who live in Connecticut, were coming down at Thanksgiving and would spend the winter at the beach house, so she'd have to vacate the place in a month.

"How is Jake?" I asked. We'd all been at Newhouse— the journalism school—together. Sophie and Jake had started dating their sophomore year and married right after graduation.

"He's good. So are the boys. Simon is in law school at Georgetown and Dave is a sophomore at Syracuse. He wants to study public policy."

"Neither of them went into journalism."

"Hell, no. Not after all the war stories about the industry they heard around the dinner table when they were growing up. But they both want to have careers in public service. I'm pleased that they're headed in that direction."

Sophie had worked in broadcast news for a few years before going back to school to get her Ph.D. in mass communications. Now she was a tenured faculty member at a big East Coast school. Jake had been editor of the *Daily Orange*, our college paper, and had gone on to be a reporter at a national newspaper. Back in college we always said we wanted to be Famous Journalists one day. Jake was the one who had actually succeeded at it.

"What's going on with Caroline?"

"She's in a special program in film this semester in Los Angeles. But Katrina happened at the beginning of the semester, and she persuaded her professors to let her come home to do a documentary on the aftermath of the storm. She wouldn't tell me about it at first. She was afraid I'd try to stop her from doing it."

"And?"

"Oh, I did try. I thought it was too dangerous for her to be poking around the city by herself right after the storm. But she decided to focus on our friend Eloise and her search for her husband Robert. His body disappeared after he drowned in their house. After that I felt a little better about the danger aspect, although it's not safe to spend a lot of time in those deserted neighborhoods like the one where Eloise lives. Anyway, Caroline spent four weeks with me after George's funeral, then went back to L.A. She came back for Robert's funeral service and did some more filming. Now she's putting it all together. I haven't seen any of it yet, of course, but I wouldn't be surprised if she wins some awards for it."

"Good for Caroline. I bet you're proud of her."

"I am."

After nearly three hours, we arrived in Wilmington. We drove onto a barrier island connected to the mainland by a bridge across the Intracoastal Waterway. Once on the island, the road curved and ran down the middle of the island, with a line of houses situated between the road and the beach.

"It's not the grandest house on the beach by any means," Sophie said. "My father-in-law built it about twenty-five years ago, fully expecting it to come down in a hurricane some season. So far it hasn't. We had a bit of a scare this week with Wilma, though."

"It went across south Florida, didn't it?"

"Yes, but then it came into the Atlantic and started up the coast. Fortunately it was far enough out to sea not to cause us any problems."

"That's good."

"Anyway, the houses that have been built along this beach in the last twenty-five years have been much grander than this one. McMansions—have you heard the term?"

"Yes."

"You'll see them when you walk the beach. Huge. Can't imagine how much it costs to insure them. This house has four bedrooms, and it's small by comparison. But it's been quite large enough over the years to accommodate all the family members who want to come down here in the summer."

We pulled up to a relatively modest white frame house. Like all the others on this beach, it was raised on wooden piers more than a story high to accommodate tidal surges. We parked under the house and climbed the stairs to the entrance.

The foyer opened to a kitchen on the right and a large living room and dining area beyond it. Sliding glass doors at the far end overlooked a deck with a view of the beach and ocean.

Sophie pointed to hallways at either side of the living room. "There are bedrooms on both sides. Mine is on the left, facing the ocean. You can stay in the one on the right and have an ocean view too."

I went to the sliding doors and looked out. In the late afternoon, the beach was in shadow from the houses and the sand dunes. The ocean tossed restlessly. In the distance I could see a yacht gliding slowly south.

George and I had stayed in hotels and houses on the Mississippi, Alabama, and Florida Gulf Coast many times over the years. This beach—and this beach house—felt familiar to me. But it also felt unfamiliar. For one thing, I wasn't here with George. I was with Sophie, someone I associated with dorm rooms, heavy coats and boots, and snowy, bitter cold days in upstate New York—not a beach house in North Carolina overlooking the Atlantic Ocean.

I set my bag down in the bedroom and opened the drapes to the ocean view. I was going to like it here.

As Sophie had promised, we took that beach walk at sunset. I was accustomed to Gulf Coast beaches where the shoreline ran from east to west. It was a little disconcerting to walk a beach where the sun was going down behind the houses, toward the land, instead of toward the right side of the beach.

"I've never seen a sunrise over the ocean," I said.

"You need to get up early one morning to see it. It's pretty amazing."

The beach sand was tan and damp from the receding tide. It was packed down enough to walk on without getting sand in my shoes—so unlike the Florida Panhandle beaches, where the sand is so fine and deep that you can turn an ankle walking in it if you're not careful, whether the sand is wet or dry.

That evening we went out to dinner at a waterfront restaurant. We sat on the deck and drank wine from large glasses. I ordered crab cakes. They were incredible.

I told Sophie of our adventures when we first returned to the city. "And we were eating canned beans heated over a camp stove," I explained between mouthfuls. "When someone brought us milk and eggs and fresh doughnuts from Baton Rouge, we thought we'd died and gone to heaven."

"I heard people at the Superdome and the Convention Center didn't have anything to eat."

I looked at my glass of cold Chardonnay, condensation forming on its sides. Guilt again. "You're right, Sophie. I never had a day when I didn't have something to eat, even if it was canned beans. What I mean is—" I swept my arm around the deck "—we didn't have this. Restaurants. Grocery stores. Electric lights. Air conditioning. All the things you—I—take for granted. And even now, very few parts of New Orleans have them. Those that do are the parts that didn't flood."

"I get it, Scarlett. You've been through a lot. I can see it in your face. But what I'm trying to say is, you had a choice. You chose to come back and live under those conditions. But the people who stayed and were trapped in the city after the storm—they didn't have a choice. They wanted to get out, but they needed help. And help took too long to get there. A lot of people died waiting for that help."

I nodded. "We thought New Orleans was part of the United States, but for four days after the storm, it wasn't. It was politics, it was bureaucracy, it was incompetent planning, it was a lot of things. It never should have happened."

"Even where I live in New Jersey, we've got people who evacuated from New Orleans. We've heard their stories firsthand, like I've heard yours. All over the country, there are people who want to help them get home and put the city back together."

"I wish it were that easy. We don't have any place in the city for them to stay right now. Even the first responders are living on a cruise ship in the port, and probably not with the amenities you get on a cruise. But one day there will be ways to house volunteers within driving distance of the city and have them come in to work for the day. Very soon, I hope."

"I'd love to bring some students down to do some work. I'll be back on campus next semester. Maybe I can organize a trip for next summer."

As I finished my crab cakes, I wondered what some of my fellow New Orleanians were having for dinner tonight. A relief organization had parked a truck alongside the empty streetcar tracks on St. Charles Avenue, not far from my house. They provided box lunches to anyone who stopped by, along with cans—not bottles—of water donated by a well-known brewery. One day I picked up lunch there. The meal consisted of lukewarm canned beef stew over rice with a piece of bread. I'd felt guilty taking the boxed lunch because I had food at home. Now I felt guilty for having crab cakes and wine on a deck overlooking the Intracoastal Waterway.

The hell with it. I was tired of feeling guilty. I'd been through an ordeal myself. There was always going to be someone who'd had it worse than me. I was here to get some much-needed R&R, and this evening definitely counted.

"Anything special you'd like to do tomorrow?" Sophie asked.

"Yeaaah," I said, drawing out the word. "Do you know of a place where I can get my hair done?"

WEDNESDAY, OCTOBER 26

We drove into Wilmington this morning for a day of R&R for both of us—Sophie said she hadn't taken a break from writing in weeks. First we went to a hair salon she recommended, where a chatty young Asian woman went over a book of hair color samples with me. With Sophie's help, we picked out a shade of coppery red that we all agreed would be flattering. The stylist did her magic with hair color and scissors, and in less than two hours I was looking in the mirror at a new me. My faded red hair, mixed with gray, now shimmered with glints of red and gold the way it had done years ago. The stylist had shaped my wild tangle of curls into a short, sophisticated look. When she was done, I hardly recognized the woman in the mirror. But I liked the way she looked.

"I wish we'd taken before and after pictures," said Sophie. "This is like one of those magazine pieces."

"Katrina survivor gets new look?"

"I wouldn't put that headline on it. But you look like you're ready for a new life."

I smiled. She was right. It was high time I had a new life. But what?

From the salon we drove to an upscale mall of new brick buildings of a classic design ringing a courtyard that served as a parking lot. Many of the shops were unfamiliar to me. We just don't have many high-end retail chains in New Orleans or its suburbs. Even before the storm, we didn't have the income levels their managements look for to justify opening a new store.

We browsed several clothing shops. In the past two months, I've lost so much weight that my clothes are baggy. I have to pull my belt to the last notch to keep the waistband of my pants from falling past my hips. I liked a lot of the clothes I saw, but I was shocked by the prices. I tried on some sale items and bought a few: two pairs of pants, a couple of tops, a jacket, and a dress. I think they'll all fit in my suitcase. I didn't bring a lot with me to the beach.

On the way home, we stopped at a small specialty grocery store to get something for dinner. I wandered the aisles, picking up a jar of this, a package of that, reading labels just to see what these things were.

"You look like you've never been in a grocery store before," said Sophie.

"My neighbors own a specialty grocery," I began. How to explain Giannini's? Since they reopened, the shelves that normally held exotic mustards and imported jams were empty. The big sellers were things like bread and milk and eggs. Sometimes a delivery truck was late or didn't arrive at all, and the shelves of bread or a section of the dairy case might be empty, too. Giannini's was the only food store in the area that was open right now. The big chains were still closed. Maybe they were negotiating insurance settlements. Maybe they didn't have enough employees who had returned.

"Things are just difficult right now," I ended lamely. "We don't have all this stuff to choose from."

"Come look at the seafood. You're the expert on that, aren't you? Let's pick out something you like and fix it for dinner."

Because of our location on the coast, the store had access to a good selection of fresh seafood. I picked up a pound of large shrimp, a box of powdered seasonings, and some corn and potatoes. "This will be easy," I said. "I can cook dinner, if you like."

"Let's do it," she said.

As we passed a refrigerated case of desserts, I stopped and stared in awe.

"What?" asked Sophie, adding a bottle of Chardonnay to the cart.

"Look at this. It's a chocolate cream pie made with chocolate liqueur, meringue topping, and a chocolate graham cracker crust. How decadent is that?"

"Let's get it."

"Are you kidding? The calories . . ." This from someone who's lost twelve pounds in the last two months.

We bought it.

That evening, I boiled the corn and potatoes with the whole package of powdered seafood boil, then added the shrimp and turned off the burner to let them cook in the hot water. The seafood boil wasn't a brand I normally used.

If it had come from Mark LeBlanc's company—I grimaced as I thought of him—the food would probably have been too hot for either of us to eat. The shrimp were quite tasty; the trick to boiling shrimp is not to overcook them. But the seasoning was quite mild by New Orleans standards.

We ate outside on the deck, with the shushing of the ocean as an accompaniment to our meal. The houses on either side of us were dark. Sophie said their owners only came on weekends this time of year. It was as if we were the only humans on the beach.

"Scarlett, you can cook! Who knew?"

"I'm from New Orleans. I know how to boil shrimp. I can make a mean gumbo if I've got a packaged mix. Don't test me on making a roux."

"Okay, I won't. But these are the best shrimp I've ever eaten."

"When you order them in a restaurant, they've often been sitting in hot water for hours, waiting for someone to order them. So yeah, they're tough and overcooked. This is what they're supposed to taste like."

"I may never order them in a restaurant again. Good job, southern belle."

We had the chocolate liqueur pie for dessert. "This is better than heaven," I said. "Oh, man. If I keep eating things like this, I won't be able to get into those clothes I bought today."

"Walk it off on the beach. I've got to get back to work on the book tomorrow."

I poured us both another glass of Chardonnay. "I want to hear about the book."

Sophie pushed back her chair and put up her legs on an empty chair beside her. "It's on the future of mass media. I've interviewed a lot of people. I've talked to executives of media organizations—you know these corporations are all diversified now. They own newspapers, television and radio stations, and cable companies in markets all over the country. Now they're buying or starting online services. It's a little scary, really. The day of independent newspapers and media outlets is long over. If a corporate entity wants to put a particular political spin on the news, they can do it across all these different platforms, in all sorts of markets."

"I've noticed that."

"When we were in school, they taught us to be objective journalists. They told us that the news is sacred and not to be tampered with. It wasn't supposed to be influenced by advertisers or politicians or corporate executives who put pressure, financial or otherwise, on a media outlet to put a certain slant on stories. Well, that's all gone by the boards. Probably was gone when our professors were teaching it to us, but they wanted us to have ideals. For years now it's been all about ratings, about numbers, about profit margins."

"What are these media executives telling you the future looks like?"

She shook her head. "We're about to see a seismic change. What we used to call journalism is going—pretty much has gone—the way of the buggy whip. Now it's called content, and it's moving away from the traditional media we've always known and going online. Remember how, when we were in school, the television-radio majors would tell the newspaper and magazine majors that print was dead? Print really is dead now. And television and radio aren't far behind. Everything is moving to the Internet."

"Huh. While I was still at the magazine, we had a website. We were starting to put articles online. But we didn't want to give away stories—content, as you say—for free that people would otherwise have to pay for when they bought or subscribed to the magazine. And people who read stuff on the Internet expect it to be free, like television used to be free, before cable. We couldn't figure out how to get people to pay to look at them."

"Exactly. Some sites are charging for online subscriptions, but to do it successfully, you've got to have a prestigious publication with high quality information people can't find anywhere else. Traditional publishers and media outlets are going to have to find a way to sell advertising on their sites. So far, many advertisers aren't convinced. I think eventually they'll come on board, when they can get reliable data on how many people are visiting these sites. In the meantime, though, traditional media outlets are struggling. Newspapers and magazines are losing readership. And they're starting to lay people off." She took a long drink from her wine glass.

It was dark out on the deck now, with the only light coming from the living room and a pair of small lights on either side of the sliding glass door. But I thought I saw tears in Sophie's eyes.

"What's wrong?"

She shook her head. "I wasn't going to tell you. We're trying to keep it quiet. But Jake got laid off from his job last week."

"Jake? What happened?" Award-winning journalist Jake, longtime reporter for a Famous East Coast Newspaper? Suddenly my getting fired from *New Orleans Now!* seemed like small potatoes.

"Downsizing. They're letting a lot of employees go, particularly those at higher salary levels with years of experience. That's code for older people—like Jake. Like you. Management says they want employees who are more flexible and comfortable with new media. Also code for hiring younger people at lower salaries. You're going to be seeing a lot of this in the coming years. Younger people are more comfortable with navigating the Internet and creating websites and learning all this new stuff. They're a lot like we were when we were little kids, fiddling with the dials on our newfangled television sets when the pictures were flipping or the faces on the color tvs were orange or green instead of normal colors. Our parents were afraid to touch the set for fear they'd make things worse and they wouldn't know how to fix it. Young people today aren't fearful of new technology. They're energized by it."

She set down her glass and refilled it. "And now, with content moving onto the Internet, management thinks they can do more with less. Run short pieces, stories without a lot of depth. Hire home-based freelancers to do a lot of it. Cut expenses associated with paid staff, like health insurance and office space. It's all about the bottom line these days. They need a certain profit percentage to keep Wall Street investors happy. The people who've put their whole lives into their careers? Well, thanks for your service and good luck." She wiped her face with her napkin. "I've been gathering all this research, hearing this was coming, and now it's hit home. Jake came down here last weekend. It was rough. We haven't told the kids yet. We may wait until they come home for Thanksgiving."

"Sophie, I'm so sorry."

"Jake got a good severance package. But he's just fifty-two. He's too young to retire and too old to have a lot of luck finding another job."

"Tell me about it," I said.

"Of course you know. Maggie, when we talked last week about your coming to visit, I was all prepared to give you a pep talk about why you should leave New Orleans and go back to New York and get your career going again. Then on Friday Jake flew down and hit me with this bombshell. He's trying to get another job. But if he can't find anything close to home and ends up having to take an offer in another city, what are we going to do? I've got tenure. I can't pick up and move. It's a mess."

"Surely he can find something. He's got a lot of connections."

"I know. That's why he only stayed the weekend. He went back Sunday night so he could arrange some face-to-face meetings with people this week. He wants to move quickly. A lot of experienced journalists are going to be flooding the job market in the next few months. The severance package is a nice cushion, but he can't afford to sit back for a few months and be—I hate to say it, but be forgotten." She took a long drink from her wineglass. "I'm sorry. This is close to home for you too."

"It is. Tell Jake how sorry I am this has happened. From the bottom of my heart. I'm right there with him."

The evening wind was rising, and it was growing chilly on the deck. We picked up our plates and wine and went inside.

Thursday, October 27

I took a long walk on the beach this morning while Sophie settled into her writing again. As I picked my way along the water's edge, looking off toward the gray horizon, I thought of those long-ago colonists who braved the ocean in tiny sailing ships and landed here to start a new life. They faced a wild, foreign land with all sorts of dangers awaiting them. Many didn't survive.

Here I am, more than three centuries later, walking the same shoreline they walked, but in a much more inviting land—a place of nice restaurants and upscale clothing stores and gourmet groceries. The beach and the water haven't changed, though. This morning they invited me to develop a closer relationship with the natural world around me.

It's so easy to believe that we in the twenty-first century have conquered nature with our technology. We tell ourselves that humans are in charge of this world and nothing can keep us from accomplishing what we want to do. The people who sailed in ships long ago respected the limitations that weather and the seasons placed on them. They avoided sailing in the winter. They had no radar, no weather forecasts to tell them when they were sailing into the path of a storm. The old sailors forecasted the weather by looking at the sky, but they couldn't sail out of the path of a storm.

The tide was starting to come in. Long ridges of sand ran parallel to the water in rows, like miniature mountain ranges with valleys between them. Here and there a deep gully cut a perpendicular swath between the ridges, connecting the shore to the water. The incoming tide swept up these gullies, flooding the valleys between the ridges.

I watched the swiftly moving water from an incoming wave race into one of the gullies. As it receded, the water sluiced out as fast as it had come in. But some water was left behind in the low valleys between the sand ridges.

This is how New Orleans flooded, I thought. Water flows toward low spots. And New Orleans has a lot of low spots.

Those television preachers who proclaimed this was all God's punishment on the city were wrong. God—if there is a God; I'm not sure of anything at this point—created the low spots, and we humans were either ignorant enough or foolish enough to build houses in them. So yes, when our human-built levees failed, the water just filled in the low spots. Like here on this beach.

Maybe there is a God. Eloise thinks so. Here on this beach, I'm wondering if she may be right.

We humans thought we'd outfoxed nature by building levees and drainage systems. We drained the ancient swamps created when the original shoreline of Lake

Pontchartrain receded to the north. We filled them with sand and built houses on them. But nature remembered where they once had been. When the levees failed, the water returned to the low places of old. Most of the city and its houses flooded. And people who trusted that human beings had overcome nature lost their houses. Some lost their lives.

I continued walking toward the north end of the island. As Sophie had said, there were some large, expensive houses along this beach. I watched workers framing a new house under construction, their nail guns making an explosive noise like repeating gunfire that echoed down the beach.

The farther north I walked, the narrower the beach became and the closer the ocean came to the houses. A yellow earth mover, like some creature out of a science fiction movie with jagged jaws at the end of a long, jointed neck, was picking up sand and piling it along the edge of the beach where erosion was threatening a line of houses. Humans were once again trying to thwart the forces of nature by rebuilding the beach that the ocean continually tried to wash away. It was a never-ending battle.

Good luck, folks. Hope you get this one right.

As the tide came in, the walkable part of the beach was disappearing, and a rocky outcrop blocked my way forward. I checked my watch and realized I'd been walking close to an hour, so I turned and headed back to the house.

I thought about what Sophie had said last night. I still hadn't gotten past the shock of learning that Jake had been laid off. His circumstances were different from mine, but the result was the same: we were both in our fifties in a world where people in their twenties and early thirties were far more employable. Their salary demands were lower, their comfort with new technologies was higher, and, I hated to admit, they had more energy than we did.

When did experience become a liability in employment? Surely someone out there wanted what we older journalists had to offer. We could be mentors and pass on our wisdom to the younger ones coming up, much as our older bosses had passed on their wisdom to us.

My job search in the four weeks between the end of my time at Parker Publishing and our evacuation for Katrina was a short one, but there hadn't been any openings at the companies I'd approached. There sure aren't any now. Media outlets in New Orleans are struggling just to stay alive. With only a handful of people living in the city and businesses closed everywhere, there simply is no advertising revenue to pay the bills. Nobody has the money to hire anyone, and many of them are laying off staff.

It's true, George left Caroline and me a sizeable chunk of life insurance. And he had investments, too, which will be tallied up after Tony can open a succession to deliver the bequests in his will to his heirs. I may never have to work again just to put food on the table. But work for me has always been about more than that. It's about who I am, my place in this world, and what contribution I want to make to the future.

Maybe I really should take my inheritance and start over somewhere else. George is gone and Caroline isn't coming back. The house came from George's family, not mine, so I really don't have a deep emotional attachment to it. I could sell it and move just about anywhere. Real estate prices in the neighborhoods that didn't flood have skyrocketed in the last few weeks, as Noreen told me, and houses are selling as soon as they come on the market.

But where would I go, and what kind of job could I get? Maybe some company would take pity on a Katrina survivor and hire me.

The incoming tide washed over my tennis shoes, soaking them. I pulled them off and walked barefoot the rest of the way to the house.

FRIDAY, OCTOBER 28

I'd bid Sophie good night fairly early last night, but instead of going to sleep, I started reading a novel from the beach house's extensive library of paperbacks left by visitors over the years. I was awake much later than I'd planned.

Sometime after midnight, my cell phone rang. Only one person calls me this late. I answered it before the second ring.

"Hey, Mags, you still up?"

"Mickey, how are you?"

"That's a long story. Not why I'm calling. I went by your house today. Eloise said you'd taken off for the beach. You're not running out on New Orleans, are you?"

"Um," I said. "Just needed to clear my head and think about things."

"Well, don't think too hard. Come back, girl."

Already this conversation had taken a strange turn, considering what happened the last time we saw each other. "What's going on? Why the midnight phone call?"

"Best time to reach you, isn't it? I'm not interrupting anything, am I?"

"No."

"I went to your house because I wanted to talk to you in person, but you weren't home. I guess I'll have to tell you this on the phone. I heard some news today I thought you'd want to hear."

"What?"

"I saw Zach today. He told me—well, you knew about Hurricane Wilma, didn't you?"

"It was a really bad storm. Went into Florida somewhere."

"Made landfall south of Naples."

"That's right. I remember now."

"That's where Howard and Ruth have been living since they evacuated for Katrina."

"Oh. Right. They have a beachfront condo, I think."

"Uh-huh. When they heard Wilma was coming, they evacuated again. They were on a two-lane road somewhere when Howard pulled out to pass someone and went right into the path of an oncoming truck. He and Ruth were both killed."

"Oh my God!" I flashed on a memory of riding in a car once with Howard driving. I never did it again. He drove a car the way he ran his business: you got the hell out of his way or else. This time it had been or else.

"Come on, Maggie. You can't be sorry he's dead. How many times did you say you wanted to kill him?"

"Stop it, Mickey. That was a figure of speech."

"Anyway, Zach has just gotten back from the funeral. Frankly, I don't think a lot of people are going to grieve for Howard. He was a son of a bitch to leave Zach behind when

Katrina was coming and to lie to Zach's parents about it. When you get past the shock of the news, you're not going to grieve him either."

"Give me a little time to digest this, please."

"Okay. Just digest this. Parker Publishing was a closely held corporation, with Howard and Ruth as principal stockholders. The corporation was in the process of declaring bankruptcy when Howard and Ruth were killed. Things are in limbo right now. I don't know how it's all going to turn out. I'm not a lawyer, and neither is Zach, but you've got some connections in that area. The assets of the corporation might be up for sale. Considering the damage to the building and its contents after the storm, not to mention the state of publishing around here right now, those assets might be purchased for a fraction of what they used to be worth. Maggie, this could be your chance. Your husband left you well off, didn't he? Buy the company."

"What? Are you crazy?"

"You already know I'm crazy. Just telling you to think about it."

"Jesus, Mickey."

"Poetic justice, babe. You can have the whole company. You know you want it."

"In case you haven't noticed, there isn't a New Orleans restaurant slash nightlife scene right now. And nobody to buy advertising, much less anybody to care about what they have to sell."

"All the more reason that you could probably pick up the assets for a song. Anyway, I'm just throwing it out there."

"Consider it thrown." I hesitated. "Listen, how are you doing? You said it was a long story."

"Yeah, it is. Look, I wanted to say I'm sorry for the mess that night when Cassie showed up."

"Nothing to be sorry about. She had every right to be angry."

"Yeah, well, I'm sorry you got caught in the middle of it."

"Reality showed up a little sooner than we expected. But it was going to show up eventually." I took a deep breath. Might as well ask, because I really wanted to know. "Has she come home to stay?"

He sighed. "She and the kids were here for a week. It just wasn't working out. I ended up driving them all back to Charlotte." There was a long pause. "Things are up in the air right now, Maggie. My marriage has been in trouble for a long time. Katrina gave us an excuse to separate. But I want you to know, if things don't work out, you had nothing to do with it."

"Mickey, I'm sorry you have to deal with all this right now, on top of all the stuff you've had to see and write about since the storm."

"I didn't want to tell you all my troubles. I just wanted it to be light and fun between us. If I'd told you, you would have thought it was just that 'my wife doesn't understand me' crap and I was trying to feed you a line. I didn't want that."

"I hear you." I sighed. "There's something I didn't tell you, either."

"What?"

"Just a few days before we . . . got together, I found out George had been having a longtime affair. Twelve years, as it turned out."

He whistled. "So I was revenge?"

Had that been it? I didn't want to think so. After a pause, I said, "I think what happened between you and me was a long time coming."

A little chuckle. "Yeah, I think you're right about that."

"I'm flattered. And, Mickey? I don't have any regrets."

"Me neither. Glad we got that out of the way."

It was my turn to have a little chuckle.

"Mags, it's hard telling you all this over the phone. Seriously, are you coming back to New Orleans? Or are you going to stay at the beach the rest of your days?"

"I don't think my old roommate would have let me stay if she didn't know I had a round-trip ticket," I laughed. "She's got her own life, got things to do. I'm flying back on Sunday."

"Come on home, Maggie. New Orleans needs you."

Do you need me, Mickey? I couldn't say it, had no right to say it. He had his own troubles to deal with.

"I'm glad you called. Tell Zach I really am sorry for his loss. And I'm sorry for all you've got on your plate right now."

"Thanks, Mags." He hung up. Did I hear a choking sob just before he did?

I set aside the novel I'd been reading and turned out the light. Of course, I couldn't sleep. I think I drifted off as it was getting light, but I was awake by seven.

I felt as if I'd been run over by a truck, and my new hairdo looked it, too. I showered and did what I could to my hair, then staggered toward the kitchen, where the smell of brewing coffee was a blessing. Sophie had been out for a walk on the beach already and was starting to pull things out of the refrigerator for breakfast.

"You don't look very bright-eyed and bushy-tailed this morning, Scarlett. Have a rough night?" She poured coffee into my mug.

"Yeah. Couldn't sleep."

"Something bothering you?"

"Just have a lot on my mind. A friend called me last night." I told her briefly about what had happened to Howard and Ruth and the possibility that the company might be up for sale.

"Wow," she said. "Do you think you could swing that?"

"Maybe," I said. "George's law partners carry life insurance on each other so they can buy out a partner's interest if he dies. I don't know how much money it's going to work out to be, but it might be enough to buy the publishing company, depending on what they ask for it. George pretty much divided his estate between Caroline and me."

"Would you want to buy it, though? It's a big leap from being an editor to owning the business."

"I don't know. I've always thought I could do a better job than Howard at running things. Of course, I guess every editor thinks that about their publisher." I took a sip of my coffee. It was hot and strong, the way I like it. "I've seen individuals try to start up magazines, though, only to go down in flames within a year. The big issue is always undercapitalization. It takes a hell of a lot of money to put out a magazine, and it takes years before it starts to pay its own way. Printing and postage costs will eat you alive. Plus, there's the overhead of office space. And staff."

I remembered what I'd told Mickey last night. "Besides, there is no market for the magazine I used to edit. I just finished a freelance piece for an industry magazine on the state of the restaurant business in New Orleans right now. Everything is in shambles. Dining and nightlife are hardly anyone's priorities."

Sophie cracked eggs into a skillet and began to scramble them. I popped slices of bread into the toaster. She said, "I'm sure you're right. So *New Orleans Now!* is out of commission for the time being. Who knows, years from now it may come back. The question is, would you still want to do that? Write about restaurants and bars? Don't take this the wrong way, but that's a young person's game. You and I are well past the age of hanging out in clubs. I hate to say it, but Howard may have been right to want a young person in that position. Maybe there's something else you ought to be covering these days. Something you have a passion for."

I got two plates from a cabinet and set them on the counter. Sophie divided the scrambled eggs and slid them onto the plates. The toast popped up. I snagged the hot slices and added them to our breakfast. We carried our food to the table and sat down to eat.

Between forkfuls of egg, Sophie said, "If you're seriously thinking about this, here's something to consider. Why buy the company? Would this be about getting even with Howard for all the hell he put you through? Because that's a lousy way to spend the money George left you. And Howard's dead, so he doesn't care what you do. Why not start your own company?"

I felt the hairs on my arms stand up. "McBride Publishing." Why not, indeed? Well, because I could fall on my face and go broke. That would be more embarrassing than getting fired, not to mention the financial consequences.

"How about McBride Media? Think big, Scarlett. Remember what I told you about publishing operations moving to the Internet? Think about it. When you publish online, you have zero printing and postage costs. Ze-ro. Hire freelancers to write for you, and you won't need all that office space. Maybe you can even start out at your kitchen table. You'll need to find people who are savvy at developing websites and maintaining them, and you'll have to learn a lot of tech stuff yourself. But I think you'll find your startup costs will be a lot less than if you were putting out a print publication."

I chewed thoughtfully on the corner of a piece of toast. "You know, since the storm, we've been getting a lot of our news online. Newspaper stories, online neighborhood forums, emails from friends, even my blog. People from New Orleans are scattered around the country and don't have access to local news. Shoot, we're not even getting magazines delivered in the city right now. The postal sorting facility downtown was destroyed in the storm. All we can get is first-class mail, and not a lot of that. And what we're getting was mailed out weeks ago. I've been paying my bills over the Internet because the paper bills aren't getting to me until weeks after they're due. You're right. The whole landscape of how we communicate is shifting out of necessity."

Sophie nodded. "These are issues Jake is wrestling with right now, too. Of course, he's not in the middle of trying to put a city back together."

"Maybe Jake could start a media company, too."

"Doubt it. We live in the middle of a market of media giants. New Orleans is quite small in that regard, as you well know. You'd probably have a much easier time getting a foothold there than Jake would in the Northeast."

"Sophie, that's a lot to think about." I finished my breakfast, took my plate to the sink, and poured myself another cup of coffee.

"The future of journalism isn't all bad news. It's just the end of the world as we knew it. There's a new world forming as we speak. That's the message of my book."

"I want to read your book."

"I do too. But I have to finish it first." She picked up her own plate and headed to the sink. "Sorry, girl, but I have to get back to work."

"And I've got some things to think about."

SATURDAY, OCTOBER 29

I finally got to watch the sun rise over the Atlantic this morning. I set the alarm to go off around six. Leaving the lights off, I pulled the curtains open, sat on the edge of the bed, and waited.

At first all I saw was the sliver of the waning moon as it rose, its shadowed area made more visible by earthlight. The sky began to lighten a good hour before sunrise. Around seven, a smoky gray line appeared along the horizon. Then a reddish-orange-pink line formed above it, like embers on charcoal. One particular spot on the horizon began to turn a deep rose and formed a little hill of color. The sun birthed itself out of the ocean, crowning like a baby's head emerging from the mother's body. Slowly it emerged from the womb of water, then rose fully above the horizon. Bright gold gave way to flaming white as the sliver of moon faded in the growing light.

I spotted a sailboat on the horizon, just to the right of the rising sun. I wondered if it had been anchored out there all night. If so, its occupants had just raised the sails. As I watched, it sailed off toward the south. Someone was living out the dream of their lifetime. It's not my dream, but I'm glad they're happy.

Today, October 29, is two months since Katrina made landfall. The rest of the world wouldn't take note of the date. But I did, and I knew my fellow New Orleanians would, too.

That's the heart of the problem, isn't it? We who lived through Katrina are now set apart from everyone else. We share this common experience of surviving a disaster and living each day with the question, "What now?" We see the world differently from others who haven't been through what we've been through. We take nothing for granted any more.

In my inner debates about whether to start over somewhere else or stay and help with the recovery, I keep coming back to the things that bind us together, even those of us living in exile. If I left New Orleans for some other place, no matter how many amenities it had, I would grieve. I would miss my neighborhood: Giannini's, City Coffee, the streetcar line, all of it. I'd miss gumbo in all its local variations, French bread, and red beans and rice on Mondays. I'd miss Mardi Gras and JazzFest and all the parades and festivals—I know their future is in doubt right now, but I'm sure they'll come back eventually. I'd miss the local accent and the jokes about flying cockroaches and mosquitoes the size of birds. I would miss living among my own people.

I thought back to conversations I overheard or took part in—the ones at the reception after George's funeral and the ones at the repast after Robert's. People who had been driven from their homes by the storm to places far away needed to gather, to talk about what had happened to them, about their fears and their needs and what they might do in the future. So many of them wanted to come home, but they couldn't see a way clear to do it.

What had Eloise's pastor said to me about the white people who didn't want black residents to return? "Talk to them. Tell them they don't own New Orleans. It belongs to all of us. And we all have a right to come back and rebuild. They don't know it, but they need us. We work in the hotels and restaurants and hospitals and schools. We work for the power company, the phone company, the cable company. We work for the city government. We work in construction. We're electricians and plumbers and carpenters and painters. We need to come back so everyone can rebuild. But to do that, we need places to live, just like everyone else. You tell them that."

Tell them that. All these people, white and black, have a right to come home. So many are craving information about what's going on in the city and how they can get back to rebuild their homes. I can help by providing them information over the Internet. Not just with my blog, but a whole online magazine. Or whatever you call it when it's electronic.

If we're going to rebuild this city, we're all going to have to work together, regardless of race or economic class. That's the message that needs to get out there. Division is not going to help a process that's already in deep trouble.

This is no time to pit white and black community leaders against each other, pointing fingers and grandstanding. I can contact people I know and do my damnedest to get them on board.

I don't need to be an employee of someone else's media company to do it. I can be my own Internet-based media company.

I'll need help, of course. I'll need someone who's more tech-savvy than I am to set this up. And I'll need writers. Wonder if Zach would like to work for me?

Would Pastor Anderson be interested? He could be a strong voice for bringing back African-Americans to New Orleans. He can blog about it. To everyone. White readers need to hear what he has to say, too.

It was still quite early, but I was ready to walk the beach. I went into the kitchen and started the coffeemaker, then got dressed as the coffee was brewing. With my steaming mug in one hand, I opened the sliding glass door with the other and headed down the steps from the deck to the beach.

Tomorrow, Sunday, will be the end of Daylight Saving Time. Spring ahead, fall back. We get an extra hour tonight. That's good, because we're leaving early in the morning for the three-hour drive to the Raleigh airport. I'm going home. This will be my last early morning beach walk. I'm going to miss this place.

A dolphin was splashing offshore as I came to the water's edge. The sailboat I saw a few minutes ago had disappeared. I didn't see any other beach walkers. Except . . .

I almost stepped on him in my bare feet, which would have been a bad idea. The little guy was pale gold, with gleaming white claws and eyes on vertical stalks. A sand crab. I'd wondered what creatures dug the holes I was seeing in the dunes among the sea oats and marsh grass. He was much bigger than the hermit crabs I see on the Gulf— almost as big as a regular sea crab. I stood there for a couple of minutes, locked in a staring contest with this amazing creature with eyes on stalks, both of us perfectly still. He won. If it was a he. As I moved away, though, he moved with me. I walked around him, giving him a wide berth, and he turned with my movements, never taking his eyes off me. Finally I waved goodbye and continued on my solitary walk.

I was glad I'd come here for these days of R&R. It was good to be at the beach, and it was good to spend time with Sophie again. For just awhile, I needed to put some distance between me and everything that's happened in the last two months. Well, three, actually, to go back to the day Howard fired me. I thought that was the worst thing that had ever happened to me. What a laugh, to think back on it now.

I have to admit, grudgingly, that Sophie is right about one thing: running around at night going to trendy restaurants and nightclubs is something best appreciated by people younger than I am. Once upon a time, I was one of them. I'm not any more. I could moan over the loss of my youth and try to compete with people twenty or even thirty years my junior. Or I could appreciate the person I am now: the woman who's learned a lot about life through her experiences over fifty-one years. Who's a lot wiser now than she was even three months ago.

I can finally say I don't want my old job back. It was never about money. George made enough that I could have been a stay-at-home mom with Caroline. I didn't have to hire Eloise and go back to work. No, it was about having a career, being proud of my accomplishments, having a sense of independence. Did my career ambitions lead George to have an affair with a woman who didn't care about such things? Now that he's gone, I'll never know. He could just as easily have been having those afternoon liaisons with Bitsy if I'd been at home, not working, and I never would have guessed.

And what had my affair with Mickey been about, anyway? Revenge? A last-ditch attempt to relive my youth with a younger man? Relief from the craziness and stress of life after Katrina?

Or was it something more? I'd had something with Mickey that I hadn't had with George. Laughter. Fun. Spontaneity. A common passion for the kind of work we did.

But if George hadn't died, if Katrina hadn't torn our lives apart, if Mickey's wife and kids hadn't been in Charlotte, it probably wouldn't have happened.

But it had. Mickey's marriage was on the rocks, and all my rational instincts were telling me to run like hell and let him and Cassie sort things out. But my heart—and my body—still wanted him.

Not now, I told myself. *Maybe later. See how you both feel a few months from now.*

As I turned to head back toward the house, I saw Sophie walking in my direction. She waved at me.

"You left your phone on the kitchen counter," she said. "You had a call from your friend Eloise. She said it was nothing urgent. The house didn't burn down or anything. Just call her when you get a chance."

It was still early in the Central Time Zone. Something must be up. I came inside and called her.

"I wanted to call you last night," she said, "but by the time I got in from work, it was too late. You're an hour ahead of us. I wanted to tell you my news. FEMA delivered my trailer Friday afternoon. Put it right on my front lawn. I can live just outside my door while my house is being fixed."

"That's great news."

"And Maggie, I was going through stuff in the house and I found some plastic storage boxes that hadn't gotten any water in them. I found Robert's life insurance policy in one of them. I think there's enough money to fix up the house, even without flood insurance. I'm going to give some to my church, too. They didn't have enough insurance money to rebuild. God has been good to me, and I want to give back to God."

"Oh, Eloise! I'm so happy for you."

But oddly, I wasn't. I had a sudden pain in my midsection. I've gotten used to having Eloise living with me.

When she moves out, I'll be all by myself. And I haven't lived alone in that house, ever. Actually, I've never lived alone. Even after college, when I was working in New York, I had roommates. When I came back to New Orleans, I lived with my parents until George and I got married. What's it going to be like to live by myself?

"I can't move into the trailer right away," she said. "They won't give me the keys until Entergy gets electricity into the neighborhood again. They'll have to put up a pole with a meter on it outside the trailer. I don't know how long that will take. Don't kick me out just yet, Maggie."

"I know you want to get back to your neighborhood and your house. But you can stay with me as long as you want. You know that."

"Maggie, I appreciate all you've done for me. I really do. If it weren't for you, I don't know where I'd be right now."

"I don't know what I would have done without you these last few weeks. Oh, shoot, I don't know what I would have done these last twenty years. Eloise, you've been a friend to me in so many ways. Going to lunch and to the movies with someone is one kind of friendship, but we've shared so much more than that. You've been there for me when I needed someone. I hope I've been able to be there for you too."

"I know. It's just . . . sometimes, you just don't get it. Things are different for you than they are for me."

I sighed. "There are things I should have been seeing all along, and I was too wrapped up in my own life to notice.

Eloise, I'm sorry if anything I've done or said has been hurtful to you."

"I appreciate that."

"So does all this mean you've decided to stay in New Orleans?"

"For now. I'm just about the only person back there in my neighborhood. The National Guard all know me by now. When I go over to work on my house, they stop by to check on me. The relief groups come and bring me water and a sandwich. Someone from a church group that's here from out of town told me they're going to send a team to finish gutting my house and help me spray all the exposed framing to kill the mold. God is good, Maggie."

"I hear you."

"Pastor came by the other day and we had a long talk. He called me a woman of faith and brave and all sorts of things. He said I could be an example to other people in the church and the neighborhood. An inspiration. That I could talk to them, persuade them to come back. He said if this widow, all by herself, could come back to her home and rebuild, then they could too. He called me Naomi—you know who she was?"

"Not really."

"Naomi was a woman in the Bible who lost her husband and her sons. She was living far from home, but she wanted to go back. And she did. She had her daughter-in-law Ruth with her, the wife of her son who had died. Ruth was a foreign woman. But she stuck by Naomi, and the two of them went back to Naomi's home town and made new lives for themselves." She paused. "Don't take this wrong, Maggie, but Pastor said you were my Ruth, the one who has stuck by me. You're not a foreigner, but you're not . . ." She hesitated.

"I'm not black," I said.

"Yes. You're not black and I'm not white, but you've been there for me through all that's happened since Isaiah died."

The nightmare didn't start with Katrina for Eloise either, I thought. She was struggling with grief long before the storm happened and Robert died. My grief over my job loss was miniscule compared to hers.

"Well," I said, "I can be your spiritual daughter-in-law if you'd like. I'm not sure how that would work, though."

"You'd have to ask Pastor about that. I guess he just sees us as two women trying to make our way together."

"You'll have to read me that Bible story when I get back."

"I can do that."

"Pastor Anderson and I talked after Robert's service. He wants me to tell the white community that the city needs all of us, white and black, to come home. I'm going to do my best to get that word out. Eloise, will you help me?"

"Help you? How?"

"You can help me get the word out. I'm going to write about it."

"I'm not a writer, Maggie. I clean houses and offices for a living."

"Yes, but you're good at talking to people. You and I—
we can be a team. We can speak to people and groups. We
can work together and tell others we've got to stop this
stupid fighting over whose city it is. It belongs to all of us.
It's going to take every one of us to bring it back. I know
we're just two people, Eloise, but we can spread the word.
Will you do that? Will you work with me?"

"Maggie, you are crazy."

"We're all a little bit crazy since the storm. But I do
think just about anything is possible right now. The old
structures, the old ways of doing things, have been hit hard.
We're rebuilding the city from the ground up. There's room
for new ways of working together. Work with me, Eloise.
Let's start a movement."

She laughed. "You are something, girl."

"Is that a yes?"

"Sure. What have we got to lose?"

The whole city. But we won't. Not if we all work
together.

Sunday, October 30

Sophie and I left early for the Raleigh airport and arrived in plenty of time for my flight to Atlanta, where I'd make a connection to New Orleans. I was surprised by the depth of my sadness at leaving her.

"Let's not take so long to see each other again," I said.

"Let's not," she agreed.

"I'll come for your book launch party."

"Academic books don't usually have book launch parties, but I think I may bend the rules on this one and give a party myself. I think there's going to be a lot of interest in this book."

"Well, you've got my interest. And let me know how things go for Jake."

"He had a good meeting on Friday with an editor. An old friend. He's hopeful."

"It's going to work out, Soph. Tell him I said hang in there."

"I will."

And then I was off, through security and down the concourse to my gate.

I had a long layover in Atlanta, wandering the shops along the concourse and standing in line to buy fried chicken at Popeye's, which had gotten its start in New Orleans. Still, it didn't feel like I was going home until I found the gate for my flight. My fellow passengers, some sitting, some standing, were world-weary souls with smiling faces, speaking in a familiar accent: Brooklyn with a Southern lilt.

Finally on board, I slid into my window seat on the left side of the plane. A few moments later, a tall, thin young black man wearing a Saints t-shirt took the seat on the aisle. I smiled and addressed him with the local greeting. "Where y'at?"

"Hey," he said. "Goin' home. Can't get there soon enough."

"Me too." As he settled into his seat, I asked, "How'd you make out in the storm?" Another local greeting these days.

"We lived out in the East. We lost everything in the flood. But we made it out before the storm, thank God. Evacuated to Jackson. We're all right. My family and I are living with our cousins on the West Bank right now."

"I'm glad you got out safely."

"Yeah. I know people who died."

"Me too."

The hour-long flight was blessedly peaceful. It was around sunset as we made our approach into the city from the east. With the end of Daylight Saving Time, night was coming an hour earlier.

The eastern side of the city, where the young man was from, had been hit the hardest by the flooding from the storm surge. He and I peered out the window as we flew over it, and he pointed out his neighborhood to me. The area showed no signs of life. No streetlights or lights in houses. I saw a couple of crumpled signs of big-box stores along the interstate and very few cars on the roads.

As we continued west, I could see some lights in the downtown office towers. Not the usual number, but lights nonetheless.

There were some streetlights working Uptown, but many neighborhoods were still dark. As we flew over the 17th Street Canal and crossed into Jefferson Parish, however, it was a different story. Most areas had working streetlights. I could see cars moving on the major east-west roadways. The plane made a slight turn to the right as we approached the east-west runway, and for a moment I could see the fire of the setting sun filtered through bands of clouds.

So much of the city lay in darkness now, but in that light ahead of us was the promise that it would not be dark forever. There was hope. With the resiliency of people like that young man sitting beside me—and all the locals on this plane—we were going to restore the city. Not simply back to what it had been, but to something better. Together we would craft a vision for a new city and bring it to reality.

A few years ago, I had gone with George on a business trip to San Francisco. It was a little more than ten years after that city had been devastated by an earthquake. I remembered seeing photos of the days right after it happened. A major expressway had collapsed. There was massive damage to buildings, especially in the Marina District. Some people were living on the streets amid rubble because their apartment buildings were unsafe to live in.

The city worked hard for years to rebuild. As casual tourists some twelve years later, we never would have guessed what devastation had occurred there. We walked along the Embarcadero, where the expressway once had been. Now a streetcar line carries passengers from the Ferry Building to Fisherman's Wharf. We laughed to find a New Orleans streetcar among the many from different cities along the route.

I'm sure there were many voices who said San Francisco shouldn't be rebuilt, because another earthquake could happen at any time. Now there are voices saying New Orleans shouldn't be rebuilt, because we could have another devastating hurricane. Those voices are right when they say that disasters can and eventually will happen again. Yet we can do things to make it more likely we will withstand the next devastation, with new technologies in construction and rebuilding the levees the way they should have been in the first place—and stronger. Develop realistic plans for evacuations.

San Francisco came back. We can, too.

We landed and taxied to our gate at the end of the concourse. When I heard the chime as the seatbelt light went out, I stood and gathered my things and wished the young man well. I straightened my jacket, suddenly feeling self-conscious. I was wearing a new fall outfit I'd bought on my shopping day in Wilmington—pants that actually fit well, a print shirt and a stylish jacket. After several days of experimenting, I'd finally made peace with my new haircut. And I really liked my new hair color, glinting with fire like that setting sun. I no longer looked like the gaunt woman with the washed-out face in the too-big pants and top, with the faded graying hair badly in need of a trim, who had gotten on another plane on this concourse less than a week ago.

Be the promise of better days to come, I told myself.

It was early evening, but all the shops on the concourse had already closed. It was like coming in after midnight. I walked quickly, headed for the exit past the security checkpoint.

There she was. Eloise looked pretty good herself. She wore jeans that fit her well and a polo top and a windbreaker.

I hugged her. "It's good to be home."

He was leaning against one of the fat pillars of the terminal, hands shoved in the pockets of his jeans, a grin on his face. Eloise shrugged and gave me a sly smile.

I laughed. "What the hell, Mickey?"

"Looking good, hot mama."

ACKNOWLEDGMENTS

I am a New Orleanian who lived through the time of Katrina. After the storm, I knew I wanted to write about the craziness of those days, but the experiences were just too raw. It was nearly ten years later that I began work on what became this novel. By the time I had a manuscript ready for publication, agents and editors threw up their hands and said, "We don't want to hear any more about Katrina"— without ever looking at what I'd written. Yet when I would travel to other places and mention to people that I was from New Orleans, they would always ask about Katrina. I guessed there were readers out there who still would read a novel set in that time, so I decided to self-publish.

This is a work of fiction set in the context of real events that took place in New Orleans from July through October 2005. Dorothy Mae Taylor (1928-2000) was a real person; her efforts as an elected leader to end discrimination are well documented online and in particular in James Gill's excellent book *Lords of Misrule: Mardi Gras and the Politics of Race in New Orleans* (University Press of Mississippi, 1997). All the other characters in this novel are products of my imagination.

So many people helped me to get this novel to publication. Thank you to the workshop leaders and participants at the Santa Barbara Writers Conference who gave me good feedback and ideas when I got stuck, particularly Dale Griffiths Stamos, Wylene Wisby Dunbar, and the late Lisa Lenard-Cook.

Thank you to Jeff Lyons, story geek extraordinaire, for his one-on-one consultations. He kept asking me the right questions to pull the story line out of me.

Thank you to Major Stephen A. Sanders, Chaplain, Louisiana National Guard (ret.) for information on where soldiers in the Louisiana National Guard would have been stationed during the Iraq war in 2004 and what dangers they would have faced.

Thanks to Rev. Alex Lewis Jr. and his wife Lucinda for information about St. Francisville, particularly what Dawson High would have been like when Eloise and Robert were students there. I originally had them meeting at a football game, but Mrs. Lewis told me the school had no football team! Oops! So Eloise and Robert started talking in the lunchroom.

Thank you to Dr. Cynthia W. Walker, professor and chair of the department of communication and media culture at St. Peter's University, Jersey City, New Jersey, and Dr. J. Michael Robertson, retired professor in the department of media studies at the University of San Francisco, for reading the section about Sophie's research for her book and what predictions about the future of journalism would have been made in 2005. Thanks also to

Professor Richard Breyer of the Newhouse School at Syracuse University for information on how Caroline would have made her documentary.

Thanks to Rev. Marc Napoleon and the congregation of Nazareth Baptist Church in Hollygrove, who were my models for Eloise's faith community. By the grace of God, they have rebuilt their sanctuary—and their neighborhood. It wasn't easy.

Thanks to my friends Maggie and Jim Eanes, who graciously invited me to their beach house on an island off Wilmington, North Carolina, in October 2005 for a week of much-needed R&R after Katrina. The descriptions of the house, the beach, the sunrise, and, oh yes, the chocolate liqueur pie came from my journals.

Thanks to fellow Newhouse alum Pam Rauscher for her careful eye in editing this manuscript. Her perspective as someone "not from New Orleans" was invaluable.

And, as always, thanks to my husband Richard for putting up with me, as the spouses of fortunate writers do, when I sequestered myself to write and rewrite and fuss a lot about how it was going.

Finally, thank you to the brave people of New Orleans who dared to return and rebuild the city better than it was before. And to those who came to help, and those who fell in love with the place and came back to live and work here.

ABOUT THE AUTHOR

K.N. CRIGHTON is a New Orleans native who majored in magazine journalism and English at Syracuse University. She worked as a business and financial journalist in Atlanta for twenty years before coming back to New Orleans. She lives with her husband, four cats, and a dog, in a house that was her grandmother's, in a "sliver on the river" that didn't flood in Katrina. *The New Normal* is her first novel.

www.ingramcontent.com/pod-product-compliance
Lightning Source LLC
Chambersburg PA
CBHW051209120726
47905CB00004B/1045